The Road

Home

Boo
The Lette

A Novel

Kathleen Shoop

This book is a work of fiction. The story is a product of the author's imagination and any incidents, documents, places, and people that inspired the work are used fictitiously. Any resemblance to current events or to living persons is entirely coincidental.

ISBN-13: 978-1511801249

ISBN-10: 1511801247

Cover photo: Susan Fox/Trevillion Images

Cover design: Natasha Brown

For my mom

Chapter 1

Katherine

1905—Des Moines

Katherine stood at her mother's coffin. The parlor was bursting with sweet pink roses, deep blue and blush-pink hydrangeas, and peonies. She drew the lush scent deep into her lungs and hoped that her mother's soul was present, that she was aware of the care taken to usher her into the afterlife. Katherine exhaled, her eyes closed, trying to suppress the grief that kept lodging in the back of her throat. It was not yet midday, and a breeze shot through the floor-to-ceiling windows behind her.

She turned toward the draft, hoping it would whisk away the tears and stop them from falling yet again. The wind twisted and then billowed the white organza sheers, making the hem lick at the hardwood floors. A warm gust made Katherine shiver. She rubbed her arms and looked to the ceiling. She had not treated her mother as she had deserved in life, so she wanted to create a loving send-off in death. *I love you, Mama. I want you to know.*

She refocused on the wood box that held her mother. It was a simple design, though made of mahogany. Katherine straightened the silken sheets across her mother's midsection, pleased to furnish fine covers after what she had understood was a difficult, luxury-free life. Her passing had been arduous. Stomach cancer had spread, debilitating her quickly, but her mother had worked hard to stay alive for as long as she could, for as long as it had taken for Katherine to begin to understand.

Caring for her sister, Yale, would be a big job for Katherine and her family. The young woman's mind had not developed much beyond a child's, and her judgment on any matter could not be trusted. But Katherine would do it because she had come to see it was right. And where her mother was concerned, Katherine had done more wrong than she had wanted to admit.

Still, Katherine counted herself lucky. Her mother showing up just before dying had given them the chance to forgive each other. From the many people she had met over the years, Katherine had learned that the opportunity to do that was a true gift—something she would hold tight in her heart.

In the last moments of her passing, she and Katherine had squeezed each other's hands, saying they loved each other with the gesture, and Katherine had felt her mother's soul leave. There was peace and sorrow, but for the two of them, the regret each had harbored faded away, like a light turned down in the dark of night.

I'm so sorry, Mama.

Katherine sighed and smoothed her mother's hair, adjusting a pin so the brown locks created just the right wave against her forehead and down the side of her face, exactly as Katherine remembered her mother liking it when she was younger. She plucked some lint from the blouse and smoothed the fabric, straightening the tucks at the shoulder.

Once she was satisfied with the styling, Katherine patted her mother's stiff hand. "Love you, love you, love you, my mama. You can finally rest. You're finally back with our sweet

James," she said and sighed. Though the regret that had been seeded in hostility toward her mother had been freed in the past few days, Katherine knew it would take time to rid herself of the sadness that she had wasted time on when her mother had been alive. There had been so much misinformation between mother and daughter. Time had allowed ill feelings to fester. Over the years, each of them had attempted to make things right, but the timing was always off, and before she knew it nearly two decades had gone by. Katherine had seen countless others make the same mistake, and yet she had not learned the lesson until nearly too late.

Tears dropped onto the creamy sheet, the moisture spreading through the fibers. Katherine swallowed the next threatening round and dabbed at the silk with a handkerchief to dry it.

"Katherine?" Tommy's voice came as he walked into the parlor and took his place next to his sister.

She sucked back more tears.

He slipped his arm around her shoulder, and she covered his hand with hers.

"Sad, isn't it?" he asked.

Katherine sniffled and roped her arm around his waist, wanting to offer comfort as much as get some for herself. She dabbed at her nose with the handkerchief. She knew her brother harbored even more regret than she did. She knew he was struggling with his work as a minister, with his marriage. "Mama knows you love her, Tommy. She knew it all along."

He looked at Katherine. His face had taken on a softness that had not been apparent when he'd first arrived back in Des Moines, when he'd still held his resentment as though it were the air that gave him breath.

"I wish I could be so confident." Tommy shrugged. "Not sure I can face the way things went. Can't seem to grasp the same peace that you have."

Katherine nodded. "It's true. The calm was there in the last minutes we had together. And now, when I take a deep breath, I feel her forgiveness, like it's embedded in the very air." She squeezed Tommy. "That forgiveness was for you, too."

He stared at Katherine, clenching his jaw.

"It's never too late," Katherine said.

He looked back at their mother and pushed his hands into his pockets. "I'm a minister, Katherine. I've said those exact words to people. I know what you mean, but I can't *feel* it. How stupid I must have sounded to all those people. I just want to laugh out loud, like it's a joke. I can't feel what you do. And I keep thinking about her life, our lives, when we were young. It's awful the way things went after it all fell apart. Remember all her friends? All the women in and out, the parties she and Father hosted, the life, the vigor? And now there's no one."

He shook his head, the tendons tightening in his neck. "I'm just so angry."

"Tommy, please." Katherine pulled him close. He put his forehead against hers, and their eyes locked the way they had when they were young. "I'm here. We're all here for you and Emma."

His eyes welled. He squeezed them shut, tears gathering between his thick lashes. Katherine could feel his tension, see his worry when she mentioned his wife's name. She pulled him into a full hug, rubbing circles between his shoulder blades the way she would when one of her children needed comfort.

"Emma's not real pleased with me right now. Not that I blame her, really."

Katherine assumed his fragile marriage, coupled with all the rest, was just too much at a time like this. "What did you do?" she asked.

He looked away. "It's complicated. And I need to talk to her, get back to her, and then I can explain to you."

"Did you tell Emma you have something to tell her?"

He cleared his throat. "Not yet."

"Well, she'll be here soon, right? You can tell her as soon as you see her."

Tommy looked down, his eyes hiding so much. He forced a smile at Katherine. "I don't know, Katherine. I just don't know if that will matter."

Katherine gripped him tight. "Well, I know it will matter. I will believe for you until you're ready. That's the least I can do."

Tommy nodded and turned back to their mother, studying her. Katherine left him in solitude, needing to gather up her brood and see that they washed up and dressed for the occasion of having to say good-bye to their grandmother before they knew her very well at all.

Chapter 2

Tommy

1891—Des Moines

Tommy Arthur had been back in Des Moines for only a couple of days, but he finally felt ready to face his future square and sure. Outside the doors of the Savery Hotel, he brushed off the front of his pants and coat for the thirteenth time. He smoothed back his hair and cleared his throat. It had been years since he'd felt the need to use the fancy manners that had once been put to daily use.

Straightening his shoulders, he pushed through the door, removed his cap, and strode toward the front desk as though he'd already paid a month's rent on the presidential suite. In the lobby, the scattered Oriental rugs complemented the shine on the rich wood floors. The brass fixtures, crystal sconces, velvet and damask upholstery, and blazing fire in the stone fireplace reminded him of the grand home in which he'd lived until just four years back.

Tommy waited behind a young couple at the front desk. The aroma of hyacinths and lily of the valley was strong, reminding him further of his former home.

When the couple was finished, Tommy moved forward, stuck his hand out, and firmly shook the man's. The clerk winced and pulled his hand back. With a sharp gaze, the man pecked away at Tommy's coat before he fixed on Tommy's hair and face. The man smirked as he registered the threadbare state of Tommy's clothing. Tommy wouldn't allow the man's glare to bother him. He had come from an important family in Des Moines. Clothes were not a measure of him as a man, and he knew it was just a matter of time before he and his family rose to the top of society yet again.

Tommy remembered the letter. "Oh, here you go." He patted his pants pocket and then his coat at the breast. He dug into it and removed a piece of paper. He unfolded it and pushed it toward the man.

"Be on your way," the desk clerk said. "Breakfast scraps are long gone."

Tommy screwed up his face and shook his head. "Breakfast?"

The clerk flicked his fingers toward Tommy, his face buried in the reservation book that lay before him.

Tommy laid the letter over the book and smoothed out the wrinkles. "This letter is my recommendation for a position at the hotel."

The clerk lifted his gaze.

Tommy pointed at the signature. "Right there. Looks like we'll be colleagues, you and I."

Picking up the letter by its corner, the clerk wafted it at Tommy. "I don't think so." He flung the letter into the air, and it fluttered into Tommy's hands.

"Say, that's not a pleasant way to season our friendship."

The clerk sighed and shook his head like he was trying to rattle away the sight of Tommy.

"Look again." Tommy pointed to the signature. He'd had to soften up harder men than this guy. "Mr. Jeremy Babcock. He was a soldier. He saved Mr. McHenry's life. The manager. Babcock wrote this letter on my behalf."

The clerk flipped several pages and ran the side of his hand down the crease in the book.

Tommy bent forward. "Did you hear what I said?"

He nodded and sighed.

Tommy's shoulders relaxed. "Good. Then tell him I'm here."

The clerk dropped his head to the side, his eyes conveying his irritation. "And you are?"

Tommy pointed to the letter. "Thomas Arthur. I come highly recommended by a spectacularly honorable man. I can do the work that is open—I'm partial to bellboy."

"Well, desk clerk is not available."

Tommy pressed a grin to his lips, not willing to let this curmudgeon sully his good outlook. "Of course not." He gave a small sarcastic bow. "I'll thank you to let Mr. McHenry know that his new bellboy has arrived."

The clerk stared for a moment, as though he were searching for another way to tell Tommy to get lost, but in the end he nodded and disappeared into a low, narrow, hidden doorway that was cut into the moldings and wainscoting behind the desk.

When the door popped open again, the clerk emerged, followed by a man so large he had to duck through the opening. His white hair was wavy but neat. His beard was full but trimmed close to his face. The creases at their corners softened his ice-blue eyes. Tommy smiled as he recalled the photograph that he had seen before. He pushed his hand out. "Mr. McHenry. I recognize you from a photograph of you with Mr. Babcock." He handed the letter to him.

As the man read the letter, Tommy's heart beat harder, faster. He hoped the man would see the recommendation as valuable, that he would see Tommy was a gentleman despite the condition of his clothing.

The man looked to the ceiling and let out a whistle. "Babcock." He rubbed his chin. "Babcock's alive and well."

Tommy nodded. "Just sold off his land. Went back East to help his daughter. Recently widowed. Sold off everything just for her."

"Sounds like Babcock."

The man crossed his arms and studied Tommy. Not in the condescending way that the desk clerk had, but as though he was curious more than anything. Then, without a word, McHenry came around the desk and waltzed right up to Tommy. Tommy tried to read his expression but could not. McHenry slapped Tommy's shoulder and guided him away from the desk. "Let's have a little talk. Some soup and sandwiches ought to hit the spot. Looks like you're a traveling man."

Tommy felt his body unclench. Mr. Babcock's kindness and glowing recommendation had achieved even more than he'd expected. Lunch. Exactly what he needed. He looked over his shoulder to see the clerk's face—reddened, he ground his teeth as he glared. Tommy wiggled his eyebrows. The clerk shook his head and looked away. This would be fun, Tommy thought. If anything, if he were offered the job, Tommy would certainly bring an air of amusement to the stuffy desk clerk's life.

**

Even with the respectful way McHenry had treated Tommy so far, he had expected him only to ask him a few more questions, hand over a piece of bread, and send him on his way. Instead, McHenry walked Tommy into the crystal-chandeliered dining room and seated him smack-dab in the center. The quiet murmur of guests talking in between bites of roast beef and mashed potatoes stopped when Tommy trod by one table and then another.

Tommy could feel the patrons' stares as much as see their gaping mouths. For the space of a breath, he felt shame. Their questioning expressions and derisive snubs made him want to scream out that he belonged there as much as any of them. Thankfully, his defensiveness didn't last long, and he stiffened his spine, tugged his coat down, and pushed his chin forward. He told himself not to fret. His poverty was a passing circumstance, not his future path. It was then he noticed a single smile from a blue-eyed teenage girl in a lavender silk day dress. Tommy nodded at her and held her eye until her mother nearly fell out of her chair, snapping her fingers to draw her daughter's attention back where it belonged.

Tommy settled into the brocade chair.

"You've got a way with people. I can see that," McHenry said. "Clothes may make some men, but some men make the clothes. I can see you are one of those in the second category."

"Sir." Tommy nodded. "Thank you." He straightened in his seat, inflated with the confidence that came when this man recognized Tommy's grace and bearing even though he was cloaked in shabby clothing. Tommy glanced at the table. Laden with silver, crystal glasses, and fine china bread plates, it took him back in time to when he had eaten at such a table for every meal, every day of the year. He touched his canvas lapel, registering its practical though unfashionable material and cut.

But he didn't feel as though that's what he wore. He felt like the man he'd been intended to be when he was born into a wealthy, educated family.

Mr. McHenry passed Tommy the breadbasket. He removed a small roll and placed it on the plate. He used the butter knife to transfer the golden cream onto the bread plate, waiting for the proper time to begin to eat.

McHenry laced his fingers and rested them on his belly. "Well, Mr. Arthur. Tell me more about your relationship with Mr. Babcock. Surely you're too young to simply be his friend."

Tommy tried to keep his relaxed feeling, pulling it around him tight like his coat. "True."

McHenry gestured toward the bread. Tommy tore off a piece, buttered it, and popped it into his mouth, enjoying the sweet cream blending with nutty, crusty bread. He sipped his water.

He thought back to the bank—to the day of the robbery. He didn't want to revisit this instance in his life, but he sensed that McHenry was a man who valued a genuine story, not something glossed over and thin. Tommy chewed and thought back to where he should start. He recalled the day, the hot wind kicking up the dirt road. He could feel it prickling like cactus against his cheeks.

He pictured the gang and their stony gazes, and then he was right back there. Noxious, horse-stomped dirt came to him as though he was standing back there now. He rubbed his arm. He could feel the pain where the infamous bank robber, Matty Sacramento, had latched his fingers, dragging him into the bank. He closed his eyes for a moment; the cold circle at the end of the gun barrel had been lodged where his ear met his skull. He touched that spot and shuddered, remembering how even in those moments of bone-deep fear, his mind had registered the cold steel against his hot skin.

"That gun," Tommy finally said aloud. "The way it felt." His fingers shook as he placed them at his temple. "Every face of every fella in the Sacramento gang is forever in my head. Not sure I'll ever return to Nebraska, for fear they're there, just waiting."

Mr. McHenry drew back and appeared to be considering what Tommy said. After a few moments, he shifted forward in his seat. He pointed at Tommy with two extended fingers. "You were *that* boy in *that* robbery?"

Tommy nodded. He had McHenry where he needed him—charmed, invested, impressed. This was Tommy's gift—persuasion—as much as his brother's had been making sense of thick, wordy books that held complicated but theoretical ideas.

Mr. McHenry threw himself back in his chair. "I read about that robbery, but they changed your names in the article, right?"

Tommy nodded.

"No wonder I didn't realize Babcock was involved," McHenry said.

"The Sacramento gang doesn't like witnesses."

Mr. McHenry pointed a chunk of bread at Tommy. "That's right. Article said you all saw his face, didn't you?"

"Matty Sacramento. Eyes black as coal and cold as ice. Still gives me nightmares sometimes."

"Well, keep talking," Mr. McHenry said. His smile lit up his face like he was on stage or some such.

Tommy was thrilled by his audience and enjoyed that McHenry treated him like a peer more than a young man in search of a job. Tommy felt his chest expand as McHenry responded so favorably. This relaxed him as he sipped his water, his neck releasing tension, knowing he'd been right to tell the whole story of how he and Babcock had met. "Once inside, the tellers got busy." Tommy mimed how they were tossing bills into dingy carpetbags. "I could see lawmen gathering outside, and instead of me feeling safer, I felt Matty Sacramento's tension like a lightning strike."

"He's a big guy, isn't he?"

Tommy nodded. "Has to be two-fifty, solid as iron, though."

McHenry's eyes were lit like candles at what he was hearing. "What happened next?"

"About the time Matty was getting ants in his pants, his brother decided a little girl who had been in the bank with her grandfather made a better hostage than me. So Matty took her on his hip and shoved me into a closet."

"That grandfather was Babcock, right?"

Tommy nodded and sat back to let the waitress set piping-hot chicken soup in front of him. His stomach rattled at the thought of such a grand meal. He saw the evidence that his social know-how was working, and he already imagined himself climbing the ladder of success within the hotel. Perhaps in a month he'd have the desk clerk position. He scooped the soup, moving the spoon away from himself, and gently took some into his mouth—not a bit of slurping, not the tiniest hint of his teeth impolitely hitting the metal.

He set the spoon on the charger and sat back, savoring the rich chicken broth. This was the part of the story he hated most. "I've been locked in small spaces before—but that's another story."

"I'm sure it is, Tommy—I can call you Tommy, right?" Mr. McHenry asked.

"Why, sure." Tommy relaxed further. He had never been more grateful for his former life as a wealthy son of Des Moines, Iowa, for all the times his mother had beaten his ears about manners being as valuable as gold itself. And best of all, somehow, this man seemed to be unconcerned that Tommy's last name was Arthur. Tommy felt as though he could confide in him. He thought of Babcock. He had entrusted Tommy to McHenry for a reason.

"I've had a rough time of it the past few years." He envisioned the closet in the bank, the fusty smell of wet mops and the vinegar they used to clean with. He remembered how he'd moved his hands around the walls, the sliver of light that came from under the door as he looked for something to protect himself. Tommy's throat dried. He couldn't expel air or take in a new breath. *Just tell the story. I don't have to feel the story.* He was safe and sound and not at all confined. At times, he could talk himself out of panic—he needed this to be one of those times. He drew and released breath purposefully.

"It's all right, Tommy."

Tommy saw McHenry's comforting, interested expression. "So at the bank, I was locked in a supply closet." Tommy could hear snatches of Matty and the other gang members' voices as they shouted and demanded their bags be filled faster. Tommy did not think he should divulge what spurred him to finally act heroically—an accidental hero was not as appealing as an intentional one.

Having developed an intolerance to tight, dark spaces, Tommy had begun to sweat profusely. He gripped the walls as he had felt as though he were spinning right off his feet. He thought he would vomit; he was sure he was dying.

Just get through the story. "I heard the Sacramentos ordering folks around and I heard the little girl cry out, and I couldn't stand it any longer. I kicked the door and burst through it like a bullet. I ran right at Sacramento like a bison, knocking him and one of his brothers to the ground. I scooped up the girl, handed her off to Babcock, and they scurried out. I was not far behind." Tommy patted his shoulder. "One of them got a shot off and grazed my shoulder."

"And so your friendship with Babcock began?"

"Right then and there. It was like we'd known each other for millennia." Tommy considered that encounter, that type of instant knowing, an otherworldly, unexplainable gift, something he'd never experienced until that moment.

Babcock's eyes had glistened as he'd thanked Tommy for making sure the Sacramentos didn't abscond with Haley. He'd noticed Tommy's tattered clothing and had taken him home with him. He hadn't seemed shocked when Tommy said he would prefer to sleep in the barn loft rather than in the house, tucked into a small room at the back.

Tommy had attempted to explain his panic, the rising swell of blood-rushing fear that hit his brain and made it impossible for him to do anything but run, run for open space. Mr. Babcock had nodded along, said he understood, that he'd been locked away during the War Between the States. Said he knew exactly what blind fear could do to a person.

He never pressed for more information on Tommy's need for space, and Tommy was grateful not to have to tell those tales. From that day forward, Babcock employed him, paying him to plow, plant, harvest, and—best in Tommy's eyes—to make and repair furniture when something was needed. This work put Tommy close to his father. Even though they were separated by miles, mountains, and rolling hills, working with his hands made him feel one with the man Tommy loved most in the world.

"Well," McHenry said, spooning the last of his chicken soup from the bowl. "In addition to you coming with Babcock's recommendation, I can see you are well-bred. You may be on hard times, but your carriage belies your tired wardrobe. You're just the kind of young man we can use here at the Savery. I believe we'll have a bellboy position opening up. Perhaps two weeks from now."

Exhilaration flooded Tommy's body. The sensation was nearly as powerful as paralyzing panic. "Thank you, sir. I'll be an asset to the Savery. In every way."

Mr. McHenry folded his hands on the tabletop. "I can certainly see that. Now, where should I send word when I know exactly when you will start?"

Tommy opened his mouth. What could he say? He turned the dinner fork over and over again. He'd been living in the woods. He liked it there, but it wasn't the type of selling point that warranted sharing. Pride was the one thing he had left to cling to, and he wasn't going to hand it over at just this important moment. Yet the man was kind. Tommy looked at McHenry, his kind eyes, the fatherly tilt of his head. Perhaps disclosing this information would serve his case better than he'd supposed. "I can stop by and check in. I'm—"

"Mr. McHenry!" a man screamed from the doorway, running toward the pair.

Mr. McHenry shot the man a disgusted look, and Tommy decided he did not want to ever disappoint this man, even though he had just met him.

"Fire. On the third floor."

McHenry pushed to standing, his chair flying onto its back. "Leave your address at the desk, Tommy. I'll be in touch. Two weeks, probably."

Everyone flew from the dining room like a herd of water buffalo. Tommy couldn't smell smoke, so he took the opportunity to let the crowd pass, and he stuffed his pockets with bread, even eating a man's abandoned cucumber sandwich—he wouldn't be back for it.

As Tommy sauntered from the hotel, he was relieved that McHenry hadn't registered anything unusual about Tommy's last name, Arthur. He dug into his pants pocket and located his lucky Indian Head penny. His fortune was swinging up, and fast. This job would put him one step closer to helping his family find their way back together. It didn't matter that he would need to sleep in the woods a while longer. He liked it there, the open sky, the animals, the river that rushed past as he fell asleep. Yes, his life was changing, and for the first time in years, he felt it was turning for the better.

Chapter 3

Jeanie

1891—Sioux Falls

I jammed my boot between the cross-hatching on the train trestle. The movement gave off a metallic ring that lifted into the navy blue sky. Raindrops pecked at the scuffed black boot tip that curled up as though it wanted to see my face when I put an end to things. The hideous clodhoppers had served me well. They'd been witness to the road I'd trekked since my family's wealth dissolved, since I came to learn there were worse defeats than losing one's standing in society and one's fat bank accounts. I curled my numb fingers around the cold bars and pulled upward. I imagined my daughter's warm hand in mine, the three squeezes we would give each other to say "I love you." It had been so long since I'd had her near. Too long.

The absence of Katherine and Tommy was suffocating. The closeness Katherine and I had shared, the way her bright eyes used to look at me, full of pride and adoration, had comforted me for much of our estrangement. But now her absence was nearly as sharp as that of my dead son James. And the last memory of her looking at me had her round eyes full of shock and sadness, her mouth hardened into a grim, straight line as she had to struggle to keep her gaze on mine.

It's almost over, Katherine. Hang in there with that nice family just a little bit longer. Your little sister can't wait to see you again… So many times I'd said those words. I thought the last time would be just that, the final need for reassurances, the last few months to live apart. How wrong I had been.

I had toiled fruitlessly to make a home that would hold all of us. My failures were heaped high and dense—a mountain of manure. The stench was ubiquitous even when I turned my back to it, even when pretending my next attempt to clear the ugly waste away would be successful. Well, no more. I could not breathe full breaths for the stink of it all. I did not want to try anymore. I did not want to have to see the sadness in Katherine's face, the disappointment in Tommy's.

I readjusted my grip. *Just let go.* The raindrops grew fatter and came faster, stinging my cheeks. I did not know if it was the frosty spring storm that numbed my face or if the deadness was due to the whiskey I'd tossed back like a coal miner set on clearing his throat of black dust.

Thoughts of my children came to mind—James, Katherine, Tommy, Yale. I had done them no good alive. Perhaps my death would release them from what felt like a curse, an Arthur family curse. In the distance, a train wailed. The fog coming from that direction obscured any visual sense of the engine that was on its way. My fingers grew tired and felt like shards of ice around the metal. I could drop forward over the trestle or backward in front of the train. I hadn't expected a choice in how I might put my life away for good.

My stomach turned; nausea dizzied me. I hunched forward and emptied everything from my stomach that I could. It was a long way down. Would it hurt? The train's whistle grew more insistent. The wind bit at my chin and changed direction, coming in sideways, tearing my hair from its neat knot at the nape of my neck. I tilted back, amazed my fingers still held, wondering why I kept them fastened. What was I waiting for?

Would it hurt?

I closed my eyes, the drunkenness comforting me in my decision. The trestle shuddered—just a hint with the nearing train. My right hand slipped off the trestle. I dangled, staring into the oncoming light. Would it hurt?

It didn't matter. Nothing could ache as much as living did. The pain in my chest pierced my resolve. If I could simply roll into a ball and die that way, I would. But I'd tried that. I'd failed at that, too. Warm tears mixed with the chilled rain, and sobs began to rise out of me, slowly, like the nearing train whistle, then fast, choking, crushing tears I should have cried long ago.

I could hear someone calling for me. *Mama!* I swore it was my sweet James. But it couldn't be him. I looked over my shoulder in the direction of the voice. The fog was thick in that direction, and I couldn't see beyond a foot or so.

Jeanie Arthur! There it was again. The voice. "Who is it?" I pushed the words out. I squinted, but I couldn't see a soul. I looked at my hands, which shook even as I gripped the bridge. *Let go. It will be over soon. My children will be free. The noose of pain will release.* As the train's light finally cut through the thick haze to illuminate the track, I felt a trace of the blackout that always seemed to appear when I could not take another minute of life.

I looked over the trestle into the rushing water below, then turned my face back into the blinding train light as the bridge quivered, jarring me. *Choose, Jeanie. Jump forward or fall back.* Either would mean the end of the grinding pain, the iron wheel that churned through my life, rolling over my chest, making nearly every breath unbearable. *Mama!* The voice came again, calling me. James? It could not be. I shook my head and surrendered.

James, Katherine, Tommy, Yale. I am sorry. I am so sorry.

Chapter 4

Katherine

1891—Storm Lake

Jab, pull, jab, pull. Katherine poked the needle through the fabric; the subtle but steady whoosh of thread passing through linen broke the silence of the deep, dark night. The dented thimble protected her finger from the sharp metal, but it did nothing for her eyes, which blurred with every stitch she'd made in the last two hours. She paused and pressed her fingers to her throbbing temple. What she'd thought might be a fine way to earn extra money while boarding with the Christoff family had turned out to be torture. If only a short break or a small meal was granted, she was sure she could finish the collars and cuffs she'd been assigned.

It was the spring season, and several families required hundreds of dresses, shirts, trousers, blouses, skirts—even new drawers to bridge the gap between winter wardrobes and summer clothing.

Katherine's head lolled forward, her eyes watering in the vanishing firelight. She yawned and wiped her cheeks as tears of fatigue ran like a spring creek. She looked at the table to her side. Just one more set of cuffs and collars after this. If she just shut her eyes for a few moments, she could finish, eat, and sleep until she had to rise and sweep the cinders, light the stove, shovel the coal in the cellar. Just a few moments' rest. She exhaled, her energy deflating further. Eyes closed, Katherine wiggled her sore shoulders, pressing against the wooden seatback, searching for comfort against the hardness. She sighed and let sleep come, just for a bit. Just a few short minutes.

A punch in the shoulder startled her. She jolted upright, stabbing her palm with the needle. She sucked at the blood, trying not to yelp.

"You're not getting paid to sleep," Mrs. Christoff said.

Katherine shook her head, trying to reorient herself. "I'm sorry. I just—" Boarding with this family had seemed like a good idea when she'd first met them. They had appeared kind and had promised that Katherine would have opportunities— school and meeting people who would pay her good money to sew.

"You have the look of an imbecile, drooling like that." She pointed at the unfinished work. "We don't get paid for work that isn't done."

Katherine had never been so tired, so famished, so drunk without having put anything into her body to make her thus. She struggled to rise, hand on her temple, trying to right her vision. "Please, just a little something to eat and I will finish."

"No. It's the middle of the night. Praise God I woke out of a deep slumber in time to stop you from wasting it."

Katherine recalled the bread she'd made for the family in the afternoon. She put her hand out, palm-up. "Just a tear of bread from the loaf. Please."

Mrs. Christoff glared at Katherine's hand. "No food. If you're so tired, you sleep—two hours. When you wake, say your prayers and finish that collar and cuffs. Then we'll discuss some eating. This is serious business. Our money tree burned to the ground, in case you don't remember. We are attempting to put this once-grand home back together. Do you even see the way it's falling apart? Look"—Mrs. Christoff swept her hand toward the hallway—"at that chandelier. Missing almond crystals, dulled brass shine. It exemplifies all that could be great in this home and all that is not. How are we to host the summer bonanza for the church when our home looks like a hovel?"

In her exhausted haze, the truth became clear to Katherine. The Christoffs had no intention of letting her keep the extra sewing money. Katherine's shoulders slumped.

Mrs. Christoff shook her finger. "And you know the Lord punishes those who take sinful advantage of others."

Katherine had heard that money tree joke too many times to feign laughter, and she'd had it with the accusing God references that were always directed at her and never reflected back on Mrs. Christoff. Katherine had begun to see herself as the only thing in the family remotely close to a mystical money tree or even a cow with plentiful milk. Each day brought a new round of milking, of pulling away at all Katherine had to offer. This turned any soft feelings she'd had toward the parents rock hard since she'd come to see the truth about her arrangement with them.

The other family members worked, too, but Katherine slaved. She cooked, baked, shoveled, washed, cleaned, and turned out beautifully finished clothing that Mrs. Christoff and Hannah had simply sewed together on a treadle machine. Oh, what Katherine would have given for a chance at sewing the clothes instead of being tasked with finishing them.

Mrs. Christoff clamped her hand around Katherine's arm and pulled her into the hall, passing under what must have once been an exquisite chandelier. They clomped up the staircase, their heavy steps making the dusty, tarnished fixture jingle. Katherine had fallen in love with its disrepair, its potential—reminding her of her, the idea there would soon be a time when she dusted herself off and revealed the fine person she had once been.

As she headed up the stairs, a strange light caught Katherine's eye. She looked over her shoulder. Through her exhausted gaze, it appeared to her that the chandelier was restored, beautifully lit, the festoons with almond-shaped crystals and prisms strung from arm to arm while diamond-shaped crystals dangled from the bend in each arm, and the fat, plum-sized pendant that hung off the finial at the bottom appeared sparkling new, almost alive as the dim light splashed off its facets.

Katherine stopped and pointed. Mrs. Christoff didn't turn to look. Her sneer deepened, and she yanked Katherine by the arm. The fatigue had made Katherine's entire existence unreal in every way—the glowing but nonworking chandelier was just one more thing.

Once upstairs, Mrs. Christoff wrenched up her nightdress, crawled over her husband, and flopped into a snoring sleep.

Katherine was too tired to undress, and so she took her spot next to Hannah Christoff. The younger girl wormed over to Katherine, her body warm. Except for the girl's cold feet, which she dug up under Katherine's dress and pressed against her legs, where the chill came through the stockings. Katherine's shoulder dug into the thin featherbed, hitting the wood floor.

As Katherine's mind further clouded, she felt the absence of her mother and siblings. The sadness in losing them was heaviest in the night, when life seemed most fragile. But in that same place where almost-sleep smudged her thoughts, she also found the soothing presence of her deceased brother, James, his strong presence reminding her not to give up hope. She clasped her hands under her chin. *Please, God, take me home, take me home, take me home.*

She pulled her knees up tight, moving away from Hannah's icy toes. Katherine squeezed her own hand three times, imagining that her mother was there to do it herself. "I love you, too, Mama," she whispered, knowing that if she fell asleep with good thoughts in her mind and love in her heart, she would find a way back to her family. As she faded further into sleep, Katherine could feel her mother brush her hair back, offer encouraging words to her and Tommy. She even thought she heard the mischievous rumble of Tommy's laugh, could hear his feet dash past, as he always seemed to be running. She never could have imagined such small things would be what stuck with her, what comforted her at night and made her ache in the daytime.

And it didn't matter what the Christoffs said about God punishing the Arthurs, that Katherine's mother didn't even bother to write to her anymore, proving indifference—or worse, hate for her daughter. No, Katherine would not give up trying until she managed to get away from the Christoffs once and for all. She didn't know where she would go, but she knew she had to leave before things got even worse. She was beginning to think that death might be superior to life with the Christoffs. She would leave before that was the option she took—that much she knew.

Chapter 5

Tommy

1891—Des Moines

The Des Moines city streets teemed with shoppers, businessmen, and workers headed to whatever store or factory in which they were employed. Tommy whistled along the sidewalk, refreshed from a good, deep sleep. It had been easy. A crisp, starry night had blanketed him with an awe-inspiring view from his makeshift quarters. To set up camp, he'd used sticks balanced against a low branch, creating a skeleton for a tent. He'd laid pine boughs against the branches and then covered the structure with a canvas sheet. A meal of rolls, walnuts and dried berries he'd stowed in his knapsack, along with cool water from the river, made his night feel celebratory, his existence cozy and hopeful.

The positive interview with Mr. McHenry at the Savery Hotel had helped most with Tommy's good spirits and restorative sleep. Knowing solid employment was on the horizon had tilted the earth so every life task seemed tinged with warm, happy light. It was simply good to be alive.

Now he just needed to do some odd jobs around town until he started his work as a bellboy. Even though he wasn't officially hired yet, he knew he would be. Clearly Mr. McHenry had liked him and wanted him in his employ. It was a matter of a job opening up—and the man had been sure that would happen soon.

At the corner near Miss Sissy's Dresses and Townside Grocer, Tommy dug through his burlap sack, pushing aside his spare cap, the small canvas drawstring bag that held a dollar in change and his tin cup. He could have sworn he had a few more walnuts buried in there. Nothing. He pressed a hand to his belly and unscrewed the lid to his canteen. The refreshing water trickled down his throat but left a metallic taste and the stale whiff of the canvas cover.

The first couple of days back in Des Moines, Tommy'd had luck getting work sweeping the sidewalks and hauling crates at the grocer in exchange for breakfast. For lunch, he'd been shoveling coal into the stoves at Mrs. Falco's Rooming House. Dinner was a delicious blend of nuts he'd collected in the woods and hot coffee—he was always exhausted enough to sleep hard even after the evening caffeine.

He shook his head and chuckled as he dug back into the sack. He'd thought it had been secured the night before, but raccoons must have had their way with the food he'd gathered. He thought of the shotgun Mr. Babcock had given him and the bow and arrows he'd traded for the other day. He'd lost two arrows while shooting at distant tree stumps just for the fun of it, and now he had only one arrow left. Not being much of a hunter but knowing a boy in the woods needed protection, he'd covered those items with canvas and tucked them into a tree trunk near his camp.

Tommy eyed the suited men disembarking from carriages and the city folk headed to work. Girls streamed by, dressed in practical boots and bland dresses, and Tommy knew they were already hours into their chores for the households for which they worked.

A man running with his paper under his arm and briefcase in hand approached as he pulled his watch from his pocket. As he looked down, he swerved and shouldered Tommy, knocking him sideways.

"Sorry!" The man raised his paper in acknowledgment but kept going. Tommy rubbed his shoulder, thinking back to the coal miner who had boarded him before Babcock. The bustling scene in Des Moines numbed his mind and seemed to be accompanied by the *whip-smack-whip* sound of a razor strop making cutting contact with his bare shoulders. He jumped as though back at the miner's house. The blows were hard and cruel, but he'd grown to expect them. The fat miner'd had a joyful expression on his red face as he'd reeled back his arm and let another blow fly. It took only once for Tommy to understand that the man enjoyed dealing out the beating to Tommy, to his own children.

Luckily, Tommy's large size gave him some measure of protection from beatings at Mrs. Henderson's diminutive hands—at least there was that. But his size also seemed to infuriate Mr. Henderson, as though every one of the six inches he grew that year was an insult to the man. It seemed to make Tommy a fine target for his fists or whatever lumber was at hand. It was in that home that Tommy became acquainted with small spaces and had first begun to feel panic when closed in.

As strange as it seemed when Tommy let himself consider it, the beatings, the physical pain, paled by comparison to Mrs. Henderson's "special place," the hole dug in the hillside behind the house. Framed up on the inside with boards to prevent it from caving in, it was no bigger than a crawl space and as dark and dank as a pit in hell. He swirled the gritty loneliness in his mouth with one final swig from the canteen. It was how they broke him, how they kept him compliant.

The door to the tailor shop slammed and made Tommy leap. *I'm here in Des Moines, away from that awful house.* He talked himself back to the present time, the door slam helping to lure him away from the panic that had been swelling inside. He shook off the awful feeling. He'd gotten good at detaching from painful loss and oppressive seclusion. It was the only way he knew to survive—he simply put the things he couldn't control behind him. Well, almost everything.

Even with Mr. Babcock having to move away, Tommy saw that things were looking up, and he would not allow sorrow to sour his day for long. He'd been offered the chance to go east with Mr. Babcock, but Tommy could not accept. He was determined to see his family put back together, not further scattered across the country.

He pushed his hand into his pants pocket and felt for the Indian Head penny his father had given him. He had promised Tommy it was lucky, and Tommy believed it. When he thought back to how he'd survived being separated from his family, the bank robbery, escaping cruel boarding homes, and then his fantastic interview with McHenry, he knew for sure the penny had brought fortune. He just hadn't been *fully* granted its luck yet. But it was coming. Next he would put his life back together, reunite his parents, and begin to rebuild their lost fortune. But James. If only the penny could manage to bring him back.

He rubbed his thumb over the rises and furrows of the feathers that were molded into the copper, picturing the face of his dead brother. Oh, how his heart ached to have his brother back. He couldn't change that, but at least he could make the other goals happen.

Tommy put the penny back in his pocket, covering it with the knife he kept there so there was no chance of it falling out. The wind kicked up, tossing particles from the dirt road into the air. Tommy squinted and turned away from the gust, but not before the unmistakable redolence of fresh-baked bread filled his nose.

Tommy followed the scent around the corner. There was an unfamiliar store—Holcomb's Bakery. It had been years since he'd lived in Des Moines, and not only was he now living off his wits and the land instead of living off his family, it seemed as though the entire town had changed, storefronts and all. The wealthy had shifted farther away from the original regal homes in the city to the suburbs, and it seemed as though half the population of Des Moines had turned over.

This was mostly a good thing for Tommy. Leaving a town in full disgrace did not make returning an easy endeavor. But it hadn't been as bad as he had feared. At his current level of society, he didn't think he'd have any chance to interact with old friends and acquaintances. Yet there was opportunity in Des Moines. Finding a real job, which he would soon have, finishing school—all of this was possible. As soon as the bellboy job was officially his, he would write about it to his father.

Just the thought of him made Tommy's heart constrict with sadness while putting a small smile on his lips. His father had left after the blizzard on the prairie in 1888. He'd returned, but for only a short time. Tommy suspected his father had been angry, sorry, and embarrassed that Jeanie Arthur had divorced him. But despite the pain between his parents, he was sure they could heal the wounds of the prairie year. He sighed. Yes, he was quite sure they could.

Tommy stood in front of the bakery window, inhaling down to his toes. He thought perhaps even a hint of the bread as its scent rose on the spring air was enough for him. How he wished it could be. The window display was laden with silver and glass pedestals of every height. Each groaned under the weight of white-frosted cupcakes, lemon custard overflowing pastry shells, tiered cakes dripping with chocolate.

But it was the simple, elegant loaves of fresh bread that made his mouth water so much, he had to wipe the corners of his mouth with the back of his hand. He balled his fists at his sides.

The bell on the bakery door rang and a barrel-bellied baker emerged.

His white hat was speckled with pastel-hued frosting. He had a loaf of bread under one arm and another half in his hands. He narrowed his eyes on Tommy and smirked. "Move along, cur."

Tommy recoiled, then looked over each shoulder. Was he speaking to him? He still wore the skin of the wealthy boy he'd been for the first ten years of his life. The last four years, though tough and unfulfilling, had taught him a lot, but he didn't feel as though it had removed who he was at his core…a fine young man.

Tommy looked back at the window and focused on his reflection rather than the treats inside. He readjusted his hat, brushed the sleeves of his dusty coat, and straightened his shoulders. The baker's sneer solidified Tommy's determination to do more with his life.

Tommy thought perhaps if he offered to work, the man would see he was not a worthless wanderer. He stepped toward the baker. The baker put his back against the door. "Move along, boy."

Tommy removed his hat, holding it against his belly. He stuck his hand forward, recalling how the manager at the Savery Hotel had been impressed by Tommy's confidence.

But the baker simply shifted the bread under his arm and tore pieces from the clump in his hand, tossing them into the sky. Tommy pulled his hand back and followed the arc the bread took in the air to the ground, where a bird snatched a few crumbs away before Tommy could finish licking his lips. A squirrel joined the feast, making the baker giggle with delight.

"Sir," Tommy said. "Could I work for some bread? I can sweep or stock your shelves when deliveries come, or I can deliver your goods. I'm hardworking and dependable."

The baker screwed his face into confusion. "I got plenty of folks working. Move on."

Tommy almost did just that. But a woman and her small son moving toward the breadcrumbs caught his eye. The child got to his knees and began stuffing crumbs into his mouth with one hand and into his pocket with the other. His mother watched, meeting Tommy's eyes for a moment before she fixed them on the boy. She wrapped her arms around her middle. Humiliation veiled her downcast eyes.

The baker tossed another handful into the air.

Three more birds joined the first, and a second squirrel followed them. The little boy brushed aside the animals to get his share.

"Look at yer animal boy," the baker said to the woman. "He's a rodent like the squirrel, ain't he?"

The mother didn't look up, but Tommy saw tears drop from her eyes, plunging into the dirt road. In that moment, he felt her powerlessness as though it were his own, twisting his gut, filling him with anger.

The baker giggled more and began to pepper the boy's head with bread, causing the birds to gather around his head, scaring him.

Tommy's mouth dropped open, disbelieving the depths of the man's malice. "Can't you give the woman and boy the scraps? You obviously don't need them."

The baker turned toward Tommy, his expression confused.

"They're hungry. I'll work for the cost of their bread," Tommy said.

The baker threw back his head and laughed.

"Please. Just the scraps." Tommy put his hand on the man's wrist.

The baker focused on Tommy, his pupils constricting.

Tommy pulled his hand away. "Please."

The baker pushed Tommy's shoulder.

He stumbled back but caught himself before falling. The sudden movement caused the birds to take to the wind and the squirrels to scurry off. The boy picked up the bread as fast as he could, his mother joining him on the ground, collecting their bounty.

Tommy breathed heavy, his heart thumping at his chest walls.

The baker stalked toward him. "You frightened off my pets, you disgusting, dirt-covered boy. Last time. Get away, or I'll shove you into the road just in time for the next wagon passing by."

Tommy swallowed hard. He was angry and embarrassed for the woman who had to allow her son to gather food from a dirt road. His blood rushed past his ears, filling his mind with ideas that would lead only to trouble. Punch him. Right in that fat nose.

"Just give them the bread you were tossing to the birds—"

The baker smiled, and Tommy's shoulders relaxed.

The man stepped closer. His stench filled Tommy's nose, making him cringe away. Without turning around, the baker resumed ripping the crust and hurling the bits over his shoulder. The birds returned, fluttering near the scavenging boy's head, snatching bread right from midair.

Tommy smiled tightly. "Cut it out," he said. The baker stepped back, cackling.

Hit him.

It's none of my business.

At first, the boy ignored the birds that hovered above, but then he looked up, and seeing them flapping so close, he began to flail. The baker increased the speed of his gleeful barrage.

More birds descended. The boy's mother batted away as many as she could, but with the steady stream of food, they were not deterred. Tommy stepped forward to block the stream of crumbs, but the little boy flew to his feet, arms flailing over his head, tripping backward. The baker crowed and laughed as the boy fell to his bottom, his face scrunching up with cries. The baker tossed more, further working the birds into a frenzy. Tommy bent to pull the boy up, but he scrambled to his feet and bolted farther into the road.

Out of the corner of Tommy's eye, he saw a coal wagon bearing down.

"Coal wagon!" he screamed.

The boy had already turned away and run blindly into the path of the oncoming wagon. The driver pulled back on the reins, causing the horses to rear up. The sudden stop made the wagon skid, and its rear end slid back and forth, finding its resting place on the sidewalk, knocking right through the bakery window. The glass shattered, shards bouncing down the wooden-planked sidewalk.

Tommy stood motionless while he took in the scene. The baker struggled to his feet after diving out of the way. Where were the mother and her boy? Tommy approached the wreck. The wagon, askew across the sidewalk, lodged in the bakery window, the horses with their back legs on the sidewalk, their front on the street—Tommy petted the nose of one of the horses. "Shush. It's all right." Was it? An odd hush over the morning bustle chilled him. He didn't want to believe the mother and child might be underneath the wagon.

The shocked driver got up from the road where he'd landed when he dove from his seat. He clutched his hat and screamed about his load. The coal had flown in every direction, and one side of the wagon was splashed with lemon custard. He removed his hat, hitting it against his leg as he pointed at Tommy. "You did this!"

Tommy ignored the accusation and hunted for the boy and his mother. It wasn't until they came up from behind him that he realized they were unscathed. The mother was crying, her boy on one hip, her other arm outstretched toward Tommy.

She latched him around the neck with the crook of her arm, yanking Tommy into an embrace. "Thank you. Thank you so much."

"You're welcome," Tommy said, wiggling away, still recapturing his air.

A clutch of policemen rounded the corner, picking up speed toward the murmuring crowd that had now gathered. Tommy scooped the woman's hat up from the road and handed it to her as she smothered her boy with kisses. It was then that Tommy noticed the focus of the group had shifted and centered on him.

The hair on the back of his neck stood up. *Run*, something told him.

But as he took his first stride, the baker and a policeman each grasped one of Tommy's arms from behind.

"This vagrant broke my window." The baker spit at Tommy's feet.

A second policeman joined them, carrying Tommy's knapsack.

"I've got him, Mr. Holcomb. He won't bother you another second of another day," the first policeman said.

"Wait," Tommy said as the baker released his arm. "It was *him*. Not me!"

"Mayor and Judge Calder are clear. Rid the streets of delinquents. We'll take care of him."

"Delinquent? I'm the furthest from it!" Tommy thought again of his upbringing. He almost blurted out who he was—or who he'd been when they'd first lived in Des Moines. But something made him refrain.

"Please. Let me tell you what happened."

The officer didn't respond.

"He saved my boy!" the mother screamed from down the road. Tommy looked over his shoulder and saw that she was still embracing her son, the boy's legs tight around her waist as she tried to explain Tommy had helped, that the accident was not criminal mischief.

"Did you hear her?" Tommy asked.

The policeman simply gripped tighter and towed Tommy away, down the road. The second officer rooted through the knapsack, plucking out items and throwing them back in as they headed down the road.

"You can make your excuses for assaulting a leading citizen of Des Moines and vandalizing his property in front of the judge. But I don't want to hear it," the policeman said. "You troubled the wrong baker, young man."

Tommy's feet were wobbly as they wove in and out of people going about their day. Even as staring faces passed by, Tommy wasn't really seeing them. He had gone numb, feeling only utter dismay that he could be accused of being a worthless pauper—a position in life that meant his story, his reasons for defending himself or a woman and her child, no longer mattered. He saw more clearly than ever that justice, the law, the good things in life, were really intended just for those with money. And Tommy had none.

Vagrant. He was not that—not in the way they meant. Being dragged away may have brought him humiliation, but he refused to show it. He kept his chest up, his gaze unblinking as he repeated silently that he had done nothing wrong. He would not live this life much longer. He was destined for something greater, even if it seemed as though the rest of the world was not yet informed on the matter.

Chapter 6

Jeanie

1891—Sioux Falls

A stream of sunshine fell over my face, drawing me out of slumber. I could see the light behind my eyelids and feel the warmth, even though I couldn't open my dry eyes. I knew where I was. I just couldn't imagine how I got back here. I lifted my head and squinted, scanning the room as best I could. I could see Millie at the other end of the attic, making her bed as she did daily.

My brain convulsed. I flopped back on the nearly flat pillow and groaned. It was then that Yale stirred. I'd slept so hard and was still so foggy that I hadn't even registered that she was nestled against me, her back curved perfectly into me, her feet pressed against my thighs. I worked my hand out from under the coverlet and pressed my cheeks, my temples, my still-damp hair. I was alive? How was it possible? I envisioned the headlight of the train coming toward me, the cold rain pelting me. I could recall the sorrow mixed with fear at the thought of tossing myself onto the tracks, thinking it was the only way.

Mama…Jeanie Arthur! Someone had called for me on the trestle. I was sure of it. I sat up, nausea gripping me. I covered my mouth and swallowed the urge to vomit. It must have been the wind. My James had been dead for years now. I'd heard his voice a million times in crowds of sons calling for mothers, but it could never be my boy calling. Never again. And yet I'd heard it last night. Hadn't I?

I wiped sweat from my brow and climbed over Yale. My heart raced. I looked down at my clothing. Parts of the chemise had remained wet and other sections had dried stiff with brown muck.

I lifted my arms and looked at my feet, still cloaked in my muddy boots. How had I gotten back here? The last four years had buried me under many layers of despair. But having lost my last boarding opportunity—when Mrs. Stevens lost her house and headed off with nothing to show for the past sixty years of her life, putting Yale and me back on the street—well, that had done me in.

I couldn't take the thought of breaking any more promises to my children, to think I didn't even know where my Katherine was boarding anymore. The weight of all that loss had turned me toward whiskey, and soon after that, pointed my feet in the direction of the trestle. *How on earth had I gotten back here?*

"It was me, Jeanie Arthur," Millie said.

I jerked toward her, chest heaving as I fought to remember any part of what happened after I'd heard someone calling me. Confused, I wondered how she seemed to know exactly what I was thinking.

"You?"

Millie dabbed at my sweaty brow with a swatch of dry linen. She held my chin as though I were her child.

"Not just me. Harvey drug you from the river after you jumped."

I licked my dry lips, searching my mind for the recollection of what Millie was describing.

Millie took my hand and pulled me toward the fireplace at the end of the attic near her cot. She sat me down and unlaced my boots.

"I jumped?" I shook my head, unable to find the memory that went with the words.

"You don't…remember?"

I squeezed my eyes closed, trying to call up exactly what happened.

"You were sauced." Millie took one of my hands in hers and turned it palm-up, examining it in the streaming sunlight that would illuminate the space for only a short time before the room was darkened by shadow and shade.

The cuts on my hands began to throb where the crusted blood oozed out of the scrapes. I had never been a lady who even snuck whiskey from a sterling flask and I was embarrassed now that I'd gotten drunk. I hadn't expected to survive the night. "I don't…I mean, I remember being there, but…"

Millie laid my hand back in my lap and dipped a rag into the pot of water beside her. "Shush. No need, Jeanie Arthur. Anyone who resides here has a story, her actions to explain. But it's not necessary. Not one bit." I nodded. Before becoming one of the women who ended up with no choice but to live in a poorhouse, I had certainly read enough about them in the paper, talked about them and their poor, pitiful children at the Women's Club in Des Moines.

Those poorhouse women found their way there by making poor choices or after having been cast off by cruel lovers or husbands, women who had been made mothers when they were barely teenagers and unwed. I had thought I could manage to make a few less-than-fabulous choices and still make a home for my children. I'd thought I was different, that the world would see me as the woman I had been when penning my Quintessential Housewife column. How could I have known that no one would allow me any position in society at all once my husband was out of the picture, useless as he'd been? Oh, how could I have known? I shook my head and studied the wounds on my palms. How could I have *not* known?

I swallowed hard. She understood? Another human being understood.

"I am so—"

Millie shushed me and turned her attention back to my hands. "Your story?" She put one fist to her chest. "I share it. I know it without you breathing a word. A woman in this world with no man ain't worth nothing."

I grimaced. Millie gently blotted at the mahogany-hued blood that had hardened in the lines of my palm. "Don't fret. You ain't worthless. But—" she circled her hand above her head, the wet rag flinging water droplets, "—the world thinks so. I'm just seeing the circumstances that would send a mother to a train trestle. It don't mean you're worthless. But it does mean you're penniless, you're tired, you're sorry about so much you've done."

The blunt words took my breath away. *Mother.* Did I deserve that title? I tried to recollect what had sent me there, what had turned me from my usual dumpy-mooded self to the self who nearly gave it all up.

My stomach turned at the memory of the whiskey hitting my innards, the sharp burn down my esophagus. I drew a deep breath. I was just now coming to realize the miracle that had occurred, that I was alive.

"It's a miracle," I said, barely above a whisper.

Millie looked up. "Hmm?"

"Nothing," I said, not yet fully believing it.

I did not know how people turned to drink for comfort. It had magnified all that was rotten in my life, and even the gentle drunkenness that I'd first felt had quickly given way to anger and hostility, hopelessness.

The flash of memory of my angry fists hitting the wall while Yale wrapped her arms around my leg made my knuckles throb. The whiskey had unleashed all the rage and tears that I'd sewn up inside me all these years. What I could recall of the evening before made me think I must have looked insane. Pounding on walls, of all things. In front of my daughter.

I opened my fingers and stared at them: red, raw, wounded like me. But unlike the cuts and bruises on my skin, no one could see the brokenness inside me. The facts were clear as print in a book—a divorced woman could not depend on herself, on a job, on determination alone. That realization was stark and left me wondering how it had taken me so much time to recognize it. My former privilege in life had left me believing the world to be more forgiving, more accommodating than it actually was.

Millie dipped a section of linen into the water again and dabbed at my sores. How shameful. How small of me, how unforgiveable that I had even thought of taking my life.

"Thank you, Millie."

She studied my hands, gently working away at the grime, delicately avoiding aggravating my wounds as best she could. Her unkempt salt-and-pepper hair, her own skin layered with filth, the sharp whiff from her unwashed body would have turned my stomach years ago. At the very least, the sight of her would have had my eyes turning away, not willing to see her as I did now. She bit her lip as she remoistened the cloth. How had she even noticed I needed her, let alone made the effort to act? I touched her cheek with my fingertips. She met my eyes with hers and smiled before looking back to my hand. Yes, she was real—skin and bones, but an angel on earth.

I closed my eyes and let her nurse me in a way no one had that I could remember. My eyes burned as I thought of the past. I had worked hard the past three years since leaving the prairie. I made money; then it was taken from me by illness, melancholy, or employers who reneged on the fee they'd promised. The depths of my bad fortune would have made for good dark comedy had it not been what had destroyed my family, my outlook, the very heart that beat in my chest.

Nothing that had sent me into the night to scale the trestle had changed. I still had nothing but a lap of broken promises, no measurable income. Yet something inside me had changed. I had my daughter Yale with me. I opened my eyes. And here was Millie. As surely as I had wanted to die the night before, there was a sense of appreciation that I hadn't. Looking at Millie, I felt something pure and loving, as though God had somehow given me a chance. I wasn't flush with empty promises and foundationless air castles.

I did not feel a surge of optimism that brought a big smile to my face as I dreamed up another plan of action. No, it was a small seed of knowing. Something told me that I had been looking at my life from the wrong angle all this time. I'd been looking down from the invisible perch from which I'd been born. My former wealth and education and standing had ensured that I'd feel a failure no matter what happened.

A seed of truth. I felt it inside my soul. That's what it was. That was what had changed. I accepted for the first time that I had no plan, no means, and from that vantage point, I might be able to see victory in simply drawing breath.

Millie dipped the linen in the water again. Her gaze met mine and she nodded. Her expression conveyed warmth and love, her heart utterly open to a brutal world in a way that mine may never had been, even if I had once thought it was.

Millie was my own living, breathing, personal angel. Thinking of her, acknowledging that she saved me, should disallow any wallowing I might threaten to undertake. I am here because of her. I looked back down to where Yale lay on our cot. I could see her dark hair sticking out from under the covers. I shuddered as the realization that I'd made the choice to abandon her on that bridge settled on me. What would have become of her? What would I have left Tommy and Katherine with had I died and permanently removed any chance to right my wrongs? I shivered and swallowed a sob that threatened to burst forth.

Millie smiled, the gaps between her teeth reminding me that I was not the only person who had a difficult life. "Thank you, Millie," I said.

She dipped the cloth into the water again. "A bit more," she said.

I nodded and thought of my ex-husband, Frank. He was drawn to laudanum, drink, lust for other women, whatever it was that could numb his senses, fulfill his desires, and allow him to forget our family even when we milled around him like stars around the moon. I'd seen him flush with drugs, an easy smile falling across his face when he consumed something powerful. He'd made it his habit, and it had helped to rip our marriage and our lives apart, yet he sought it out as though the drug had made his life precious, not ruined. Now, suffering from overdrinking myself, I wondered how the man had gotten up at all.

And while Millie nursed my tender hands, I had to admit that I missed that man. Not his soul or his heart or his body, which he'd laid on mine countless times. But I missed what he was supposed to be, what I'd thought our marriage was, what I had believed love to be. I squeezed my eyes shut, dug deep inside the memory that lived in my skin, and pulled up the feeling I'd had when we'd run away and eloped as rash fourteen-year-olds.

There it was—a flicker, like a spider I didn't notice had landed on my arm until it was ascending back up its silken web. Oh, that love had been strong, and I'd felt it so wholly that I'd run off to marry Frank in secret. I trembled. This momentary snatch of remembered love chilled my skin, then skittered away. It left me to wonder if I'd ever feel it again, feel it truly, deeply, feel it with a man who would honor his vow and hold me more dear than his ambition, his air castles, his desires to try all things new. Millie patted my palm dry with an unused cloth. She laid my hand in my lap and started on the other. Perhaps it was not my lot to share love, to have a united family that flourished.

I had managed much of my life to ignore these shortcomings, to plod on and do my best to put my family back together again. I had thought this was the only way to go on after Frank's part in James' death, after my husband chose another woman over the rest of us. I had thought the resulting separation from Katherine and Tommy would be temporary, days at most. And here I am, years later, barely having been able to put my gaze on them. I had thought it was the only solution—to oust Frank permanently. I thought I was bigger than the rules of society. I had believed I was smarter, savvier, harder-working. And yet here I was.

Feeling grateful to be alive—like a miracle had visited me last night. But I needed to be honest with myself, to question how it was that I'd gotten to the point where I was slugging back whiskey and taking to a train trestle on an icy spring night.

How could I be sure I could hang on to the grace that I felt? It was so easy to feel my loss. Each time Yale and I were turned out of a home yet again, when the full weight of my dead son, James, shook my bones like the wind rattled tree branches, I would be suffocated by regret that I had erred when I hadn't taken Frank back.

This last time, the desperation had been worse. Things had been good with Mrs. Stevens. I had been saving money, so hopeful as I helped her gardener work the land and learned how to sustain my daughter and myself. But Mrs. Stevens was a widow with lavish tastes, and her money had run out. I hadn't seen it coming—certainly the gardener hadn't, either—but perhaps I had just closed my eyes to it.

I also hadn't seen the disgruntled maids who'd stolen the money I'd hidden away in the carpetbag in the tiny closet in the attic where I hung one dress. How could they have stolen from me—from someone with even less than them?

The day before I took to the trestle, I watched Mrs. Stevens leave her substantial home with nothing of value. My knees had weakened so much, I had to grab the railing for support. Seeing that once-proud, wealthy woman on her porch, waiting for her soon-to-be-laid-off wagon man to drive her to the train station, where her last dollar would take her back to where she'd been born, Chicago—the experience took me back to when I stood with nothing, with my grand home at my back, knowing that I would never be the same again, not understanding what that really meant.

To see Mrs. Stevens' chin held high, her hand clasping the suitcase handle, me knowing that it held just five items she'd managed to hide from the constable who'd come to claim her assets—one set of stockings, one chemise, one blouse, one skirt, and the silver hairbrush engraved with her initials.

The indignity had lain dormant under my skin, but in seeing that, seeing her, remembering, knowing I had failed my children again—even if not by my own actions. I should have been smarter, should have put the money in the bank. On the porch that day, the words, "I will start over; it won't be long," came again, as they always did. But this time, they were wholly bitter, no sense of the sweet hopefulness that had been there the other times.

The thought of beginning again had assaulted me, dizzied me. I had believed that I'd scraped the bottom of the dry well years before, but in that moment, I understood that I had not. I wondered how much deeper I would have to go before I was permitted to simply die.

That was the first time, in the midst of my decimated life, in the endless blizzard of unfortunate happenings, that I considered surrendering. I had thought in relieving the world of me, my children might have a chance to thrive.

It was in the giving up, that night with the whiskey, at the saloon down a ways from the poorhouse, that I offered myself to death. Death may have been all that kept my image in the eyes of my children the slightest bit warm and worthy. If I drank enough, I could amble over to the railroad trestle and have a little accident. Miss Millie could care for Yale until my Katherine and Tommy were notified of my demise.

In the desperation, in the panic that caused me to easily carve away all reason, all desire to live another day, I had planned such a thing. My death was the only condition that could make up for not following through with having money and a home to call Katherine and Tommy back to. I had broken enough promises in the past three years; there was no way I could willingly break another. Air castles. I used to deride Frank for putting up one useless dream after the other. And now I was no better than he.

The shame was hot, like a lightning bolt striking a tree, tearing the bark away, leaving a black slash, evidence it had been there, that it was in charge of the tree's stunted existence from that day forward. I mentally inventoried the letters I'd sent and received from my children.

Several months back, Katherine had stopped answering my letters. She was living in Yankton with a family named Turner. I could only guess she'd had enough of my fractured promises. When Tommy actually wrote, his letters were laced with hopeful ideas that his father and I might reunite and live happily again. He misunderstood the condition of happiness, the circumstances that had torn us apart. He was living with a large family where the father was a coal miner. I imagined him enjoying the experience of living with a hardworking man like that, but I knew it was his own father whom he held in highest esteem.

I hoped Katherine and Tommy were safe. I worried that it would take days for me to get word in the case of an illness or worse. And lately, I had begun to worry whether I even knew exactly where they were. Even hot with anger at me, I couldn't imagine why Katherine wouldn't drop a short note. *Was she all right?*

My letters to the Turners asking if all was well had not been replied to. Not having my living children near me was nearly as bad as James being dead. I knew where he was; I spoke into the air at times, watching the weather shift over my head, knowing he was up there somewhere with a hateful God or no God at all.

Recalling Katherine's face hurt the most, seeing the agony in her eyes when I had first boarded her out, and then when I failed to bring her to me again and again. The lack of letters, her disappointment—it was too much to keep going. The drinks had gone down, slicing through the flesh in my throat and belly.

Punishing myself. I can't even say when I stopped being able to see, to follow thoughts, when exactly blackness dropped over my mind, but if forced into court, swearing to tell the truth to the judge, I'd have to say I had no idea how I'd come to find my bed, how my daughter had found her way into the curve of my embrace. The sun lit a small section of the room near the fireplace. I watched as Millie swept the cinders and replaced the tinder in the fireplace.

I shook as I fully realized how fragile life was, and yet I was alive. A wave of emotion coursed through me as I comprehended that I had survived and caused me to drop my face into my hands, to let the tears rush forth, crying like I can't remember ever having done.

Millie pulled a coverlet from off the cot, tucking it around my legs. *I am alive.* I was alive. She pulled me against her.

"You're alive, Jeanie Arthur. Now you must live. For that little one over there. She's slow like winter sap. Needs her mother or she'll suffer the world in ways you don't want to know. Slow ones are worse off than divorced women. But you know that."

A flash of memory caused my eyes to fly open. I had asked God to show himself on that trestle. I had been six years old the last time I believed God existed, that he cared about the earth he supposedly created, but there I was, my stomach punishing me for the whiskey, and I began to think perhaps there was a God, and for some reason, on the other side of sanity, he seemed to think I should be alive.

Chapter 7

Katherine

1905—Des Moines

Katherine stood in the foyer of her home already feeling the heat of the day growing thick, the humidity beginning to saturate her skin. The funeral would not be long due to the small number of friends and family Jeanie Arthur enjoyed. Katherine was grateful that she was able to give her mother an attractive, proper service and burial. She glanced to her right, into the parlor. The flowers that surrounded the coffin were happy even if the occasion was somber.

She smoothed her skirts. The embroidered silk was smooth and rough at the same time. She'd rehearsed what she wanted to say at the service, but as she stood there waiting for her family to gather, she found that every word inside her brain had dissolved, fluttering away like dreams upon waking.

The rumblings of her children reverberated throughout the house. The boys' screams of protest as Aleksey scrubbed them down and combed their hair came from upstairs, their feet pounding down the hallway as they scattered once released from their father's hand. Katherine smiled, feeling grateful that Aleksey was there to help at a time like this. The sound of her daughter Beatrice's feet clicking across the dining room floor made Katherine turn.

Beatrice came into the foyer, her mourning dress too tight as she hadn't worn it in nearly a year. She wrapped her arms around her waist. Her violet eyes held cloudy sadness, her brow furrowed, her mouth formed into a little o.

Katherine's heart seized at the sight of her. She opened her arms, walking forward. Beatrice broke into a run and smashed into Katherine's embrace, her body shuddering as she sobbed. Katherine smoothed the back of her hair. "Shush, my sweet pea. It's all right. Grandma Jeanie is at peace now."

Beatrice's body jerked as her sobs morphed into hiccups. "But she's gone, Mama. She's gone now. We didn't get to know each other as well as possible. She even said."

"I know. I know." Katherine pulled away and studied Beatrice's face, cupping her cheeks, rubbing away tears with her thumbs. Beatrice was a sensitive soul, always rescuing things—birds with injured wings, cats who seemed hungry even if they were fat and happy, butterflies that were well on their way to the end of their short days on earth, and even other children she deemed in need of spending time with the Zurchenkos. Beatrice seemed to feel others' emotions as though they were her own. It was as if she could not hold enough things against her or share enough of the warmth she felt inside. Katherine hadn't realized how much time Beatrice had spent with her grandmother during the short time she'd lived with them, snuggling into her grandmother's bed with Yale to listen to their stories, their reading of the letters.

Katherine took Beatrice's hand. "Why don't the two of us have a moment with Grandma Jeanie before everyone comes down?"

Beatrice sniffled and nodded. "I don't want the others here. Just us."

Katherine pulled her by the hand into the parlor. "It's just family, Bea. No need to worry. The minister will speak.

I'll speak, and if you or Tommy or your brothers want to say a word, they can."

"I mean the others."

Katherine pulled her toward the parlor. "No one but us, Bea. Grandma didn't have a wide circle of friends."

"Will Auntie Yale speak?" Beatrice's eyes were hopeful.

Katherine and Beatrice stopped at the foot of the coffin. "Auntie Yale?" Katherine cocked her head, then shrugged. "Does she want to? I hadn't considered it. But that makes sense, doesn't it, my sweet pea?"

Beatrice nodded, dropped Katherine's hand, and went to Jeanie's side, where she patted the silky cover that lay over her belly. "The pain is gone, Grandma. You are free."

Had she heard her right? "What did you say, Bea?"

"Just that the pain is gone, the pain is past." She swiped at her tears. "And that's good. I know that part is good."

Katherine held Beatrice tight against her. "Sweet pea, sweet Bea, you are a kind soul. I know Grandma appreciated the time you spent with her."

Beatrice nodded against Katherine's chest.

"The minister should be here any moment. Why don't you let your brothers know—"

"Hey, Mama. We're ready," Asher said. Katherine turned to see her eldest son and his younger brothers standing tallest to shortest in the doorway. Each one had tamed their normally moppy blond hair with grease. She released Beatrice and opened her arms to her boys. They came forward, legs stiff, as they disliked the crisp fabric of their Sunday best. Katherine chuckled as they collapsed into her. "Oh, my, who are these fresh, clean boys in my arms? Someone must have done away with my real sons." They chuckled and nestled in for another moment before Asher grew as stiff as his woolen pants and pulled away, the others following him.

Katherine took Asher by the arm. "Let your father know the minister is freshening up and make sure Yale is on her way down. I did her hair and checked over her clothing, so she should be ready."

"I will," Asher said, proud of being trusted to help.

**

Tommy and Aleksey entered the parlor with Yale between them, supporting her as she approached Katherine. Katherine reached out for her and absorbed the weight of the woman with the mind of a child, a woman Katherine worried would not understand death or recover from what it meant. Yale had been lucky to have lived with her mother her whole life. Most people with her low intelligence would have been stowed away in a sanitarium like Glenwood. But for all the good being with their mother had done throughout Yale's life, Katherine wondered what this loss would do to her going forward.

"Yale, would you like to sit?"

She shook her head and turned toward the coffin. Katherine guided her toward it as Tommy passed by.

"Tommy," Katherine said, "any word on Emma?"

"She can't make it. Telegram said she is ill. Devastated, but too sick to travel." Tommy's voice cracked as he spoke. Katherine stepped closer to him and saw his eyes shining behind tears that were rising past the lids. He wiped the fallen drops from his cheeks and cleared his throat, his expanding chest telling Katherine he was trying to hold back his pain.

Her heart constricted at the thought of Emma being too ill to travel. She saw the ache in Tommy's eyes, the worry carved into his face. None of them had known how much Emma had written to Jeanie until Katherine found the letters when she went through them over the past couple of weeks.

Over the years, Tommy's wife and mother had become close through the correspondence. Katherine supported Yale as she looked at her mother. "Oh, I'm so sorry, Tommy. I know Emma would want to be here."

He nodded, his face even more sorrowful than before. This wasn't the moment to dig into what seemed to be her brother's very broken life. Perhaps it wasn't only their mother he could not forgive.

Tommy moved back to the doorway, leaning against the doorjamb, looking away from all of them. Katherine watched the sister she barely knew, seeing her in a whole new light since learning the truth by reading all the letters their parents had written. She gently pushed some wayward tendrils of black hair back under the hat Yale wore. "Tell me if you have questions. You can say good-bye to her even though, well…" Katherine sighed. She didn't know how to explain.

Yale nodded but didn't ask anything. Katherine kept her hand at the small of Yale's back in case she grew weak at seeing her dead mother or in realizing she was not coming back, ever. Yale's gaze slipped from one end of their mother to the other. After looking back at Jeanie's face, she stretched across their mother's body and adjusted the very same pin that Katherine had and kissed their mother's cheek. Then she petted her hand. Tears dropped out of Yale's eyes, splashing over the silken sheet, same as Katherine's. She was comforted by the fact that Yale did not suffer under the weight of regret. Her life with their mother appeared to have been pure and loving, full of all the knowing that Katherine's had not been.

Yale choked and covered her mouth.

"It's all right, Yale. Mama will always be with you; she'll always be part of you. A mother's love is special," Katherine said. "It doesn't simply go way because the mother is no longer around."

Now Katherine choked. Those words were thick and suffocating, full of wisdom she wished she'd heeded when her mother was still alive, when Katherine was fully immersed in the work of continuing the estrangement.

The minister entered the parlor. He began speaking with Aleksey while Tommy sat with the children, waiting for the service to begin. The boys on either side of their uncle sat close as though wanting his body for support, and Katherine wished so much that Tommy and Emma had been able to have children. Katherine settled Yale in a seat and went to where Aleksey spoke with the minister.

"Is there a problem?" Katherine asked.

The minister turned his attention to Katherine. "We need to begin the service. I'm due at a second service at the Langstons' later today."

Katherine narrowed her eyes at him, not understanding. "Well, let's begin," Katherine said.

Now the minister narrowed his eyes at Katherine. "But we can't. We're not ready yet."

Katherine shook her head, confused. "Not ready?"

"For the guests," Aleksey said, appearing as confused as Katherine felt. "Reverend Daniels informed me there's a line of people around the corner, waiting for the service."

Katherine drew back. "Line of people? Where?"

The minister went to the open window, pushed the sheer aside, and pointed. Katherine lifted her skirts and strode across to the window, where she could see what the minister was looking at. A line of people, silent as mice, had formed, snaking down the sidewalk and around the corner at the end of the block.

Katherine's mouth fell open. She put her hand up to the screen, fingertips pushing through the tiny squares of woven wire. *What on earth?*

"What's happening?" Katherine asked.

"Why, they're mourning. Same as you. They've come to send a sister into the afterlife."

Katherine looked at the minister. Was he joking? His gaze was warm and understanding but certainly not mocking. She had heard of this happening, where a church sends members of the congregation to a funeral that would otherwise not be well attended. Katherine hadn't known the minister would be doing this for her mother.

She was flushed with gratitude that the minister would make such a gesture for her mother. She grasped his hands. "Thank you, Reverend."

Now he appeared confused. But there was no time to ask more questions. "We'd better get more chairs," Katherine said. A smile came to her and she kissed Aleksey's cheek.

Aleksey hugged Katherine. "This is good," he said. "Really good." Then he gestured at the children. "Let's move. Fast."

The boys raced into the hall, and Tommy rose and crossed to where he could see out the window. "What is going on?" he said.

"I guess Reverend Daniels thought Mama should have more mourners than just us," Katherine said.

Tommy rubbed his chin. "That's kind of him. We do that at our church for the most desperate cases."

Katherine took Tommy's hand. "I'm glad he thought of it. Makes me feel much better."

"Me too," Tommy said as though he were somewhere far away. He took Katherine's hand and led her toward the door. "Let's get those chairs."

"In the cellar," Katherine said, now feeling as though it were she who had been sucked into another world, far away from the reality of what was happening right in front of her.

The line of people, with heads bowed as they quietly awaited the service, made Katherine smile. She pulled herself from the window and went with the rest of the family to gather chairs for the people who'd come to say good-bye to a woman whom all except Yale barely knew at all.

Chapter 8

Katherine

1891—Storm Lake

The Christoffs' kitchen was hot with the fires that heated the stove for Katherine's baking. She'd been working for hours before she stopped and stretched her aching back. With barely a full breath's break, she bent forward again and rolled the cookie dough in short pushes and sharp pulls. Eleven-year-old Hannah Christoff yanked at her collar. "You're starching these too stiff. I can't move without the material slicing at my skin. Then I get red as the devil."

Katherine chuckled and swiped at her sweating forehead with the back of her hand. "Go on and finish your studies, Hannah. Your mother will not be pleased to find you lazing about." Katherine butted the small girl with her hip, shooting her a smile. Hannah grinned up at Katherine and affixed her gaze on the table before them. The younger girl may have been spoiled and a bit dense, but somehow she was sweet—something her parents were not.

Katherine floured her pin and rolled again while Hannah attempted to sneak her hand onto the kitchen worktable and stab at the sugar crystals that had escaped the nippers used to cut the loaf. Hannah poked at the nearly invisible sugar particles that had scattered over the surface and licked her fingers with her eyes shut, moaning at the delight.

"Kat, tell me again how you lost half your finger. Tell me about Aleksey and the cow."

"Hannah." Katherine gripped the girl's shoulders. Every time Hannah called her Kat, she smiled, feeling like they were sisters.

Hannah's eyes were alight. "And the blizzard and how Aleksey was there when they had to take your finger and how he held your other hand and—"

"That's enough. Your mother will have my hide if I don't finish this." Katherine had told Hannah the story of the blizzard that stole her finger so many times that Hannah probably remembered more of the details than she did. "Go on. You have your report to write. You'll get a swat if your mother catches us commiserating. She doesn't like me distracted."

Hannah narrowed her eyes as though considering Katherine's arguments.

Katherine pointed her rolling pin at Hannah. "Besides, I'm sure you haven't forgotten the visit you had from Doc Landry last month, have you?"

The little girl hesitated, eyes widened, just as she was about to pop her finger into her mouth, a crystal of sugar catching the midmorning sunshine like a diamond. Katherine could see that Hannah was recalling having been held down while the doctor dug a wrench into her mouth and came back out with a tiny white piece of her very own body.

She shrugged. "A baby tooth. No matter."

"But—" Katherine said.

Hannah responded by pushing her finger into her mouth. She closed her eyes and grinned.

Katherine's stomach growled. She thought of all of Hannah's wistful dreams of marriage to a wealthy man someday. "Boys don't really like toothless girls."

Hannah reached under the table and came back out with a gleaming red apple. She held it up to Katherine in the palm of her hand.

"Your mother said nothing to eat in between breakfast and luncheon."

Hannah shook her head and sidled up to Katherine. Hannah's perfumed hair filled Katherine's nose with the fragrant roses as she laid her head on Katherine's shoulder. "For you."

Katherine stopped rolling. Her mouth was instantly full of saliva; the sensation as she imagined the apple juice on the back of her tongue made her look away. Hannah pulled at Katherine's skirt, lifting the cotton. Katherine sprang back and pushed the fabric down where it belonged. "What are you doing?"

Hannah shrugged. She pointed the apple at the skirt. "I know your secret. I saw you sew the pockets into your underskirt when Mother was in town."

Katherine's face heated up, dizzying her. She swallowed hard and began to roll the dough yet again, ignoring Hannah's accusation.

Hannah put her hand over the roller. Katherine froze.

"I won't tell."

Katherine shifted her eyes so she could read Hannah's face. Her lifted eyebrows and kind expression caused Katherine's posture to soften. She was ashamed but grateful. She couldn't remember the last kind thing someone had done for her. Her breath caught with shame and gratitude. How could such a kind girl be born of such awful parents?

Hannah tapped Katherine's hand with her slim, soft fingers. "Mother is stingy. I can hear your belly rumbling. I'm eleven. I'm not an ignoramus, Kat. I'm not."

Katherine gave a little smile. Hannah pushed the apple toward her again. This time, Katherine took it. She didn't want to lift the skirt and hide it away in the pocket she'd made. It didn't matter that Hannah already knew, that she didn't seem to judge Katherine; the act of hiding food, of acknowledging her need to, was humiliating. Hannah stole a piece of the dough and turned her back, busying herself with the drawer that held the hand towels.

Katherine yanked her skirt up, had the apple nestled in the pocket inside of five seconds, and was back at rolling.

Hannah lifted her hands and spun around, her dress ballooning as she did. "I adore sugar. Rotten teeth or not! Mother says I'm suitable for many—bad teeth or not. A proper upbringing and a fat dowry will open doors." Hannah shot an uneasy look at Katherine as she moved around the table, searching for more wayward sugar.

Katherine shook her head. "Just be sure to keep up on your studies, Hannah."

"What do I need with studies? You're smart as a whip, and see where it's got you?"

Katherine stopped rolling and straightened, recalling her mother's words. "They can take your house, your jewels, your everything—except for what you learn. Once you learn something, it's yours; it's embedded in your body like the blood that blazes through your arteries."

Hannah put her hands on her hips. "Now, that makes me think you're dumb. That hogwash only matters for boys and men. And that's why you're here serving even though you're smarter than anyone I ever met. I told Mother I had no need for writing reports or studying history."

A lump formed at the base of Katherine's throat, cutting off her air. She bowed her head at the truth of the statement. "Oh, galoshes."

"Even your beauty hasn't kept you from this life." Hannah cocked her head at Katherine. "Don't you want a man to tend your heart and bring you riches? Or a knight in shining armor like your Aleksey?"

"He's just a boy, Hannah. I don't even know where he is. And no. There are no knights in this world. Not really." Katherine thought of her mother, the many conversations they'd had about education and its importance. She thought of her parents' decimated marriage. She considered the fact that the splintered marriage had scattered each living Arthur child like the sugar crystals littered over the tabletop.

She missed her mother down to her toes—their quiet conversations while cooking or sewing by the firelight. In many ways, the prairie year was the worst of their lives, but Katherine held dear the simple things she'd shared with her mother when they were not pressed into social obligations as they'd been in Des Moines. Katherine touched her temple. She could still feel her mother bending in to show her a new stitch, the way their heads would touch, the way her mother smelled of cinnamon after cooking dinner.

When was the last time Katherine had heard from her? Ages. Was she all right? Was she even alive? Katherine forced herself to breathe, to ignore what may have been correct about Hannah's words.

"Hannah!" Mrs. Christoff screeched from upstairs. Katherine jumped and realized she'd begun rolling again and had thinned the dough practically into the marble worktable. Mrs. Christoff's tone sawed through Katherine's skull. Hannah took a final swipe at the sugar and dashed from the room, wiping her hands on her skirt.

As Hannah's footfalls faded, Katherine balled the dough and began rolling again. The pin flew back and forth, and her mouth watered at the thought of the sugar grains inside the white mixture that would end up providing the Christoffs with the sweet treats they desired.

Katherine thought about the letter she was ready to post to her mother, eager to think that somehow this one would reach her and that she would write back. None of it made sense. Her mother was not one to shirk correspondence, even if just to be polite. Though she worried maybe the Christoffs were correct and her mother's affection for her children had dissolved, she knew in her heart that could not be. Had something happened to her mother and sister, Yale? Oh, how Katherine hoped they were safe.

She tried to focus on what was good in her life, just so she could survive, but lately her life seemed flooded with more awful than even all right. She enjoyed Hannah's company but wished Mr. Christoff had continued to ignore her. Boarding with the Christoffs had not been bad at first. The Christoffs simply treated her the same as they did the broom in the corner—twice a day and on the occasion of a spill, they would notice she was there to serve them in some way.

After the last house where Katherine had boarded, the abuse and the yelling... Oh, the yelling had been mind-numbing. After all of that, the flouting she received from the Christoffs felt nearly like love. But recently, with the unpaid tax bill, things had begun to change.

Jeanie Arthur, Jeanie Arthur, Jeanie Arthur. Katherine whispered her name, wishing that the words sent into the air could conjure her mother, could take them back to a time when their lives had been linked in every way. If only Katherine's mother had come for her when she'd said she would. No. Katherine swallowed the thought and squeezed her eyes closed. She shouldn't dwell on the sting of disappointment. She knew her mother was doing her best.

Each precious letter her mother had sent was tucked away in Katherine's travel case, along with a few horsehair paintbrushes and the drawings she made every chance she could. But in the past few months, Katherine had received no word at all from her mother. Not to be deterred by the lack of communication, Katherine had taken to sending letters to the last home she knew for sure that Jeanie had boarded in.

At first, those letters had come back inside other envelopes with a nice note from Mrs. Terry saying that she could no longer afford to keep her mother and sister. Mrs. Terry said that her original promise to allow Jeanie to keep a portion of money along with earning room and board had been squashed when the woman's father needed the excess cash to cover doctor's bills, that she was sorry and she would help find out where Jeanie and Yale had gone.

Again. This same story unfolded every time her mother seemed to be close to saving enough money to call them all back to her. It wasn't fair that it never worked out, but it was true that an unmarried woman with children was turned useless as an old stump at nearly every turn. Katherine was angry that it was not easy for a woman to make a living without having her name and hand attached to a man, and she would do her best to get back to her family by her own doing instead of waiting for someone else to make it happen.

Katherine thought of the last note that came—a short one that said they had taken room and board with a well-heeled widow named Mrs. Stevens. Then the letters had stopped coming back at all. Where had her mother gone?

Then…nothing. About the time that letters stopped coming from Jeanie, everything changed at the Christoffs'.

"Katherine." Mr. Christoff's voice stabbed into the quiet of the kitchen.

Katherine startled. She hadn't realized she'd faded into memories and stopped her work. She inhaled, straightened, and began to roll again. "Morning, Mr. Christoff."

Katherine crouched down to look at the dough and noted the thickness. Too thin again. *Concentrate. Pretend he isn't there. He must have hours of work to do in the fields.* "The canteens are set where you like them. They should all be full," she said.

Katherine folded one end of the dough over like paper and rolled again, finding just the right thickness. She grabbed the cookie press and started her way around the dough, twisting the wooden mold into the dough, a perfect circle with the indentation of an iris left in the middle when she lifted it up.

"Don't let me catch you basking in the glow of Michael Turnbill's attentions again. Your duty to that family began and ended with your finishing of his shirts and pants."

"Yes, sir," Katherine said.

"You will not leave us and get married, not with all that's due us, our taking you in when you were frightened and alone. We could have chosen any girl to come here and left you back in Yankton. We are the ones who've—"

Katherine turned to look directly at her employer. She considered saying nothing to him at all. She had become frightened in his presence. Not only did he himself strike fear in her, but his interest in her caused his wife's ire to grow as well. But being mute hadn't proved as useful as she thought it might have been.

"Marriage doesn't interest me in the least, Mr. Christoff."

He stepped toward her. She reached for a second cookie press in order to move farther away without looking as though she were doing that—not wanting to anger him.

He gripped her elbow. She froze. He stepped closer, his thigh pressed against her hip. He bent toward her, his breath on her ear. She fought the urge to wrench her elbow free and put it into his ribs or to turn and thump him on the head with the cookie press as she had once before. While it had discouraged his attention in that one moment, Katherine had feared he would beat her. He did not do that, but instead he had punished her without food for three days while he spent those days draping his ever-longing gaze over her, passing his fingertips over any patch of exposed skin that he could reach without anyone noticing, rubbing at his own pants as he watched her toil for his wife, telling her that her weakened, hungered state only increased her attractiveness to him.

Katherine rolled her shoulder to shrug him off and pushed the cookie press into the dough, plopping each round onto the sheet, moving as quickly as she could, wishing just this once that Mrs. Christoff were hounding her, wishing the woman were there simply to keep her husband kenneled.

"Your wife wants these baked before lunch."

The mention of his wife caused him to back off. Katherine walked to the stove, slid the metal sheet of cookies onto the grate above the fire, and wiped her hands on her apron. "So much to do today, Mr. Christoff." She shot him a smile, hoping that it would be satisfying enough that he would be on his way back to the fields. She had learned her lesson about asking him what she could do for him, so she would not ask that question again.

She sauntered to the parlor, where she was to begin a new order of collars and cuffs.

But instead of him heading out the back door to his work, he followed, fast on her heels. She scooped up her needle basket and began to dig through it for the thread that matched this set of pale pink ruffled cuffs. "Where is that pink spool?"

"Sit."

Katherine kept digging in the basket. "Your wife was very clear about the number of collars I was to complete." She held a spool of thread up to the light coming through the window. *Go away*, she pleaded in her mind.

He stepped closer. Katherine's hand shook as she replaced the spool in the basket and drew the pincushion out.

"You grow more heavenly each day."

Her stomach turned over. She gripped the pincushion, imagining shoving the whole thing into his cheek, piercing him with the back ends of needles and pins, leaving holes to seep blood and scab over. Instead of acting, she examined the needles for just the right one to attach women's lace cuffs to spring dresses.

Out of the corner of her eye, she saw Mr. Christoff worm his fingers into his waistband.

"Look at me," he said.

She took a spool from the basket, acting as though she did not hear his raspy request.

"Put your eyes on me," he said. His tone caused Katherine to shiver.

The order gave her no room for choice. She turned her gaze to his face. Without looking down, she could tell he'd stuffed his hand fully into his pants. His chinstrap beard held breakfast crumbs; his body was perfumed with perspiration. She knew he wanted her to look at where his hand was, not at his face. She knew his religion was the only thing that kept him from laying his body on hers—and his wife, the one thing he feared beyond God. Katherine swallowed hard and forced her gaze to his crotch long enough to satisfy his need and send him on his way.

With his free arm, he belted her waist, his fingers kneading her as he tried to release her blouse from the waist of her skirt. He inhaled, his nose whistling, making Katherine's urge to vomit seem all the more probable. He hadn't gone so far as to pull her to him before. She was paralyzed, not knowing what action would result in getting him away with no further punishment.

"You need to soften your heart and open your arms to me, Katherine. You're a woman now, and it's your duty to learn to love a man. I think you'll be surprised at my prowess."

She shuddered and swallowed the gagging that gripped her throat. With his lips so close to her ear, it seemed as though his words were forming right inside her head, reverberating off her skull.

No. Please, no. Katherine held her breath, trying to separate her mind from her flesh as she was held in his revolting embrace. *He is not touching me. He is not even in the room with me.* Katherine fixed her eyes on the chandelier that hung in the hallway at the bottom of the stairs. The faceted ball at the bottom caught the morning sun that streamed through the transom, splashing jewel-toned colors over the floor and walls. Katherine's shoulders tensed as she stiffened in his grip, letting the dancing colors take her thoughts from the room, allowing a calmness to come over her, a sense that her soul was somehow protected even while her flesh was breached.

Mrs. Christoff's voice rang out from the room above. "Katherine Arthur! What is that stink?"

Mr. Christoff snapped away from Katherine, freeing his hand from his pants, adjusting them. Katherine let out a sob she hadn't realized she'd been holding inside. She pressed one hand against her chest; the other was draped around her waist. Feet pounding overhead coming toward the stairs sent relief through Katherine's body. She breathed heavily as Mr. Christoff scratched his beard, trying to appear as though he had not been doing anything untoward.

"What is that wretched *smell?* It's like the devil's breath."

Mrs. Christoff came stomping down the stairs, causing the rickety chandelier in the foyer to sway, the almond-shaped quartz jewels jingling against one another like music, the crystal ball at the bottom swinging wildly, making Katherine think it was going to fly right off its tiny metal link.

"What is on fire?" Mrs. Christoff screeched.

Fire?

Katherine covered her mouth. With her senses returning, she realized what Mrs. Christoff was talking about. The cookies. Katherine knew this would mean scolding, yelling, punishment, but it was nothing compared to what Mrs. Christoff had interrupted. Katherine would take the beating in exchange for being sprung from the disgusting man's arms.

Mrs. Christoff passed under the chandelier, her angry face settling on Katherine, who was stunned to inaction. Her shoulders relaxed as Mrs. Christoff crossed the space that separated them and pinched the back of Katherine's arm, twisting the skin. Katherine thought she might hug the woman.

"I just asked our Katherine to darn my socks tonight. I've put an awful hole right through the toe, it seems."

Like a writhing snake, a vein in Mrs. Christoff's neck popped as she looked between her husband and Katherine, clearly uneasy that the two of them had been alone.

"Why don't you just write that on the list next time, Abner? That way, Katherine won't lose track of what it is that she's doing."

She pushed Katherine between the shoulder blades and Katherine left the room, rubbing the back of her arm where the pinch throbbed. She went to the oven and removed the tray from the grate, thinking the aroma of burnt cookies had never smelled so wonderful to anyone in the world.

Chapter 9

Tommy

1891—Des Moines

Tommy shivered. The turn of events from the point he'd met with McHenry to now, being tossed in jail like a seasoned criminal, spoiled his positive outlook on the world. How was it possible that trying to help a mother and her young boy ended like this? He pulled his arms into his shirt and bit down hard, trying to stop his chattering teeth. He pushed his back into the jail cell wall, knees folded in, jutting his chin forward, shoulders back, eyes scanning the nine grown men, swallowing every urge to whimper and cry out. He wanted to disappear. Thoughts of his mother made him feel stronger and sadder at the same time.

Mama, Mama, Mama, please. Come get me. He wiped away a fallen tear, hoping none of the men in his cell would notice. Memories of his mother's strength, her iron spine and problem solving, reminded him he was not made of parchment. He was born of that same vigor, and with her blood coursing through his body, he knew he could survive this terrible turn.

Mold grew over the damp cement; the emanation, mixed with urine and feces, was suffocating. A channel of light slid through a narrow rectangular opening along the top of one wall. The light there captured dust particles and created shadows that fell over the men scattered around the space. Tommy watched the sunbeam migrate across the floor, making sure to keep as still and silent as possible.

The sun had nearly moved completely away from where the window could seize the light, and Tommy hoped the ensuing darkness would mean he could close his eyes and sleep, if only for a moment.

But as the sun slipped away, the guard in the hall lit a lamp, and it brought a wave of energy that swept through the small space. The men turned their gazes to one another, staring, posturing, daring each other to encroach. One of the nine men slipped down to the floor, his head propped against the corner opposite Tommy.

The man stared blankly ahead, his raspy, choppy breath providing the baseline for the conversation that was turning bitter. His cellmates' once-jovial, collegial way with one another grew strained with taunts and derision. And Tommy seemed to be the only one who noticed the man with his head wrenched into the corner appeared as though he were fighting for the last air he'd ever breathe. Tommy covered his mouth and averted his eyes.

A scrawny, long-haired man puffed up his arms and circled the perimeter, spitting, marking every few steps he took. Tommy wanted to tell him to just sit down and forget his "I am king" routine because there was no way even the next smallest man couldn't whip his tail in a second.

As the little man drew his circling in tighter toward the group, the others barked at him. "Sit down, you slogged pile of shit."

"Find a slice of wall, or I'm gonna use you for my davenport," said a bulky man with a tattered hat. He took it off and rubbed his backside with it. "That floor isn't quite comfortable enough for the tender likes of me."

"Mongrel," a disembodied voice called from somewhere in the huddle.

The largest, a man the size of a mountain, stood in the center of the clump, his head extending over all the others. He puffed his cheeks and blew out his breath as though he'd had enough. "Christ, Smithy. Same routine in every grog shop, every damn time we land in the clink."

"You're always doing that." The slight man stopped circling and pointed his finger at the mountain man.

"I'm gonna allow you to hang up your fiddle," the mountain man said, breaking through the group and leaning against the wall across from Tommy.

Smithy walked away, mumbling.

There was a marked release of breath and tension, and the men broke into small clumps, deportments now relaxed.

Tommy's nose began to itch. He tried to rub the itch away. *Please, no. Don't sneeze.* After he swiped a few more times at his nose, the sneeze roared forth. Nine sets of eyes turned in Tommy's direction, as though they'd just noticed he was in the same cell with them.

The bulky fellow stooped over, hands on his knees, squinting at Tommy. He felt the tone of the room coil like a spring fresh out of the box. The scraggy man, Smithy, stepped forward and let a smile slip across his lips.

"Look at the little guy in the corner. Looks as if he's hiding. Trying to find his way into a rat hole."

Tommy rubbed his eyes, wishing they were referencing the dazed drunk in the other corner rather than him. He didn't respond, hoping that if he behaved like a submissive animal and allowed them their age-earned dominance, they would keep their distance.

"I'm suffering an insult, I believe," Smithy, spreading his feathers as wide and tall as a small man could.

Tommy pushed harder against the cold wall. The slight man swaggered closer, putting the toes of his boots against Tommy's.

"Looks like Smithy found the guy he can rightly mess with." The bulky man chuckled.

"You too good to talk to us fellas? Little boy?" Smithy reached down and smacked Tommy's knees.

Go away, go away, go away, Tommy said to himself.

The other men began to laugh, the noise growing as each man added his voice. "Yep. Finally, a fella Smithy can whip."

Tommy decided to defuse the situation. He looked up at Smithy. "I don't want trouble."

Smithy bent down, hands on his knees. Tobacco clung to his serrated teeth; his breath smelled like horse-tramped dirt. "You won't be trouble for none of us," Smithy said, grinning. He grabbed Tommy's arm and yanked. Tommy resisted, writhing out of Smithy's grip, wishing that his plan to blend into the plaster had worked. But he remembered the other rules of dominance—there nearly always came a time when a dog had to fight his battle, like it or not.

Smithy smacked Tommy's head and pulled at his arm again. It was no use trying to dissolve the tension by minding his own business. This time, Tommy allowed Smithy to bring him up to standing. He watched Smithy's face register surprise as Tommy rose slowly, unkinking his limbs, finding his full height, somewhere around six feet. The others hooted, but their dropped jaws confirmed they were just as shocked that Tommy was taller than most of them and bigger than some.

"Well, Smithy. Looks as though he could whip his weight in cats. You done lost before you even start."

Smithy shook his head, erasing the dumbfounded expression. He rolled his shoulders back and paced, looking at his contemporaries while gesturing at Tommy. "He's a *kiddie.* I can take him easy."

A man with an eye patch kicked at Tommy's foot. "Yeah, look at that baby face."

Another man standing only in his drawers and shoes stepped in for a closer look. He drew his hand up the length of Tommy. "Size of a man. That much is true."

"He's a kid," came another voice. "Let 'im be."

"Baby face. Easy pickings for Smithy," Bulky said. "He needs a win to earn back his confidence."

The mountain man pushed off the wall and shuffled forward, narrowing his eyes on Tommy. He scratched his chin, his fingers against his stubble sounding like sandpaper. "My brother had one of them baby faces." He pinched Tommy's cheek. Tommy resisted balking away, holding the man's gaze.

The man chuckled. "Watched old baby-faced brother slice a man's belly open like a screaming mouth. Just because." He scratched his chin again. "I'd leave this one be, Smithy."

Smithy's shoulders pitched as he seemed to consider whether fighting Tommy would be worth the risk that he wouldn't be able to beat him. Tommy fisted and released his hands, trying to stay as relaxed as he could, to exude confidence but not cockiness. Smithy twitched and jerked at thin air, and Tommy understood what was going to happen even before Smithy did. There was no way the little man could back down from a boy and not have to hear of it for the next ten years.

Tommy pushed away from the wall. Smithy took a step back and then forward again, opening his chest as wide as his skeleton would allow. Tommy smiled as friendly as he could. He hoped his charm would work on these fellows as much as it had on McHenry. He spread his hands wide and tried to convey an easy posture. "I'm sure you don't want to fight," Tommy said. "I don't care a hooter to fight you. You're a wiry fella. Strong as an ox, even if compact. That's plain as anything. Don't need to be Rocky Mountain big to beat up someone like me. Just a kid."

Smithy cocked his head and bit down on the corner of his mouth. Tommy wanted his charm to do the job, but there was a flicker of fear that warned him that might not be the case.

A few moments passed, a calm coming over the cell, and just as the thought that he may have managed to defuse the situation spun through Tommy's mind, Smithy launched himself chest first, smacking Tommy into the stone wall, his head hitting hard. As he rubbed his skull, a lump rose under his fingers. Stars shot through the room as he felt the lump forming on the back of his head. He squinted and then opened his eyes wide, trying to find his way through the blurry fog.

He'd had enough unfairness for one day. Any fear he had felt turned back on itself, and Tommy was filled with blinding anger. "You're not going to do this to me!" He roared and rushed forward despite his vision. He landed a punch on a cheek, but when he backed away, he saw Smithy was laughing and Bulky was the one rubbing his cheek. Tommy hadn't meant to poke at Bulky. He shook his head, trying to disperse the fog in his mind. He backed up, light on his toes, fists up like he'd seen others do in street fights. Smithy came forward, fists bouncing, too.

"All right, you want a fight?" Tommy asked. "You got one." He raised his fists.

Smithy hocked up some mucus, swallowed, and smiled. He glanced away, then took a swipe at Tommy, catching his cheek. Tommy felt the knuckles open his skin, but before Smithy could punch again, Tommy unleashed a barrage of punches, landing his fists on Smithy's lip, his chest, his eye. Smithy got a couple more in on Tommy, but not as many, not as damaging.

A kick from one of the men off to Tommy's side doubled him over and forced his breath out. But even with no breath, he vaulted up and managed to belly punch the bulky fella and then deck Smithy in the face one more time.

"Hey, hey, hey!" a guard called from the other side of the bars. Most of the men backed off. Smithy took another swipe. Tommy could hear the jingling of keys as the guard tried to unlock the door. Smithy backed away, his hands in surrender. Tommy fell back against the wall, heaving for breath.

He surveyed the room. The guard was warning Smithy he would put him in isolation if he kept up his nonsense. When the guard moved to the side, Tommy could see Smithy's lip was bright red and his eye was swelling. Though every membrane in Tommy's body throbbed, he was satisfied that he'd managed to prove himself satisfactorily.

There was nothing he wanted to do more than ball himself up in the corner, but he knew that was not smart. He straightened against the chilled stone and uncurled every inch of his height.

Though Smithy kept his eye on Tommy, the others had grown bored of him as Tommy had hoped they would. Relief came for the moment. He crossed his arms against his tender ribs and put one foot against the wall. He wanted to cry. Again, he wished for his mother to appear, for her to take him into her arms and cradle him, whispering wonderful things in his ear.

He thought of Babcock. "The world awaits you, Mr. Arthur. You'll find your way. You're sturdy, intelligent, savvy, and kind." Perhaps Tommy should have gone east with him and then sent for his family. But he couldn't do that. He wasn't even sure where they all were.

He rubbed his shoulder. The pain that had taken so long to heal in the first place was inflamed. Tommy's shoulders drooped. He pushed them square again. Far worse than the physical pain was the knowledge that he was helpless to stop it...unable to fight back. In his entire fourteen years, he'd never felt so alone, so abandoned. Or perhaps it was just the first time he allowed himself to fully accept that was exactly the situation at hand.

Chapter 10

Jeanie

1891—Sioux Falls

I sat on the poorhouse cot I'd been using the past week with Yale nestled on my lap. I couldn't separate the ripe stench of the well-worn canvas bed from the grime that had formed on my own clothing. Yale's cheek warmed the skin at my collarbone, her breath even with sleep. My stomach turned over its emptiness, and I could hear Yale's tummy rumble, making me feel the weight of my failures even more fully.

Still, running just below the surface of my humiliation was a sense of wonder that I was alive. A surge of gratitude came each time I marveled at the fact I'd been saved from drowning the night before. On that trestle, I'd thought I'd somehow heard James' voice, but aside from knowing that was impossible, it turns out it was Millie and her man, Harvey, who were calling. The whiskey, the storm, and the train bearing down had played tricks on my mind, but the fact that I fell forward instead of backward made me certain a miracle had occurred.

Harvey had jumped into the water after me and pulled me to safety. He and Millie then dragged me back to the poorhouse, dried me off as best they could, and tucked me into bed. At some point, Yale had made her way from the pallet on the floor near the fire to me on my cot, where I'd wakened with her in my arms.

I was awed, appreciative, stunned. Millie had said they were repaying a kindness offered them the year before. I did not understand what another person's favor to them had to do with me, but she was adamant that benevolence, like money, was useful only in its spending.

A miracle was what it was. I was beginning to see that the least of us give so much more than the greatest of us. Even with this gift I'd been given, I was paralyzed. Fear and lack of a plan stopped me from taking action of any sort. I had started over so many times. I'd broken countless promises. I hadn't meant to, but I'd learned the world was cruel to a divorced mother.

But I am breathing. Yale stretched in my lap, eyes closed and her face placid. What to do? Normally, my first thought when I was given a clean slate was to write to Tommy and Katherine, to tell them things were better, that I would soon be saving enough money to bring them out of boarding, that this time would be different.

This time *was* different. I wasn't even sure where Katherine was. Tommy, yes. He was with a family on a farm just outside of Des Moines. I could get word to him easily, asking him to join me in Des Moines. But Katherine, no. For the first time I could remember, I didn't scratch off letters to say all would be right in no time, that I would surely be able to rekindle my writing career, that I would find even the tiniest abode where we could all shelter, where we could be a family again. If they just believed in me a little longer.

I kissed the top of Yale's head and exhaled. I focused on my miracle but knew I wasn't in any better of a situation than before I'd imbibed and decided to end my life. The sense of a miracle had descended fully, but it didn't change the reality of my dirt-floor-poor life. "But we'll find a way," I whispered.

"We'll scrape up a few pennies, have some scrambled eggs at Murphy's, get a paper, and we'll make a plan. We'll make some money, and this time we will save and find a tiny little place where we all can live together again."

I did not survive jumping into the river just to shrivel up and die a slow, humiliating death. That would be wrong in the face of what Millie had said.

The sound of feet stomping up the stairs that led from the bar below startled me. Millie lumbered into the room where I was sitting, her arms laden with items wrapped in brown paper.

"These come fer ya."

I shook my head. No one even knew where I was—no one with the means to send packages.

"Listen, Mrs. Arthur. I just saved yer pack here from the likes of Dave the Drunk, so lighten my load and open the parcel."

I smiled at Millie's insistence at calling me Mrs. Arthur or Jeanie Arthur even when I told her not to. I moved the now-wakened Yale beside me and rose to relieve Millie of the parcels.

I sat back down, running my hands over the brown wrapping. Yale popped her thumb into her mouth and snuggled against me, putting her hand over mine as I smoothed the paper.

Millie peered closer, hands resting on her knees. "Open 'er up," she said, her jack-o'-lantern smile big and warm.

I pulled one end of the bow and released the twine that kept the whole thing together. I turned the smaller package over and opened the flaps. Inside was a salesman's sample of a painted chest. I'd seen it a million times in Mrs. Stevens' home, and I would have sworn in front of a judge that it had been carted away with all of her other belongings. I opened it and pulled a stack of letters from it.

"Letters is all?" Millie's sour-apple smile made me grin. She stood straight and shrugged, hands now on her hips.

I paged through them. "Oh my, yes. Letters, Millie." I turned to Yale and gave her a peck on the forehead. "We love our letters, don't we, Yale?" She nuzzled my shoulder with her cheek. "We've read these until the envelope flaps nearly came off from overuse." I sighed at the sight of Katherine's fine handwriting and Tommy's sloppy scrawl. Yale smiled around her thumb. "Our letters." I had left another trunk full of them with the Zurchenko family when we left the prairie three years back.

I continued to page through them and almost passed one particular letter right over. The rose color of the envelope sent me back through the pile. I'd received it three weeks back but had refused to open it. The last thing I needed to do at that time was subject myself to Mrs. Mellet's hateful words, as she no doubt would have written a screed, demonizing me along with my family. She had been especially cruel after my father's bank collapsed with her money in it. Why she felt the need to continue to blame me for my family's actions, I could not imagine.

But this time something made me consider opening it. What did Mrs. Mellet's derision matter after all that had happened? There was no more stubborn pride or ego for her poisonous words to penetrate. I even chuckled at the work she must have done to trace my movements to Mrs. Stevens' home.

I slid my finger under the flap and gently tore it open. A breath of lavender escaped when I freed the paper from its home.

"Woo-wee!" Millie slapped her knee. "That smell. Somethin' wonderful there. That there's a special letter."

"From an awful, vacuous woman." I laughed at Millie's assumption.

"Don't that beat all," Millie said. "Can't be everything, I s'pose."

I unfolded the letter and began to read. Just a few words down and I found I could not breathe.

Millie shook my shoulder, her grasp tight and jarring. "Yer cryin'? What's got you cryin'?"

I swallowed hard, barely able to move the saliva down my throat.

I covered my mouth. I couldn't get the words out. It couldn't be possible. I put my gaze back on the words, rereading. And for the first time since I was a little girl, I let another adult see me cry. I could not keep the sobs from choking me up, from spilling over my lids, from relieving my body of the tension I'd held for the past four years.

"I can get Katherine and Tommy back," I said.

Millie narrowed her eyes on me and grasped my chin, forcing me to meet her gaze. "Who's Katherine and Tommy?"

I tried to tell her, but I couldn't get the words out. I tried to keep from withering away right there, but all I could do was thank God, for in that moment, in the space of a short time of witnessing no less than two miracles, I thought I owed God the kind of gratitude that lifted right out of my chest, not even passing by my lips, but feeling gratitude deep in the core of my being, deep in the broken shards of who I used to be, feeling as though someone, somewhere, was putting me back together, seeing me for who I truly was.

I drew a deep breath. "I can get my children back. Finally." Millie pulled me into an embrace. She patted my head, and I decided there must be a God for this letter to have found my eyes.

Chapter 11

Katherine

1891—Storm Lake

Katherine had been asleep for some time when she woke, her mouth summer-prairie dry, so hungry that she could feel her stomach shrinking. She yawned, her hip digging through the featherbed to the floor as Hannah turned over and snored softly. The Christoffs were in the raised bedstead next to the pallet on the floor where the girls slept. Katherine's penance for the burnt cookies had been no more food or water that day.

Mr. Christoff passed a burst of gas like a honking goose, causing Katherine to gag quietly. She tried to fall back asleep but could not. Due to the slow crawl in restoring the once-grand home, the only room that received heat from the coal furnace was the front room where they all slumbered each night. Katherine once suggested she and Hannah use wood to heat the back bedroom for them but had been met with a slow twist of the back of her arm.

Katherine's stomach rumbled. She recalled Mrs. Christoff's angry face as she ordered Katherine to scrape the charred cookie remains into a slop bucket. She paired her demand with another twisting pinch to the back of Katherine's arm. Painful as that was, Katherine was grateful that the cookies had burned, that the stench had called Mrs. Christoff down those steps, interrupting her husband as he attempted to find sexual pleasure with the unwilling Katherine.

Though the remnants of the cookies would have been inedible to a person who was fat with rich meals, as the Christoffs were, a dream of the sugary, crisped treats had awakened Katherine. She had been careful to stow that particular slop bucket under the dry sink when Mrs. Christoff stomped out of the kitchen, barking Katherine's next set of orders for the day.

Now, in the quiet of night, the Christoffs' sleep, aided by whiskey before bed, gave Katherine her chance to sneak to the kitchen. Over the past few months, she'd become accomplished at keeping the pump quiet, making sure it was greased when they withheld water. Katherine began to slide out from under the blanket she shared with Hannah.

But as she was extricating herself from the cocoon, she realized she was not the only one awake. A swatch of material came flinging from above Katherine and landed over her head. It had the distinct body odor of Mr. Christoff. Katherine swallowed her disgust and moved the garment away. She knew what was coming next. She quietly positioned her body so she would appear dead asleep if one of them looked.

Hearing the sounds of Mr. and Mrs. Christoff rooting around, the groan that rose from deep within him and the gasp that caught at the back of Mrs. Christoff's throat caused Katherine's belly to lurch yet again. Since being taken in by them, she'd heard their gropings, gasping breaths, and whatever else she could not imagine but somehow knew was happening frequently. So often that Katherine marveled that they did not have dozens of children.

There was a lull in the activity and Katherine craned her neck to see if she could begin her crawl to the door. And as though Mother Nature had been cooperating, she dropped the glimmering moonshine right through the room's large window, draping the bed and its occupants in slivery-blue hues.

Mr. Christoff's naked body hovered over his wife's. She kicked her fat leg out from under the cover, hooking it around his milk-white buttock. He bucked and threw his body back and forth. Katherine buried her face in her hands, covering her eyes with her fingers and plugging her ears with her thumbs.

Even with such measures, it wasn't enough to block Mr. Christoff's escalating grunts. Katherine tamped down the urge to hum to block out the noise. She wished for the ability to vaporize and reappear somewhere else.

Once the pairing ended, Katherine's guardians fell into their telltale snore patterns—his high-pitched and hers raspy, punctuated with a cough every so often. Thirstier and hungrier than she could have imagined until that moment, Katherine began her attempt to leave the room again, passing Mr. Christoff's cast-off nightshirt. She crawled toward the door, knees scraping over cracked wooden planks. She sucked back the scream of pain she wanted to let out, and panic skipped over her skin. What if he got cold and searched for his nightshirt?

She halted, head drooping, and fished a splinter out of her knee, flicking it from her finger. Should she go back to bed? She smacked her tongue off the roof of her mouth. No, he'd had three whiskeys over the course of the night. Not enough to make him fall into his snore before the groping and the panting, but enough that he would probably sleep past sunrise and Katherine would be ordered to take on extra daybreak chores.

She finally made it into the hall, got to her feet, and crept down the stairs, hand on the banister, high on her toes, stepping in the middle of the treads so they wouldn't squeak. Once in the kitchen, Katherine exhaled. The full moon lit the space enough that she could move without banging into a stool or the worktable in the center of the room.

She worked the pump gently and put her mouth to the spigot, eyes closed. A metallic taste came with the liquid, but the quenching water satisfied like nothing she'd felt before. She wiped her mouth with the sleeve of her nightgown. *Food.* Her bare toes were cold against the wood floor as she moved to where the bushel of apples sat below the table. She fished one out and bit into it. The juice dripped down both sides of her chin. She spun it, her teeth snatching at the fruity flesh, disposing of it in seconds. She set the core on the center of the table so she would remember to get rid of it.

Even hungrier now that she ate the apple and drank the water, she thought of the dried meats in the basement. But Mrs. Christoff tracked that food as though it were gilded. She couldn't eat another apple because it would be noticed.

Her mind flew to the chocolate cake she'd made for the evening dessert. She covered her mouth, thinking that was as risky as any food she might take. She padded over to the pie safe. There was a padlock on it, as there was each night. Katherine pressed her nose against the screened door and drew a breath, her mouth filling with saliva as she imagined the taste on her tongue.

The burnt cookies would have to do. She opened the door to the cabinet under the dry sink and pulled out the slop pail. She reached into it. There was nothing there. She spun around to capture the moonlight and turned it over. Empty. She shook her head. Mice?

It could be. Maybe she'd grabbed the wrong bucket. She bent down and drew a second pail from the cabinet. She stuck her hand in it and smiled when she felt the blackened shards under her fingertips.

She collapsed onto the floor, sitting cross-legged, nightdress strained against her bent knees, the bucket perched on the muslin material stretched across her lap. Using both hands, Katherine jammed the food into her mouth. The burnt taste hid most of the sweetness, but it didn't stop Katherine from filling her belly, chasing the elusive sugary taste of the morsels that had escaped the blackening. Katherine emptied the pail and stared into the bottom of it, feeling the heaviness of having to forage for food. She shook her head and looked to the moon.

Her rush to devour the cookies left her breathless, her shoulders heaving as though she'd run a mile before taking the spot on the floor in the moonlight. She slowed her breathing and felt a warmth gather in her tummy even as she shivered in the chill of the cold kitchen. She would add coal to the stove before heading back upstairs—insurance in case someone woke when she returned to sleep.

But instead of moving, she sat looking into the night sky. It was in these quiet moments that Katherine felt a calmness envelop her. A peaceful manifestation permeated the kitchen as though it arrived on the moon rays that streamed through the glass. *James.* In these precious moments, she felt and often saw the presence of her brother, who died three years before. She lifted her hand into the light, closed her eyes, and waited for the sensation of her brother's hand wrapping around hers, his palm against hers. There it was. In spite of the humiliation and fear she felt much of the time, she could count on her James, what she thought of as his protection of her. It was all she had to count on since her mother had boarded them out, especially since things had gotten so bad at the Christoffs'.

She believed in God, and she believed that somehow her brother was watching over her.

"Katherine," a woman said.

Katherine's eyes flew open. Had the lead-footed Mrs. Christoff snuck down the creaky steps without a peep? Katherine's heart pounded. She bobbled the pail in her lap before saving it from crashing against the floor.

She looked over her shoulder. No one was there. She shook her head, thinking she was going mad. She stood, shivering now that the warmth she'd felt in James' presence was gone again. She put the pail back into the dry sink and gently closed the cabinet doors. She straightened and put her hand on her pelvis. Cramps pulled at her gut, reminding her of the last time she ate too much too fast after not being permitted any food.

She began to sweat, the pain doubling her over. She squeezed her eyes closed until the wave of nausea passed. She straightened, hoping that would be the end of it. She glanced around the kitchen to be sure she didn't leave crumbs or any sign that she'd engaged in unsanctioned eating. She opened the stove door and scooped some coal into the iron belly. She adjusted the damper and watched as the additional air stoked what had been a fading fire.

Pulsing nausea hit her again. She pressed her stomach, hoping that might quell the pain. But the cramping made her sure she would need the privy or a chamber pot. One more glance around the kitchen and her eyes went to the worktable. The apple core. She hobbled to the table and swiped it. That sealed it for her—she would go to the privy, where she could dispose of the core along with the food and water that was ripping through her body.

She turned to the back door and let out a small scream at what she saw. Standing in front of the window was a woman holding a dark-haired baby. Katherine had seen them before, near the general store.

She froze despite the urge to use the bathroom. The woman's face was partly obscured by a shawl, and the baby was cradled in her arms. Katherine couldn't breathe. Her insides ached with threatening diarrhea, but she couldn't make her feet run. What were they doing in the Christoffs' kitchen, of all things?

"Go," the voice said again, and Katherine knew then the voice she'd heard call her name had come from the woman.

Katherine felt a mix of confusion and fear. She swallowed.

The woman turned her body as though she were directing Katherine to go past her to the door. The pain in Katherine's bowels seized. She could not wait any longer. She dashed to the door, slid the bolt, and as she pulled the door open, she saw the woman and baby simply disappear from sight like mist on a cold river. She ran across the cold, wet grass to the privy, where she collapsed onto the seat just in time to release the food and water.

She gripped the wooden slats on the walls as the pain forced her eyes closed. Her body tensed and sweat poured from her hairline even as the cool air lifted bumps on her arms. And as Katherine let her stolen dinner run its course, she tipped forward, pushing the door open with one hand, just a crack, to look into the yard that separated the privy from the house. Nothing was there. No misty figures, no voices calling. No one had followed her. She let the privy door close and waited out the purging, oddly comforted by what she'd seen, even if she was more confused by it than ever.

Chapter 12

Tommy

1891—Des Moines

Tommy pressed against the jail cell wall, keeping upright as best he could, catching scraps of sleep when the others were occupied and at a safe distance. The rough, uneven plaster against him made the muscles in the small of his back scream with fatigue, while his ribs pulsed with pain each and every time he drew a breath.

"Zachary Taylor," the guard said as he jammed the key into the lock. Tommy opened his eyes enough to see the guard bending down, turning the key back and forth, the others on the ring clanging against the bars. Tommy began to sit up and realized Bulky had fallen asleep against his shoulder. Tommy's eyes widened. He cradled the man's head in his hands and moved to get up, trying not to wake him.

A man on the other side of Tommy rolled over and got up on his elbows, yawning. "Hey, look. Jeb found a snuggle-bunny."

This roused Bulky, who appeared horrified when he realized Tommy was gently laying his head on the ground. He drew his legs under himself and sprang up like a frog.

"Keep your paws off me, boy," he said, pointing at Tommy.

The guard swung open the cell door and kicked Smithy's leg to the side. The lean man rolled to his other side, and the guard walked by unfettered. "Zach Taylor!"

Tommy swiveled toward him. He'd forgotten he'd given a phony name when he'd been arrested. He'd chosen the name of the twelfth president of the United States because Tommy admired his status as a war hero.

Tommy wove between the sleeping bodies of his cellmates, catching sight of the man in the corner, his eyes still staring, glassy. He was surely dead, Tommy decided. He raised his hand. "Here. It's me. Zachary." His ribs smarted with the waving movement. Smithy stuck his leg out as Tommy passed, and he stumbled, the searing pull of bruised muscles causing Tommy to cry out.

"Milksop," Smithy said as Tommy wove through the splayed men. When he reached the door, the guard took his arm and pulled him into the hall, locking the cell door behind them.

"Turns out it's your lucky day, Zachary Taylor."

Tommy patted at his cheek, the swelling thick and raw under his fingertips. "I suppose so," he said. He was not sure *lucky* was the right word.

"Six men caught robbing the Express are coming in, and Judge Calder said to swap you out. He made a visit a few hours back and saw you half asleep against the wall, face all swollen, and decided you had punishment enough.

"That, along with the mother of that boy you apparently saved from being run flat over by that coal wagon. But the judge said if you get caught up in any more mischief, you'll go straight to the workhouse. If you're lucky, that's where you'll go."

Tommy hadn't realized he'd even fallen asleep to not notice Judge Calder peeping into the cell. None of that mattered. "I'm free?"

"For now."

Tommy exhaled. He looked back at the cell, noting the men splayed this way and that, bodily air being passed by those still slumbering.

The guard pulled open a drawer at his desk and removed a stack of letters and his knapsack. He slapped the letters into Tommy's palm and then tossed the sack to him. "Best stay out of trouble. Keep out of Judge Calder's courtroom, and keep clear of my jail cell."

Tommy nodded. "I sure will." He dug through his sack. Everything was there. He paged through the letters.

"They're all there. Why in coal-mine hell would I want your blessed letters?"

Tommy nodded. "I see your point." He pushed the straps of his bag over his shoulders, sucking in air as the pain stabbed him. No use explaining why the letters mattered so much.

The guard threw Tommy his cap. "Get out before I stuff you back in that cell."

The guard opened the door and signaled Tommy to walk on through.

Tommy doffed his hat. "No need to put me back in there. You will not see me again."

"That's what they all say," the guard said with a sigh.

Tommy emerged into the sunshine, the warmth embracing him in a way he'd never experienced before. The surge of happiness made him think of McHenry. He had seen the best in Tommy. The past day would not define Tommy. He turned and stepped back into the shade of the building to address the man. "No, really. Not me. I won't be back. Not ever."

The officer looked at his feet, shaking his head, then raised his eyes, sweeping his hand through the air. "I just might believe you, Zachary Taylor. I just might."

Tommy covered his eyes and went on his way. His vision adjusted to the light, and he drew a deep breath, the sunshine feeling like oxygen itself. He squinted, and it made his cheek smart even more. He patted his cheek and winced. Fitting his cap onto his head, he felt a surge of elation bathe him despite the pain from the fight the night before—*the captive is free.*

He lifted his arms and walked, the spring air carrying the essence of budding trees, blooming bulbs, and hope. He'd never felt anything like it. He would never go back to jail, not for anything. He was free. Oh, man, there was nothing like that feeling.

He thought of the camp he'd set up near the bend in Rock Creek, near the spot where it swelled with the spring thaw and tunneled right through the banks of the Des Moines River. Even with his body aching at the intersection of every bone with another, in the hard muscle of his belly and the soft flesh of his soul, he determined if he could bottle this sense of freedom and douse himself with it every day going forward, he would. He turned his face into the hot sun yet again and smiled. Yes. This was something he would not forget.

He stuffed his letters into his back pocket and whistled a tune. He felt rich in that moment. Full of the feeling of freedom. He dug into his front pocket. The Indian Head his father had given him was still there. Miraculously, it had escaped the hands of the deputy who had been tasked with settling Tommy into jail. What a great day. He would head to the woods and gather his thoughts, revisit his plan, and figure out how he would manage to live until he was officially offered the job at the Savery Hotel.

**

Tommy strolled along the banks of the Des Moines River, its roaring waters lifting and pushing the trunk of a fallen tree here, swirling a pine branch there, sucking one or the other under the water before releasing it to reemerge. He selected a smooth, flat stone and skipped it across the surface, making it dance even though the water was rough and frothy. This was the life. He lifted his arms in triumph only to have his smarting ribs remind him of the awful time he'd just spent in jail. *Mama.* That's all that was missing—his family. He sighed. He wouldn't allow himself to dwell on what had gone wrong.

He mentally inventoried the items he had left back at his camp. Would any of it still be there? He'd traded for a small stove that came with all the parts packed into a rectangle, easy but heavy to carry. He'd bought a trap for, well, any animal he could lure into it. And he'd left his shotgun, bow and one arrow there, wrapped in canvas, entombed in a hollow tree trunk.

He wasn't the first fellow to have taken to the woods to weather a personal economic depression of one sort or another, but he wondered if the others were the sorts to trade off their honesty and take things that weren't theirs. Would someone think his camp was abandoned? Perhaps everything would be gone after he'd left it unattended for more than twenty-four hours.

As Tommy's path took him closer to the edge of town before it would wind deep into the woods, he could see two boys huddled up with a man and a woman. That section of town looked to be largely abandoned, paint peeling off of facades, storefront windows turned opaque with dirt.

The woman looked in Tommy's direction. He was turning away even as he realized who she was. Mrs. Hillis. Was that her? He looked back to confirm. She was staring at him. He looked away. This woman had been a friend of his mother's, a cornerstone of the Women's Club, and he was sure she was one of the families who'd lost money and blamed his family for the loss.

Today was not the day to have to explain his sorrow that her family lost money when the investments fell through. The entire town seemed to misunderstand what had happened. They must have been mistaken in order for them to turn such rage at them, driving his parents right out of town. He remembered the anger, the way it felt—the idea that it was possible to feel another person's ire as though it were made like the dimensions of an actual object that you could throw at someone. No. Today was not the day for that. When the man offered his arm, Mrs. Hillis returned her attention to him, and Tommy felt relief that she didn't seem to recognize him.

Tommy wanted to pick up his pace to move past them, but a pebble in his shoe forced him to his knee to dig it out. He untied his shoe and pulled his foot out, watching all the while.

The man with the boys and Mrs. Hillis was Reverend Shaw, in his signature black overcoat with the expensive cut, but worn just enough that he didn't appear to be dipping into the collection basket for the sake of fashion. His lanky build and pencil neck, which held the head that balanced the weathered, out-of-fashion tall top hat, made Tommy think he'd never even left town. The reverend was always ready when life went wrong for folks. If he had recognized Tommy, he would have come at him with love and forgiveness, and Tommy was not in the mood for that, either. He'd lost much of his faith in religion in the last two years and was not ready to rekindle it or be obligated to do charity work when he had to focus on feeding himself and earning a living like a grown man.

Tommy had seen the two boys on the first day he arrived in Des Moines. They were swimming in the river with some others when Tommy passed them by to find a place to set up camp. Without even spending much time with them, he could tell they were mischief-makers, the kind who were always a mess of laughs, but the sort Tommy wanted to avoid in order to stay on a straight path. This stint in jail certainly made that promise all the easier to keep.

He guessed they were staying with the reverend, working for him and trying to right what must have been formerly wayward lives. As Tommy recalled, those were the only boys who had ever spent much time with Reverend Shaw.

He shook out his shoe, held it in the sun, and noted that where the ball of his foot hit the sole, the leather was nearly worn through; a sliver of light shot right through. As he put it back on, he watched the huddled group out of the corner of his eye. Standing on the edge of the dirt street lined with formerly opulent homes and bustling stores, they shook hands and separated. Reverend Shaw walked Mrs. Hillis toward her gleaming black buggy, helped her into it, and she was driven away. Reverend Shaw went to his wagon and fussed with its cargo. And the two boys jogged toward Tommy.

Tommy finished tying his shoe and lifted his hand in greeting.

When they reached him, the taller boy doffed his cap. "Say. What's your name? You need a place to stay?"

Tommy drew back, surprised. Did he appear to be without a home? Without a plan?

The minister came toward them as well. "I know you. You've grown like a weed, but I remember your face."

Tommy straightened his shoulders. "Tommy Arthur, sir." He stuck his hand out. He didn't have to be ashamed. He was a good soul, a fine man.

"That's right, Tommy Arthur." Reverend Shaw paused, and Tommy assumed he was running the details of the scandal through his mind. Tommy hadn't realized how odd that would feel for him, that he would have the urge to explain away what happened, even though he'd had no hand in it and wasn't even sure he knew all that had happened.

Reverend Shaw flashed a grin. "Glad your family's back in town."

"Well, just me. For now."

"Just you?" The reverend nodded again, appearing to be sorting through a complicated problem. He snapped his fingers. "We need an extra set of hands. Care to help? You'll get some cash and a place to stay."

Tommy held up his hand. "I'm fixed for housing, thank you."

Reverend Shaw jerked back, looking shocked. "You look like you need a place to stay."

Tommy rubbed his aching ribs. He needed to eat. That was for sure.

"You look hungry." The minister slipped his arm around Tommy's shoulder and squeezed. "I see you're a proud young man. Strong. Capable. Think of this work as buying you reinforcements. I'm sure you're settled for the most part," the minister said.

Tommy tasted a subtle condescending tone, felt the slow squeeze of manipulation at work. He didn't like it, but he had to be honest with himself. He was in need. Even if everything he left at camp remained there after his absence, he would still need to earn money and replenish his supplies. He'd spent nearly everything Babcock had given him when they went their separate ways. He could use some flour and fat to make some slapjacks. That would keep him afloat until he trapped or shot something to eat.

And though he had no intention of living with the minister the way typical wayward boys did, he thought perhaps doing some odd work for him would be a solid way of filling in his financial gaps until he was fully settled. It made sense, and since he would not be living with the reverend, he did not have to see himself as a charity case. This was an opportunity, and that was good. There was nothing wrong with honest work, no matter what type it was.

"All right. I'm settled for quarters, but I could certainly use some money for other essentials." Tommy smacked his hands together. "What kind of work are we talking?"

The minister grinned and rocked forward on his toes. "Praise God, I knew you were heaven sent, happening along like that just when we needed another set of hands."

Tommy had grown to hate such flowery use of godly words. They had once seemed sincere to his ear.

Money. You need the money.

The minister pointed the boys in the direction of the wagon that stood outside a townhome with a sagging porch and sooty siding. The wagon was far too flashy to be paid for by someone living in that home. Tommy squinted, wondering if he should inquire.

"I see your mind churning," one of the boys said. "We just detoured here for a moment to deliver some goods to the very kind and charitable Mrs. Hillis. You must remember her?"

Tommy smiled. "Of course. I saw her."

"Well, that corpse…"

Corpse? Tommy craned his neck to see the wagon, but he couldn't see that there was a coffin in it.

"The woman who passed away in that home was once very wealthy. She refused to leave the home she built with her husband, ramshackle as it had become. Turns out she willed some furniture and goods to the Women's Club and the church, so when we took her body out we arranged for the rest to go to the assigned people. Her family is sour on that news, but the Lord's work is the Lord's work."

Tommy shrugged. He wasn't so sure about that. But he supposed the reverend's work and certainly Mrs. Hillis' work was worthy. *Just do the job, get the money, and burrow back into the woods. Money.* He said the word to himself repeatedly. Just enough to see him through.

"So what is it we need to do? Drop off the donations to the church?"

"Why, no," Reverend Shaw said. "Mrs. Hillis is handling all of that. You're going to drop the body at the burial site."

"For the ceremony?"

"No. Ceremonial good-byes are complete. All that's left is to send her on her way."

Tommy wondered why the family would not have wanted to see to the burial, but he did not really want the answer, so he did not ask. He jammed his hands into his pockets and shuffled his feet. "Well, all right. I suppose I have the time today. How much?"

"What price would you put on an act of compassion as you lay a woman to rest?"

Tommy started to question what the going rate was for the two boys already working, but just as he opened his mouth the minister's words settled in his mind. He swallowed his question. This was what Tommy had been worried about—getting roped into acts of forced charity. But how could he say that?

"I'll be along later to bless the site, but it's time to get the body in the ground, and the gravedigger has already prepared the grave. It would be much appreciated. Two boys to lower the body, one to guide it in smoothly. God is waiting."

As much as he'd lost his vigor for Scripture and such, Tommy had no intention of appearing as though he were stingy. On the other hand, he'd had enough of death in his short life, and he wasn't so sure he wanted to bury someone. He envisioned his camp—cozy, but possibly not for long if the weather turned. He remembered the nuts he had collected and kept in his knapsack being taken the night before by raccoons. He could fish, but he was not a hunter in the way many boys were.

"What do you say?" The bigger boy hiked up his pants.

Tommy nodded.

The two boys smiled and slapped Tommy on the back, introducing themselves as Hank and Bayard, as though they were instantly great pals. And truthfully, Tommy liked the sense that maybe they could be. It had been ages since he'd had time to spend with friends. He crammed into the front of the wagon with them. He was careful not to bend or stretch too quickly and irritate his ribs.

As the boys pulled away, Reverend Shaw waved. "I'll go back to the church. Paperwork is piling high." Riding to the cemetery, Hank shifted and his elbow brushed into Tommy's ribs, causing him to gasp and grab his side.

"Rough night in cell two, was it?"

Tommy's throat dried. He didn't know how to respond. How could he have known?

"Aww, it's all right," Hank said. "I was in cell three. Heard every punch you took."

Tommy felt his insides contract at the thought of someone out here in the public world having been witness to the most humiliating night of his life in *there*, that this person dared to speak of it as though it were a perfectly normal topic of conversation. Tommy looked at Hank's profile as he drove. His face was blemish free, his straight posture was easy, and his placid expression indicated he'd suffered none of what Tommy had in cell two.

"Don't be embarrassed. Everyone does time in the clink at some point. For me, it's every other week. Just a little mayhem, a little disorderly conduct, or lifting an apple. No need for hanging your head about it."

Tommy bristled. "I didn't do anything wrong. They tossed me in there without even interviewing a witness. Other than that fat baker—"

"Holcomb?" Hank and Bayard said at the same time.

Tommy looked at one and then the other. "Yeah. How'd you know?"

"Well, he's always getting someone tossed into jail for some dumb thing. He's pals with Judge Calder."

Tommy thought of how the judge had seen him in jail. He was grateful Judge Calder had not recognized him but was angry that he'd been locked up at all. "Well, I saved a little boy, and the mother came to my defense. I'll never go back there, and certainly not as some"—Tommy circled his finger in the air—"in and out operation to make the judge look good."

"Don't knock it. I enjoyed a warm, pleasant night in jail, a fine job—this is what being in snug with the minister and Judge Calder gets you."

Tommy wrinkled his nose. "I'm never going back there." Not for any reason.

"Don't turn your nose up, Tommy Arthur, jailbird."

Bayard cackled. Tommy deigned himself a charmer, able to turn a conversation in or out of any topic he saw fit, and his current inability to find the words brought an unfamiliar sort of discomfort. He shifted in his seat, rearranging his pants, which had bunched at his crotch.

Hank clicked his tongue at the horses and turned back to Tommy. "This is how it works with people like us."

Tommy grimaced. He wasn't so sure he wanted to be lassoed into Hank's definition of the word *us*.

"I get in a little scrape, I get tossed in a jail cell by myself, enjoy a nice meal, a nice chat with the officers, a card game, a shot of whiskey, even. They stuff me in there just for show, so it appears the judge is cleaning up the riffraff and the minister is ministering to the dead-soul types like onlookers decide I am, and we are all happy. The reporters write an article or two about how fabulous the adults are, and I get rewarded for playing the fool. There are worse roles in life to play."

"I don't get it. Isn't there plenty of riffraff without faking a case?" Tommy asked.

"Sometimes the hassle of reality is not worth the trouble. Perception is all that matters when the reverend is scraping together donations and the judge is fumbling for votes."

Tommy was disappointed. It all sounded like more work than it was worth. He certainly wasn't stepping onto some sort of continuous trip through the jail doors. Not for anyone. He imagined his mother's face if he were to engage in such a thing.

Hank elbowed Tommy again. "Don't get all riled. Mostly it works like it will today. Reverend Shaw employs Bay and me and some other boys. We stay at the church in a room in the cellar. We get meals, do odd jobs, sell some prayers. It's fulfilling."

That relieved Tommy a bit. "I agree. Reverend Shaw lays a fine road to follow when needed. But I'm sure you boys are like me. You have dreams and plans, and I'm sure eventually you want to live on a salary instead of odd job to odd job. You boys have to want more than this for your future."

Heck, he'd even go to school like his mother wanted. *His mother.* How he wanted them all back together. Katherine. Her, too. And Yale. And his father. He longed for his family to gather around. "I have plans, too—like you fellas, I'm sure."

Hank elbowed him again. Tommy pulled away, his muscles starting to tighten now that he'd been sitting for a bit. "You just wait and see. Odd jobs pay more than you think."

Tommy shrugged. No point in arguing with boys who lacked vision.

"Almost there," Bayard said.

Tommy pushed his hat off his forehead and squinted into the sun, stealing glances at his new cohorts. The boy driving the wagon—Hank—had the reins draped over his hands, easily controlling their journey as they bumped along. Hank lifted his arm and wiped his nose on a worn shirtsleeve.

Tommy looked at his own sleeves. They didn't look much better. The second boy, Bayard, hocked up some mucus. Apparently, the filth originated so deep in the boy, his body shuddered from top to bottom to get it up and finally out onto the dirt they were traveling over.

"You are precious, aren't you?"

Until Bayard said that, Tommy hadn't realized his face was creased with disapproval. His night in jail had exhausted him more than he'd realized. He softened his expression.

"Tough as nails." Tommy reset his hat.

Hank clicked his tongue at the horses and didn't take his eyes from the road ahead. "You better hold your lunch, then, 'cause if a little mucus turns your insides, just wait till you get a load of us lowering this body into the ground."

The second boy punched Tommy in the arm and cackled to the sky. "Oh, this one here, this Tommy's a pretty boy, a mama's boy. I can tell. I put it at thirty seconds before he's inside out."

The first boy laughed and smirked, still keeping his eyes ahead. "Ten. I give 'im ten seconds."

Tommy thought back to the past few years. He'd seen plenty of bodies—grotesque, frozen corpses of people he'd come to love on the prairie, the red, dead face of his own brother. But this wasn't something he wanted to relive right then; this was not something he needed to share. "I've seen plenty of dead folks. Matter of fact, one fella in cell two was dead as the corpse behind us. Died right in front of my eyes just last night."

Hank cackled. "That's Boozin' Byron. He ain't dead any more than you or me."

"I saw him die. I saw him lying there—"

"Eyes staring off at nothing?"

Tommy looked at Hank.

"I'm right, ain't I?"

Tommy felt another rush of relief.

"Byron's fine. A sideshow act, the way he sleeps with his eyes open. Something wrong with the nerves in his eyes, they say."

Tommy thought of his brother, of all of them who had died in the blizzard. He knew a dead body when he saw one.

"Ten seconds," Hank said again. Bayard threw his head back. "Ten, yes sirree, I hear ten, myself."

Tommy shook his head. Once you see your older brother buried along with neighbor after neighbor brought in from the snow, frozen in all manner of movement—midstride, curled into a ball, kneeling in prayer, cradling a sibling. He scoffed. Lowering a wooden box into the ground, well, that was nothing to a young man who'd seen all that Tommy had.

"Oh, I'm fine, boys. I can lower a box in the ground without blinking an eye."

The boys continued to mock Tommy, and he let their jabs blow right past him on the dusty wind. He was every bit as qualified for a burial as any guy on the street, and so he entertained himself with thoughts of his cozy campsite. He lifted his finger into the air and thought of his brother and the way he'd been enthralled with the idea of predicting the weather. Felt like fair weather to Tommy. Tonight would be a good night under the peaceful black sky.

**

Tommy hopped off the wagon while it was still crawling to a stop, relieved that his gasping pain was covered by the sound of the wheels crunching over rocky terrain. He met Hank and Bayard around the back of the wagon, and they lowered the hatch. Tommy took the first end and pulled the metal handle on the box while the other two boys latched on to the wood, and they all slid it from the wagon.

Tommy followed their lead as they moved toward a tree behind the wagon and lowered the coffin. He stood, hands on his hips. "Reverend Shaw said this woman was going to her family mausoleum. Said it was quite a walk from the gate."

"Easy does it, do-gooder—"

"I'm no do-gooder. I just want to—"

"Told ya," Hank said. "He's a broken wheel buggy." Hank was a wiry fellow, built tight like Tommy. Hank's voice sounded like wagon wheels turning over cinder, crackling and rough.

"Hey there, Tommy," Bayard said, his face brightening with his words. Bayard was as big as a Des Moines mansion on Grand—thick and square. But his voice was high-pitched, like an eight-year-old girl's. "Why don't you fetch us some water, and we'll check out the directions the minister left us? After all, we been working fer him much longer than you." Bayard pushed his chin in the direction from which they had just come. "There's a pump thataway."

Tommy removed his hat and wiped his forehead with his arm as he considered what they'd said. Hank pulled a paper from his pocket and unfolded it; the directions from Reverend Shaw, Tommy supposed.

Tommy scratched the front of his neck. "I am parched," he said.

"*Parched.*" Hank hit Bayard on the arm and they covered their mouths. "Grab that pail and slug us some water. We're parched, too." They bent at the waist, laughing.

Tommy grabbed the bucket and slugged off toward the water. "You two figure out where to put that body, and I'll be right back." A little chuckle at his expense did not bother him a bit. Tommy pumped the handle. Besides, it wasn't as though he would spend much time with these two. Once he was settled into his job at the Savery, his fortune would more fully turn, and his friends would certainly occupy a higher place in society than that of orphan boys working for an old minister. Tommy put his face under the splashing water, cooling his skin, gulping it as some slid past his mouth, the rest dropping into the bucket.

As long as he got paid something, he would look at the day as a success, especially in light of how the day before had unfolded.

**

Back at the wagon, Tommy heard hooting and hollering, but he could not see Hank or Bayard. Tommy hung the bucket on the hook that jutted from the side of the wagon. He dipped the ladle into it and took one last drink before heading toward the tree, toward the voices.

The giant maple hid the laughing boys. Tommy figured their game was especially childish since he was quite sure they were older than him, but they apparently hadn't had easy childhoods. He snuck toward the tree, remembering a lesson his mother had repeated when they'd lived in Des Moines years back. The children who worked and lived with preachers and such never had parents—so perhaps they enjoyed an impish game once in a while. Tommy skulked over to the tree, hiding on one side of it, listening.

"Wow!" Hank's gravelly voice came with Bayard's squeaky, "Oh, yes!" accompanying it. Tommy crept around the bottom of the thick barked trunk on hands and knees and finally got a look at what the boys were up to. He shook his head at the sight of the two. They were bent over the now-open box, lifting up the woman's hands, giggling.

Tommy didn't much care if Hank and Bayard got in trouble, but he didn't need to bring any more attention to his own behavior, not after his night in jail. But playing around with a dead body? That he couldn't tolerate.

He sat back on his haunches and then sprang from behind the tree. "Take your hands off of her!"

Hank and Bayard startled and froze in place, their hands gripping the corpse's wrists and fingers. With this closer view, he could see that the boys were not playing with the body, but were in the middle of removing her jewelry. Each looked over their shoulder, then resumed their work.

"Leave her alone," Tommy said.

Tommy held his breath, waiting for them to back away. The two boys exchanged a glance, and just as Tommy was getting the feeling that they were going to stop, they rushed at him, tackling him to the ground. Tommy had never felt such pain before, as the impact aggravated all the injuries he'd suffered the night before. Bayard rolled Tommy over onto his stomach, shoving his mouth into the dirt.

"Easy, easy!" Hank bellowed. "He's been drug up and down the creek enough for one day."

Bayard released Tommy's head and stood. Tommy rolled to his back and sat, coughing into his arm, wiping his mouth with his sleeve. His ribs felt as though they were splitting his skin. Even taking shallow breaths hurt.

"She's somebody's grandmother! Leave her be!"

"I just don't want him gettin' no bright idears, is all." Bayard spread his hands upward, clearly the weaker of the pair even though he was bigger.

Tommy tasted blood mixed with the dirt.

They chuckled. "He won't be getting no idears," Hank said. "That's what we're hired to do, Tommy."

Tommy's mind raced. Hired to steal? Did they think Tommy belonged in jail and so he'd go along with such a thing? He replayed what they said about how they cycled through jail, the way the minister and judge helped them. Tommy rubbed his ribs and thought of the grown men he'd fought in jail. He'd done all right, even though that was not how he appeared. Now these two were shoving him around. Tommy was not afraid to fight, but the pain might as well have been shackles around his limbs.

"Look at him. Worthless," Bayard said.

"Me?" Tommy asked. "Just because I don't steal from the dead doesn't mean that—"

"Yeah, you're soft. Somewhere along the line you had money, didn't you? I can hear it in your voice. Your ratty clothes don't hide it. You're a soft rich boy left to fend for himself. Whatever happened to you sapped your good sense. If you ain't gonna help us, then just be on your way."

Tommy began to feel anger spin inside him.

"Soft little rich boy," Bayard said, chuckling.

That and the fact that Bayard had wiped the dirt with Tommy's mouth, back and forth, the grainy film unwilling to wash away with his saliva, caused the intensifying anger to build and grow.

Tommy was a lot of things, but he was not soft. Incoherent thoughts spun through his mind, and before he let the pain hold him any longer, he burst up, latched his arms around Bayard's midsection, and plowed him into the ground, a plume of dirt rising up around them. They landed with such force that Tommy could tell Bayard had his wind knocked from him. Before Bayard could collect his first breath, Tommy flipped him to his stomach and sat on his back. The boy writhed and then stopped struggling as he tried to get his breath back.

Tommy noticed Hank standing near the tree watching, smiling, hands on his knees as though taking in a baseball game rather than watching his good friend get pummeled. Tommy stood and kicked Bayard in the butt, finally bringing Bayard's pip-squeak voice back in the form of a girly screech.

Tommy kicked Bayard's seat again. "Don't mess with me." Tommy pointed at Hank, then at Bayard, who was straining to lift his head and make eye contact with Tommy. "Ever." Tommy stared at Hank before kicking Bayard in the backside one last time, angered that he had resorted to fighting for the second time in twenty-four hours.

Hank fell back against the tree and exhaled, eyes still wide. "Woo-wee! Tommy Arthur." Hank removed his hat and ran a hand through his hair. "Looks as though we got us another partner, Bay—a full thirty-three percenter—the Three Musketeers ride again! Wouldn't you say, buddy?"

"Can't breathe," Bayard screeched. His feet kicked, hitting nothing but air.

Tommy rubbed his knuckles and stalked to the coffin to look inside. The woman's hand was lying off to the side unnaturally. He placed the hand back with its mate across her midsection. He snapped his fingers at Hank and held his palm out. "The jewelry. I'll put it back."

Hank looked away.

"Do you really want this on your mind for the rest of your life? Disturbing the dead?"

Hank sighed. "Put this bracelet back, but I have to take the rings. I'm obligated."

Tommy stared at him for a moment and saw a flicker of worry pass over Hank's face. He shifted his feet, and Tommy understood that Hank needed to return with something or face punishment of some sort.

Tommy turned to the body, pushed the woman's sleeve up a ways, and clasped the gold-linked bracelet around her wrist, cringing every time his fingertips brushed the woman's papery, lifeless skin. "Why on earth would her family bury her with all this jewelry?"

"Her stupid son is some sort of Spiritualist or some cockamamy thing. They think their dead might have use for their possessions in the afterlife. Me? I see their childish beliefs as an opportunity for the living, not a tool for the dead. Stupid man."

"I don't know about that." Tommy shuddered. It did seem unwise to adorn the departed with valuables, but he couldn't shake off the sensation that taking anything from someone's casket would result in something awful—the worst kind of luck.

"Leave it for the dead. Last thing I need is some lady's ghost chasing me around," Tommy said. "Just tell the reverend what is happening. I mean, he'd help you deal with whoever hired you, right?"

Hank sputtered.

Tommy met Hank's gaze. It was then Tommy put it all together. "Reverend Shaw hired you? This is part of how you pay your room and board?"

Hank took his hat off and slapped it against his thigh. "He knows exactly what the family wanted to bury her with. If we come back with less than that, we ain't gonna eat tonight."

Tommy's throat constricted. He scratched his chin, feeling nauseated. He looked at the woman's arm, where he'd just returned the bracelet. Tommy was not interested in stealing, but he didn't want to be the reason Hank and Bayard didn't eat. Clearly, their options were limited.

Tommy began to unlatch the bracelet. "You better take this, then."

Hank put his hand on Tommy's. "No. Rev must not have known about it."

Tommy saw a softness in Hank's expression. "You sure?"

"Sure, yeah." Hank backed away. Suddenly, Hank appeared to be a little boy again, his face devoid of hard angles and angry tension as shame spread over him.

"Why don't you fellas find another way for room and board?"

"Live in the woods with the ne'er-do-wells?"

"I don't know if I'd call those who take to the woods *ne'er-do-wells.*"

"What else are they?"

"Free," Tommy said.

"Poor," Hank said. He shrugged. "He depends on us. We depend on him. Took us in when we were small. Like a father now. Can't imagine turning my back on him."

Tommy straightened his hat. He understood that aspect of it. Loyalty was important. He felt naïve. Though he was surprised about this scam, he understood how difficult it was to turn away from someone you loved. He remembered Mrs. Hillis being with Reverend Shaw and the boys when he'd first seen them. A kernel of numbness took hold in his stomach. He knew the world was full of people with rotten cores and selfish motives, but Mrs. Hillis? He supposed no one was immune to greed if they needed something enough. "Mrs. Hillis is part of this?"

"Aw, shucks, no way." Bayard made a clownish face. "Mrs. Hillis is one woman I'd never take for a dummy or a meanie. Her trouble is her belief that there is good in everyone."

"Yeah," Tommy said. "That's how I remember her. I used to…well… She used to come to my house all the time before…well, before, yeah." He didn't want to go into his tales of woe.

Hank shrugged. "I don't know what the heck *before* means, Tommy, but had I met her before Reverend Shaw, I just might be respectable. It breaks my heart to see her help him, not knowing what he's about. But the time is not yet right to let her know what that man is working in the back room of his church. We do good deeds, too. And be honest with me; can you really say this dead woman here needs this expensive jewelry? The money in trade for this stuff will feed seven boys for who knows how long."

Tommy cleared his throat but kept his thoughts to himself. He'd learned so much in the last two years. On one hand, he'd seen a minister lose his life to save a church member who'd fallen on a train track with the engine bearing down, but he'd read all about a certain East Coast minister who bilked the world with a charming smile and just the right words when called upon. He should have realized he didn't need to live in New York City to find himself in the company of people who preyed on the vulnerable. He did agree about her not needing the jewelry, but this was not the same as lifting a loaf of bread when he had missed two days of meals.

"Just turn away, Arthur. You don't need to witness this. Go get more water or something. You don't have to be in on it."

Hank started removing the rings again. "But no matter what your opinion, Tommy, I have to take these to the reverend. He'll cut my work in half, won't allow me to sell prayers, and keep the extra and…well, I don't cross a man like Reverend Shaw, and that's that."

Tommy shook his head. He saw fear in Hank's face as Bayard whimpered like a chorus in the theater.

Money. Just get paid for delivering the body, and when your job starts at the Savery, you will never be part of anything sordid again.

"You won't go run yer mouth to Mrs. Hillis or someone like her, will ya?" Bayard said. "We don't want to have to hurt you. Or see you find your way back to jail."

Tommy drew a deep breath. Self-preservation was paramount at this point. That and the fact he saw good beyond the bad in these boys made it easy for Tommy to promise not to reveal their dealings. "Tell Mrs. Hillis?" He shook his head and knew he would not tell anyone of this. Survival might be the argument that kept him out of hell, but the courts did not care for flexible law-breakers.

Hank jammed the jewels into his pockets and straightened.

Tommy gently closed the coffin lid. *Rest in peace, lady.* He took his place at the head of the box. "Let's get this coffin into the ground before I shrivel up and die of heat right before your eyes."

Hank grinned and pushed his head in the direction of Bayard.

Tommy looked at the large boy. He had nearly forgotten he was there, humiliated in the dirt. Tommy felt a tug of guilt for what he'd done to Bayard, but he didn't want to be the one to help him back up. He knew this kind of boy needed to know he would not ever have power over Tommy.

Hank jerked his head toward Bayard again—this time more exaggerated.

"Oh, all right," Tommy said. He got down beside the whimpering Bayard. "I'm sorry I kicked your backside. Three times. And punched you, tackled you, too." Bayard didn't reply. "How about you fill me in on this 'prayers for sale' business, whatever that is? I bet you can write a mean prayer."

He rolled Bayard onto his back and brushed off his shirtfront while Bayard covered his face with his hands, coughing and, Tommy suspected, crying a little bit. "You can't be hurting that bad. Plenty of cushion on your seat."

Tommy helped him to sitting and wiped off Bayard's back. Bayard sputtered as though he'd just been dug out of a grave.

"Now, that's enough, Bayard. It's not like you didn't get a few good licks in on me. Let's get this woman in the ground before that perfume of hers wears off and the corpse rot poisons us all."

Hank laughed, a deep giggle rising out of his belly as he slapped Tommy on the back. Tommy felt a twinge of happiness inside him. A sense of community, of belonging, no matter how tangential the acquaintance was, no matter the fact he didn't really want them to be his people, to be the people he turned to in a time of need. But for now, this was what he had, and this was what he would use just to survive.

Chapter 13

Katherine

1905—Des Moines

The parlor was stuffed end to end with mourners who were unfamiliar to Katherine and her family. Upon seeing the crowd who had arrived to attend the funeral, the Arthurs gathered every extra chair they could find, lining the room with them. The temperature rose as people without seats filled every open space, standing behind the family, along the walls, even stretching back out into the hall.

The minister began with a standard sermon about life and being born a child of God and returning to his side when called. His words were reassuring and typical of what was said at every funeral Katherine had ever attended. Katherine closed her eyes, wanting to feel the presence of her mother's spirit. But she only experienced a widening sense of emptiness as the service went on.

Katherine grew nervous at the thought of speaking in front of strangers. She scraped her memory for the missing words she'd planned to say. *Love, sorrow, fear, strength.* What *had* she wanted to say about her mother? She could feel the weight of the words, but couldn't remember how she had linked them together so that they made sense, so they would convey the love she wanted to express.

When their essence hid further and further from her consciousness, panic nicked open her composure, leaving her feeling out of control. Her hands shook as she imagined her life path forever separate from her mother's earthly trace. Could she say that?

Katherine had expected to be able to wrap herself in the surety that her mother's soul would somehow be closer than ever now that they had made their peace, that she would simply know the right thing to say even if she forgot the planned words. She clasped her hands in her lap and did her best to suppress a rising sob. She squeezed her eyes shut, trying to calm herself, to ready her voice for the words she'd wanted to express.

But by the time the minister finished, Katherine couldn't camouflage her shuddering shoulders. She covered her mouth with her handkerchief and drew deep breaths. *Please, God, bring me my calm. Grant me this moment to say good-bye as my mother deserved.*

She looked up to see the reverend close his eyes and lift his hands upward. "In the next months and years, I will have many moments to consider Jeanie Arthur and what she meant to our church, but I think those who have gathered here to say good-bye should have the pulpit."

Katherine's throat closed and she stole a glance at Aleksey. He squeezed her hand and offered an encouraging nod. But she couldn't move. He smiled and pulled her closer, his lips near her ear. "It's all right. You don't need to say the words aloud for her to have heard them. You know that."

Katherine melded into him, comforted by his acceptance and understanding. Still, she was unnerved by the thought that no one in the family would have anything to say at this sacred time. Beatrice had felt particularly close to her grandmother during the last days of her life, but she was too young to speak at something like this. The boys were quiet souls and also too young. She tried to straighten up. She needed to speak. Someone needed to make this right.

She couldn't move her feet. She couldn't even signal to the minister that she had something to say. She thought of the kindness the minister had done, inviting his congregants to fill the room. This crowd was spilling into the hallway, but there was not a familiar face in the group. Most of the guests were dressed in respectful, but inexpensive, clothing. Katherine's gaze went around the room. There were several women dressed finely. What would they think?

One woman caught Katherine's eye. Their eyes met, but she quickly turned away. *Cora Hillis.* What would she be doing at this funeral? Katherine's mind worked to remember. She knew her mother and Cora had collaborated on some committees and had been in the Women's Club together at one time.

But Mrs. Hillis occupied a space in society that Jeanie Arthur had not known in decades. Mrs. Hillis was a benevolent woman—accomplished, nationally regarded for her speeches, writing, and development of women's organizations that benefited the welfare of children. Katherine looked back at Mrs. Hillis. Their eyes met again. Mrs. Hillis forced a smile through her tears, dabbing at her face before looking down to her feet. What a nice woman she was to have come to a funeral on behalf of the church. It seemed she never tired of doing good deeds.

Absorbed in watching the fellow mourners, Katherine didn't notice Yale rising in her seat until it was too late to stop her. She shuffled up to the pulpit, where the minister stepped aside to make room for her.

Katherine stifled a yelp, wanting to save Yale from the embarrassment of speaking publicly when she was surely not capable of such a thing. Katherine moved to the edge of her seat. Yale looked at Katherine with a steady gaze, and the look in her eyes made Katherine stop. She watched as a single tear trickled down Yale's face. Her lips quivered, and then she pushed her chin forward in that way Katherine had seen their mother do a thousand times.

Yale flattened her paper in front of her. "My mama. I am here to say good-bye."

Gasps and sobs began to ring out from around the room. Tommy lifted his eyebrow at Katherine. Katherine looked around the room. There was deep sadness on every face. Were these people really sobbing at listening to a few words from Yale?

"I want to read something she wrote. Something that she told me over and over. Here it goes: 'For the longest time, I couldn't feel anything. The death of James was like a weight on my chest, cutting off all feeling to all parts of my being. I wanted to be strong. James was not the first boy to die in the world. I'd seen so many mothers act with dignity and grace in the face of putting their children in the ground. Before…I had imagined that would be me, that I was made of iron or grit, or ever-bending rubber, but it turned out that my soul was cotton, and when wetted with an endless store of grief, it could hold nothing else, dripping with sadness that nearly took my life, sapping me, leaving me useless. Still, all my life I've comforted myself with the weather passing by, thinking of James' interest in predictions. I've soothed myself with warm glows from fires and bright stars and unexplained golden flashes that tell me my Katherine is near. And it is with the intensity of the world—someone's quick smile, or sharp ire, or wide grin—that I see my Tommy each and every day. Yale was with me always, same as my very heartbeat, but so were the others, and I know, as my Katherine knows deep in her soul, that we never really leave one another.'"

Yale paused, biting back a sob. She wiped her cheeks, exhaled, then drew her finger along the paper, clearly looking for the spot where she'd left off reading. "And my mama wrote that she never stopped thinking of or loving her children for *one second*."

She paused and looked at Tommy. "Mama made me underline that for you." Katherine stole a glance at her brother's face as he registered a moment of surprise before smiling.

Yale cleared her throat. "Not one moment. She said," Yale moved her finger along the paper again and then kept her eyes there, following along as she spoke, "each person takes a road or a path. Sometimes we are hand in hand, and other times our roads stretch out toward opposite poles. But even as our feet travel away, as we watch the back of a son or daughter disappear from sight, it is in our hearts that we carry our home. No matter where we go, the road takes us home in some way."

Cries came again from around the room. Katherine could not breathe. She stared at the floor and held every muscle in her body tight to keep from keeling over.

Tommy stared ahead, his eyes glistening as tears dropped off his lids, splashing over his pants. Katherine groped for Aleksey's hand and squeezed tight, hoping it would keep her from bursting into the loud sobs that threatened in her throat. His face was sodden and red. Death had marked his childhood far more than had been fair and she was sure he was reliving that pain right then.

"So," Yale said, "my mama read that to me, and I read it back to her to practice over and over. She wanted me to say she was sorry the path seemed too far away at times. She was sorry for being spongy rather than iron or metallic."

Yale covered her mouth, and it looked as though her knees were about to give out, but she drew herself up taller, both hands latched on to the sides of the podium. "I think metallic means strong like metal." Yale met Katherine's gaze, her eyebrows raised as though wanting confirmation.

Katherine nodded. "Yes. Strong," she said, unable to comprehend how Yale came to be able to offer this reading with such dignity and strength. Katherine felt a smile soften her as it came to her lips. Her veins filled with pride for her sister.

A grin stretched across Yale's innocent face. "Okay. Strong." She pressed her chest with her open hand. "But I want to say that I liked my mama's softness, her sadness. I liked that she was not hard like silvery iron. I liked that she was just like cotton." She grasped her blouse, gripping it tight in her fist.

Yale's legs began to give way, and Katherine and Aleksey rushed to the podium, catching her before she fell completely. Beatrice hopped up from her chair, and they settled Yale into her abandoned seat. Asher changed seats with Tommy, and now Yale could lean against him. Katherine sat on her other side, relieved that the service was nearly over.

She patted Yale's face with the handkerchief, marveling that she had managed to say anything at all, let alone such beautiful, heartfelt things at such a stressful time, in front of such a large audience. Katherine could only guess at how long Yale and their mother had rehearsed that reading.

When Katherine looked back at the minister she expected to find him readying to finish. But instead there was a woman at the podium. Her hair was swept up and knotted at her crown. Her white starched blouse was neatly tucked into a brown skirt with a barely there bustle. She was a young woman, probably in her early twenties.

Katherine looked at Aleksey, who bore the same surprise as Katherine. Bea snuggled into her father's lap, her head against his chest. Tommy shook his head as he looked on, wonder on his face. None of them knew her.

"My name is Libby Tuthill." She cleared her throat and smoothed a paper on the podium. "I am deeply saddened to hear of Jeanie Arthur's passing. It's been years since I've seen her."

Katherine squinted. Years since this woman, clearly educated and well-dressed, had seen Katherine's mother?

The woman forced a smile at the crowd. "I'm a college graduate. I have been working in a law firm for two years. I am getting married next month."

She smiled around the room as people, sniffling and crying, looked on.

"And…" She popped her hands on her hips, looking toward Jeanie's body before putting her gaze back on the mourners. "I would not be alive today were it not for the help Jeanie Arthur gave me. I would certainly not be a college graduate. I…" She covered her mouth. She gripped the side of the podium with one hand and straightened, her expression showing that her mind was full of a story that no one knew but her. "Jeanie Arthur helped me when no one else would. Not *could*, but *would*. And I would not have a life at all if not for her. In fact, I'm sure I would be dead."

The woman's neck grew tense, the tendons there clearly tight as she looked around the room. "I don't know if I'm the only one Jeanie Arthur helped. But even if I am the only one, I can still say that her life meant more than that of most people I know and meet every single day. She made a difference in a way that so many others simply chose not to."

Libby Tuthill cleared her throat and put her eyes back to her paper. She folded it one section at a time, running the side of her hand over each crease. One, two, three, four folds, as though the woman did not want to take her seat. Katherine did not know what her mother could have done to have so significantly changed this woman's life, but the thought of it caused a wellspring of tears to release. Katherine held her breath, wanting to run from the room so she could let it all out where no one would hear or see.

The room was hushed. Katherine sprouted silent tears and waited for it all to end.

The woman bit her lip and then gave a single nod to Jeanie, who lay in the casket to her right. "Thank you." The woman began to step away when a voice came from behind Katherine. "She helped me, too!"

Katherine winced but didn't turn to look.

A deep male voice rumbled from the back corner of the room. "She helped me, too."

Before Katherine could turn around to see who'd spoken, another declaration came from the left. "And me."

Katherine moved forward in her seat to get a look. *What was happening?* The man who'd spoken raised his hand at her. She waved back.

"She gave me her coat," someone shouted from out in the hallway.

"She saved my house." Another affirmation came from near the windows.

Katherine's mind tangled. Her mother barely had anything of value. How on earth was she able to help so many people?

"She gave me every single ear of corn she grew one year," a hoarse-voiced lady said.

"*Me!*" A quivering chirp made Katherine look down past Aleksey to see an elderly woman with wispy angora curls looking upward, a small smile on her lips. "Gave *me* respect." She spoke fiercely this time.

And before Katherine could fully process what she was hearing, the proclamations came like corn popping over a hot fire. She could hear their praise for her mother, but emotion swamped her ability to fully appreciate the depths of what this meant for her. When it stopped, the silence sat heavy, and finally Katherine shifted in her seat and felt her chest tighten even further. Looking around the room, she began to feel faint, to be filled with a rush of love and awe that she had never felt before. Like sentries, every single person in the room was standing or had raised her hand stating as clear as a Sunday church bell that Jeanie Arthur had changed their lives in some enormous way.

"Oh my heavenly God," Katherine said. Each person she made eye contact with gave her a nod. Her mouth fell open in awe, confused but utterly touched by the sight. It was as though her mother was present in every single one of these people.

She turned back toward the minister, who was smiling down at the family. Katherine wanted to keep it all in, to save her sobs for later, for private. But the unexpected crush that came with seeing these people give tribute to her mother caused her to fold over, to drop her face into her hands. Stunned, unable to speak, Katherine finally absorbed the honor these people were showing her mother, a woman for whom Katherine felt the damning weight of not knowing at all.

She forced herself to straighten and looked at Tommy. His face bore the same condemned expression that she knew she was wearing. Without a word spoken, they both understood each other—their shame and sadness. They knew one thin layer of who their mother had been. But there was so much more to her that they did not understand. Yes, they'd each tried to reconcile with their mother at different points in time. But something always got in the way. Sitting there, witnessing this outpouring of love from strangers, made it spring-water clear that Katherine had much work to do in getting to know her mother.

She looked around the room again. She was met with warm nods, forced but heartfelt smiles through pain for the loss of a woman these people obviously felt strongly about. Katherine lifted her gaze to the ceiling and closed her eyes. *I am so sorry for how I treated you, Mama.* She recalled the last breaths of her mother's life, the gift it had been to witness her pass from this world into the next.

Katherine clasped her hands in her lap and allowed herself to feel the three squeezes they'd exchanged to say they loved each other just before she died. Katherine cherished that moment like a priceless jewel. It was all she had to know her mother had forgiven her, that she understood Katherine's regret and wanted to release her from it. She held that realization tight in her heart in order to keep from falling over, from wailing like a lunatic for all she'd done wrong to a woman who had deserved so much more.

Chapter 14

Jeanie

1891—Sioux Falls

The poorhouse had grown stale with the hot sun pouring through the painted-closed windows. The heat unleashed the reeking smell from careless chamber-pot users, perspiration soaked linens, and the vinegar that Millie and I used to try and clean the space. I could not wait to get back to my letters and reread the one from Mrs. Mellet for the thirteenth time, making sure each word had been written the way I'd interpreted it, trying not to fool myself into thinking what she wrote was not what she meant.

Mrs. Mellet of Des Moines, Iowa, former partner in my father's and husband's misdeeds, was ready to tell her story. She promised to fatten my purse for my trouble.

And most important, she swore she would do her best to restore my name, to be sure the leading citizens of Des Moines understood that, though related to those who'd had a hand in a bank collapse and investments that returned nothing, including the initial contributions—many folks' life savings—I myself was not part of the operation in any way, shape, or form.

I couldn't believe it. Mrs. Mellet had sent enough money for me to purchase train fare for three children and myself, plus some extra for expenses—whatever that meant. This had stunned me, unable to fully accept that her letter was true, that this was not some sort of trick to get me back to Des Moines to suffer further humiliation. I ignored my fears and had already sent a telegram to Des Moines for Tommy in care of the coal miner with whom he was boarding when he last wrote. I'd sent one also to the Turners in Yankton—the last place I knew Katherine to have been boarding. Then I'd written letters to each child, sending those to every address I had for them, knowing that one of the letters or telegrams would have to reach them. I did not allow myself to dwell on the idea that perhaps none of the correspondence found my children safe and ready to meet me in Des Moines.

I smoothed the letter on my legs. Things were changing, and this time for the better; this time it was real. It didn't make sense for Mrs. Mellet to call me back there simply to berate me. Surely there were plenty of folks she could lambaste without having to make a special effort to have me stand in front of her again.

She had to have been sincere when she wrote this, when she sent cash for my use. But my life had gone so wrong that I believed anything bad could latch on to me, embed itself into my life. Yale tapped two wooden spoons on the pine floor of the poorhouse while I read the letter again. I lay back in the sagging cot that we shared and put the letter over my chest. A soft wind snaked through the dormer and made the paper flap in the wind.

Could this be why I was spared on the train trestle? Could something of great power and love have had my interests in mind when Millie and her man followed me, when they called to me and I fell into the water instead of backward on the train track with the train bearing down?

My heart pounded with doubt and hope. So much had gone wrong. My mind went back to my father's funeral, back to when I began to realize how dire our situation was.

I remembered it clearly, standing at the coffin, fingers gripping the smooth sides. I could not let go. Reverend Shaw's hair flopped over his brow as he huffed and pried at my fingers, wrestling one hand away. But as soon as the minister removed one hand, I slapped the other back onto the wood. The bracing under the mahogany box buckled, and the body shook inside. With a grunt, the minister finally stepped away, leaving me there while he offered a short service.

Safe from the minister's attempts to remove me, I listened, clutching my father's stiff hands while tears careened down my cheeks, off my nose, from my chin, speckling his navy blue suit in blotted shapes.

Behind me, ten-year-old Katherine sobbed while Frank hushed and comforted her and our sons. The crying grew louder, and I imagined the church filling behind me. I couldn't turn to face the congregation. I couldn't stand the idea of making eye contact with people I'd known my whole life. For if I did, I might never stop crying at the sight of them doing the same.

The minister brought his words to a close and glanced at me. He appeared frightened. I wouldn't make him tussle with me again; I'd said my good-bye. I drew a deep breath and choked back sobs. There would be no more weeping. My father had suffered, yes. So much that he'd salved his soul with opium, too much of it, but he was at peace finally. His accidental death had freed him. I focused on all the lessons he'd taught me over the years.

I wanted to honor him by living a good life in the home that stood beside his. "We are not quitting people," he'd always said. I grasped my pearls, a gesture that always soothed me. I willed the tears away and recalled my father's words in times of trouble. "We are not crying people." He was right. Tears only served to weaken a sad condition further. *Keep it in.* I pushed back my shoulders, patted my father's arm, and moved to join Frank and the children.

I turned. The sight of the church made the hairs at the nape of my neck tingle. I'd thought the sight of weeping friends would take my breath away, but what I saw—an utterly empty church—did the job instead. I grasped my chest with one hand and cradled my forehead with the other, feeling as though my brain were made of seltzer, with incoherent thoughts darting about. Frank rushed toward me, slipping his arms around me, helping me down the aisle. The children trailed behind, sniffling.

Outside, we stopped under looming oak trees where chutes of sunlight streamed through the boughs, mottling our skin with odd shadows. I began to understand what I'd seen in the church. Our friends, lifelong friends, must believe my father took his own life.

"It was an accident." My words were stilted. Intense remorse filled me on behalf of my father. He'd crumble if he knew the people he'd helped so much and so often believed he killed himself. I bore the pain for my father—we'd been so close I was sure I felt the exact regret that he would have if he were alive.

Frank took my face in his hands, his smooth thumbs brushing my skin in his attempt to comfort me. "You have to understand what happened. You must know. You are not a stupid woman. You have to face up. We have to leave."

He was wrong. I'd never felt such anger gather inside me. We had done nothing wrong, and I would not just run away. I smacked Frank's hands from my face and shot quick, embarrassed looks at our children. James, Tommy, and Katherine melded together, eyes wide, clearly filled with the same disbelief that I felt. I put my back to them.

"Don't say that." I balled my fists, trying to keep all the emotion stowed inside. "Why would we run? I've lost my father, your father-in-law. Des Moines owes him. Is this the thanks they give my father for paved streets, a library, modern utilities, loans? And us—my newspaper column, your commissions, our children's very existence is due to Father's good works. And you're telling *me* that not one person in this town is capable of understanding he *accidentally* ingested too much opium?"

Frank shook his head and looked away.

Katherine snuck up and took my balled-up hand, clasping it inside both of hers. I looked down at her, her cheeks sodden but placid. "I believe it, Mama. It was a mistake. I believe you. We'll be all right. I know it. We can carry on Grandfather's work, and you can write, and—"

"Enough!" Frank said. Katherine and I jumped at the outburst. "We are leaving, and that is that. I made the decision, and we will go. I am the man of the household."

Katherine squeezed Jeanie's hand harder.

"There are times," Frank said, "when you have to recognize the fleas in the dander, pluck them out, then move out of the infested space. This is one of them. We're done here. Your father…" Frank bit his lip. "Let's just get home. I'll explain the rest. Everything."

"It's not possible," I said. "Everyone loved my father."

Frank pulled Katherine and me toward the buggy. "They loved him until he lost their money."

"But Mrs. Mellet said she believed in my father. She spoke for all of them."

Frank stopped short and turned, taking me by the shoulders. "Pull your head out of the oven and look around, Jeanie. Our dear Mrs. Mellet was part of the problem. She got half the town to invest, and she knew it was not a sound deal. She put your father in touch with Mr. Jackson. She knew and she plotted with your father. What you saw was her pretending she had nothing to do with it to save her standing."

Rage blurred my vision. Frank pulled me along, Katherine still gripping my hand.

"Let's not embarrass ourselves further," Frank said as he pushed Katherine up and into the buggy.

The boys followed, and then I lifted my skirts and Frank helped me into my seat. I looked around; the fresh spring air rustled the treetops, but midday should have meant the street was filled with people shoulder to shoulder headed to or from lunch. But the streets were vacant. Still, knowing we should not expose the inner workings of our family, of myself, to the public, I fought to further tamp down the tears.

We had lost nothing up to this point. If we maintained decorum we could make this work in this town. People would forget what my father did. People would start over, just like us. We, too, had lost some money in the investment. It wasn't as though we ourselves were unscathed.

I held my breath and straightened in my seat, projecting all the calm and grace I could manage. Though no one stood there with us, no one turned their gaze upon us, I knew people were somehow watching, listening. And for that second, I thought it might actually be possible that the town would turn against us simply because of my father's disgraceful death.

I hugged myself, then shoved my hands in my lap and straightened my posture. I would not crumble in town. The buggy jerked forward. We passed a tree with green buds opening to the world. One brown leaf remained from the fall, dangling there, alone among the new life around it.

I quieted my speeding heart with thoughts that my father would at least lie next to my mother. The minister had promised. We would manage with what was left of our fortune. Even if we sold Father's belongings and holdings to pay our friends back, we would carry on. We were strong, and I would make Frank stay in Des Moines. I would show him we could go on. Running was never the answer.

By the time the black buggy pulled up to our grand stone home, I had gathered my wits, accessed my common sense, and was certain I could right whatever perceived wrongs my father had committed. I could explain that he hadn't intended to die. He had plans and dreams. Men who have plans and initiative don't kill themselves. I averted my gaze from the redbrick home next to ours, the one my father had occupied until three days earlier. I saw the curtains move in a bedroom on the second floor as though someone had been looking out of it. It must be a draft in the room. I would check on that after the wake.

"I will not leave here," I whispered. "We are *not* hiding people." I shifted in my seat and took Frank's hand as he offered it to help me down. I lifted my bombazine skirt. A tan layer of dust had discolored my black silk shoes. I stepped out of the buggy. The thought that I'd clean the shoes after I helped Vera prepare for the luncheon made me grimace. But I reminded myself that even when mourning, one must be immaculate.

I silently forgave my friends and neighbors for not attending the service. I understood that many people—deeply religious, nearly superstitious, in fact—were afraid for their souls. If they believed the sordid details of Mr. Scholler's death, they'd not sit in a church with the corpse. But surely they'd come to luncheon in droves. Surely.

Frank kissed my cheek and reached over my shoulder to help Katherine out of the buggy. Tommy and James hopped from the back and scrambled down the street to the Renaults', where they were to spend the next hour. "Go on, Katherine. Skedaddle." I forced a smile to convey that all was well.

Katherine nodded, then tore after her brothers.

"Frank, darling," I said. I felt as though my vocal projection, its normal tone, was a sign that I could handle this. I'd been named the Quintessential Housewife, after all, and wouldn't this be the ultimate opportunity to show the title was deserved? We entered our home, deafening quiet filling the foyer.

I plucked at my gloves one finger at a time, pacing, gathering determination. "We need to reach for normalcy. Re-create our existence. And the first step in doing so will be to offer a pious, loving wake. Then as Teeny, Vera, and the rest are cleaning up, we must dive full-bodied, headfirst back into our daily responsibilities. No exceptions. We have lives to live. We will live fully, as he wanted us to."

Frank grabbed my hands. "You aren't listening. We have nothing. Your father took everything with him when he ended his life."

I squinted at Frank. A chill worked its way up my arms. "I don't even know what that means."

"It means we have to leave. Your father disgraced us—"

I tore my hands from Frank's grip. "Jed Tumulty lost his life at his own hand last year. Elizabeth and her family did not hightail it out of here. No, Frank, what I hear you saying is that this is your chance to fully entertain your air castles, to develop a town called Frankton or Frankville or what have you. But you know as well as I that your gifts live in your hands, not in your head, and that all the town-worthy land near the railroad, if there ever was decent land to homestead in Dakota Territory, is long, long gone."

Frank squeezed his eyes shut, and I took it as acknowledgment that he agreed. I tucked my gloves into the silver box we kept by the front door. I held my head high, ready to mend our fractured life. There was nothing breeding and good works couldn't transform. I headed toward the back hall and saw Vera watching me, her face sad and creased at the forehead. I shook my head, struck by my harshness toward Frank and the fact that Vera had witnessed it. I rubbed my temples.

It would never do to let things settle that way. If I didn't offer Frank his dignity back, I'd surely have to live with the blue mood; perhaps it would even turn black, oppressed by fat, industrial-sized clouds that settle on a person, on a family, like a heavy box, blocking out all that might be good in the world.

I needed to apologize and wished that the feelings of lust, love, and romance I'd once drowned in would return, that I could once again feel excitement and compassion for the man who was my husband of twelve years.

I retraced my steps, but Frank had left the house. I stopped at the front door and closed my eyes, searching out dormant emotion, and though the old feelings stirred, they were gone the instant I opened my eyes. If only the feelings would stay at the surface. If only I could force them to.

I poked my head out the door. "Frank?" He wasn't near the buggy. I walked to the edge of the porch and craned my neck to see down the sidewalk. Under the canopy of bulky elms, Frank and Elizabeth Tumulty Rowe stood. Their heads were bent over a piece of paper, so close together that Elizabeth's perfectly curled bangs touched Frank's forehead. He pointed at something on the paper, and Elizabeth smiled up at him.

I felt as though the ground had been shaken, and I was barely able to stay upright. Elizabeth, my oldest friend, flirted with any man she saw fit. She always chose Frank when he was around, always brought their past puppy love into conversation, making me question whether Frank's former blue moods had sent him into Elizabeth's company. But this felt different. Their intimate posture, their familiar gestures, made my stomach ache with the realization that they seemed more like a couple than friends. I forced myself to head down the steps toward them.

Bitter bile collected in my mouth. Though I had no idea what they were speaking about, my body seemed to understand. I grasped my pearls, fingering the fat balls strung in two strands, brought from Japan expressly for me. I'd seen a similar set on the wife of a gold rush millionaire one day, and my father had produced the same set weeks later for my fourteenth birthday. The memory combined with the silky feel of the little orbs threatened me with new tears. *Don't cry.* I blotted under my eyes with brisk finger strokes. *We are not crying people.*

As I neared my husband and dear friend, a smile flashed on Elizabeth's face, her lips pulling wide before she glanced at Frank, stepped away from him, and then put that smile right back on her face along with a pitying expression as she came toward me, arms extended as though wanting to comfort me.

Frank walked beside her. The sight of their synchronized gaits further unsettled me, as though I were the outsider in the Frank G. Arthur marriage.

"Oh," Elizabeth said. "What a dark, sad day."

I nodded, trying to discern why her words felt sarcastic more than comforting.

"I'm so glad to be able to help you in this horrible time." Elizabeth hugged me tight, her lemon-verbena perfume strong in my nose.

I sniffled and nodded. "Thank you, Liza. But there's not much to do. Death needs to be weathered and moved past. No one can do that for me, unfortunately. I know you understand that."

Elizabeth covered her mouth with her gloved hand and lifted her eyes to Frank. "You didn't tell her?"

Beads of perspiration formed on my upper lip. Her tone had gone from comforting to nearly taunting. I could tell she meant more than to just offer support. Suddenly outside the clasp of friendship, I felt dismayed that Frank and Elizabeth shared a secret. I drew straighter, stilling a torrent of sickening fear.

"Tell me what?" I asked.

"About your father."

I shrugged. "The doctor's report was inconclusive. It said—just like *your* father, I recall—it was... Why would you or anyone else judge..."

Elizabeth wrapped me in her arms tighter than before. Her French perfume filled my nose again. I was too shocked to pull away.

"Dear friend," Elizabeth whispered in my ear. "I will be sure to do what I can to keep your name in conversation, and I know one day you'll be able to buy your things back. I will be here to remember your life, to remember you like no other."

"What does that mean?" I wiggled out of Elizabeth's embrace.

Elizabeth grabbed my hands, her expression soft, familiar, comforting. Except for what she'd just said, except for the grip of confusion and fear that made my hair stand on end.

"You've lost so much with your father's death. I understand that. But I want you to know that I will help you. I still have money, and I want to make sure you are on sound ground."

Frank nodded. I tried to stop my jaw from falling at the sight of my husband and my friend having formed some sort of alliance, sealed with a hidden plan that turned my stomach without even knowing what they had arranged.

"Des Moines," Elizabeth said, "can forgive a man's weaknesses. As you said, my father's good memory remains intact. But when a man's weakness results in his own death, and before that death he snatches away the savings of nearly everyone else in town, well, that man is harder to mourn."

I grasped my pearls as my knees buckled. Frank caught me around the waist. His moist cheek brushed against mine, and I inhaled his soapy-clean skin.

"Is that what you were trying to tell me?" I asked.

Frank nodded.

Elizabeth patted my shoulder. "People can be cruel, and I was just trying to help."

Frank took the paper he and Elizabeth had been looking at and turned it so I could see it. It was an inventory of familiar items, things that defined and shaped our lives.

Elizabeth patted my shoulder. "Frank thought in light of your mourning, it would be best if you accepted my offer. He's got a way for you to all start over. And I'd be pleased to contribute and fund your trip into the great Western expanse. I'll even purchase some of your things—"

Frank shot Elizabeth a look, and she stopped talking.

"What does she mean? What does any of this mean?" I said.

Frank sighed. "We've lost everything. Any money we make from selling our things goes to the investors or we will go to jail."

I couldn't respond. I stared at the paper and the scribbled rows and columns of household items, family heirlooms, all that had given shape to our lives. This could not be accurate. He must have overlooked an option. "Frank, you can't have agreed to this nonsense. Surely Judge Calder will put a stop to this. He knows our family. He knows *me*. He understands our position."

Frank and Elizabeth looked at each other. Frank shrugged. "It was Calder's decision."

I couldn't believe that it was true. I'd known him since I was four years old.

"You know he never liked me," Frank said.

But it was impossible that dislike could lead to something like this. There had to be another way for us to make amends—to pay my father's debt over time. It was well-known that Judge Calder never liked Frank and had always had feelings for me, but this could not be right. I would make the judge understand.

Elizabeth put her arm around me. "I spoke to the judge myself. Frank may not be his close friend, but this was not a punishment. It's a gift."

Frank flinched and crossed his arms.

"A gift?" I asked.

Elizabeth squeezed my shoulder, jarring me against her. "You and Frank could be tied up in court, serving time, the children on the street. *Imagine.* This was Judge Calder's way to ensure that you could simply leave, unscathed, family intact. There's simply too much owed."

Unscathed? "*I* haven't agreed to any of this. I would not be in jail. I did nothing! I certainly didn't agree to give up our things and go west. We can dispose of my father's home, his things, in an appropriate manner, but *my* things? We are our own family. My father, though generous, never completely tied our assets into his. This is an abomination." I stomped my foot, crushed at the thought that Elizabeth and Frank had arranged all this, excluding me. I was terrified at the thought my life had been dismantled, that all I knew was true just days before was suddenly shown to be false.

I looked at Elizabeth, further disconcerted at the level of knowledge she had about the inner workings of my life. Elizabeth tilted her head and offered a look more pitying than understanding. I suddenly felt as though I did not know her, as though she had abandoned our friendship in a way I could never have imagined.

Frank nodded toward the house. "Go ahead, Elizabeth. The faster this goes, the better."

Elizabeth took the list and stepped away.

Wait a minute. What was she doing? I could see her running her gloved finger down the paper as though ticking something off in her mind. Was she really going to take my things? "You can't!" I reached for Elizabeth's arm, gripping it.

She turned back. "Everything will be all right. You'll see."

I shook my head, but she was pulling out of my grip, walking toward my home.

"Frank! Stop her!"

"I tried to tell you."

"You didn't try to tell me this. The time to tell me was when all the decisions were being made."

Frank held his hand out to me. "I tried. You were grieving. You didn't want to hear it."

I would have sworn in court he never even hinted he was going to court to hear a decision on how our things were going to be sold off. I certainly didn't hear Elizabeth's name mentioned in any context other than that she'd dropped off her famous chicken salad and butter biscuits to feed us. But I didn't have time to fight about this right then. Elizabeth was already heading up my front stairs.

I grunted and chased after her. Frank raced around and blocked my progress as I reached the porch. "Don't embarrass yourself, Jeanie. I read the papers. Your father sank every person's money into—"

I covered my ears. My chest heaved, but no air came in or out. I lifted my skirts and moved around Frank. I had no time for his words after he'd kept them to himself for such monumental choices.

I entered the foyer, watching as Elizabeth pointed to items that Vera and Teeny then removed from their resting places. Paintings, tapestries, the silver box where I'd just tucked away my gloves—all of them were being taken. Frank appeared in front of me again. He grasped my arms. I looked around him and finally simply pushed him aside.

"No!" I seized the candelabra that had been beside the box and tossed it to Frank. I ripped the gilt-framed oil landscape away from Teeny.

Elizabeth stepped back. "It's better if you don't watch, Jeanie. It must be simply awful. Go with Frank and it will be over soon, and you'll be on your way. If anyone can make a go of homesteading, it is you."

Her sincerity struck me. I kept the tears back and nodded. "That may be true, but I don't want to go. This is not right. I didn't do anything wrong."

Then, as I started to explain further why this should not be happening, the door swung open behind me. The wind rushed in, and with it came so many familiar faces, rushing as though headed to catch a train. At first I thought they were coming to offer condolences, but when each and every one of them breezed past me, heading into every corner of my house, even up the staircase, I realized what was happening.

"The family portraits, too," a man who seemed to be checking off a list shouted to some men dressed in work clothes. "They were commissioned by fabulous artists—one is even a Sargent, I believe. They will do nicely in any fine home."

I shook my head, watching the paintings of my proud father, of my children, of all of us together, trotted out the front door. The frames alone were worth enough to feed a modest family for some time.

Before I could process what was happening, I was bumped from behind as people streamed in. A trail of men wound into the house like ants at a picnic, following Elizabeth up the cherry staircase that Frank had carved himself. Nickolas Kuban, Elias Stout, Zachariah Thomas—their faces flashed by, though each man avoided my gaze.

My skin prickled with sweat. I would not let them raid my home as though I were not even alive, not even standing right in the same room as them.

"Frank. We have to stop them. Just long enough for me to meet with Judge Calder. If I talk to him—"

"It's over, Jeanie. You have known that man for your whole life, but he is not your friend. He certainly has never been mine."

He dug his hands into his pockets, standing there like a child. Over the years, he had often been weak, but he had never been cruel or so utterly impotent. How could he let this happen?

I shook my head. "This is wrong."

He didn't reply.

"I will not allow them to pillage our home simply because—" I strode to the wall, mumbling as I rehung an oil landscape one of the men had set against a bench.

Frank shuffled his feet, his voice washing over my back. "Be reasonable. Elizabeth has the papers from court. I saw them. Your father lost everyone's money. Ours included."

"Elizabeth didn't even have half her money in Father's bank. She had nothing in his investments. Why would she do this?"

"She's trying to help us by holding on to our things instead of letting everyone take them willy-nilly."

I couldn't get the look on Elizabeth's face out of my mind—that sympathetic expression laced with the smile she could barely keep back. I wasn't so sure this was her helping us at all. "She's punishing us because you chose me over her. She is spiteful… I will not—"

"It's not *that*," Frank said. "We were children then."

"I'm *not* leaving this town," I said. "You'll build exquisite furniture, and I'll write the column." I lifted my arms and spun around once. "We don't need this expansive home. We'll take a sweet cottage near the river. We don't have to suffer for Father's sins. They aren't our crimes."

"People lost everything. The Kaplans, they put everything into your father's oil scheme—"

"Scheme? That was *your* scheme, if I remember correctly. You were part of this?"

"Your father tricked me, too—"

Stung as I was by my husband's punishing words, the last crumb of my pride dissolved away. I wanted to smack his face. I stepped closer. He crossed his arms, as though bracing for my hand. "I should have known your air castles were nothing but—" I snapped my fingers, "thin air."

Frank shook his head and looked up the staircase. Shouting came from the rooms upstairs.

I would not fight with Frank about his bad ideas right then. I suddenly imagined people rifling through my jewelry box, my children's things. Another brigade of men filtered into my home, trailing up the stairs without a glance my way. Our possessions were not simply a collection of things. They'd been amassed over time. Each item symbolized a milestone, an event, an achievement in some way.

"No!" I ran into the kitchen and grabbed the shotgun from the corner. I jammed two rounds into it, lifted my skirts, and dashed up the back stairs, following the sounds of murmurs down the hallway. I found Elizabeth and her troops in my bedroom. She stood in front of the dress-length looking glass and admired herself, fingering my sapphire necklace.

"Elizabeth," I said. How could she appear so satisfied, gazing at herself, pride all over her face? I couldn't breathe. Elizabeth was not sorry one bit about my loss. Had I overlooked her hate for me all these years? How could I not known? The whiff of betrayal I had sniffed out between her and Frank just moments before was now superseded by what I saw on Elizabeth's face right then. The rage that had been coursing through me gave way to choking sadness. I let out a sob that I hadn't felt rising in my throat. My eyes stung. I told myself to inhale, to push my air back out.

Finally Elizabeth turned from the mirror, staring at me, mouth gaping.

I cocked the gun. "How could you?" I asked.

Everyone in the room froze.

"Now, wait a moment, Mrs. Arthur," Mr. Kaplan said, slowly lifting his hands. I thought back to his jovial face when'd he arrived at our yearly Christmas party, always so grateful to have been invited.

I stepped back and turned to him, gun trained. "Mr. Kaplan?" I shook the gun at the bundle in his arms. "Stop. Look at yourself, digging through my house. After what my father did for your mother?"

Mr. Kaplan cleared his throat and shrugged, holding his treasure tight against his belly. "Way I see it, I have to go on living. Everything here is now everyone's who lost money at your father's hand. I have my paperwork. So do these fellas." He looked at his feet. "I'm sorry that your losses are wrapped up in mine, but the papers—the court papers—are clear. There's nothing you own that isn't really your father's."

"Not my own?" That could not be true. I thought of Frank going off to work with my father, the salary I was sure he drew, the windfalls that came when an investment paid off, the small but regular fee I was paid for my column. I had never paid attention to how Frank was handling our finances or considered that our money might not actually be ours. A new wave of fear swept over me.

I raised the gun, my arms quivering under the weight. My gaze flicked over the bundle in Mr. Kaplan's arms. Katherine's jewel box was on top of lace linens. *Katherine. My children.* I wanted to protect them from this onslaught. I wanted to kill this man, the rest of them, too. But then what? *Katherine. Tommy, James.* What would they do without me? I lowered the gun, my arms tingling and leaden.

"Your things can be distilled down to your newspaper articles," Mrs. Jones said from her place near the front windows. She wagged her finger at a stack of papers and books on the shelves near the window bench. "Oh, and your personal letters, probably those books you wrote. If no one wants them, then they are yours. And you have your title as the Quintessential Housewife. You'll always have that."

I had never been so angry in my life. They had to leave if I told them to. This could not be happening. I raised the gun to my shoulder again, my finger shaking as I placed it over the trigger. Just one shot at one of them. I would feel better then. "I'll shoot you. Sure as I'm standing here. I haven't seen one paper that says any of you can even enter this home, let alone take anything—"

Hollering grew louder, rising in pitch as people climbed the staircase, ran down the hall, and into the bedroom, and I finally understood. Tommy burst into the bedroom with a shouting mob on his heels. His eyes widened at the sight of the gun at my shoulder.

"Mama," he said.

"Stay back, Tommy. I told you not to come here until you were called."

He straightened, his fearful face transformed to something calm, something altogether foreign to what I'd seen in him before. But then he took off running, threw his arms around my waist, almost knocking me off my feet. "Come on, Mama! Wagon's set for us to leave." He grabbed for the gun. I pulled it away from his grasp.

I looked down at him. Of all the children, he was certainly the one who wouldn't follow my instructions and stay where he was told. He yanked on me, his eyes filling. "Please, Mama." He looked at the gun again. My gaze followed his to the Winchester in my grip. What was I doing? I looked back around the room.

The mob filled the room, not noticing or caring that I held a loaded shotgun. I lost all strength.

"Mama." Tommy grabbed my arm, then worked his hand down to mine, his calloused palm against my skin clarifying my thoughts. Suddenly drained of the feelings that had me nearly pulling the trigger scared me more than compelled me. Shooting people would not bring my father back or change what these people thought. There were other ways to take care of that. I let the gun barrel fall to the ground as people jostled me, rooting through every inch of the room, taking pillows, linens, dismantling the bed, even stuffing my underthings into coat pockets.

Tommy pulled me toward the door. As we moved that way, Elizabeth slipped her arm around me. "It will all be all right, Jeanie. You are the strongest woman I know."

I stopped. Tommy kept going, pulling me toward him. I yanked away from him and glared at Elizabeth. "You might be holding my things for me as you say, Elizabeth." I tore out of Elizabeth's feigned affectionate hold. Then I took her by the arms, my fingers digging into her so hard, I thought I hit bone. "But you will never have my trust again, never have my friendship, never have any of the things that really matter. Never."

Elizabeth quivered. I let her go. She grabbed her arms where I'd clamped them. "You have nothing I want, Jeanie. Nothing."

Tommy came to my side again, slipping his arm around my waist, guiding me from the room. As we entered the hallway, I envisioned my children's rooms and buckled as I imagined these people ripping through their things. Tommy caught me. I looked into his face. His boyish features were the same as I remembered, but his manner with me seemed wholly different from ever before. I remember wanting to thank him, ask him where his siblings were, where his father was, but before I could, the crowd surged, growing before my eyes, the wild-eyed friends and acquaintances bumping and barreling by.

I shouldered through the mob, dragging the gun like a child with a baby blanket trailing behind, Tommy's arm slung around me as he protected me. So overwrought with what followed. Sitting in that poorhouse right then, I recalled Tommy shedding his boyish discontent, revealing a protectiveness I would have always bestowed upon James instead.

I hadn't let myself revisit this moment in years. I could not remember a single other time Tommy had behaved in this way.

I closed my eyes, going back into that memory again. I could envision Tommy and me latched to each other as we wended down the hallway. My vision had blurred, my sight choppy as the scene in front of me jumped as though it were a fantastic carnival sideshow. I rubbed my eyes, then focused on Tommy. I took his chin. "Go on ahead. Get the trunks from the cellar. It might be all we can get away with. I'll be right behind you."

He began to protest. "I'm okay. I won't shoot anyone—I swear." I held my hand up to him as though taking an oath.

He put his palm against mine. I folded my fingers over his. He nodded and took off, weaving in and out of the crowd that was coming at us like ocean surf. I was filled with gratitude for him at that moment.

I bumped my shoulder into a corner of the wall as I turned to fight my way past the landing that overlooked the foyer and head down the stairs. My progress had been halted. I was jerked back by the throat. Someone's fingernails ripped into my skin, pulling my pearl necklace. It tightened across my throat, digging into my flesh before exploding like fireworks.

The white balls bounced like pearled sugar, *click, click, clicking* over the wood floors. I fell to my knees, trying to scoop the snowy balls into my palms. But some of the looters joined me on the hardwood, snatching the pearls right out of my hands, while others crawled around, searching for even one of the beautiful jewels that once graced my neck. Empty-handed, I inched to the edge of the stairs, where I pulled myself up by the banister. I lumbered downward, drawing Frank's gaze. He held his arms out as I approached.

"Tommy's getting the trunks from the cellar. We have to get them," I said through the whoops and inhuman growls that swelled behind us.

Frank took my arm. "Elizabeth gave us enough money to get a sturdy wagon, some supplies. We're loaded up and ready to go. I suspected…"

His voice incensed me, killed me little by little with every cowardly word he spoke. He walked on, and I turned to gather a final view of my beloved home, the sight of the animals who were once my friends, or at least acquaintances, eviscerating it with anger and greed. My stomach lurched. I reached for the missing pearls to comfort myself and realized for the first time how deeply, how fully, my life had been transformed.

If he wasn't going to help with the trunks, the children and I would handle them ourselves. I'd had enough of letting him control the direction of our lives. He eventually followed us as we took to the cellar, gathering all that we could.

And that was when the shift had occurred. That was when I knew I had to make the best of awful circumstances. I had been so sure of myself at that time. Then losing James, shedding my husband, being separated from Katherine and Tommy for so long had all taken its toll.

Sitting on that poorhouse cot, recalling the way my life had been undone, I wondered if I could manage a return to Des Moines. When thoughts of James, his sweet face, his dead body, came, I was reminded again that some things were worse than losing all your possessions and your good standing. Yes, I would return to Des Moines, get what was owed me, gather up my children, and make a life for them.

I had learned my lesson, and humility was now my partner in life. There was no more stubborn pride to keep me away. Perhaps being somewhere familiar, even if awful, would make it easier to start over. *Tommy.* The thought of him made me smile. I tried to locate another memory of him taking charge, helping out, being so mature. But nothing came. Funny how memory worked that way. All I could do was hope that we would make more memories, that we would have the chance.

I thought of Millie, her craggy smile. She had little, but she'd given me everything. She embodied peace and contentment all in the center of scarcity. That lesson was something I needed to carry with me going ahead.

Once again I was filled with strength. This time it was born of surviving the leap from the train trestle, from knowing someone like Millie. I felt the slow burn of iron will harden inside me again.

"Come, Yale." I scooped her off the floor and kissed her forehead. "We must ready for travel. We are going to bring Tommy and Katherine back to us. Finally. We are going home."

Chapter 15

Katherine

1891—Storm Lake

It was a perfect night for a revival. Mr. Christoff had thrown back his head and bellowed that phrase repeatedly as he drove Katherine and his family to the tent in the field where souls would be cleansed and the soil blessed.

When they reached the part of the field where folks parked their wagons, Mr. Christoff moved with more energy than Katherine had ever seen as he jumped from the wagon and dashed to the other side. He offered his hand to his wife and supported her as she descended from the carriage onto the spring soil. She brushed her woolen moss-green cape. Next he reached for Hannah, making her giggle as her legs swung upward before making a soft landing.

Finally, he stretched toward Katherine, snapping his fingers at her. She took his hand for balance but wiggled it from his grip as soon as her boots hit the ground. His gaze lingered on her face, making her want to run.

In order to move away quickly, she laced her arm through Hannah's and pulled her toward the opening to the great canvas tent.

Mrs. Christoff's voice came from behind them. "Hannah. Remember we are to be seated in the front, with the important congregants and special guests." Hannah stopped walking and turned back, forcing Katherine to do the same.

"Katherine, you'll find a seat in the rear of the tent with...well, with the others."

Katherine nodded and smiled down at Hannah.

Hannah sighed. "I'm sorry. I wish you could sit with us."

Katherine straightened Hannah's hat and plumped a ribbon that had lost its puff. "I look forward to the solitude."

Hannah narrowed her eyes on Katherine. "You'll hardly be alone."

They began to walk again. Katherine didn't try to explain that a thousand people could surround her, and if none of them expected her to do anything for them, she would consider it solitude. Their pace slowed as they reached the line that snaked out of the tent.

Katherine turned her face to the sky and smiled. The pincushion lights flickered and danced like angels, filling her with hopefulness. She searched for an especially bright point and wished to be with her mother again. The revival would give Katherine just the chance to lift her prayers to God, who she imagined was watching, listening, delighting as he drizzled the stars from his fingertips into the velvety heavens just for her.

She had never been to a church gathering of this magnitude. The Christoffs had told her it would draw from hundreds of miles, bringing people bearing handfuls of soil to be blessed, hopes and dreams to be fulfilled.

Katherine's family had not been deeply churched, though her brother Tommy had spent much of his talking spouting off Bible verses while they lived on the prairie. The worshipers Katherine recognized at the revival seemed excited and alight in ways she had never witnessed in them before.

Fresh, airy feelings flooded through her, infusing her with the confidence that God would make himself present at such an event as this, that he might enter Mr. Christoff's heart and transform him from a man who spoke much of religion but did not live its tenets in any meaningful way.

They edged closer to the windblown flap of the tent. Murmured voices, piano and fiddle music, and clapping rolled out of the lantern-lit space where the Spring Up! Revival would usher in a blessed growing season.

Katherine shut her eyes and inhaled the sweet, warm air. Yes, tonight would bring good things. She could feel it.

**

Soon after they entered the tent, it became stuffy. They meandered through the crowd, and Katherine deposited Hannah near the front with the other important elders and deacons. She kissed her forehead. "I'll see you afterward."

Hannah nodded and folded her hands in her lap. Katherine started through the crowd toward the back. She exhaled at the thought of being free of the Christoffs, even for a short time. Katherine's heart sped up. She began to feel the excitement that was pulsing through the crowd. *Alone.* Her balled-up nerves loosened then untangled. How long had it been since she was more than one screech of her name away from them? Katherine searched for a seat where she could retreat into her own quiet peace.

Across the tent, she saw Mrs. Christoff nodding at women who were greeting her while Mr. Christoff crossed his arms, looking stern, his gaze searching the crowd. Katherine should have felt sad at being separated from the family. She knew they meant it to be forbidding that she did not enjoy a special seat at the front of the venue with them. But for Katherine, the idea that she would have time without sewing, without Mr. Christoff's penetrating gaze or violating hands pressing at her, was like being transported to a tropical island with nothing but warm sand under her feet and sweet surf to fill her ears.

Katherine removed her cloak and set it over her arm, hiding the worn material of the calico dress she wore. She would have kept the cloak on had the heat not been rising so quickly. She took a seat at the end of a row near the back. Seated next to her was a mother with a babe in arms, three more boys, and what Katherine guessed was their father next to them.

She nodded hello and then retreated into herself. After fifteen minutes or so passed, the crowd began to hush. She sat straight in her seat and watched as Reverend Banks entered the tent from the back of the stage and stood at its center, waiting for the murmurs to fully dissipate. When the last mumbling subsided, he lifted his hands to the sky and dropped his head back. "Sin has entered our community."

Several gasps came from around the audience. "Cast it out!" someone yelled from Katherine's left. She craned her neck to see who'd said it but couldn't identify exactly where it had originated.

Reverend Banks pointed in the direction of where the shout had arisen. "And we will not have flowering ground until we seek it out and destroy it. Cleanse our souls, Jesus. Scrub our hearts."

Two women seated at pianos that were angled toward the minister banged on their keys at just the right time to highlight his words, as if they'd rehearsed it many times before. Katherine moved to the edge of her seat, trying to see better. For at least twenty minutes, Reverend Banks bounced and dashed around the stage, pointing, sweeping his arms to the sky, kneeling down, hopping up, even spinning like a top at one point.

Perched forward on her chair, Katherine suddenly felt exposed. She shivered with fear but was unable to look away.

In spite of all the upbeat music and cheering, she felt a darkness envelop her, as though she were experiencing something different from everyone else. She wrapped her arms around herself, digging her fingers into the boning underneath her thin dress, feeling as though she might be going crazy as she withdrew at the same rate that the rest of the crowd seemed to engage.

The woman in front of Katherine stood on the chair, arms stretched upward. She lost her balance and toppled backward. Katherine pushed her hands up and heaved the woman upright again. The woman turned back and stared down, latching on to the back of the chair, bouncing as though she were the very thing that made the piano music emanate from the front of the tent. Katherine grew chilled, her heart racing in fear.

The woman screeched and wailed, her eyes glazed and somehow unfocused even as they fixed on Katherine. She drew back, scooting her chair away as much as possible, forcing herself to break her searing gaze as though that might protect her from the woman's frenzy.

Across the aisle, a man was stumbling down his row to the center aisle, where he collapsed onto the ground, flopping back and forth like a fish tossed upon the shore. Katherine was petrified. She could not understand what she was seeing and felt as though her breath had been snatched right out of her lungs. *What was happening?*

She saw the minister on Sundays, and he had never revealed the smallest hint of this side of him—this fiery force pacing the length of the stage like a bull. She certainly hadn't expected some of the people she'd seen regularly in church to bounce and chant and *amen* in a way that was in stark contrast to their typical dark, monotonous services.

She had expected to have hours to sit with her thoughts, to beg God to put her back with her mother. But her desire for quiet had been thwarted as her attention pivoted from each jarring movement of the minister to the unexpected shouts reverberating around the room as though watching a dance choreographed for everyone but her.

"Lord, cleanse our ugly souls. Jesus, take what is worst in us and make it known here. Reveal our sins so you can blot the pain away like a mother dabs her child's tears." His voice rose and fell and burst forth as he emphasized words with pounded fists on the pulpit, veins popping in his neck as the congregants mirrored his exuberance. Katherine felt frightened in a way that made her insides rattle.

"Or is it too late?"

Gasps filled the room. Katherine's throat felt as though it was closing.

He shook his finger, pacing back and forth. When his slicked-back hair fell forward, he stopped and smoothed it back with both hands. He drew a deep breath, hands rising upward. "Prostrate yourself before the Lord. Or forever tread the fiery waters of Hell's hot lake. The devil—your only companion. Your pain, all you feel and see. Without Jesus and only Jesus, you are worms of the dust. Nothing more. Rotten hell is your future if you hold any besides Christ as your king. *That* is the only fortune awaiting you and your evil soul."

Katherine's hands began to shake as fear grew inside and around her. *Could any of this be true?* This was not religion as she had seen it. Her church experiences had been quiet, staid, prescriptive.

"You." He pointed into the audience. Katherine put her hand to her chest, where a pain formed as though his searing finger were actually pressing into her sternum.

"You, in fact, are beyond redemption. You are unworthy of forgiveness. You stand there, unmoved."

Katherine tried to swallow. *Was he speaking to her?* Katherine covered her mouth. Was he looking at her? She looked side to side to discern if anyone else was drawing his attention.

Sweat curved down cheekbones, faces were flushed and pushed skyward, heat emanated from the tight seating arrangements—yet her body grew chilled; the very blood rushing through her body iced her.

"And there shall be weeping and wailing and gnashing of teeth."

The woman behind Katherine grabbed her shoulders and shook her so hard that her vision blurred. "That's Matthew, thirteen forty-two!" She screamed in Katherine's ear. Katherine jerked out of the woman's grip and hugged herself.

Then, like wind that abruptly dies down after whipping wildly through trees, the minister put his back to the audience, silenced his ranting, and grasped the pulpit, his shoulders heaving with each breath.

The audience followed suit, calming their movements, quieting their mouths as they waited, watching, blotting sweaty brows. In this silence, weeping began. The frenzied screams were gone and met with silence or choking sobs that poked through the hush like thorns through skin.

A man fell to his knees and walked forward on them, his hands clasped and pressed to the heavens. "Have mercy, have mercy, have mercy." It was Mr. Smalls, the banker in town.

Katherine's stomach lurched as she thought of this man as she'd seen him before, running his bank, now on his knees, raw, vulnerable, begging for forgiveness. It seemed as though the world had been upended, reminding Katherine of when her family had been brought down by scandal in Des Moines. Suddenly she was back there again, four years younger, frightened, grasping for the only person she knew could protect her—her mother. But this time, her mother was not there.

Mr. Smalls struggled to his feet and stumbled the rest of the way to the stage. Reverend Banks reached down for him, and Mr. Christoff helped hoist the man to the stage. Katherine was nauseated, feeling as though she was witnessing a living creature mauled rather than a celebration of the spring plow.

The choral sobbing quieted, and the congregants rose on the balls of their feet to get a better look. Unable to look away, Katherine slid her chair to one side to get an unobstructed view. Reverend Banks placed his hands on Mr. Smalls' head and pushed him to his knees.

"Forgive me my sins. The money I took that was not mine. Please find mercy for me."

He stole? Katherine's stomach filled with acid at the thought of the betrayal, at the fact she now knew of it. The reverend closed his eyes and tilted his face upward. The veins in his neck distended, snaking, pulsing with the blood that rushed through them. Katherine wanted to turn away, to run out of the tent, but she couldn't make her feet move; she could not stop staring.

Reverend Banks' fingers curled like claws as they dug into the man's skull. "Oh, Lord, have mercy on this poor sinner's soul, even though he is not worthy of your forgiveness. Satan has claimed him for one of his own, and he has fallen into temptation."

Then the man crumpled to the stage and began to twitch as though having a fit.

"The Holy Ghost is upon him." The audience threw their hands into the air, cheering as though taken with the same ecstasy as the man flopping onstage. All at once, Katherine could hear the collective mumbles of hundreds of prayers lifting into the air and also hear their singular cries for forgiveness—individual voices crying out for God to forgive all manner of ills.

Katherine had originally thought the revival was a heavenly idea. A way to sit in reverence of God, to ask for his help, to connect with her brother James, to pray that her mother and siblings were safe and that she would soon be reunited with them. But she hadn't been prepared for what she was experiencing.

The Christoffs alternated between being sharp and wooden, and their Sunday services mirrored their personalities—staid, punishing affairs. But this, this was unexpected. Still, she had hoped perhaps this would open a new avenue to view them, that this might be a chance to see them differently. Even though Hannah had told her there would be raucous singing and smiling faces, Katherine had not imagined this.

Another man dashed from one side of the tent and took the steps to the stage two at a time, sprinting past the pulpit. He emptied his pockets onto a table that had been fashioned from found tree limbs and fallen trunks as a gesture to God that this revival was all about the land and its resources. Katherine stared at the people around her. She seemed to be the only one who was not drawn into the spectacle, the only person disconnected.

Reverend Banks spun around, his hands out, fingers spread. "The Holy Spirit is with us."

One after the other, people shot to their feet, arms thrust into the air, spiraling, chanting, completely lost inside themselves. The *whoosh* of the emotions surrounding her sucked Katherine's breath away. She felt as though she'd been slapped; every nerve seemed forced to the surface of her skin. Where she felt icy-cold fear, dark confusion, and actually *saw* swathes of black drop down from the ceiling like smoky organza sheers, the others seemed to levitate with hot passion. She pressed onto her toes to see what had drawn the crowd to their feet. A young girl was being dragged into the aisle by what looked like her mother. A man jumped into the aisle and took the girl's feet. She kicked at him, catching the man's chin.

The man dropped her feet and rubbed his beard, his face crushed with pain. The girl wrenched free of her mother and bolted back down the aisle toward the rear of the tent where Katherine sat. Wanting to save the girl, Katherine opened her arms to her but the girl didn't seem to notice.

Her crazed, terror-filled eyes were focused beyond Katherine, on the flap at the back of the tent. Katherine stepped into the aisle to follow the girl, but a man had already scooped up the girl and flung her over his shoulder, heading back toward the stage, hauling her like a sack of potatoes.

He passed Katherine with the bellowing girl, and she reached out for Katherine, her fingers stretching. "Please," she said as she passed. Their eyes remained locked until she was tossed onto the stage.

Katherine covered her mouth. Was she the only one who was appalled at what she saw? Surely this young girl could not be so full of sin that her soul required scouring. *Soul-cleansing.* She had thought they were flowery words tied to nothing but prayer and the hope to be better people. Instead, this soul-cleansing felt more like a hunting expedition, the prey an innocent girl no older than Katherine.

Once the girl was restrained, supine on the stage, Katherine got a full view of the two who were holding her down—Mr. and Mrs. Christoff. The reverend put his foot on the girl's belly to stop her wriggling while her arms and legs were pinned. Katherine wanted to run up and rescue her, but her fear was paralyzing.

She looked around. *Did anyone else think this was wrong?* Everyone was either riveted to the action on the stage or their eyes were closed, faces upturned as their lips moved in prayer. No one seemed at all concerned that there was a girl on the stage, her dress working up over her drawers as she tried to wrench free.

"Stop struggling," Katherine whispered. The girl flailed harder.

"You've brought temptation to your home," the reverend shouted. "You've welcomed Mr. Sandhill into your bed. You have created temptation like that born of the devil."

Katherine squeezed her eyes closed and prayed for the girl to stop trying to free herself, to be calm and wait for a moment to flee. Hot wind whipped through the tent as people pushed closer together, taking Katherine with them, pushing her up against the chair in front of her. When she opened her eyes, she saw that the girl on the stage was twisting back and forth as hard as possible, her face red. Spittle flew from her mouth, and she began to take on the appearance of a rabid animal. "*He* took me. I *ran* from him."

Katherine felt as though the girl were speaking for her. What if someone ever said Katherine was luring Mr. Christoff? Katherine felt sure this girl was in the same situation of having done nothing wrong. Tension grew with the heat the crowd generated just by standing together. Shoulders pressed against shoulders and someone grabbed Katherine's arm, tight like a clamp that had been screwed down to her bone.

She slapped at the person's hand and peeled back the fingers, but the grip remained tight. Finally, she bent down and bit. The hand was pulled away and when Katherine turned to see who had been holding her, there were so many people pushed up close to her that she couldn't determine who it had been. She'd never felt so trapped, like being in a box that was somehow alive with its sides folding in on her.

The minister held up his hands, his fingers bent into claws, as though he were holding some invisible soul. "This young lady's soul is soot-black, full of sin. Her fight is fueled by the strength of the devil. She won't stop struggling until our prayers penetrate her skin and soften her tempting, disobedient heart. Look at her fight even as these good people hold her for cleansing. Imagine the same power in her temptation of Mr. Sandhill. She is evil, a gifted temptress."

Something caught the attention of the people who had been pushed up against Katherine and they filed away, heading up the aisle. Katherine grasped her chest, heaving for air. The woman next to Katherine chortled, then shook her shoulders as though tossing off a coat. "Good people."

Katherine looked at her. The woman didn't seem to be bothered by how they'd been shoved by the crowd before many of them had moved onward. The woman turned to Katherine and rolled her eyes. "The Christoffs? Good people, my eye." She rocked back and forth, the toddler on her lap somehow napping through the ruckus. Had the woman been mocking the minister's characterization of the Christoffs? Perhaps Katherine just misheard the sarcasm in the midst of the penetrating chaos.

Katherine tilted her head toward the woman, lifted her voice, but kept her eyes on the stage. "The girl hardly looks like a temptress to me."

The woman shrugged. "She must have done something."

"She's only struggling because they won't free her."

Katherine finally turned fully and stared at the woman, wondering if she'd been in the position of having a philandering husband for her to believe that a young girl could so easily be evil in any way at all. "How can you watch her struggle and not be affected?"

Katherine looked past the mother at the three boys sitting next to her. "You have four children." Katherine felt as though her chest were being compressed. The woman ignored her and gawked at the action at the front of the tent.

"Bear your ugly soul for cleansing." The minister got on the ground, straddling the girl. The Christoffs backed away. The minister pinned the girl by the shoulders. "Bear your sins, girl!"

The girl turned her head, squeezing her eyes closed, and sputtered, her kicking slowing. Katherine saw the fight in her dissolve as she stilled almost completely. "I did it." The words were thin and the audience quieted, leaning forward to hear the now-soft voice. "I did what you said with him." The crowd gasped and pressed closer to the stage again. "Please," she said through sobs. "Get off of me. I'm going to vomit."

He sprang up and lifted his arms, nodding as he walked from one end of the stage to the other. The girl curled into a ball, choking.

Katherine grasped her chest. She did not know that girl or her situation, but deep in the center of her being, she knew that girl confessed to a sin that was not hers.

Petrified that someone could be made to reveal an obvious, horrid lie made Katherine shake from head to toe. She wrapped her coat around her shoulders, attempting to chase away the cold. But as the crowd cheered the balled-up girl, Katherine ran to the back of the tent, toward the exit, unable to watch another second.

As she reached the table where several women had sat, welcoming guests as they arrived, Katherine saw a young man about her age watching. He was large as a grown man, but his baby face was sweet, young. His flame-red hair was unkempt. His arms were crossed; his legs formed a wide stance.

The crowd thrust their fists upward, their voices laced the air with "amen!" and "cleanse her!" Katherine couldn't help but stop and stare at the man who appeared to be the only one in the audience not enthralled.

Katherine cinched her hand around his arm. She'd never felt such desperation for an explanation. "Why are they doing this to her?"

"They lack trust in the land."

He doffed his cap with his free hand.

Was he serious? He wasn't taken by the uproar, the threat of evil?

Katherine nodded. "Yes. That's it, isn't it? They say they believe but they don't trust at all, do they?"

Katherine released his arm and he backed away.

"It's good to see there's one person in the tent who isn't a fool. Now, I'm heading back to my parents' farm to do the only thing that will actually ensure a harvest—work."

Katherine watched him disappear into the night, and she turned back to the mayhem on stage, relieved that there had been someone who viewed the events as she had. This alone comforted her to some degree. With the audience standing, Katherine couldn't see it clearly, and the tide of rising voices hid any sign of what the girl might currently be experiencing.

For the next two hours, she stood at the back, covering her ears half the time, trying to find that calm that normally came when she needed it most. But the bedlam never allowed her to settle into the peaceful stillness she enjoyed so much. Still, thinking of the redheaded man, she knew it was not she who was taken by lunacy or the devil. By the time dozens of attendees had been dragged to the pulpit or had run up on their own two feet, the audience was depleted and Katherine was famished.

They welcomed the break from the soul-cleansing to enjoy snacks that had been arranged in a small space off to the far side of the tent. Katherine moved quickly down the table that held tiny sandwiches, buttered bread, sugar cookies, and cold milk.

She ate quickly, her stomach lurched with its fullness, and Katherine wondered if she would need to run for the privy. She blotted the corners of her mouth and wiped crumbs from her bodice, not wanting Mrs. Christoff to see her eating and withhold even more food the next day.

As Katherine walked away from the food, she saw the woman with the children who had been seated next to her. They were both moving through the river of people, and each smiled. In the distance, Katherine could see the Christoffs greeting folks as they funneled toward the refreshments.

"Awful, aren't they?"

Katherine shook her head. "Excuse me?"

"Them." The woman used her elbow to point toward the famished crowd.

"I don't understand this, I will admit."

"Well, you tell my sister to be sure to plant a rosebush this year. She needs something to bring color to those cheeks of hers."

Katherine narrowed her eyes on the woman. "I'm sorry. Your sister is who?"

"Why, Ida Christoff, of course. You're working in her home, right?"

Katherine drew back. "Well, yes, but how did you know?"

"You came with them, right?"

Katherine nodded. "I didn't know Mrs. Christoff had a sister. I suppose I don't know them that well." Katherine tried to recall if Hannah had ever mentioned an aunt, but nothing came to mind.

The woman shifted her child from one hip to the other. "They probably don't mention me because I owe my sister an apology."

Katherine didn't know what to say, and she didn't want to pry. She had never envisioned her keeper as anything other than a difficult, harsh woman, never as a sister who might be owed an apology. The woman rambled on about her children and her husband as they worked their way through the crowd, and when they finally reached the Christoffs, Katherine hurried ahead to bring Mrs. Christoff to see her sister. Katherine grabbed her hand and dragged her to the woman.

Mrs. Christoff slapped Katherine's hand away.

"She said she wants to apologize to you."

"Who?"

"Your sister."

"Helen?" Mrs. Christoff looked horrified.

"Well, I suppose. I didn't ask her name, but she said... Well, come on. She's over there near the Murrays."

Mrs. Christoff moved her body to see past the shifting crowd.

Katherine lifted up on her toes. "Right there." She pointed.

Mrs. Christoff craned her neck and then scowled at Katherine. "My sister is dead."

Katherine poked her finger. "She's right there."

Mrs. Christoff pinched Katherine's ear. "She's dead."

Katherine pulled away, covering her ear with one hand, looking back at the woman with the brood of children surrounding her, the husband standing at her side. "She said she owes you an apology and that you need to plant roses to bring pink back into your cheeks."

Mrs. Christoff's mouth dropped open. She shook her head. Mr. Christoff came to her side. "Reverend Banks is asking for you, Ida." She grasped his hand and backed away. "Yes. I'm coming."

She whirled around, winding through the crowd, Mr. Christoff looking over his shoulder at Katherine, his smile full of the very lust Reverend Banks warned the world against.

Katherine turned back to where the family had been standing near the Murrays, but they had all disappeared.

Hannah stepped up to Katherine and pushed a glass of water toward her. "You look ill," she said.

Katherine took the water and swallowed it all without a breath. She patted the chignon at the nape of her neck.

"Are you all right?" Hannah asked.

Katherine looked deep into Hannah's face. Could she trust her? "Your aunt. She's here."

Hannah lifted the corner of her mouth, her eyes narrowed. "No."

Katherine paused and thought about all that had transpired. "She is. I talked to her, too."

Hannah belted her waist with her thin arms. "That's impossible."

Katherine stared off into the crowd before fixing her gaze back on Hannah. "Because your aunt is dead?"

Hannah nodded.

Katherine's heart pounded. She brushed her fingers over her forehead. She thought back to the woman who had appeared in the kitchen the other night. Was that the same woman who had been here tonight? No. She was sure it was not. What was happening to her?

"Yes. Remember the photograph book I was paging through? I showed you her photograph."

Katherine's hand shook as she covered her mouth. "Yes, that's right." Katherine still could not fully grasp what she had experienced. "That must be it. I thought I saw someone who looked like her." But Katherine knew that was not true. The woman mentioned needing to apologize...and the roses. Katherine could certainly not have gleaned that from a photo. Certainly, she could not be hearing entire conversations in her own head.

"Did they have a poor relationship?"

Hannah's face whitened. "I'm not permitted to discuss that."

Katherine turned her hands palms-up, fingers spread. "Why, of course. Every family has its arguments from time to time."

Hannah looked relieved. "You understand, then. What with your mother not contacting you, your brother being in the wind somewhere?"

"I do." Katherine put her hand over Hannah's. "I understand. Could you get me more water?" Katherine needed a moment alone. "Please, Hannah?"

She put the glass back in Hannah's grasp, and she skipped off, smiling over her shoulder at Katherine, her soft, wavy hair bouncing down her back.

Katherine surveyed the crowd. Where was the woman? Had she misunderstood her? She would find her and ask for clarification. Where was she? Katherine's gaze stopped when she saw a familiar figure. Even from the back, she knew it was him. Slowly he rotated, turning her way. James. There he was. And seeing him she began to feel her calm, the warmth that settled over her when he came to see her.

It was her. James' voice came to her as clear as Hannah's had just been. What was happening? Was he saying it *was* Mrs. Christoff's sister?

Could Katherine find a way to deny that the woman and her family had been there at all? Could she convince herself that they were not Mrs. Christoff's relations? She stared at James standing there and suddenly it was solid as a fat oak tree.

She *had* seen Mrs. Christoff's sister—she had been there, and Katherine had spoken to her as though she were still alive and well. She didn't know why she'd experienced such a thing, but she had, and that she could not deny. It would not be something she shared with anyone else, but knowing it herself brought a veil of sanity to her.

Even amongst the crazed revivalists, she felt seeing her dead brother was saner than what she'd witnessed with the girl on the stage that night.

Chapter 16

Jeanie

1891—Sioux Falls

I stood at the train depot with Yale at my feet and my friend Millie, with her mostly toothless smile. I had gotten off half a dozen letters since the first round I sent: one to Tommy, who I was fairly certain was still staying just outside of Des Moines. The letter would easily reach him if he was staying there. Running for the mail was exactly the kind of chore I imagined him doing for the family. The remaining five letters were sent to all the homes in which Katherine had boarded—all the homes I knew of.

I hadn't heard from Katherine since I'd sent word that Yale and I had moved to Sioux Falls to board with Mrs. Stevens in her great home with abundant gardens, where I had thought I was finally pulling my life back together. I wondered how I lived all those years before heading to the prairie, barely aware of death and its impact on the world. Since my father's death, I'd come to know how one soul leaving the earth left so much pain in its wake.

I patted the bag where the garden journal Mrs. Stevens had sent with the letters was pushed up against the inside flap. It was the only item I had of any value, and its value was not easily realized—it couldn't be traded or sold for cash. But it was precious, full of the hopes and wonders that came with learning to work the land. I didn't know where I'd plant a garden, but with the money from Mrs. Mellet and her promise to pardon me, I looked forward to creating a garden that was both fragrant and useful—somewhere.

I had no idea how much money was at stake with Mrs. Mellet. But I wasn't naïve enough to hope it would be adequate to secure a grand home with gardens to tend, as I had at Mrs. Stevens' home. Still, I allowed myself to imagine it would be enough to keep the children under one roof—that was most important. And a potted plant or two would be enough to start.

The train neared the platform, calling into the dark night. The bright headlight flung me back to that night on the train trestle. I turned to Millie and took her hands. Soon Yale and I would be back in Des Moines. "Thank you so much for…that night. You know…"

Millie squeezed back, causing my gaze to drop to my friend's blackened fingernails.

I patted her hand. "You saved me," I said. "Like an angel right here on Earth. I…"

Millie smoothed my hair back. Her hand smelled of kerosene. "Life is a wonder. I see you were a great woman before. Like them stories you tell. They were about you. Right? The rich woman in a big house? I see it clear. Your bad dream has ended."

I couldn't speak. I agreed that the nightmare was ending, and I was buoyed by Millie's certainty. Greatness was no longer important, just ordinary life. I reached into my pocket as the train arrived and passengers began to disembark, jostling us as they did. I pulled the paperweight button that Millie had frequently admired from my pocket.

The glass fastener wouldn't change her life, but I hoped that it would be something pretty for Millie. I pressed it into her hand. Her mouth dropped open as she stared at it. She lifted the orb by the metal loop and turned it back and forth in the overhead lamplight, the flower inside turning deeper shades of pink as she moved it. She offered it back to me. I shook my head. "It's for you."

Millie put it back into her palm and smiled as she shook her head. "No need. I don't need a thing. I got a cot in that old poorhouse. And I got a man named Harvey."

Her hand quivered as she lifted it toward me. I curled her fingers around it. "To remember me by, then. Just to remember me like I will always remember you."

Millie's fingers opened like a starfish when I pulled away. "I don't have anything for you."

I moved Yale to my other hip and pressed my hand against my chest. If not for Millie, I would not have been alive to read Mrs. Mellet's letter. She'd given me the chance to make a life for my children. She gave me hope like no one ever had. I folded her fingers back over the button, pulled her hand to my lips, and kissed her fingers. "You gave me *everything*."

Millie's eyes grew moist. She rolled the button back and forth with her forefinger and grinned. "All right." She pushed the button into her pocket and patted it. "But nothing you hand me will help me remember you." Millie patted her heart. "I will keep you here, stuffed away like money tucked inside a featherbed."

My eyes burned. I swallowed hard, my muscles tensed. I'd felt this way when I left my friend Greta behind on the prairie. I wished I could gather the two women into a bright garden. Like fragrant flowers and hardy plants that could be counted on to bloom even when they had given over to winter, they were always there, waiting to show themselves again.

"Jeanie Arthur. Jeanie Arthur. That's a name to remember."

"Millie Standhope. Millie Standhope. *That's* the one I will recall."

And with another surge of travelers bursting past us, Millie backed into the crowd, lifted nearly off her feet with the wave of people pushing by. She struggled to turn back in my direction. She put one hand into the air, fingers wiggling, leaving me to smile a big, warm, real smile. Great woman, as Millie saw me, or utter failure, as I did, I was going home. And I was sure this time things would be different. Things would be better. They just had to be.

Chapter 17

Tommy

1891—Des Moines

Tommy, Hank, and Bayard headed to the river to cool off. They stopped the wagon near a towering, budding oak tree and watered the horses. They'd had a busy day. After using ropes to lower the dead woman's coffin into the hole and covering it with the mound of dirt the gravedigger had dug, Tommy and the boys went to sell the prayers Reverend Shaw had written for several families.

While in two fine homes on Grand Avenue, the spring air turned humid, summer thick, suffocating the sweet spring breeze Tommy had enjoyed earlier.

They were passing the river, and it was too hot not to take advantage of it. They would hide the money under their clothes until they were finished swimming.

When they neared the shoreline of the Des Moines River, Bayard jerked his head toward a line of trees. They stripped off their coats, and Bay wedged the money into the ropy roots of an oak, covering it with all their coats. They kicked off their shoes and peeled away their clothes, leaving only underclothes.

Tommy hooted, feeling good to have made some friends. The smarting ribs and swollen cheek were not enough to keep him from enjoying a swim. He had not enjoyed dropping off the corpse, but the job they did after that had been fulfilling. Since they were driving and needed to deliver the prayers, Tommy went with them. At first he just watched Hank and Bayard as they read the words aloud that had been written by Reverend Banks. Then they listened to the stories the elderly people had to tell.

They let Tommy handle the prayers at the second home, and he found that offering thoughtful sentiments to people who needed them was fulfilling. While Hank and Bayard shoveled hay into the privy out back, Tommy scribbled a prayer of his own right on the spot for Mrs. O'Malley.

She'd been so pleased with the personalized invocation that she jammed a dollar in each of their hands while clasping the paper with the words to her chest as though it were magic. She then fed them to bursting with bacon and toast and eggs. He had no intention of living odd job to odd job, but if he needed to sell prayers to bridge the gap between now and when he was officially given the job at the Savery, he could live with that.

At the shoreline, Tommy, Hank, and Bayard greeted other boys who'd gathered to swim. They went to a small rise in the bank where they could jump into the rushing water. There had been rain a few days before, and it had helped melt the stubborn snow. The extra water swelled the river higher than it had been in months.

Hooting and hollering, a dozen boys dunked and chased and floated along with the current, letting the force of the water have its way with them for a while, and then they would clamber up the banks, their wet feet and hands turning the dirt dark brown as they did. They would run back upriver and leap back into the water, letting the current carry them down again.

They'd done this several times when they began to get bored. Tommy was making the trek back to where they jumped into the river when he saw several boys tying a rope around a rusty iron.

Tommy, Hank, and Bayard squatted down beside them. "What're you boys doing?"

"We're gonna see how deep it is out there in the middle."

Tommy scratched his chin and wiped some dripping water from his eyes.

"I'm Gus." The boy shook Tommy's hand. "And this here rope is sixty feet long, to the inch." Gus pulled the rope into a tight knot.

"So?" Tommy said.

"So we'll drop the iron into the water, swim it over to the middle, to where those cold patches of water are, and we can figure the number of feet deep this here water is by what's left over."

Tommy stood and crinkled his nose, looking down at them. "Well, I gathered that much. Just don't know why you're doing it, is all. Why not just enjoy the rapids and leave it at that?"

Bayard stood. "With this heat, in two days, the river will be as still as that body we just dropped at the graveyard. We could drop the rope then."

"Nah." Gus grinned at the group of dripping boys. "I want to know how deep this here water is right now with the best of the spring thaw." He stood and started to drag the iron to the edge of the riverbank.

"Aw, hellfire," Tommy said. "Fine. You'll break your back, you weakling." He and Hank helped Gus pull the rope.

The iron moved easily with that much manpower. The three boys clasped the iron and swung it back and forth to the count of three and let go, watching it sail over the water and plunk into it with a sound that seemed to echo.

They hopped back and away from the rope that was snaking wildly across the dirt as the scrap iron sank, drawing most of the rope with it. They were cheering it on as it went deeper under the rushing water, and they'd gotten so excited about the river being deeper than they'd thought, no one noticed that the smallest boy in the bunch had his foot in the wrong spot, and it became wrapped in the rope, pulling him right into the rushing water.

At first they laughed, watching Shorty's body fly through the air, his yelp as hilarious as the funniest sideshow any of them had ever seen. But it didn't take long for Tommy to see Shorty was not resurfacing. Perhaps the river was much deeper than they had guessed.

Tommy dove into the water right where he saw the boy go under. The only good part of this was that the river wouldn't move the boy's body if he was tied to the iron. He should be right where he went into the water.

Tommy stroked downward through the brisk water. His eyes stung. His lungs burned as his air depleted. He pulled at the water as he swam down farther into the blackness. He strained to see. A cloud must have shifted away from the sun above the water, because suddenly there was a stream of light bolting through the darkness, and he could make out a cloudy version of a body just a little ways off.

Tommy swam to the body that bobbed up and down, the rope still attached to his ankle. Tommy grasped Shorty's leg and tugged, pulling him downward to release some slack on the rope, and with that, the rope easily fell away. Tommy moved as fast as he could, kicking and swimming with one arm as he held the boy in his other arm, moving upward as quickly as he could.

Grasping for water, to propel him upward, Tommy resisted the urge to let his body take a breath. He repeated to himself that he was underwater, that taking a breath would result in both their deaths. He squeezed his eyes shut, lungs exploding in his chest. *Please, God. Let me live.* The cobalt sky burst into sight above the sloshing current and finally his head popped through, his mouth fell open.

Heaving for air, he felt as though he were still underwater, as though his lungs no longer knew how to work. All at once, there were hands grabbing at him, pulling at him. Weakened and out of breath, he let the hands have control. He tried to look over at Shorty, but all he saw were hands and backs and wet heads pulling at him. Finally, Tommy closed his eyes and stopped fighting for anything at all.

**

Tommy's consciousness came back as he was vomiting silt-laden river water. Hank rolled him to his side, slugging him between the shoulder blades. His gaze went to the boy lying beside him. Reverend Shaw and Mrs. Hillis were bent over him as they each barked orders to the wet boys.

Mrs. Hillis had gathered the boy into her arms and cradled him. Tears dripped down her face, reminding Tommy of his mother cradling James when he died. Was Shorty Mrs. Hillis' son? Did she even have a son? He couldn't remember.

"Go get this boy's mother. Now," she barked in the general direction of the gang of boys. When they stood frozen in place, she boomed again. "One of you boys, go get his mother now!"

Two of them took off running as Tommy continued to heave for breath. Mrs. Hillis bent her cheek to the boy's head, rocking him.

The reverend moved closer to them. "I'll take him, Cora. It's all right. I'll make sure his mother—"

"No! When she gets here, I'll give him to her. But this boy..." Her voice cracked. "He needs to be held, and I won't let him lie here, half naked."

Tommy began to crawl away, toward the tree where his clothes were, wanting to turn his gaze from the lifeless boy. As he did, he could still hear Mrs. Hillis. "Every spring and summer, we go through this. We need a swimming pool, Reverend. Something for these children to use safely."

Tommy was far enough from them that he couldn't hear Reverend Shaw's response. He could not stop his body from quaking. The idea that the little soul was dead washed over Tommy, taking him back to his brother's death, as though it were happening all over again. Being underwater in the darkness put him right back in the musty dugout behind the miner's home. All of these events seemed to collide with what he felt right then. Panic set in, and he couldn't inhale deeply enough.

Tommy heard someone say, "That boy there, he brought him up. He tried to save him... He nearly died himself!" Tommy wanted to disappear. The sensation of air being pressed out of his body was so familiar.

His heart raced, and he stumbled to the tree where they'd stowed their clothing and the money they'd earned. He pressed his hands against the tree-trunk, the bark thick against his palms, his teeth chattered, the humidity no longer influencing his body temperature as it had when they had arrived at the river. He knelt by the clothes and finally was able to draw deep breaths.

Someone grabbed Tommy's shoulder. Tommy whipped around, startled.

Hank raised his hands in surrender. "Whoa, whoa, whoa. Reverend Shaw said he wants..."

"Sorry, Hank. I just have to get out of here." Tommy did not hear Hank's response. He jammed his arms into his shirt and his legs into his pants. He pulled on his shoes and then dug through the pile of coats for his. As he did, the clang of metal gave him pause. He shook out the bottom coat and saw glinting silver mixed in with the money. Tiny salt wells, coins, baby spoons.

Tommy ran his thumb over the engraving on one salt well. He looked at Hank. Where had this come from? The engraved initials were ACO. He bounced it in the palm of his hand. O'Malley. Tommy couldn't believe they'd stolen it and he hadn't noticed.

Hank squatted beside Tommy. "Where'd that come from?"

Tommy glared at him. "I think you know."

Hank shrugged.

Was he really going to try to lie? "Acknowledge the corn, Hank. I'm not that stupid."

Hank shifted his feet and pushed his hand through his dripping hair.

"Well?" Tommy said.

Hank nodded. "We took it. But we had to."

Tommy didn't even want to know what he meant by that. Surely there were times that Tommy lifted an apple or even a loaf of bread when he was between meals for too long. But that wasn't the same. He shook his head and sorted through the pile of clothing to gather up all of his things.

"We make a fine team, don't we? You penning those godly words while we…well, you know," Hank said.

Tommy met his gaze. "I don't steal. Not from elderly folks seeking some sort of comfort." Tommy rubbed his sore ribs. "Sweet jeez. She paid to have people in her house who then stole from her."

Tommy stood. Hank did, too. Tommy did not want trouble or hard feelings, but he needed to be on his way. He needed the solitude of his woods, to be alone but not confined.

He offered his hand to Hank. "Thanks for the chance to sell prayers. I enjoyed it. Forgot what it felt like to actually think that way. But I gotta pull foot."

Hank hesitated and glanced at something behind Tommy. Finally, he took Tommy's hand. "If that's the way you want it."

Tommy nodded and shoved his hat onto his head. "Yeah. Thanks. I'm better off on my own. I like it that way."

Hank pointed to Tommy's coat. "There's payment in the right pocket of your coat. Reverend Shaw would want you to have that. Might need it. Only in a pinch, of course."

Tommy knew people did things when they ran out of choices. He wouldn't hold it against Hank, but he didn't need the hassle for himself. Tommy dug the object out of his coat pocket. A silver salt well glistened in the daylight. He slapped it back in Hank's hand. "That's all right. I have plenty of what I need. Thanks again. And I'm sure I'll see you around." Tommy felt the other coat pocket, wondering if the boys stashed anything else there. But it was empty.

Hank shoved the salt well into Tommy's trouser pocket. "Just take it."

Tommy pressed his pocket where the object had settled against his leg. Maybe he should keep it for insurance purposes. As soon as he made his first pay at the Savery, he would return it to Hank. "Thanks," Tommy said.

And he dashed away, heading to the grocer for flour and maple syrup to make himself some dinner. All Tommy could think of was being alone, of hiding himself away in the woods where life was safer, where he could chew on all the ways things were about to get better.

Chapter 18

Tommy

1905—Des Moines

Tommy stood in his sister's parlor as funeral guests circled the room and orbited him and Katherine, dabbing at tears, sniffling back sobs, offering stories and thoughts on his mother, Jeanie Arthur. When he had begun his visit at Katherine's home, his mother's health had been rapidly declining. He had arrived flush with anger and blind to the very short time he had to set things right with his mother before she died.

He wiped his mouth and stuffed his hands back into his pockets. He told himself it was part of grieving to feel an onslaught of emotion ranging from regret to ire to sorrow, to deep abiding love for his mother, the first woman he'd wanted to protect in his life.

Andrew, Katherine's son, hid behind Tommy, trying to avoid Asher, who had been charged with keeping the younger children in order. Andrew's fingers dug into Tommy as he latched like iron clamps onto him, using Tommy as a safe base. A woman had just come up to Tommy and Katherine, wanting to tell how she knew their mother. Tommy's mind had grown foggy with these unfamiliar but loving stories about his mother. Each tale struck him with awe and disbelief that the destitute mother he'd seen when he'd arrived at Katherine's could have worked so much of what was coming to look like magic in all these strangers' lives.

"Please excuse me for a moment. I want to hear this, but let me settle this little guy first," he said as he hoisted Andrew onto his hip and tousled his hair, which had long since lost its slicked-back style. "Just a little longer, Andy," he whispered in his ear. It had been hours since the funeral began. Oh, how he and Emma had wanted a house full of children, but all of that had ended with loss and sadness. Being with his sister's children opened wounds and salved them at the same time. "Believe it or not, little Andrew, it's not just children who want to leave funerals as fast as they can."

Andrew's eyes widened. "Can you take me fishing? At the bend in the riverbank where you used to camp?"

Tommy pinched Andrew's nose between two fingers. "Fishing? You want to fish?"

Andrew nodded wildly. Tommy threw his head back, laughing. "Oh, I'd like to go fishing for sure, but I'm not sure it's possible." He wanted to say yes, definitely, but he could not. His stomach had churned itself into nearly nothing, his mind was stuffed with cotton batting, and he was choking on every emotion a human could feel. If Tommy managed not to run from the funeral before it ended, it would be a miracle. He was not sure he could do anything but run once it was over. Tommy pushed his nephew's hair back from his eyes. "Be good for your mama. This can't go on much longer. Sit over there like a gentleman and I bet she'll reward you with a peppermint stick."

The boy broke into a smile, nuzzled into Tommy's neck, and kicked his legs to be set down. "Okay, Uncle Tommy. I will."

Tommy set Andrew down and the little boy slunk over to the chairs and sank into one, arms crossed, face folded into a frown. Tommy smiled at him, feeling another sharp pain in his chest at the thought that he had no children, that his marriage was currently as fragile as china teapots in an earthquake.

Katherine turned toward Tommy and waved him to her. He nodded but didn't yet move. He watched as Aleksey passed by Katherine. Without her even looking, Katherine's hand found her husband's and she gently pulled him back toward her. Aleksey was never improper with public affection, but seeing how naturally they found a way to touch, it occurred to Tommy that if Aleksey were within an arm's reach of Katherine, they would have some physical contact. Tommy had never noticed it before, but now, watching them, he could see Aleksey anticipate Katherine's need for a sip of water, his gaze holding his wife's as he held her elbow or squeezed her hand, telling everyone in the room he adored her, that she was precious to him in every sense.

Katherine turned back toward Tommy again, gesturing.

He nodded and joined his sister, brother-in-law, and an older woman who'd been weeping since she sat down for the service. Her hair was snow-white and, though fine and wild, rose off her head like stems in spring soil. She broke into a wide smile, showing off missing teeth as though it were the fashion of the day. Instantly Tommy was absorbed in her warmth. He could not help but step toward her, right into her open arms.

She smelled like talcum powder, her flesh tight against sharp bones. She squeezed his arms several times and backed away, still grinning at him.

Katherine stepped beside the woman. "Tommy, this is Millie Standhope."

He took her hand and patted the top of it. "I'm Jeanie's son."

She nodded. "I know. I knew your mother quite well."

Tommy pushed his hands into his pockets. "Thank you for coming," he said.

"Couldn't miss it. Told her the other day I thought I'd be in the ground long before her, but she knew that cancer had a grip of her innards and there was no pretending it wasn't so."

Tommy liked Millie instantly. "You were close?"

She thrust her fingers into the air. "Two peas in a pod, we were. She told me about all her children. I knew sweet Yale, over there, but I heard lots about you and Katherine. So proud of you both, she was."

Tommy felt sick. Proud of him? That was something he'd wished for so badly early in his life and there was a time he succeeded in eliciting it. But that was long past. Or so he thought. She had told people she was proud of him? The swell of emotion—gratitude and sorrow—stirred, making him feel like a fourteen-year-old again. Jeanie Arthur had lived two lives it had seemed; one life that he knew and understood well and another newly exposed that left him wondering if he even had the right to claim her as his mother. He searched his heart for the last time he'd felt she'd been proud of him, for the last time he deserved it.

"She was lucky to have you," Tommy said. *I wish I had been a better son.*

Millie lifted her hands, palms-up. "Her lucky to have me? No, it were me who found fortune with your mother. Why, take a look at this." She dug into a pocket in her threadbare skirt. She pulled something out and put it in her palm before she pinched it between her fingers and lifted it into the air, the sun catching it, illuminating it clearly. Katherine angled forward for a closer look and gasped. Tommy bent in, but he felt no knowing gasp, as his sister had.

"What?" Tommy said, squinting.

Katherine straightened and put her hand at the base of her neck. "May I hold it, Millie?"

"I brung it for ya," Millie said. "All yours."

Tommy shook his head and narrowed his eyes on Millie. "What is it?"

"A button," Katherine said, holding it by its tiny metal loop. It was glass and held a pink prairie flower. It seemed familiar to Tommy, but he could not call to mind anything as powerful as Katherine clearly had.

"Mama kept these in the trunks when we went to the prairie. It was one of the few things that she managed to keep. The paperweight buttons. You don't remember, Tommy?"

Tommy shrugged. "One button is like another to my eye."

"No, no. Remember how Mama always said these held a whole world inside them? Not precious pearl or ivory or painted china buttons, but her favorite of all."

Katherine seemed mesmerized by this insignificant item. Millie, too, stared at it, glistening in the sun as though they could see something completely different in its existence than he.

"Even with all your father did to her, how he hurt her," Millie said, "she survived. She found her little patch of happiness and cultivated it."

The mention of Tommy's father, hearing that phrase casually released into the air, caused something to clamp down on his heart and paralyze his lungs. He had been naïve for many years, not fully accepting his father was an imperfect man. But there was something that made him keep hold of the idea that his father had not been at fault for the family falling apart. Now that he knew that was not the case, he had to face his own part in the anger he'd held so fast over the years. Still, he was unprepared to hear his father's failures spoken of in casual conversation.

"Uncle Tommy. Uncle Tommy," Andrew said. He yanked on the bottom of Tommy's coat.

"Tommy," Millie said, drawing his attention back to her. "You don't have to worry. Your mama loved you and knew your road through life was not hers to choose. You don't have to carry sorrow about being a good son or not. She knew you were. Your feet turned on the path that was to be yours. You're where you should be."

Tommy scooped Andrew up, shaken by hearing these comforting words from the mouth of his dead mother. "She said that?" He felt another kick of sorrow that there was yet another layer of his mother, something apparently significant that had escaped him.

Millie nodded and patted Tommy's hand.

Nausea undulated through his belly. So much had happened since he'd arrived. He'd never really thought he would feel such heavy sadness at his mother's passing. In some ways, he saw her as having been selfish, as turning from his father and their marriage, sacrificing their family for some invisible sense of security that she claimed to feel without their father there. He now knew that his father had contributed to the death of James—at least in theory, if not directly. He could understand how that would keep his mother from being able to have their father around.

Tommy wished he would have known sooner. It might have changed much about how he'd lived his life. Why couldn't she have just told him what happened in the exact terms that he'd learned through the letters in the attic?

He knew the answer to the question—not the specific answer, but the general one. His mother had tried to tell him that she'd had no choice but to divorce. But she had also been determined to allow him to keep a positive image of his father and gave vague explanations that never quite satisfied Tommy. He couldn't have imagined that she was protecting him all those years—that she had meant to do just that. He had lived apart from his mother for so long, not talking enough over the years, that he believed to have already been separated from her in many ways.

What difference did death make if they had spent so little time in each other's company anyway? He would have sworn on ten Bibles that he'd made peace with the way his life had turned out but, yet, since arriving, he was battered with a truth he did not recognize until it was too late.

And yet Millie's words both comforted and haunted him. What if they had all been honest right from the beginning? His mind went back to something Millie said. *Even with all your father did to her...* Tommy should not have been surprised at hearing his mother might confide in a friend about how her life had evolved over time.

Still, something about it humiliated Tommy—he should have been open to hearing about what had transpired that year on the prairie. But he had been a boy then.

And now there was something unseemly about a stranger bundling up what she thought was the essence of a relationship and presenting it to the world as if entirely true when he himself was only learning the truth. He thought of the letters Katherine had read, about how his father had been planning to leave them. That newly learned fact angered him beyond any coherent words he could cobble together, but he was suddenly mortified that all these mourners, not just Millie, might very well know something about their family that he was not willing to share, something that he hadn't even known until just before his mother died. It wasn't as though his father had always been there for him. *You can stop defending him. You can let go of his failures. They aren't yours.*

Heat emanated from deep inside him. Sweat burst from every pore, dripping down the sides of his face. He wiped it away, but his heart thumped as if straining to push right through his ribs and skin. The panic. He hadn't felt it in years.

But here he was, thrust back into a circumstance he thought he was equipped to face but was not.

Tommy held tight to Andrew, knowing it was holding him that kept him upright. Millie was insisting that Katherine keep the button, that she had decided long since coming to Des Moines, when their mother had so generously brought her there, that the button wasn't hers to keep; she was just watching over it.

Tommy began to back out of the conversation. He would say he had to leave for the sake of Andrew. The clutch of mourners, their stories, their weeping had been too much. As curious as he had been to talk to the rest of them, to hear each tale, the whys and hows of their mother helping others, it had suddenly become too much.

"Tommy," Katherine said as he was moving away. Tommy met her gaze, doing his best to keep from falling over or dropping Andrew. Andrew squashed Tommy's cheeks between the palms of his hands. "Squish the banana," he chanted.

Katherine held her hand out to him. "Mrs. Hillis said she has some of Mama's things and will need to drop them later."

He nodded and forced a smile at Mrs. Hillis, not wanting to stay in that room another second. "I'll take care of Andy here," Tommy said. "He's had enough."

Katherine pulled her hand back and nodded, watching her brother with a confused expression. Tommy was doing his best to keep his voice light and not let on to the swell of fear inside.

Katherine nodded. "Check on Yale as well. She's disappeared."

Tommy nodded as he finally was able to turn and leave the parlor, leave the mourners who had in some ways offered patches of his mother's past. They left him comforted that she had not been alone in these years they'd talked only sporadically. Yet his body rebelled as though it were not ready to absorb all of this information about his mother.

He wasn't sure if hearing these stories from her friends, in really understanding his mother in a fuller way, would allow him to release his regret or make him clench it ever tighter. Forgiveness. He wanted it more than he could have believed possible. And for the first time, he was willing to fully give it. If only it were not too late.

Chapter 19

Katherine

1891—Storm Lake

Katherine inventoried the amount of kitchen work she had to finish before getting back to her sewing. She was worried. She had too much sewing to do after the revival had taken her away from it. If they were late getting the clothes back to the customers, they would reduce their pay. Katherine felt as though the extra money she might be earning to fund her way back to her mother was falling away like finely ground flour through her fingers.

She told herself to be grateful. For once, Mrs. Christoff had given her a hearty breakfast. Maybe that meant something—maybe the revival had softened the Christoffs' charred souls and they were ready to loosen up on what they expected from Katherine.

She scraped the remnants of eggs, biscuits, sausage, and gravy into the slop pail. For the first time in weeks, she did not nearly keel over with hunger or desire for scrumptious food she had prepared but was not permitted to share.

"Once you've finished cleaning the kitchen," Mrs. Christoff said, shoving a pair of worn boots toward Katherine, "you'll be in the fields today."

Katherine's throat closed and she let out a cough. She could not imagine a worse predicament than being alone in the fields with Mr. Christoff. She tried to maintain her composure.

"I have an order of cuffs to finish," Katherine said. "Then the Wescotts' shirtwaists are due."

"Yes. Hannah can certainly do away with those tasks while we make up for the hands who've taken ill and can't show up to plow or plant today. The seeds are tarred, so we'll be working by hand. They'll clog up the seeder with the sticky tar."

Katherine nodded at Mrs. Christoff, feeling considerably more amiable to the work if the wife would be there—protecting Katherine whether she knew it or not. She put the final scraped plate into the bowl of steaming water. "You'll work with us?"

"Of course. Mr. Christoff will drive the horse, I will drop the corn, and you will cover the seeds. We need to make short work of this so you and I can get back inside to sew. Mrs. Ash just ordered thirteen shirts for her husband's spring wardrobe."

"Fine," Katherine said.

"And Katherine. Not another word about my sister to Hannah. You must have been taken by the spirit at the revival, but you've confused her wholly."

Katherine nodded. "Of course. No, I won't. I haven't mentioned it since that night."

Mrs. Christoff smoothed the waistband of her skirt. "See that you don't."

Katherine didn't know what made her bring that up, but Mrs. Christoff's displeasure when Katherine told her about her sister made it clear that it was not to be discussed. Katherine did not have to be told twice. She wanted no reason for the Christoffs to haul her to a revival to have her soul cleansed. She felt as though the revival was born of something secret and foreign, but she knew deep inside not to ask questions, not to draw any attention to herself in regard to what had unfolded that night.

**

The sun beat down on Katherine's back as she worked the hoe to cover the seeds Mrs. Christoff dropped in front of her at the point where the furrows crossed. The land was hard, full of thick, grassy tufts that reminded Katherine of the year they homesteaded in Dakota Territory. She knew the Iowa land was generally rich, but she couldn't help thinking the Christoff land didn't look as fertile as it should have.

The work of covering the corn with the plowed dirt strained her back muscles. Every so often, the shrill call of Mrs. Christoff screeching Katherine's name into the air came as her husband brought the sulky to a stop when the coulter was rendered useless by clumps of earth stuck to the blade. Mrs. Christoff would rest herself while Katherine was tasked with clearing the wheeled blade of its debris. Mr. Christoff would watch Katherine as she worked right in front of him. She could feel his gaze on her, and when she accidently made eye contact with him, his lusty expression would turn Katherine cold even under the sweltering sunrays.

With Katherine back behind Mrs. Christoff, the woman would signal for her husband to get the horses going again. The work was difficult, but the monotony gave Katherine an opportunity to consider all that had been happening to her since she lost touch with her mother and brother Tommy.

In her desperation, Katherine had begun to believe that her brother James' spirit came to her, often soothing her, offering comfort when she was lonely. He seemed to bring patience and hope. This sense of *him* being with her provided an understanding that answers would present themselves in time. She tried to keep a grasp of that faith when she was most fearful or sad, but that wasn't always easy to do.

The woman and her baby who had appeared the night Katherine ate the burnt cookies were more perplexing to her. Until the mother had shown herself to Katherine, she had seen only two others besides James. The first had been a little boy whom Katherine saw the day of the fire on the prairie. She and her brothers had climbed and clung to a bee tree as a fire raged past them, nearly taking their lives as it did. Filled with confusion and fear at having almost died just a short time after arriving on the prairie, Katherine's parents hadn't paid much attention to what Katherine had seen—a little boy. Katherine had been only ten years old, but she got the message clearly—that was not something she was to think about. She knew she was to pretend it hadn't happened. And there were plenty of times she wondered if it had happened at all.

Then, under quarantine at the Zurchenkos' home, flaming with fever, she was visited by a little girl who she knew to be Anzhela Zurchenko. The little girl had been laughing, her white-blonde hair blowing in the wind, her dress lifting as she happily spun in the thick grasses—the same sweeping grasses that she'd strolled into but never returned from.

Katherine and Aleksey Zurchenko had been charged with watching over the little girl. Neither had their back turned for long, but it took only a moment for Anzhela to disappear. And hours of searching, yelling for her against the thick prairie winds, did no good.

It happened all the time out in that odd, flat-looking yet undulating land. She carried the regret and sorrow with her in the same way she carried her heart and lungs. And so when Anzhela appeared to Katherine in the midst of illness, she felt forgiveness in the event, in seeing the girl's gleeful smile, her raspy laugh.

She told Aleksey about it and saw that he was soothed by her revelation. He was skeptical that it happened, but Katherine could see he wanted to believe.

But the others hadn't. There'd been so much death on the prairie, the dead children in the blizzard, the animals, even Lutie Moore.

When Katherine had thought her vision would ease some of Mrs. Zurchenko's grief, she found that telling her what she'd seen only opened the wound further, salting it, sending the woman into deeper despair, filling both Katherine and Aleksey with fear.

She never treated Katherine the same after that. Katherine never spoke of seeing Anzhela or James or the little boy again. And, until recently, she hadn't seen anyone other than the spirits of those few people.

But now, with the woman and baby in the kitchen and Mrs. Christoff's sister appearing to her at the revival, Katherine was taken back to the other events, recalling the mix of awe and confusion that came with those experiences.

Katherine stepped into a freshly turned furrow and twisted her ankle, causing her to gasp. She knew the Christoffs would not allow her to rest. So she carried on, breathing deeply, trying to court the calming condition where James seemed to find her easily.

She wondered if he was able to show himself to their mother, if she was comforted by him as Katherine was. She needed to find her. She needed to get away from this horrid couple. By the time she was tasked with covering over tarred corn kernels with the soil that would start them growing, Katherine had been fully educated in the way the world mistreated children.

She also understood that many children were passed along to seemingly responsible adults who, when it counted, could feign concern and affection for their charges but would never again employ or even feel such things once the family was away from the gaze of others. But she was an adult now, really, fourteen years old. And if her mother had stopped writing, had stopped promising her she almost had a place for them all to live, then Katherine would grasp matters on her own. She would go for her mother, and she would make all that was wrong right again.

Her attempt to reach her mother had yielded no information. Tommy had written once since losing track of her mother, but now even his most sporadic and thin of letters had come to a halt. As she moved with the rhythm of the hoe and a gentle tap of her shoe to tamp the dirt, her mind searched for answers. She would not believe they stopped corresponding on purpose.

The conditions with the Christoffs were becoming more and more inhospitable. She had no access to money or valuables to sell to at least make her way back in the direction she knew her family had last lived. Mr. Christoff was growing more aggressive.

Katherine felt heavy with the uncertainty of leaving, leaden with the thought of staying. She pushed the anemic dirt over the kernels that sat in the crosshatched intersection, the broken roots clumped in the dirt like tiny arms reaching upward. So much death. The land seemed to hold it all; the turning of it seemed to release the awfulness Katherine thought was below.

The blue sky was cloudless, and the air was still—a peaceful day like that would have seen her mother writing on their patio in the shade while the children were at school. So long ago. She tried to reach back to that time, to feel those days when a household staff met their needs and their worries seemed nonexistent.

Katherine stopped walking and looked upward, her hand shielding her eyes as a chill worked through her body. The sky was as blue as the glistening sapphires that used to adorn her mother's neck. The velvety expanse stretched on, never interrupted by land until it just disappeared in the horizon. Beautiful in a way that one has to see to understand. Yet under the blue heavens there was blackness, a darkness that caused Katherine to feel a coming storm—one that was visible.

She looked over her shoulder as far as she could see in the other direction, squinting at something drawing her attention that way. But there was nothing of note—nothing looming, no churning clouds or pushing winds, no person calling her name or hazy outline of a person who had passed on. And yet there it was, that sense that something was wrong and she was in danger of losing the only thing she had left in the world—herself.

Chapter 20

Tommy

1891—Des Moines

When Tommy reached his camp, he was elated to find the Winchester and ammunition were still there, tightly wrapped in the canvas sheath he'd made to keep it dry, still stuffed inside the tree trunk where he'd built his tent. Tommy was disappointed but not surprised to find the half loaf of bread he'd wrapped in a muslin bag had been ravaged, the bag strewn in the thorny bush across from the tent. Hungry raccoons.

He went to the point where Rock Creek met the river, where an old room in an abandoned beaver dam was used as a refrigerator for the squirrels he'd traded for. He dipped his hand into the rushing water, wrapping his fingers around the rope that had the meat attached on the other end. A fellow named Donnie had caught these and then left them for Tommy, hopping a train to find his love, some girl in Chicago he'd been waiting to hear from for nearly a year. Tommy couldn't imagine abandoning his food for a girl, but this fellow couldn't get out of Des Moines fast enough.

"You'll understand someday," he'd said. "You'll meet a girl and love her so much that your insides feel like they're outside your body and someone's just punching them silly or filling them with such joy and love... Well, love, there's nothing like it, no way to explain, so I'll just take my leave and let you figure all of that out for yourself. But trust me when I say you will find out."

Tommy was beginning to feel exhausted. The high he'd felt when released from jail was still there, but he needed sleep. He knew he should prepare something to eat so when he was hungry again, it would be ready. He pulled the rope one hand over the other and knew before he even had the whole thing up that something had got to the meat in the water. It was too easy to bring up.

Oh well. He could always fish when he tired of pancakes.

He ripped a piece of grass from a clump of sprouting greens and chewed on it. He was still satisfied from the lunch he'd had while selling prayers. He would be fine. He rarely went without a meal even when he went without a proper bed. It was all part of the luck that his father's Indian Head brought.

The birds chirped, the river rushed by, and Tommy sighed. *Take the good with the bad.* He chomped down on the grass, the fresh taste of greens filling his mouth.

He sighed and stood. It was too early to bed down for the night, so he would take a walk and get a better look at his surroundings. He'd already discovered the remnants of what must have been a tree house. Now only the base survived, but Tommy thought that was a good spot to sit and relax, to collect his thoughts and enjoy nature.

Tommy followed the deer path that hugged the river. He could see where another man had traveled, his boots kicking off the moss that had grown on the tops of the tree roots and rocks. And he could see where the deer had gone, their hooves making a different path where they went in between the mossy rocks instead of on top of them. The raccoons often sipped at the riverbank. He didn't have any particular connection to that animal. Perhaps he could shoot one.

He reached a great oak tree. Its branches extended over the riverbank, and the mud below was a brown canvas of deer and raccoon tracks. Tommy swung the shotgun over his back and dug his feet into the bark where he could get a hold and shimmy up.

Where two thick branches met the trunk, someone had added planks, a seat that was the perfect spot to sit and reflect. He relaxed against the trunk, feeling the solitude. He felt a surge of excitement at the thought of being self-sufficient. His time in the woods would be a nice complement to the life he would build as a bellboy at the Savery. With room and board paid, he could save money.

Maybe he would go back to school, as was the tradition in his family. He could become an engineer, a doctor—No! He would own things...property, businesses, anything. He would have a family and pets, and his sisters and mother and father would visit regularly, enjoying enormous meals and good stories. He thought of his mother's brilliance, the way she'd been a writer in Des Moines before all had gone badly for his family. He thought of his brother James. He missed him deeply, the sharp pain of his loss raw and penetrating to the point that he often had to keep from thinking of him just to avoid the pain.

Thinking back to when their lives were whole and happy, he realized it was the men who owned things who were really well off. Even the men who'd lost money when they invested with Tommy's grandfather were able to survive if they also had property holdings or mills to run or coal mines to exploit. He shuddered as he remembered the twisted, anguished mouths on women, and even some men, when they realized all their money was gone, when they understood that having saved for a lifetime had netted them nothing but losses if all they'd saved was paper.

Tommy's eyes were heavy, and if not for the telltale snort of a deer off to his left, he probably would not have even noticed it was there. A buck stood near the edge of the riverbank, majestic. He knew hunters sometimes waited for days for a deer, employing all manner of stealthy plotting to lure them or simply not scare them away. And yet, this one had simply wandered right into Tommy's path.

He held his breath as he sat up, careful not to let his trousers rub against the bark and give him away. He twisted his body and lifted his gun firmly against his shoulder. Tommy hesitated. What was he doing? It wasn't like it was a doe with fawns nearby. One deer in the scope of things was not bad. He could eat for three weeks off this one deer.

He'd grown up on food prepared by someone else. On the prairie, they made do with whatever they could secure, but big game was not on the menu there. Certainly, in the homes where he had boarded, hunting was never on his chore list.

He knew it was silly. The strange hitch he felt in his heart at the thought of shooting a living thing embarrassed him. No one was there to know of his reluctance, yet it bothered him. He had flour to make flapjacks. He hardly needed to shoot this animal.

His breath skipped like a stone across the river top, sounding in his ears. *Don't be stupid. You have nothing and need to eat. This deer sauntered by just for you.* He exhaled and dropped his gun, unwilling to shoot. But as he did, the plank under him shifted and Tommy flinched, pulling the trigger.

The weakening boards under his body and the gunshot shocked him. But that shock was nothing compared to what he felt when he saw the deer had lost its footing and was splayed out by the river.

Tommy hustled down the tree. *No, no, no. Please. I can't possibly have shot the deer. I wasn't even aiming at that point.* The deer got to its feet and dashed away. Tommy's heart ached. He knew seeing the deer's tail tucked instead of flashing white meant that he'd hit it. He shook his head. It couldn't be possible. Perhaps he'd only grazed it.

He went to where the deer had momentarily dropped. There was blood on the mud and rocks. Perhaps a small wound? He could nurse it if necessary. Why did he feel this way? He ate meat all the time. It was ridiculous, he knew, but it was his heart that didn't seem to grasp the sense it made to hunt a beautiful animal, even if his head did.

He didn't give chase immediately. He knew that making a ruckus when the deer was close would only spook it, sending it running for its life. Better to let it think it was alone. Then it would run a bit and lie down to rest its wounded body.

After some time had passed, Tommy followed the deer, seeing the tracks it left as well as smelling it, the putrid odor that an animal releases when it's been wounded. Stepping carefully down the deer's trail, the thoughts that always came to him when he'd shot an animal twisted in his mind.

It was for food. It was life. It was just the way things had to be. The weaker are prey for the stronger. Tommy reached a point in the woods that opened into a clearing. He doubted the deer would have collapsed out in the middle of the grassy field. It would hide or run for its life.

He looked at the ground, closed his eyes, and listened. The sound of crows cawing and sparrows singing filled his ears. He strained to hear the crash of twigs breaking. Nothing. He lifted his nose to try to catch the scent of the wounded animal. He was about to follow the trail to the left when he heard the distinctive snort again, off to his right.

He moved slowly to the brush that certainly hid what would now have to be his dinner. If it died, he was obligated to eat it.

He rounded the brush and stopped short. In front of him was the buck, lying on its side. Its great chest heaved, exhaling with a shudder that caused the thick body to quiver. Tommy felt his breath leave him. The deer opened its eyes and looked around, knowing someone had arrived. Tommy lifted his gun and prepared to shoot again.

The deer lifted its head and looked at Tommy straight on. Tommy narrowed his eyes on his target. *Shoot it.* The deer's lips pulled back as if trying to say something. Tommy had thought shooting a buck would be less of a problem than a doe, but being close up to it, he felt its…well, its humanity or *something*. He felt as though he'd taken down a man, a fellow human being.

Tommy sidled up closer, gun steady. *Shoot.*

The deer tracked Tommy's movement as he shuffled around its side.

A pain formed in Tommy's shoulder. His arm shook as he held the gun. The deer shuddered and let out a whimper that sounded human to Tommy. He felt connected to the deer, another living thing, just trying to survive. The deer wasn't old or feeble, and Tommy hadn't even been really hungry when he shot it. His eyes filled. James. His brother had died before his time as well. Suddenly, the deer seemed one and the same as James.

He lowered the gun. How stupid. There was nothing he could do. The deer was not going to live if Tommy walked away. And yet, in this moment, Tommy felt the dying deer's body as if it were his own. He raised the gun again. *Shoot it.*

Hot tears overflowed his lids and his eyes burned as he aimed straight down at its head. His hands shook, making the rifle buck. What was the matter with him? The deer held

Tommy's gaze, then finally its head just dropped back to the ground, eyes open, still watching Tommy, but it was as if it had come to the realization that its life had ended.

Tommy watched as each breath caught and shook its body just before it exhaled and struggled for the next gasp of air. Tommy didn't know what was happening to make him hesitate. He couldn't stop himself from feeling this pain in his gut, this remorse in his soul. The way it looked at him. He shook his head. The deer lifted its head again.

Tommy was suddenly weak. His legs gave out and he dropped to his knees. His eyes teared up as the deer held his gaze. Tommy put his hand on the deer's neck, energy coursing through his body. *I'm sorry. I'm so sorry.* He wanted to hold the animal, comfort it. But that was ridiculous. He put his hand on its warm side, feeling the fight to live or allow death to come. Tommy couldn't move. He knew he should have finished it off, that it was crueler to let it struggle; yet he couldn't do it. Something made him just sit there with it, comforting it, a silent apology for ending this great animal's life.

And as Tommy felt the life leave the deer for good, it nodded at him as if saying it forgave him. Tommy felt a wave course through him. Had the deer really acknowledged him in some way? That was crazy, he knew, yet he'd felt it. He'd felt the forgiveness as though it were made of warmth, as though it were possible.

Tommy smoothed the fur on the deer's neck. *I'm sorry.* And he knew he'd hunted his last animal. Silly as it was, he'd felt something in those moments that changed the way he saw his own life. All the families he'd boarded with, the aimless way he'd been wandering through life, the little boy he'd kept from getting hit by the wagon the day he was arrested. All of these things crammed into his mind. *It's not where we live; it's just where we live now.* His mother's words came to mind. Mama. He would make her proud. He was destined for something better than all this.

Where his destiny lay, he did not know, but he was sure there must be something for him that didn't leave him feeling disgusted inside.

**

Tommy tried to get to his feet. Prickly heat stung his toes where he'd cut off the circulation kneeling beside the deer, foolishly attempting to comfort it as it died, until its last breath raised and lowered his hand. Tommy fell back on the ground and let the feeling come back to his feet. He laid face up, hands over his eyes, willing his stomachache to go away.

"Hey there, Tommy Arthur."

Tommy flew to his feet, grabbing his shotgun as he did, training it in the direction of the voice.

It was the girl from the post office. She threw her hands into the air, a clutch of envelopes fluttering to the ground around her mud-caked boots as she surrendered.

He exhaled and lowered the gun, not wanting to be startled into taking yet another life. He let the gun fall to the ground and bent over, hands on knees. "It's you. You scared me to… Well, why are you sneaking up on people?"

She slowly lowered her hands as though not sure he wasn't going to point the gun at her again. "I ain't gonna take the deer from ya," she said.

Tommy's body was hot with surprise. "What in heaven and hell?"

She shook her head. "Just got yer mail, is all."

Tommy squatted down.

"First deer, is it?" the girl said.

"What?" Tommy looked at the buck. "No." How much had she seen? He rubbed the front of his pants, then straightened, pressing his chest out, wanting to be impressive, not soft, as Hank and Bayard had suggested he was earlier that day.

"I can dress it. If you, well, you know. If yer stomach ain't up for it. You look sick."

Tommy raised his arms. "What on earth are you doing here?"

"I saw you lugged off to jail. That baker's got a reservation in Hell. I saw what he did to that boy."

Tommy drew back. The admiration in her voice made him smile as his cheeks warmed.

"Yeah. I saw what you did," she said. "Most folks don't stick their neck out for no one, let alone some lady poor as Job's turkey."

The sun shifted between the trees and made Tommy shade his eyes. Her eyes shone, holding all the smarts her appearance belied. "Mr. Holcomb doesn't seem worried what others think of him."

"He'll get his. Makes me sick when those with the most give the least. He should share his crumbs with folks who need it, not the birds."

"Birds are good. But I agree." Tommy had seen this girl several times over the months he'd been in Des Moines. But usually just at the post office, where she organized the mail.

She bent down and gathered the letters. "You're always coming in looking for letters that ain't arrived yet, and then this did." She licked her finger and paged through the envelopes. "So I went looking for you. Those fellas Hank and Bay said you been camping out. So here I am."

She held a letter out to Tommy.

He snatched it away, embarrassed at his earlier display of weakness. He saw the familiar, pretty slope of his mother's handwriting. *Mama.* He stuffed it into his pocket. He did not want to read the letter in front of the girl. He motioned toward the other letters in her hand. "And those?"

"Not yours."

"There are more fellas in the woods you need to deliver mail to?"

She fanned her face with them, making the tendrils of hair that fell around her face rise and fall with the air she generated. "Nah. These are undeliverable. I read 'em. I think of them as mine."

Tommy jerked back. That didn't sound right.

"Dead letters, we call 'em. I ain't in the position for schoolin', so I read letters. Learn spectacular words from some. You can't imagine the pretty language in some of these. I plot out a list of places I'm going to visit someday after—"

"You can't just read people's letters. Dead or not. They're not yours. That's against the law."

She rolled her eyes and wrapped her arms around her middle, tapping her toe.

"Why don't you just sit and read yer letter?" she said. "I'll start on the deer."

She pulled a knife from her apron pocket and opened it. The pearl handle glistened in the sun. She was clearly poor, uneducated, but that knife… The pearl handle didn't fit her life situation at all.

He watched her slip the blade under the skin of the deer, still feeling the heavy death, still confused by the whole thing. Perhaps he'd just felt the results of the beating he'd taken in jail. Perhaps his mind was soft, and it played on his feelings in a way that made no good sense whatsoever.

Perhaps for that moment, he just identified with the deer, its position in the world of being shot by some fellow who'd been hiding in a tree, unable even to defend itself… Perhaps that's exactly what the last three years of Tommy's life had felt like.

He began to open the letter.

The girl looked over her shoulder at Tommy.

"Let's make a deal, Tommy Arthur."

"I don't make deals."

"Really? Well," she slid the knife into the belly, moving up toward the head, "let's just say if I don't tell no one 'bout yer crying over this buck, you don't tell no one about my reading other people's letters."

Tommy pulled his mother's letter from the envelope and considered her offer.

She stopped cutting and grinned at him, squinting into the sun. She stood and stuck her hand out to him. "Pinkie promise."

He guffawed and shook his head. "That's ridiculous."

She shook her little finger at him, the deer blood dripping from it. "Pinkie promise."

Tommy's stomach flipped in an unfamiliar way, his skin alive in a way he'd never felt as this girl looked at him, her smile both knowing and demanding.

He hooked his pinkie into hers. "Stupid pinkie promise."

She nodded and squatted back by the deer. "Now, you read that letter. I think it's important. And let me work here."

"What's your name?"

She held the knife up to him. "Pearl."

"Like your knife?"

She nodded and went back to work, her body jerking as she dug inside the animal's body. "My father dropped me at the Widow Smith's house when I were a baby." She paused and sighed. "*Was* a baby, not *were*, with nothing but my naked body swaddled in a feed sack and this pearl-handled knife." She worked her way around the buck.

Tommy unfolded his mother's letter, trying to imagine such a thing. "Sounds like a fairy tale."

She turned and shot him a black, angry-eyed look. "Well, it ain't a good tale. Not like Cinderella and such."

Tommy did not know what to say.

"Cinderella's life ain't nothing to fret over. Why, if I could…" She shrugged. "Never mind. Now, go on." She dug back into the hide. "Read that letter of yours and then help me out. I ain't yer slave, you know. I still got to get to these glands."

She shot him a smile. The wind swirled a cluster of her red locks past her eyes, and warmth filled his insides. He didn't like anyone knowing his business, but something about this girl Pearl…Pearl. Pearl. Pearl. He repeated her name, liking the way it felt to think it as though it meant something, as though she did.

Chapter 21

Katherine

1891—Storm Lake

Working their way over four acres of land, the Christoffs and Katherine plowed, planted, and covered neat rows of earth that would someday feed the family with tall shoots of sweet corn. The plodding steps left Katherine's feet aching and her legs numb from the repetitive movements, but the change from work in the kitchen and from squinting as hours turned into entire days of sewing was welcome.

The physical activity revealed to Katherine her strength. Seeing Mrs. Christoff's exhaustion and Mr. Christoff's boredom gave Katherine a sense of empowerment. Her mind hadn't been idle as they plowed a grid and planted in each intersection of the grid. She used the time wisely, plotting ways to stow away money she earned taking on side jobs from women who desired just one more set of cuffs or another collar for the spring season.

If she didn't hear from her mother in the next month, she would simply go back to Yankton and retrace her mother's movements in person. Someone had to know something. She figured it would take her a month to earn the extra money that she would have to hide from Mrs. Christoff.

She was going to leave the Christoffs with or without word from her mother.

Katherine recognized for the first time how strong her muscles were, how her body seemed to have been calling out for such activity, growing loose and limber as the sun moved overhead, as the Christoffs grew more depleted.

After a luncheon of salted pork sandwiches and mashed potatoes, which Hannah had prepared, they headed back outside. Mrs. Christoff limped as they started the second half of their day and repeated prayers until she could no longer walk any farther.

"Abner!" she said.

He stopped the horse and turned in his seat. His eyes were full of irritation. "Dear Lord, woman, what do you want?"

She wobbled, putting her arms out to steady herself. Katherine rushed to her side, supporting her.

Mrs. Christoff pulled a square of cotton batting from her bodice. "A blister. Just let me put this in my boot."

His mouth formed a straight line, his eyes cold on his wife. "We're wasting time. You should have done that while we ate." He tossed his head toward Katherine. "She can plant and cover while you tend your foot."

His eyes traced over Katherine's body, making her feel as though he were actually touching her with his gaze. Katherine glanced at Mrs. Christoff, who was looking back and forth at each of them, finally settling a scowl on Katherine.

"You just keep to the land, Katherine Arthur. Thou shall not covet another's husband."

Katherine drew back as acid rose into her mouth. She almost guffawed at the thought of longing for such a repulsive man.

Mrs. Christoff's mouth twisted as her eyes hardened. "God keep you in your time of employ. For sinners rot in the lap of the devil."

Mrs. Christoff pulled her arm out of Katherine's supportive grip, sat down, and began to unlace her boot. Katherine picked up the pail of corn and took her place behind the plow. Mr. Christoff snapped the reins to start the horse. He began to whistle, and Katherine wondered if he'd been whistling the whole time and she had simply been too far back to hear him.

With the pail and hoe in the crook of one arm, she dropped four kernels in each intersection they passed. Then she hoed the dirt over the seeds and moved on.

"You need to move faster." He had stopped the sulky and turned to watch her.

"Mrs. Christoff must be almost done with her boot." Katherine looked over her shoulder at her keeper. The woman had hiked her dress up past her knees and looked to be pulling her shoe back on, wrestling to reach past her barreled middle. Her plump thighs glowed like snow under the shine of the hot sun. Katherine squinted, thinking she saw someone standing near the woman, looking in the direction of Katherine and Mr. Christoff.

She looked back to Mr. Christoff. "Do you see that?"

Mr. Christoff sneered. "I see my fat, lazy wife trying to get us to do as much work as possible without her. Yes, I see that."

Katherine turned back and shielded her eyes, squinting harder. James. There, sure as he always arrived when she needed him. But other than the general sense of need that she experienced just in living with these rancid people, she did not feel particularly threatened at that moment. She smiled at the sight of her older brother, still appearing like the eleven-year-old he was when he died. He'd always been insightful and wise.

Despite her being older than he'd been when he passed on, Katherine was sure he still embodied wisdom that was meant to guide her. Perhaps it was simply the loneliness that bit at the marrow in her bones, making her ache to believe he was with her, or perhaps somehow the dead never really left the living.

Go back. Those words materialized in Katherine's mind, sending chills down to her toes. She rubbed the back of her neck.

"Move it," Mr. Christoff said. "No time for two lazy women. Even a beauty like you needs to earn her keep." He leered at her as he often did, but this time Katherine was too distracted by what she'd heard. She shivered and brushed her arms, looking upward as though the blue sky held some clue as to what she was experiencing.

Katherine looked back at Mrs. Christoff. She had gotten onto all fours and was struggling to stand, her bottom pushed into the air as she did. James was no longer beside her. Katherine exhaled. Perhaps she'd been seeing things? She picked up the pail and the hoe and waited for Mr. Christoff to get the sulky rolling again.

Go now.

Katherine dropped the pail. The voice was clearer, almost as if it were emanating from inside her skin. "Did you hear that?" Katherine shouted at Mr. Christoff, who had clicked his tongue at the horse and snapped the reins to start it moving.

"I hear money draining from our accounts. That's what I hear."

She closed her eyes, trying to discern what she was experiencing, waiting for the calm that came when she opened up to it. Nothing. She wiped her brow with her sleeve and wondered if the heat was getting to her or if she was getting ill. Today of all days, with a full belly and having slept well, she should not be growing sick. She nodded and picked up the pail. When she looked toward the sulky to begin walking, she saw that Mr. Christoff hadn't turned back toward the horses. His stare penetrated her like a needle through a knit weave.

"The coulter's clumped. Clear it so we can get this done."

Katherine nodded and stomped to the coulter. She bent over to brush away a stubborn chunk of mud that stuck to the metal of the round blade. She picked up a stick and was using it to loosen the soil when she felt Mr. Christoff's hand on her shoulder.

She spun around, ready to slug Mr. Christoff. No one was there. She covered her mouth and shot a gaze back to the sulky. He was still seated there, wiping his brow with his hat. Katherine pressed her chest where her thumping heart beat against her insides.

"What on this hot, green land are you doing?" Mr. Christoff asked.

Go now. Go back. Don't wait.

A rush of fear swept through her like she'd never felt before. Yes, James had "spoken" to her before. He'd done it at the revival. There, it was comforting. Now, her skin pricked and stung as though it were being poked with sewing needles. Katherine heaved for breath, trying to puzzle through this confusion and dread.

Go now.

James was suddenly beside her. He looked toward the house as though directing Katherine to go that way. She couldn't very well tell the Christoffs she would be heading back to the house because her dead brother's voice was inside her mind, telling her there was some unseen danger afoot. She focused on Mrs. Christoff, who was lumbering toward them. Mr. Christoff rose from his seat and pointed behind him. "Get back to work!"

Her thoughts snarled, confusing her. This made no sense. There was no reason to go anywhere.

She kneaded circles into her temples. Another wave of shuddering fear shook her shoulders, and she knew she had to heed James. She knew something about them being there was unsafe. She turned to Mr. Christoff. A board-stiff wind blasted her, pushing her back a few steps. She spread her arms to balance herself, pressing back against the gusts. "Something is happening," she said.

He pointed again. "Get your pail and hoe and get this work done. That's what's happening."

She shook her head, knowing what she said made no sense, that she would receive worse punishment than before. He hopped from the sulky and ran to her. He picked up the pail and jammed it in her hand, closing her fingers around the metal handle.

"We have to go back," she said, her words halting.

He gripped her shoulders. "If you go back to the house—"

Katherine couldn't hear the rest of the sentence he spoke because the wind came at them even harder, ripping her bonnet off her head, anchored only by the string tied under her chin.

Go now.

She gripped his wrists and pulled him. "We have to go!"

She expected to feel him yank her back or to wrench free of her, but instead he yielded and was quickly running along with her. Katherine picked up her skirts and jogged, Mr. Christoff keeping pace for a moment before he suddenly circled back. "I need to get the horse!"

Approaching Mrs. Christoff, Katherine could see the confusion on her face.

"What's wrong?"

Katherine could not speak—the terror ripped through her body and muted her. They both turned to see Mr. Christoff had unyoked the horse, but once unleashed, it ran off as though it had been kicked in the rear with a pointed boot.

Another wave of fright made Katherine's teeth chatter. Even the horse knew it was time to seek shelter.

Now.

Without another word, she kicked into a run. Her feet pounded over the land, her strides lengthening. Every few steps, her foot turned in a furrow, booting up some of the planted seeds. She pumped her arms as every sense seemed numbed; all she could do was make her feet go.

As she neared the farmhouse, she saw Hannah on the back porch, which led to the kitchen. The girl looked up from her sewing. Her face first registered a smile and then surprise. Katherine looked over her shoulder to see the Christoffs running behind her. Katherine was heading straight for the porch. "Hannah!"

The girl stood and walked to where the steps led down to the grass.

Cellar.

The voice echoed against Katherine's skull.

Without slowing, Katherine veered toward the storm door to the right of the porch. When she reached it, she wrenched the heavy wood open, straining her shoulder. "Hannah! This way!"

The girl arrived at her side. Katherine tried to guide her into the basement.

Hannah looked to the sky, her hair plastered to her forehead by the gales. "It's just windy!" she shouted over the noise.

The shutters ripped off the side of the house. Katherine followed Hannah's gaze to the blue sky. She swallowed hard as her heart throbbed. She considered again the insanity of what she was doing. She couldn't find the words to explain her actions to Hannah. The Christoffs were still running toward them, anger folded into their faces. Katherine was only fully realizing what would result from this event—her employers may never give her access to food or water again.

But as their strides turned to limps just twenty yards from the house. Mr. Christoff stopped short, reaching out to keep his wife from going farther. He turned his face to the sky and motioned beyond the house, where Katherine and Hannah could not see. Mrs. Christoff grasped his arm, leaning into him. Both of them wore expressions of fear and disbelief as they clutched at each other.

Then came the sound of a train bearing down, its call shrieking like metal scraping against metal. The Christoffs fixed their gazes on where Katherine and Hannah were standing, bolting toward them.

Katherine and Hannah looked to the sky yet again. Katherine's tongue smacked off the roof of her mouth. The very air had taken on an iron taste, as though it had thickened and coated the inside of her mouth.

The clear blue sky had been swept away and was now alive with soot-black, roiling clouds. Katherine grabbed Hannah's wrist, and they tore down the cellar stairs, leaping down the last few. They huddled with arms around each other as Mrs. Christoff beat a path down the stairs. Mr. Christoff stopped just long enough to slam the door shut behind them.

In the center of the musty space, Katherine and Hannah huddled together, arms latched around each other as Mother

Nature's lashing storm railroaded past the house. Katherine held Hannah tight, the girl's face buried in Katherine's shoulder.

She recalled James' warning, the sense of him standing at her shoulder, as close and as real as the roaring weather that sent them down the cellar stairs. Katherine pressed her eyes closed. *Please, God, keep us safe*, she prayed silently. She'd always been certain James was her protector, full of wisdom and guidance, but never like this, never giving a clear sign that she had no choice but to obey.

Listening to the unexpected, blistering storm quiet as quickly as it appeared, Katherine opened her eyes. Mrs. Christoff was on her knees, her clasped hands held skyward as her lips moved, no audible words emanating. Mr. Christoff's hands were pancaked together. "Lord, save us. Lord, save us all," he repeated. Katherine exhaled deeply and rubbed Hannah's back, her chin on the top of Hannah's head. "It's all right," she said. "The storm has passed." Katherine eased Hannah's grip and found the girl's frightened gaze. She took her cheeks and dried Hannah's tears with her thumbs. "We're safe. We're safe now."

Hannah nodded, and Katherine looked to the adults to join her in comforting their daughter. The two were still mumbling, begging for grace. "Protect us, oh Lord. Keep her from our souls." Mrs. Christoff pulled Hannah away from Katherine, her eyes still full of fear. Mr. Christoff's expression held suspicion, and only then did Katherine realize that the Christoffs' prayers were not in reference to the fear of dying from the storm as much as they were in fear of the girl who had warned them it was coming. Mrs. Christoff lifted her quaking finger at Katherine. "The devil whispered in your ear, didn't he? That's how you knew."

"No." Katherine shook her head. "It wasn't that. It wasn't anything…" She knew the words weren't a helpful defense. The fear on their faces took her right back to the revival, to the people who willingly ran to the pulpit and those who were dragged upon the stage. She felt darkness settle on her moist skin, chapping it, stinging it like a cold burn. No. There was nothing for her to say.

Chapter 22

Katherine

1905—Des Moines

Katherine gripped the sides of the kitchen sink, trying to steady herself. The open window let flower and herb-laced wind gusts brush over her. The familiarity of the fragrance, the quiet in her home was comforting. The funeral had tornadoed past her. At various times during the funeral, Katherine was left to feel as though she were inside a spinning funnel, where smooth, rotating sides left her relatively calm but aware of the death all around her. The presence of people like Millie resulted in a sense of comfort for Katherine.

But other mourners had approached her, evoking feelings of her being ripped apart, mortified at the stories people told her about her mother. It wasn't that these unfamiliar people carried awful, hateful, searing stories about her mother. It was in hearing them that Katherine felt again the humiliation that she had let so much time pass unresolved, unwilling to share her life with her mother the way she once had.

She and Aleksey had spent much of their time away from Des Moines, away from Jeanie, but Katherine could not have imagined the breadth of the divide until meeting all these people who embodied this loving, generous spirit that they attributed to Jeanie Arthur.

With stark clarity, Katherine saw that her mother had lived two lives—the one Katherine had been witness to as a younger girl and a second life she knew nothing about.

Aleksey came into the kitchen at some point, but Katherine didn't notice him until he was behind her, his body warm against her back. He rubbed her shoulders, then roped his arms around her, pulling her tight. "I love you, Kath."

She felt yet another swell of emotion, but this time it was pure love and gratefulness that Aleksey had been a part of her life for so long. There was no one she trusted like him, no one who had cared for her as he did. The day's emotions swirled inside her, making her want to be as close to her husband as she possibly could. She turned to him and took his face in her hands. His gaze was penetrating and loving as he dotted her with sweet kisses.

"I love you always," Katherine said.

He smiled and kissed her harder. His mouth was soft and gentle on hers. His strong hands caressed her back, warming her body all over. Katherine pressed against him, wishing they were alone in the house and could hide away in their bedroom. Her limbs grew heavy as Aleksey's gentle touch seemed to allow her to fully feel the exhaustion she'd been ignoring. He absorbed her body weight.

She rested her cheek against Aleksey's chest and let him cradle her. Her fatigue was rooted in emotional turmoil. And the feelings took her back in time to a place she had tried to forget for most of her life. She realized this fatigue she felt right then was matched by few experiences in her life, including the days she'd spent with the Christoffs.

All of the energy it took to reconcile with her mother and survive the funeral forced Katherine's mind back to when she was just fourteen, causing her to recall the way every inch of her ached and screamed for sleep and food. Now, though, the exhaustion was tinged with relief. She knew deep in her bones that her mother had passed on to a better place. Katherine was confident that her mother had been met by James, that Jeanie Arthur could finally rest in peace.

Aleksey kissed the top of Katherine's head and pulled her close. "You all right?"

Katherine shook her head. His body was warm and strong against her as he swayed her gently, as though wanting to lure her into a dance.

"It was a beautiful service," Aleksey said. "Were you happy with it? All those people. It was amazing. I feel like I know your mother better, and it reminded me of her when we first met your family way back when."

Katherine gripped him tighter, feeling the full length of his strength. "I agree. It was unnerving at first, and to see Yale as composed as she was and I was barely keeping it together. I felt her there. The sense of her was strong."

"I know. I felt the same way."

He kissed the top of her head again. Then he looked into her eyes, holding her face as he gently brushed her lips with his thumbs. "Now let's get you some peace and quiet. Yale's asleep." He kissed her. "Tommy and I put most of the chairs back. The boys and I will handle the rest of them tomorrow. After a good sleep, what do you say we go to the Lighthouse for brunch tomorrow?"

She let him absorb her weight as her body pressed into him. She could have stood there all day with his arms around her.

"But right now," he said, "it's time for you to rest."

"You're right," she said. "But I can't sleep. I'm beat like a rug, but my mind won't shut down." She drew a deep breath and exhaled with her whole being. "All those wonderful people. All that I learned about my mother. And still so much

I don't know. Cora Hillis said she has things we will want to keep. And that Millie woman. Something about her just felt…" Katherine rubbed her arms and looked off into the distance. "Warm, loving. Different from most people. Her energy and, well, you know what I mean. She was like an angel."

Katherine pulled the button from her pocket and held it up. "This button. It's something that should make me feel rotten—thinking back to that year on the prairie—but it doesn't."

"That makes sense. By that logic, being with me should make you think of the awful year on the prairie. But it doesn't."

She shook her head and then pointed her finger at him. "You're right. Maybe it's just that I'm finally ready to remember the good with my mother that year and not just chew on the bad. That's it. Thank you, Aleksey."

Tommy came into the kitchen. Katherine and Aleksey continued to hold each other but turned to him. He drew back, and Katherine wondered if their affection made him uncomfortable. She stepped away from Aleksey and turned to the cupboard, pulling a mug from the shelf and turning back. "Tea?"

Tommy pushed his thumb over his shoulder. "Listen, Katherine. I'm gonna head out."

"Head out? It's nearly dark," Katherine said.

Aleksey pulled a chair out from the table and gestured to it. "Sit. You probably need some sweet tea instead of hot?"

Tommy shook his head and pushed his hand through his hair. "No, thanks, Aleksey. You've been kind and opened your home to me. And, Katherine, I realize you've managed some sort of feat in that you've softened your heart and forgiven Mama's mistakes and absorbed the letters and the fact that our family breaking apart was not all Mama's fault, but I haven't done that yet."

"Please don't just run away."

"I just need some air."

Katherine remembered the way he would take to the woods as a young man, the way he flew across the prairie lands as if he thought he could take off flying if he just ran fast enough.

She stepped toward him. "It's hard, I know. You haven't said exactly what is happening with you and Emma, but let's get some sleep and we'll send a telegram to her tomorrow. Maybe Aleksey can send for her. Or we'll go to her if she's too sick to travel."

Tommy's eyes welled and he gripped the table edge. "Did you hear those people? That woman Millie with the button? She mentioned our father as though she knew him, as though everyone in that room except us were actually Mama's family instead of us."

Katherine shrugged. She agreed, but she did not feel anger about it, simply regret. "Don't you think that was partly our fault?"

"Our fault?"

"Not completely, but somewhat, yes."

Tommy puffed his cheeks and blew out air, glaring at his sister. "Sure. Partly us, yes. She reached out and I wasn't able to... Well, the timing was wrong. And then I tried to reconnect and it was like she couldn't be bothered." He exhaled again.

"I know what you're feeling, Tommy. But won't it be better if we bring Emma here? You said you were in the process of giving over your church. Maybe if you both got away from your regular life, it would give you a chance to sort through all your troubles with Mama and Emma? Aleksey and Asher can go for her. It will be two days' trip and then—"

Tommy waved his hand at her. "I see your disappointment in me. I'm a minister, and I'm full of all the wrong words, all the wrong feelings, all the wrong choices."

"That's not what I was saying," Katherine said. Perhaps that was the truth, though, if he felt she was indicating those very things.

Tommy grasped his shirt placket. "I feel like I'm on fire. I'm a fraud, Katherine. I was angry and put off by what that Millie woman said. But how can I judge? I'm a fraud in every area of my life. I feel like the only way to shed my failures is to run until the wind shaves it right off my back. I just need to get out."

He went toward the kitchen door. Katherine caught his hand and pulled back. "Please stay. We don't have to talk. I don't think *anything* of your feelings, and I wouldn't say you were a fraud. I'm not judging you. You should know better than anyone that I don't judge a person's ability to follow a religion. I am the last person who would look down on that."

Tommy laid his head against the door.

"Stay, Tommy," Aleksey said.

Tommy turned and sighed. "I want to. But I just can't."

He wrenched free of Katherine's grip and was out the door.

She watched him disappear into the moonlight and was again reminded of a time long ago when Tommy would take to the open air for sleep. It was as though their mother dying and then the funeral thrust Tommy back in time, as though he were fourteen again.

Aleksey took her hand and kissed her fingers. "Let him go. It's not his first time taking to the night for some air."

She swung his hand. "No, it certainly is not." She and Aleksey headed up the stairs to the second floor. When they reached their bedroom, Katherine stopped him. She hugged him and pulled his face down so she could kiss his cheeks and nose and forehead. "You go on and get into bed. I need to do something."

"The attic's dark. Not enough light up there to dig through boxes and—"

"No, no, not the attic. I just want to sketch. Just for a minute. In a lot of ways, I feel just like Tommy. I'm scattered and disconnected, and I just need to put some things on paper before I sleep."

He kissed her, his hand caressing the nape of her neck. Katherine's stomach fluttered, and she ran her hand around his backside, pulling him close. "I'll be in soon. I promise."

And as she headed down the hall to the room they were using for her studio, she heard the bedroom door close. She entered the room. The moon was framed in the floor-to-ceiling windows, flooding the space with the otherworldly light that only a full moon could offer.

She pulled the paperweight button from her pocket and held it up in the moonlight, the pink basque flower illuminated inside the glass orb that held it. She cut a piece of twine from a spool and threaded it through the metal loop so it hung like a gem on the end of a necklace. She pushed the twine over her finger and smiled at it. Millie. The woman who held a quiet warmth that intrigued Katherine.

Millie certainly wasn't the type of friend Katherine thought of when she pictured her mother's world, but none of the mourners were. In Katherine's mind, her mother's world of friends began and ended in Des Moines back before they left for the prairie.

Katherine held the button between her thumb and finger and remembered some of them being used on Lutie Moore's dress the year they homesteaded. Her mother had made a beautiful dress in a dark, awful time of their lives.

Katherine let the button drop, and it swung back and forth on its new twine. So pretty, bridging her past to the present, taking her back to a time when all she wanted was to find the path back to her mother, when Katherine spent much of her time sewing, her fingers bleeding, her eyes watering from strain. She pushed the twine that held the button over the window latch so it would dangle in the morning sunlight.

She sighed and went right past the projects she'd been working on lately. She reached into a cupboard and pulled out something she hadn't touched in ages. Her burlap knapsack. She held it against her. Suddenly, that knapsack felt as though it held exactly what she needed to cast out the confusion tangled up inside her.

She sat and began to draw, almost as though dreaming while awake. She did not know how long she had been sketching, but when she stopped, she was surrounded by drawings, the white pages like snow piled high.

Each page was shaded with charcoal figures and scenes. She held the last one up as the sun was rising and chuckled. It was Tommy and his wife, Emma, with a child. She smiled at it as she sat with the feelings she was experiencing.

She feared her brother and his wife could not have children, yet she felt hope for them. Perhaps they would take in a needy child? Something had made her draw them that way, and she couldn't help but feel hope for them. She couldn't ignore the sense that something had to change for the better for her brother.

Chapter 23

Tommy

1891—Des Moines

The woods were growing cooler, fast. The spring evenings settled in chilly and more like winter than near summer. Tommy and Pearl dragged the meat from where the deer had fallen to the abandoned beaver dam, the place where rushing, frigid water should have kept the squirrel meat safe but hadn't.

The river water slapped the shoreline, jumping out of its banks, splashing him and Pearl from time to time. Had he thought he would ever eat the meat, he might have been leery of showing Pearl the old beaver dam, might have been worried that it could disappear like the squirrel meat had.

When they had it safely stowed, they went to the shoreline and each submerged their hands, letting the water clean away the remnants of the dead animal.

Pearl fished a stone from the bottom and used it to scrape at some filth she could not remove otherwise. She let out a long whistle and smiled at Tommy. "That's some setup with that old beaver dam making a well for you to store your meat."

"Well, I just sort of lucked into it."

Pearl cocked her head and shook the rock at Tommy. "You hit me as a lucky fella, you do."

Tommy thought of the Indian Head in his pocket. Maybe it was finally doing its work if someone noticed that he seemed fortunate. He looked at her small face; her emerald-green eyes and the strawberry hair that flew out from her pins, long and unkempt, struck him in a way a girl's appearance never had. Her smile lit her up like a full moon on snow.

Each expression that swept over her face was different from the last, making it impossible for him to look away, impossible for him to stop the word *beautiful* from coming to his mind. He jerked back as though someone had spoken the word aloud.

Pearl straightened and looked over each shoulder. "What?"

Tommy picked up his own rock and skipped it across the river.

She poked his arm with the rock. "Well, what is it?"

They both sat near the shore, plucking stones from beside them, skipping them across the water. He looked at her. Had she been a boy, all the nudging and questioning and supposing she did would have surely annoyed him. She grinned. He noted the dirt that gathered on the crests of her cheekbones and at the point of her chin, which turned her face into a distinct heart shape.

"Well?"

"Your teeth."

She squinted at him and rubbed them with her finger. "What about 'em?"

"They're perfect. Straight, white, together. Perfect."

She stood up and turned fully toward him. Her dress was too short, the hem tattered and dirty, but her looks made none of that matter. Clearly she lived no better than Tommy, yet her lack of fashion took nothing from the power of her looks.

She slammed her fists onto her hips. "That's how I know I'm destined for great things."

Tommy narrowed his eyes on her and rubbed his forehead, confused. He looked up at her and shaded his eyes with his hand.

She spread her lips apart, showing her teeth. "My teeth tell me so. Working that post office," she waved one hand back and forth in front of her, "women and men come rollin' in wearin' the best silk and softest wools." She brushed her hand over the bodice of her dress as though imagining it were as fine as the images in her mind. "Each dress in the most magnificent colors of the rainbow." She looked up as though she could see the scene in the sky somewhere. She fixed her gaze back on Tommy. "And yet every five or six of 'em is missin' at least one tooth. Or they're all scattershot." She wiggled her fingers at her mouth. "Like God just tossed them into their mouths without paying a lick of the attention he tends to pay to things."

She nodded and straightened her posture in a way Tommy had never seen her do. "I lack plenty, but good teeth I got." She gave a final nod.

"You do, Pearl. That you do."

She reached down toward him, offering her hand. He took it and stood, feeling awkward silence take hold of the moment. He looked at her hand in his. He cleared his throat and backed away, drying his hand on the back of his pants. "I best get back to camp," he said. "You best get back to…well…wherever it is you go at night. It'll be dark soon, and you won't be able to see a thing—"

She grabbed his arm, the fabric of his sleeve tight in her grip. "So you ain't invitin' me to yer camp?"

"Why, no. You have a place to stay."

"Even with my good teeth, you ain't gonna?"

He threw his arms up. "What's teeth got to do with the fact my shelter's built for one?"

She stared at him and shook her head.

Tommy felt defensive. "You can't just invite yourself to a fella's camp like he's boarding out rooms and such."

She pursed her lips and pegged her fists on her hips. "Well, don't think for a blasted minute that I'm gonna let that deer meat slip my mind."

He put his hands up in surrender. "I wouldn't expect that you would."

She tapped her temple. "I don't forget a thing. Fox trap I got myself up here. I don't forget."

He chuckled. She made him feel things—happy things. He had an urge to rub his trousers, to adjust them where they were growing tight. He'd felt that before, but never for someone like Pearl.

"And don't think I'll forget that pinkie promise." She shook her pinkie at him. He nodded.

She put her thumb and forefinger against her temple and turned them as though turning a key. "Steel trap."

Tommy was struck dumb, as though he'd never in his life had words to speak. The word *pretty* came to him. *Angel.* That word came, too. But beautiful and angel and this Pearl made no sense at all to Tommy, because if he were ever to deem a girl attractive, it would be the sort who arrived in a tailored dress, in sugary-hued clothing, with smooth, shiny hair. The kind of girl who found a way to put some pink in her cheeks. Pearl was more a friend type of female, like the kind he'd had when he was eight years old, like his sister Katherine. Yet...pretty. It kept coming right to his mind as though the word were a magnet and his brain made of iron.

He turned and waved her on. "Let's get going. Or we'll both be cold and unsheltered tonight."

He heard her feet trailing behind him. He could tell she was kicking at the ground. He turned to see her launch a stone off the toe of her boot. It pegged him in the thigh.

"Ouch, Pearl. You hit me."

She lifted that heart-shaped face at him as though deflecting something off her chin. "Yer all right."

He was all right, but that hurt. He rubbed the spot and turned away, walking forward again. He thought he heard her mumble that she would keep him warm in the event he got cold that night. He looked over his shoulder to see if there was any hint that she'd really spoken those words.

But she rabbited right past him, studying the path her feet were taking, her arms pumping like mad. Perhaps it was in her carriage that Tommy saw her lack of grooming most. She stalked away with purpose, for locomotion, not as a means to lure a fella's eye like other girls he'd known.

She took another glance over her shoulder at Tommy, and it was as though his gaze kept hers for hours—in all of seconds, his mind registered her jewel-green eyes crisp against the fading day, her reddish locks spread out from her like kite streamers whipping through the air. "I know my way around these here woods, Tommy Arthur. So if I ain't welcome at yer camp, I'm gonna make myself scarce."

Feeling scolded, he threw his hands in the air. "Pearl," he said. Tommy didn't know what she wanted to hear, so he said nothing. He watched her disappear into the brush ahead of him, wondering what had turned her so sour so quickly. He rubbed the spot where the rock had pelted him. "Girls." They required the attention of a hothouse orchid. So if she was taking her leave, then the faster, the better.

He sighed. *Pearl.* Saying her name, he remembered what had brought her to the woods in the first place—a letter from his mother. It had been weeks since he'd heard from her. The last time she'd written, she had placed a bloom of some sort in the envelope—grown with her own hands, she'd said. And she was certain that it would not be long until she'd saved enough to afford all her children's room and board right under the same roof.

But then…nothing. Her regular correspondence stopped like the rock that had just smacked off his thigh. He drew the letter from his pocket, eager to read it.

He looked to the sky. A laugh coursed through him. Dormant excitement bubbled up. He rubbed his sore ribs. He could not wait. His mother was coming, and she had great news. He hadn't allowed himself to wish that she would get to Des Moines before it was he who sent for her. Yet her letter said she'd found a way. *Mama. Thank you, God.*

Once he read the letter several times and the idea fully settled in, he thought again of Pearl, her face suddenly in his mind. For some reason, that very idea of seeing his mother again made him think of Pearl. She had a plan. More than Hank or Bayard had, and that impressed him. It made him more fully understand the greatness from which he came.

He folded the letter. It didn't matter that the great had become the small in the last four years. He was certain that his mother returning, and him bringing his father back, would mean they would enjoy the kind of greatness they used to take for granted. For even someone like Pearl had goals and desires and ambitions. And even though he didn't think she ought to read people's letters, he admired that she'd learned something that way. Even someone like her had potential.

And for some reason, all that prospective greatness made his thoughts swirl around Pearl, imagining his fingers working through her hair like the wind on a hot summer day. Somehow, after only a few meetings, Pearl had worked her way onto the list of people he hoped to impress someday.

Chapter 24

Jeanie

1891—Des Moines

Finally! We made it to Des Moines. The train depot was dusty and dank. Yet it had its own pulse, its own breath as travelers and their families shed tears and found joy at reuniting just as I imagined my family would in a very short time.

On the train, I'd made a list and sorted through all that I would need to do to make sure I set up a proper home that was comfortable and affordable. No matter how much money Mrs. Mellet returned to me, I was no longer in the business of overspending and following fashions to the tune of four hundred and thirteen dresses per year.

To simply have a warm home, delicious food, my children at my side, and a garden, a simple garden. All of that—only that—was what I needed to feel again as though the world is a safe and wonderful place to be.

I hoped Tommy and Katherine would meet me at the depot when I reached Des Moines, as instructed. If they did not arrive, I would check the post office for letters, since I had instructed them to begin sending correspondence there to reach me. It was not ideal, but I felt sure they would show up, that they must have received at least one of the many letters or telegrams I'd sent.

Having disembarked, used the privy, and paid a few pennies to freshen up Yale with linen dipped in herbed water at the bathhouse nearby, I was ready to greet my children. I checked the arrival times for trains coming from Yankton in the hopes that Katherine would be on the last one for the day. I thought Tommy would surely be there waiting or would show up shortly, as he was situated just a short distance outside of Des Moines.

I shivered and rubbed Yale's back. The warm day had turned chilly, and crisp night winds tore past us, pushing my skirt flat against my legs one way, then digging up under it, lifting it, ballooning it. Down the way a bit, a boy dressed in tattered clothing played a violin, the sad song lifting over the gusts as if riding on the bursts of air that pushed me one way and then the other. I would have thought this shabby fellow had stolen such a finely tuned instrument if not for the elegant way he played it.

I tried to keep from smiling so wide, to stop myself from looking like a circus clown. This day! To think I was finally reuniting my family, that I had finally found a way to make things right. Hope and accomplishment swelled inside me. I wiped the tear that wound its way down one cheek, stopping at the corner of my mouth. I wrapped my arms around myself, trying to hold in all the excitement.

"Mama." Yale grinned and pointed up at me. She sat on the suitcase at my feet, leaning against my leg, warming it right through the worn skirt and tattered stockings.

"Yale." I squatted down and pulled her into a hug, catching a whiff of fresh lavender-water. "Mama loves you dearly, my darling."

I sighed. It was a great day. Even Yale felt it, speaking the only word she ever did despite her already being three years old. *Mama*. It was heavenly to hear that word float off her lips.

A ruckus not far away, down near the ticket window, drew my attention. Where the fiddler played, four older boys had arrived. They circled the fiddler, snapping their hands out, poking him, attempting to disrupt his playing. The fiddler continued, shutting his eyes against the prying hands. Playing ever fuller, richer, louder.

The four teenagers doing their best dirty work were clothed in fine wool pants and navy blue jackets with gold buttons, and each wore a cap, tilted this way or that to announce their mischievous ways in case their taunting didn't tell you enough.

Even from this distance, I could see tears running down the fiddler's face, as the wetness had cut a swath through the dirt that should have been washed off days ago. I patted Yale's head and stood, entranced by the scene.

"You stole my mother's apples." The biggest boy pushed his target's shoulder, knocking him back, making the violin wail like a dying animal as the bow tore away from the strings. Another boy caught him and then tossed him back the other way, the rest of the group forming a circle around him, pushing, prodding, taunting. The fiddler wrapped his instrument tight against his body as though only concerned for it, not himself.

I waited for a moment but was soon sure they weren't going to leave the boy alone.

"I didn't take her apples," the fiddler yelled. "I didn't take nothin' from any of you."

"If I say you did, you did." One of the four, the one with white-blond hair, took his hat off and thwacked the violinist about the back and then the belly, forcing him to double over to weather the barrage, his instrument brushing the ground.

I covered my mouth and looked around the platform. Was I the only one seeing this? Others looked on. A woman with a cage full of clucking hens turned her back to the scene.

A man with his overcoat slung over one arm and a newspaper in the other hand finally turned to see what was happening. I stole a glance at Yale, who was happily studying the hem of her skirt. "You stay sitting right here, Yale. Mama needs to speak to someone."

I headed toward the derelicts and the fiddler. One boy picked up the hat that had been collecting the fiddler's pennies and shook it, promising that the money was not his. Another tried to wrench the fiddle away from the bent-over boy.

"Hey!" I screamed. "You leave him alone." The wind took my words and threw them in the opposite direction, having no effect on the marauding ruffians.

"You leave that child alone!"

The wind dropped away, and this time everyone within earshot turned and looked at me. The boys even stopped for a moment before one of them fired off a sarcastic salute and another shot me a fisted gesture. My breath grew heavy as anger swirled in me. I shook my head, arguing with myself that this was none of my concern, but before I could even think, I was stalking toward them.

"You back right off of that boy. He's younger than you. He's..." I swallowed my next words as I passed the chicken lady, who laughed, but the man with the paper joined me in moving toward the boys.

"Stupid derelicts," I said.

"You're right about that," the man said, keeping pace.

I reached the circle of boys, who resembled wild dogs with their snapping and nipping. "Now, you all be on your way. You leave this young man alone."

The largest boy stepped up, nose to nose with me, glaring. I felt a surge of fear. I let it sweep up through my body and out. I stepped around him and pulled the poor child out of the grip of one of the other boys. The man who'd been walking with me took two boys by the arms and started down the depot with them, past the ticket window.

The smaller boy's face was awash in relief. He wrapped his arms around his instrument and looked up. "Thank you, ma'am. Thank you. I didn't swipe nothin', I swear. The grocer down the way, he gave me a sour green. I played his favorite tunes for 'im, I swear."

I brushed his unkempt hair back from his face and wished that I still had the cool, wet linen I'd used to refresh Yale earlier. The man with the paper returned and escorted us back toward Yale, past the woman with the chickens, who scowled at me. When we reached my suitcase, where Yale sat slumped against it, sleepy from our early-morning train ride, I scooped her up, her tired head on my shoulder, and cradled her.

"Thank you, sir," I said.

He nodded and smiled. "Everyone all right?"

"Mr. Hayes. Professor Hayes!" A voice came from behind the nice man. He turned and put his finger up to signal he would be there in a moment.

He turned back to me. His kind eyes and concerned expression felt reassuring. His gaze lingered on mine, like I remembered men used to do, back before. I felt warmth spill through me like the sweet wine we used to drink at dinner in Des Moines. I pressed my cheek, hoping the blush I felt inside was not turning my face red as cherries. I stuffed my hand behind me, realizing that my ungloved hand would paint a clear picture of who I was, or worse, who I was not.

"We're fine, sir. Thank you for moving those boys along."

I took the little boy's chin and lifted it, turning his face back and forth to check for injury. "You're not hurt?"

He shook his head. "I ain't learned like them. I ain't even got a home. That's why those boys pick at me like that. My ma put me out to Glenwood, to live with the other soft young'uns. Said I'm soft in the head, soft in every way."

I looked around. "No one who's soft in the head can play like that."

Hoots and hollers rose and fell in the distance, the other boys continuing to bellow, as if to warn everyone they were still watching. Before long the gang had reappeared down the way and were moving toward us again, swarming forward, like bees heading for the hive.

I reached for the fiddler. "Keep near." My fingers brushed over his arm, missing a full grasp, and before I could take another try at pulling him toward me, he was gone, his feet beating over the wood planks, echoing like bullets leaving a gun.

Swooping in like birds of prey, the gang targeted their quarry. As one of them passed by, he knocked the brim of my hat, but I caught it before it fell. I readjusted it, worried. *That poor soul running for his life. Please keep him safe.*

Had I forgotten what Des Moines was like, or had it completely and utterly changed in just three years? I wanted to run after the boys. I strained to listen for the screams of one boy attacked by this gang. Nothing came. I could only tell myself that the boy had gotten away, that he was safe for the time being. I picked Yale up again and rocked back and forth, holding her as tight as possible.

The four taunting boys were dressed so nicely. I shook my head at the thought that being dressed well and being kind, considerate human beings were not the same thing. I tried to place their faces. I was sure I must know their families from before; I would have had tea with the mothers of boys so finely dressed. But the years since we'd left our proper life had either stolen my memory, or their transformation from boys to young men had rendered them unrecognizable. Either way, it saddened me that well-to-do, educated young men with the world at their disposal would bother with such a vulnerable little thing as that fiddler.

I wouldn't let the fear that something awful could be happening to my children, that they might be vulnerable to a gang of fancy, awful boys, settle in. I knew they were in safe homes, with families who cared for them. Although I hadn't heard from Katherine in too long, I felt a twinge of jealousy that she was so comfortable and happy with where she was boarding that she might not want to return after so long. I counted that as a blessing, no matter if it stung that my children's contentment came at a cost to me.

I could save my true worry for Yale, the most vulnerable of all. She needed time to grow stronger, to catch up to children her age. Now that Mrs. Mellet was offering to pay us back, I felt sure I could provide a good family home, even without the help of a man. That Yale survived so far showed me she would be fine in the end. I knew she would. Everything was going to be all right.

"We're all right, little Yale. I'll protect you from everything in this whole wide world. I will." And she turned her head on my shoulder, her plump cheeks sweaty, her red lips parted as I smiled down on her, watching as she peacefully let sleep find her and make all that was wrong in the world go away.

**

The train that I thought might have been carrying Katherine was late. I shook my hands out as though the motion would expel all the nerves swirling inside me. The gasman had lit the lights in the depot, and the soft glow reminded me that the prospect of seeing my children that night was growing slimmer by the second.

I could not wait to see Katherine, to press her into my body, hold on tight, laugh and share ideas, and start our lives all over again. I hadn't heard from her yet, but I hoped she would send word to me at the post office if she couldn't make this train. I would need to keep my faith strong if I was not going to crumble at the sight of an empty train pulling away with none of my children having met me. I knew it was a possibility, but until then, I hadn't considered how that might feel, not after all that had happened so far.

I picked up Yale, hitched her onto my hip, and paced. A train had stopped and dispatched its passengers, puffing and belching soot as it snaked away. Its waste lifted and dropped over us, mixing with the stink of the chicken woman's cage.

My heels clicked over the wood, echoing in my ears. What if things didn't go well? It had been years since things had gone well for us. No. I would not let that thought play in my mind. I would make things right.

My stomach churned. I pressed the spot where the acid gathered. The pressure quelled the pain that habitually seared my innards. When I'd first felt the pain years back, I'd blamed my body's rebellion on the loss of my family fortune, the ruination of our once good name.

I shuddered. I shook so hard that the chicken woman glanced twice to be sure I only appeared as though I would vomit and pass out right there and not actually do it. I patted Yale's back, nodded, and lifted my mouth into as much of a smile as I could. I'd gotten used to doing that—smiling to hide the fact that my mind was lost behind a gray veil of grief I could not throw off no matter how hard I tried.

"The wind. Chilly." I rubbed my arms.

The chicken woman mumbled and growled and picked up her poultry cage, agitating the hens until they were flapping and chattering, scolding me with sharp voices as their owner turned away from me.

I shrugged and set Yale on the ground again. She folded her arms on the suitcase and laid her head down, closing her eyes. I didn't have the energy to assure the woman I wasn't full of flu or tuberculosis, that my shuddering was set about because I was aggrieved. Truthfully, people were less inclined to allow for one's emotional tumult than they were to sympathize with physical pain of just about any sort. I was once that type of person myself.

Thunder rumbled in the distance. I looked into the sky, where rain clouds folded and then unfurled before stilling, threatening, reminding me of the way anguish had worked me over in recent years.

James. In just thinking his name, sorrow rolled through me making the terrain of my son's absence as tangible as the planks under my boots. I closed my eyes and let the pain pass through—at least now it *would* pass through. For three years, his death had defined my every breathing moment.

Even waiting for the train, the dark swirling clouds made me feel as though James was nearby. I had come to regularly survey the sky, feel the winds, and notice atmospheric changes as though I were employed at a government weather station. It allowed me to feel closer to James, to recall his life instead of to only feel his death.

He and a friend of ours on the prairie, Howard Templeton, used to spend time trying to predict the weather, reading the indications that might tell us what to expect. Trouble was, the weather was often sly, giving one sign and then doing something else, like the day of the blizzard that killed my James and so many others. He was not supposed to die. I buried a chamber of my heart with him and I did not know how to get it back—I did not even know if it was possible to recover it.

Thank you, Millie. A chill crept up my arms. Because of her, I was alive. And today was a day for joy. Yale pulled on my ratty hem, and we exchanged the same smile we did a hundred times a day. She shifted against my leg again. I patted the top of her head. I heard the distant howl of the train. I rose to my tiptoes to see over the chicken woman's head.

I kneaded my hands. Nervous to see my daughter? Well, I was just as excited and happy and hopeful that we could put the past at our backs once and for all, that I could shed the shame I felt for not managing to make a go of starting a household that could keep us all.

I had promised my daughter countless times and broken those promises each time. I had comforted myself with the knowledge that my Katherine the Great was intelligent and practical and strong as prairie winds. That was the blanket I covered my guilt with, trying to smother out the truth, the demoralizing failure of not raising my children right.

I blamed myself for that. Although, when I allowed for it, I let the truth bubble to the surface of my mind, that I shared the responsibility with Frank. Really, I could have seen myself hoisting all the responsibility onto his shoulders, as he was the one who'd had the affair. He was the one who'd caused the death of our son. And he was part of the swindle that had sent us to the prairie in the first place. It was time to put that behind us, to fully start again.

I could see now that courting blame—holding hate for Frank so close—opened the door for helplessness, wasted energy. It was time to walk away from all the desperation that his betrayal had wrought. At this point, it was me who was latched to it. It hindered my ability as much as the divorce itself. A new start for us. It was finally here. I was finally ready to accept it.

Yale whimpered. She pawed at her throat.

"Thirsty?" I asked her.

She nodded. I had weaned her only recently, forced to nurse her for longer than was right for reasons tied to my personal economy. I bent down and took her chin, lifting it so she'd look me in the eye.

"We'll get a drink soon. Just a few more minutes and Katherine will arrive." Yale pulled her chin from my hand and nestled back against my leg, worming her hands under my skirt so she could wrap her tiny arms around my leg.

The whistle blew again, forcing the acid back up. I cleared my throat, swallowing it back down my burning esophagus. I squeezed my eyes shut. This was my chance to make up for all I'd done wrong when I was just trying to keep Yale alive. Time to let it go, to uproot my feet, which were so tangled in regret.

I heard the sound of a violin playing in the distance—a staccato, happy tune. I smiled. It must have been that little boy. He must be all right. The sadness I'd felt when he bolted away was replaced with hope. Clearly that child was a survivor, too, and that omen made me think I was right. Nothing bad would befall us again. We'd paid our tab on bad in the world, and we would only find good and plenty from this point forward.

**

The crowd waiting for loved ones was growing. I craned my neck to catch a glimpse of the train coming around the bend. Nothing yet, but I heard it calling, its haunting tone the exact sound I'd heard in my head for the last three years, the calling of my children who I could not reach. I tried to imagine what Katherine looked like, how she had changed. My heart pounded as my excitement grew. A smile pushed across my mouth. I allowed the full sense of happiness to take hold. I tried to picture Tommy, the way his eyes narrowed with unexpressed irritation, the way he used to take off running for the Zurchenkos, looking for something entertaining to do.

A gust of wind blew my hat nearly from my head and made me giggle. *A sign from James?* Somewhere in heaven, he was watching the atmosphere swirl and push and suck at the land, sending me messages with the wind, reminding me he was there, excited for the reunion of most of his family.

My hands shook and I tucked them around my waist, holding myself together. Where was Tommy? He should already be here. He was the least reliable of the children; perhaps he was simply late. I imagined seeing Katherine leap from the train and run into my arms. I hadn't let myself picture it until I was sure everything was in place. Oh, to share every breath of our lives the way we had the first eleven years of Katherine's—I could not wait.

Yale dozed and fell away from my leg, startling herself awake. I scooped her up and settled her on my hip, kissing the top of her head as she nestled it onto my shoulder. Her eyes closed, her mouth went slack with sleep, and I was back to my thoughts.

Steps one, two, three. It was a simple sequence—do the next right thing—that I'd offered to women in the years I was the Quintessential Housewife. For the first time in a long time that determination was back, and the thought that my simple steps to a simple life could actually lead to the good life I knew we deserved returned. I exhaled long and deep. This was it.

The crowd inched closer. The mix of squalid bodies and perfumed attempts to cover it up combined with the soot Des Moines was famous for. I turned my body to shield Yale from a pushy man who nearly elbowed her in the face as he stuck his arm in the air, waving at a train we could still barely see.

Excitement rose in me. I deserved this hope and happiness. I knew that. I had punished myself from the inside out.

I would serve a life sentence without my sweet James. But the absence of Frank did not require the carving out of a piece of my heart. No. His presence had been the reason I'd had any loss at all. I eased images of him out of my mind—this was my day to be joyful, optimistic in a way that thoughts of Frank would not allow.

After we left the prairie, after the divorce, I'd pushed one man who had seemed to love me, Howard Templeton, from my life as hard as I could. The timing had been wrong. I thought I could navigate the world as a divorced woman. And I simply hadn't trusted him, even though something told me I should have. How could I ever trust another man, even a seemingly good one, after what Frank had done?

Now I was left to wonder if I should have put aside principles and simply done what was smart. As much as it soured me, I had grown to see that a divorced woman could not easily create a household in the manner children should—or even could—be raised. I had not been able to afford to keep my children. There were times I thought they were old enough to earn their keep right alongside me, but something would go awry—the family I was boarding with would not need extra hands, or the poorhouse I'd have to sleep in was full to the brim with unsavory folk.

Many nights leading up to this very day, I'd sat in the rocker in some family's attic room, Yale straddling me, her head resting against me, sleeping hard as prairie ground, and I'd considered my strengths, my weaknesses, my options for earning a living.

The train's whistle grew louder. I moved the suitcase forward with my foot as the throng squeezed closer. I patted Yale's back.

Yes, I would make up the lost years to Katherine and Tommy. I stopped trying to imagine what Katherine might look like and simply pictured Katherine's round face the way I remembered it. Her unusual eyes that held all the colors of the prairie right inside each iris. I saw her slow smile, which she unleashed when all was right in her world, the cock of her head when considering women's liberation or what color paints she should use to create just the right shade of green that lit the early-summer grass.

"She's almost here, little Yale." I bounced her gently, my excitement rising out of me as the train slowed to a halt. Tommy must be on his way, just a few minutes away, I was suddenly sure.

The train came around the bend, slowing further. Excited voices rose and fell as loved ones burst from the train openings. I couldn't recall a moment I'd been so excited. I held my breath, marking this moment, this feeling, actually being able to note the sensation of my heart swelling—love swirling right there in my chest, palpable.

It was as though the muscle had shrunk since I'd boarded Katherine and Tommy with families who could afford to keep them, as though I hadn't allowed myself to feel this love in their absence because my yearning would make it impossible to draw my next breath even if I wanted to. I felt alive.

I watched the passengers trailing out of the cars like ants to a feast, voices rising and falling as they neared and then passed. A young girl hopped from the top step and flew into her father's arms as he spun her so her feet thwacked at those too close. Her mother came behind and hugged them both. A young man greeted his love with a handshake under her parents' heavy gaze. Another family disembarked, looking exhausted but content to meet relatives bearing embraces and picnic suppers.

I was grateful to have my arms full with Yale, to have a reason to stay upright. I smoothed back her hair. My throat closed as the number of passengers disembarking began to dwindle. The porters were pulling luggage from every crevice of the train, and the once-overflowing mound of baggage was down to nearly nothing. Was Katherine still on the train? Had I missed her going by? My head filled with unconnected, jarring thoughts. I spun around, searching the remaining faces for my daughter.

I trembled. Had Katherine missed the train altogether?

"Are you all right, ma'am?" A porter took my arm.

"My daughter," I said. My eyes widened and my voice shook.

I moved down the depot, going up on my toes to see through a steamy window, stepping into the doorways and then moving down again.

The porter had followed, and he gripped my arm again. "What's her name?"

I looked at his hand, then focused on his face. "Katherine Arthur. She's not very old, just, well…" I closed my eyes and pictured Katherine. "Well, she's fourteen now, but she's alone. She's still a girl. I'm just…" I wiggled from his grasp and worked my way back down the train, looking into the same windows and knocking on the now-closed doors.

So familiar, this black dread that dropped from my heart at the same time it shot into my head, causing me to nearly collapse. Where was Tommy? I held Yale tighter, worried I might drop her. Perhaps Katherine wouldn't ever come to me. Perhaps she'd had enough of my promises and had stopped opening my letters.

"Mama?"

I spun around and squinted.

A man stood ten feet away from me. I saw those narrowed blue eyes, the lift of one corner of his mouth, and I knew it was true. I grinned like an imp but could not run toward him. It was Tommy, I knew it even if my eyes couldn't mesh his new height and build with the memory of who he had been the last time I saw him.

Finally, I moved my feet and Tommy began toward me. We each broke into a shuffle then a jog, and when we finally met, I held him so tight that Yale was squished between us, causing her to whimper.

I pulled away to get a better look at him. I ran my free hand down his arm and reached up to cup his cheek, stretching so far, my arm had to straighten to make contact.

"You must be six feet tall!" I pulled him into an embrace again, squeezing a cough right out of him. "And big. You're the size of your grandfather!" He'd grown much thicker than his father, looking like Frank in the face but clearly favoring my family in height.

He hugged me back just as hard. "Mama. I missed you. I love you so much," he said.

Such beautiful words—it had been so long since I'd heard them directed at me.

We released each other. He smoothed Yale's hair back, studying her. "You're so big," Tommy said, kissing her forehead. She buried her face in my shoulder but then turned her head to keep an eye on her brother, offering a little smile.

It was then I noticed Tommy's swollen eye, the faded blue and black of a bruise dotted around it.

I touched it. "What happened?" My heart stilled at the realization that there had been so many happenings over the last years, and I was struck by the odd sensation that I had to ask about it instead of having been with him to already know the details.

"Just a little fun with the boys is all." He smiled, his eyes alight and his grin just as easy and open as it had been sour the last time I saw him, when I broke yet another promise to bring our family back together.

"I'm so sorry about everything, Tommy. I just want—"

He held up his hand. "It's all right, Mama. And there's so much we need to discuss. But I want to hear about Mrs. Mellet. Your letter said she wants to give us back what's ours. Is that true?"

I nodded. "But…" I craned my neck to see if Katherine was anywhere in sight. "I sent word to Katherine, but I haven't heard from her in a long time, and I have no idea if she got my letters or if she's just ignoring them or…"

Tommy shrugged. "You sent one to the Turners? Last letter I got from her was from their home."

"Me, too," I said.

I gripped Tommy. "You don't suppose that—"

"No, Mama." He gathered me in his arm. "She's fine. I know she is. Somehow I just know."

I nodded, feeling secure in the strength of his clutch.

He released me and bent for a suitcase. "I'm sure she got your letter and her reply is on the way."

"Oh, Tommy. I hope so." I took his free hand and squeezed it three times—*I love you*. But that was something Katherine did with me, not Tommy. And he didn't register that I'd done it. My eyes burned at the thought of my missing daughter.

Tommy kissed the back of my hand. "She'll arrive soon, Mama. We'll check the post tomorrow for word."

I nodded. I felt as though a piece of my heart had been sectioned off, stilled, numbed, unable to beat until I knew my Katherine was safe, until she was back with us. But, having Tommy with me was a good start toward healing.

"I want to hear all about what you've been doing."

I scooped my arm through his. "I have just enough money to rent a room until we go to Mrs. Mellet's tomorrow."

Tommy kissed my cheek. "Time to start our lives anew, Mama. Fortune has turned its bright face upon us."

I smiled. His positive outlook made me feel as though, even with Katherine not yet with us, there was new vigor, a promise that my life was about to be transformed all over again.

**

Yale and I got a good night's sleep in a small room in a broken-down boardinghouse near the train station, using nearly the last of the money I had from the letter Mrs. Mellet had sent. Tommy had begun the night in our room, sharing the slender bed with us, then going to the floor, then, sometime at night, slipping out. When I woke and he was gone, I panicked, afraid that seeing him again had simply been a dream. But when Yale and I went downstairs that morning, we found Tommy sitting on the porch in a rocking chair, waiting for us.

He treated us to breakfast at the boardinghouse and told us that he had been doing odd jobs for Reverend Shaw. "But I have a good job waiting for me. Well, I think so anyway. I need to check back in and see when I will start."

I pushed the remains of the oatmeal I didn't eat toward him. "A job? You are really something."

His camping out worried me. He told me all about it over breakfast. He promised to pack up his things and leave the woods just as soon as we rented rooms, which we'd do later that afternoon, after Mrs. Mellet settled her debt to us. He looked uncomfortable at the thought.

"Tommy." I squeezed his hand across the table. "I can see how you've grown, but you're my son, and I can't have you sleeping outside. You'll be hurt or... You've already been hurt out there. I can see you're all bruised." My heart soared and ached at the sight of him. I could see him smiling past what must have been stiff pain. I began to wonder what other hurts he might have suffered in the years since the prairie, but I stopped myself. I could not visit the space where my failures were so evident. Not right then, not so soon after getting together, not when this felt so good.

"I like it outside, Mama." He inhaled, expanding his chest, shoulders going back. "The fresh air, the freedom. Father used to say the fresh air gave a fresh start. Now I know what he meant."

He looked away.

"Well. Now that I'm here, it's time for a proper home."

Father used to say...

Those words shook me. It had been so long since I'd heard mention of Frank by one of my children.

Tommy grimaced and pushed his hand through his hair like he did when he was keeping some silent sliver of anger to himself. I suspected he wished to reminisce about his father, wanted me to say I wanted him back. Knowing I could not satisfy Tommy with my thoughts on his father, I asked him about the coal miner he had been boarding with instead.

"They were inhospitable in the end, Mama."

Without elaboration, he went on to describe how he met Mr. Babcock.

His mention of the bad experience at the miner's home circled back in my mind and settled on my heart. "I'm sorry about the miner."

Tommy shrugged. "Babcock's place was good. Really good." He shrugged again. His face lit up, and he began to tell another story about living with Babcock and how wonderful it was. But as his telling of a pleasing day and restful sleep in the barn came to a close, his voice softened.

I was relieved that he'd found such a welcoming household with the Babcocks. I would have to write them and thank them for caring for him when I could not.

"But not wonderful like when we're all together, Mama," he said. He took my hand in both of his and held it against his chest, reminding me of the day he'd helped me at the house, when the mob had come to claim "their" things. My heart lurched and my eyes filled with tears. "Being with the Babcocks was just wonderful compared to some other families I boarded with."

I lifted his hands to my mouth, kissing them. "Oh, Tommy. I so agree. There is nothing like family. And soon Katherine will be here."

He relaxed back in his seat. I sipped my coffee as he rambled on, telling more stories, his eyes wide, gesturing for emphasis. Yale snuggled against me, and I let the moment embody peace, fill me with contentment—the most satisfaction I could experience while not knowing where my Katherine was.

"After I meet with Mrs. Mellet, we will send telegrams to each home where Katherine might possibly be. I've done all that already, but we need word on when she will arrive."

Tommy finished off his water. "And I'll retrace her steps, if that's what it takes, Mama. She'll get here soon, or I'll go get her myself," Tommy said.

Once the bill was paid at breakfast, we headed toward the trolley. When we passed the grocer's, I looked through the window and caught a glimpse of the clock over the counter. We had forty minutes to catch the trolley that would take us to where we could walk to Mrs. Mellet's home.

When I turned forward again, I stopped short, almost running smack into two women toting pastel embroidered parasols. They swerved past us, but two boys whipping down the sidewalk forced several gentlemen who were deep in conversation to split apart, one of them sending me, Yale, and our suitcase into the muddy road, where I fell to my knees.

Suitcase strewn, I managed to keep Yale out of the mud except for one foot. My free hand had plunged into the muddy rise and fall of wagon ruts; I looked over my shoulder to see the back of one man chasing off after the hoodlums. "It's all right, Yale. I have you."

Tommy jumped into the street, splashing more mud over all of us.

He reached down. My chest heaved as the stench of horse-droppings stung my nose. I inhaled through my mouth to avoid retching and lifted my foot to stand. "Take Yale." He did and extended his hand to me as my boot caught the inside of my skirt, making me fall to my knees again. The man who pushed us was suddenly at my side. He and Tommy lifted me to my feet.

"Thank you," we said to the man who helped me up and set the suitcase near my feet.

"Sorry about that. This town is going to the hoodlums and dogs, isn't it, now?" the man said, shaking his head.

"Sure has changed," I said, but the man was already stalking away, late for an appointment, I assumed.

"Now, don't fret, Mama." Tommy held Yale and dotted at my face with a handkerchief. "I have you."

I took his hand. "Thank you, Tommy." The feel of his man-sized fingers and palm forced me to look. It seemed as if I was no longer holding his hand, but he was holding mine. Fourteen years old was too old for him to hold his mother's hand in public. But still, I didn't want to let it go.

His hand dwarfed mine. I had to keep looking down at our entwined fingers, marveling that his grip was now that of a man. I felt as though I were dreaming, as though none of what I saw in him was real. He was my boy, yet I wondered if I knew him at all anymore. To see him holding Yale like that, her comfort with him having come so quickly, was a gift to me.

I sighed. "Katherine. We need to hear from her."

He guided me back onto the sidewalk, where I stood against the wall, bricks digging into my spine. "We will, Mama."

I brushed at my skirt with the hanky and noticed that Tommy was suddenly nervous.

Tommy bounced Yale on his hip and glanced over his shoulder, pacing like a caged animal, then ducked inside the grocer's door before coming back out. His skittishness did not fit the ease he had displayed just moments before.

I grasped his arm and pulled him to me. "What's got you so jumpy?"

He shook his head. "Just happy to see you. That's all." He pulled away and looked over his shoulder again.

I nodded. "Let's move on. Mrs. Mellet was direct about us arriving before her nap. Not to mention Des Moines has changed. It looks to be bursting at the seams with rabble-rousers."

Tommy flashed a lightning-bright grin, taking me aback. His sudden ease was a bright spot—but another way I no longer knew him.

He picked up the suitcase. "It's full of 'em, Mama, chock-full of scalawags. Let's move along before we're knocked off-kilter all over again."

I nodded and stared at the backs of my children as they headed forward. I was unable to believe what I was seeing with my Tommy, my once-moody son now full of charm. That smile that covered his unease in a blink.

Tommy stopped and turned. "Let's not miss the trolley. We'll get tickets and then I'll stop in the post office to check on mail from Katherine."

I nodded, struck by his take-charge attitude, which reminded me of James. A stiff wind pushed at my back, prodding me along as though the universe knew I needed a little nudge into this new phase of life with children who were mine but whom I did not know anymore.

**

Nearly at the trolley stop, Yale was back on my hip, head buried in my neck, when a strong wind swept over us. I looked to the sky. "This makes me think of James."

"The weather? The wind?" Tommy asked.

"Yes. James." I couldn't remember the last time I'd said his name aloud.

Tommy took my hand and squeezed it. "Me, too, Mama. When I sleep outside and the night closes in and all I have to do is stare at the stars, or try to see them through the clouds, all I can do is remember James, the way he was, the way he still seems to be around, even though…"

"Shh, shh. I know exactly what you mean."

Tommy exhaled a breath and grinned. "My goal is to be much more like James, Mama. I've been working that out, being industrious and ambitious, and, well, you can be proud of me, Mama."

"I am proud of you, Tommy."

Tommy cocked his head; a flash of ire lit in his eyes. "No, Mama. I want you to be proud like you always were of my brother, not just relatively proud based on how you saw me before. I can do it."

I shook my head. "It's not a matter of being proud, Tommy."

"I'm a man since you saw me last." The words tumbled from his lips as though being pumped like water. "Oh, and I forgot I picked up a newspaper for you early this morning. I know how much you like the dailies. I thought now that we're here, you can write again." He pulled a paper from his back pocket and presented it to me as if he were a waiter offering a tray of appetizers at one of the parties we used to throw.

My breath sucked out of my chest. "Tommy. Thank you." My eyes welled. I was touched that he had such faith in me, more so by the fact that he thought such a thing would be important to me. But I was not sure that staying in Des Moines after we got the money was the wise thing to do. I steadied myself, smoothing my hair away from my face. The movement deposited some of the cool mud I had missed in wiping off my hands onto my cheek. I wiped it away with the back of my hand.

It was then that I caught the distinct sensation of being watched. I looked to my side and saw a couple had stopped, but they were looking at a map, not at me.

"Well, well, well. What *do* we have here? Jeanie Arthur?"

An icy feminine voice blew over me from behind, sending chills up my spine and down my arms.

I knew that voice as though it were my own. Hearing it caused my innards to turn to custard, forced any confidence I'd regained recently to melt away like spring snow. I could run, but my worn, curled boots would only trip me up.

Tension hunched my shoulders nearly up to my ears. I hated that my posture, even from behind, would have betrayed my stress, my loss, my grief. I wasn't ready for this meeting, not yet. A stab of pride reared up inside me. I would not satisfy Elizabeth this way.

I pushed my shoulders down, ignored the odor of animal waste that wafted from my clothing and skin, smoothed the front of my skirt with one hand, and turned to face the woman I had hoped to never see again.

"Oh, my. It *is* you." Elizabeth Rowe tilted her head in just the right way to properly gaze down her nose at me, to attempt to carve away at my already vulnerable spine. We had perfected the expression as young girls when we thought being generous in thought and spirit was a sign of weakness, that arrogance was in kind with confidence.

Tommy was busy at the fruit stand, oddly interested in produce. He stood close enough to hear my conversation, but his posture told me he was not going to join me in greeting someone we'd once known well. I could not blame him.

I swallowed fear at being seen in such condition as I was. But then Millie's face, her easy grin and openhearted way, came to my mind. I now knew what was important in life, and I would not let Elizabeth attempt to shame me. "Elizabeth. It's been some time." I pushed my voice out strong and steady. Hearing it, I recalled who I used to be—that woman, the socialite writer, the Quintessential Housewife—it was still inside me somewhere. The part of me that wanted to run the other way and let Tommy bring all my baggage was fierce. But it was time for me to face my past.

I reached my muddied hand out to shake hers.

She bent forward, peering at my hands as though examining a cut of meat at the butcher. "No gloves? Or mud gloves, as it seems. The height of prairie fashion, I suppose?" Elizabeth swept her gloved hand over the back of mine.

"I'll be sure to check my attic," Elizabeth said. "I must have something from last year's fashions that you could use. I can't do enough for a dear old friend."

Elizabeth sighed as though frustrated with a child. "It is good to see you. It certainly is." She started past us, her gait happy with every springy step she took away from us. She looked over her shoulder and came back.

"Do let me know if you need something." Elizabeth lifted her skirts just enough for me to glimpse the hourglass heel on her perfect silk shoes.

I met her mocking grin, waiting for whatever it was she needed to say before heading on. Her gloved hand flashed over the ocean-blue brocade jacket that nipped her waist in the most fashionable way.

Shoes were nothing, clothes frivolity. I drew myself up. I carried my riches in my mind. "We don't need a thing." I wiped away a bit of eye crust from Yale's face, hoping Elizabeth would move along and end the interaction.

Elizabeth's silence forced my gaze from Yale. I watched as Elizabeth plucked at the buttons of her jacket collar, waving air toward her face in between each unbuttoning, pretending that a heat wave had settled on the April chill. The sound of each ivory button forced through its rigid hole let me know the garment was brand-new that season. That sound! I hadn't heard it in years. It still delivered a thrill.

Two buttons down and I saw the real reason she was unbuttoning. The unmistakable flash of blue stones, winking, teasing me. The sapphire necklace. The one I'd been forced to hand over as part of my family's repayment to the people my father and Frank had swindled. She had promised to keep my things safe…by wearing them, I supposed. With the glint of those gems, I was sent back in time with all the humiliation and shame that came from our friends and acquaintances taking our things, turning their backs, shunning us. Every inch of my worn dress was heavy on my bones.

My throat closed. My hand shot to it as it used to clasp around my pearls. Of course, the jewels long gone, the empty gesture caused me to slump a bit. Sudden grief and embarrassment startled me.

"Well." Elizabeth stepped up to me and wiggled her forefinger at my face. I flinched away.

Elizabeth grinned. "Just some mud there on your cheek."

I brushed my cheek where she was pointing, feeling the cool slickness as I removed it. I hid the embarrassment that rose up in me. I still had pride, even if mud-splattered and bruised.

Elizabeth shrugged and sighed. "Well, I've a meeting at the *Register* this morning. I'm nearly late with all this chatter. I'm meeting my husband there."

Wondering what business she could possibly have at the *Register*, my old newspaper, but not wanting to inquire, I sighed. "Well, tell Alfred I said hello."

"Oh no." Elizabeth looked to the ground and put a sad face on. "He passed. Shortly after you moved." Then, as though she'd rehearsed this before, she snapped her gaze to mine and smiled. "I've since married Judge Calder. He's adopted my children, and we've had another."

My stomach seized at hearing the name. Tommy's attention locked on Elizabeth and me. He stared at the back of Elizabeth as though her mention of her new husband brought up the same bad memories as it did for me. But I would have sworn in court that we had managed to keep the information related to Jeremy Calder's order to liquidate our entire life from the children. Fury swirled in my belly at the thought of what that man did, at how Elizabeth had treated us.

"I am late." Elizabeth *tsk*ed and rolled her eyes as though it were me who'd forced her to stop her day and take the time to demoralize another human being. Elizabeth turned, her shoulder nudging mine as she began to saunter by. At the last second, before she was completely past, I slid my foot out. Before I could even process it, let alone stop myself, I slipped—no *shoved*—my ugly, curled boot into evil Queen Elizabeth's path. Her shoe caught mine.

She stumbled. Her arms shot out to her sides as she circled them. It was as though the world had slowed on its axis as I turned to watch. Elizabeth twisted just enough to one side that her massive bustle took her completely off balance and face-first into the mud.

She pressed both hands into the mud and pushed upward, screeching for help.

I almost started walking again, but a giggle in my throat got the better of me. I wanted to enjoy another few minutes of this. I lifted my unfashionable, unbustled, raggedy skirt and bounded into the street, splashing her again. I circled my arms around her waist and heaved her up. When she got her feet under her, she turned. I wiped a clot of mud from her chin. "Oh, my, what a mess," I said. I felt glee in what I saw.

"Don't you smile at me, Jeanie Arthur." Elizabeth raised her hands and looked downward at her skirt.

I lifted my skirts again and reached toward Tommy, who was offering me his hand. He pulled, and I easily regained my footing on the sidewalk, above Elizabeth. Seeing her standing in the street, no passersby willing to hop into the muck to help her onto the mud-free planks, sent a surge of energy through me. I felt good. I shouldn't have, but I did. I could taste her disgust at being mud-covered and helpless, and it was delicious in my mouth.

I closed my eyes and took inventory of what I felt just then, seeing someone from my past after all these years, someone who had betrayed me. Was it worse than I'd imagined? With another gust of wind, humiliation passed over me, and then it was gone. I opened my eyes with a smile. I was alive. No, seeing Elizabeth was not worse than I'd imagined. I'd withstood infidelity, the death of my son, divorce, and separation from my living children, so seeing the woman who found glee in all I'd lost was nothing. Nothing at all.

The sapphire necklace was worth no more than a pen-and-ink drawing of it to me. My children were my jewels, and our determination to rebuild was the golden filigree that would hold us all together.

I finally offered my hand to Elizabeth. She accepted it and I pulled her up on the sidewalk. She wiped at her skirts, straightened her crooked bustle, and ripped off her mud-caked gloves. "You did that on purpose."

"I did not. I'm sorry you fell, though. I am." *What else could I say?*

"You're mean, Jeanie Arthur. You always have been."

I almost agreed. There were times in my life I had been vacuous and awful. This was not one of them. I would not yield on this matter. This did not come close to what Elizabeth had done to me four years back. "Good to see you, Elizabeth." I wiggled my fingers at her.

She glanced over her shoulder and shook her head. "Where is my girl? Jessica?" She screamed at no one, but her voice lured a young girl with arms full of fruit to her.

"Look at me. Where were you?" Elizabeth stomped her foot.

"You told me to purchase some apples for—"

"Shut up! Let's go." Elizabeth stormed away and the girl tossed the fruit back into a bin and followed quickly, glancing at Jeanie, confused.

I pulled up my skirt enough to see the curled tip of my weathered black clodhopper. For once, the ugly thing had come in handy. For once, I fully felt my presence in them— and it was fine. I was the woman who wore such shoes, and I could be proud that I survived. Somehow I had, and that was something to behold.

**

Mud-caked and tired, we finally reached Mrs. Mellet's home. Tommy stood behind me, quiet. I glanced over my shoulder. He was smiling. He stood with Yale in his arms, far enough from the house to appear respectable and well-behaved but not close enough that when Mrs. Mellet opened the door, she would engage him in small talk. I felt good that this much of my family had been reunited. Now we just needed to reclaim what was ours and get Katherine back, too.

This quick visit would not be about old times or new friendships. I would get my money and settle into a clean boardinghouse until we located Katherine. Then we would make a sensible plan. We would be free to go anywhere, to do anything. But I was getting ahead of myself. I was owed a significant sum of money. It would not be nearly what I had lost when we lost it all, but Mrs. Mellet said it would be a fine amount.

I kicked the riser of the first stair to dislodge the mud caked to the bottom of my boot. I drew a deep breath as I stood in front of the house. Remembering their grand New Year's parties and large summer picnics, my eyes traced the peaks and slopes of the stately, wood-sided home, falling over the intricate moldings that highlighted the home in a way that made me linger, remembering the grand house we once owned.

My attention slipped and slid over each angle, waiting for the next visual surprise. No matter how slim or short, each carving was carefully painted in one of several different hues—greens, blues, and creams.

A final glance at my demure children and I was sure Tommy understood how important this meeting was. They had been told so little about the scandal that sent us running to the prairie years back. I knew a time would come when they would ask questions about their grandfather's part in the loss, as well as their father's.

When we were still firmly entrenched in Des Moines society, Mrs. Mellet had been a coarse, overbearing woman, a woman to avoid whenever possible. She had a quick eye for noting juvenile misbehavior and a lightning-fast hand to match. She had been a wealthy woman who showed up every time my family invested, wanting a piece of whatever deals Frank and my father were working. And then, when it fell apart, she could not have been harsher. When I received her apology, I had been stunned. It was full of claims of yearning to set things right.

I'd thought it was a ruse or a joke. But a telegram sent and received and I was assured that Mrs. Mellet had turned some sort of moral corner in her life and was prepared to give me enough money back to make a difference in how we had been forced to live our lives recently.

I stepped onto the first stair and looked over my shoulder at Tommy. "I'll just be a few moments, and we'll be on our way. If she comes out and asks you questions, please employ your manners."

Tommy nodded and grinned. "'Course we will."

I drew a deep breath. *Don't fret.* I was there to accept an apology, not vice versa. This was the first time in ages that someone would make amends to me; this was something that should carry with it glee, not the angst and fear I could not seem to shake out of my body.

I climbed the stairs, pausing on each, swallowing the bile that rose into my mouth. Even though it was Mrs. Mellet who had contacted me, full of good news of her own redemption, I still couldn't settle my searing nerves. I thought I'd been prepared. I'd rehearsed all manner of conversations we'd have.

At the door, I looked over my shoulder at the children again. My mind flashed back to a family photograph we'd had made shortly before the scandal broke in 1887. I squeezed my eyes closed and opened them, swearing I'd seen James standing beside Tommy just then, just a hint of him, of what I imagined he would look like if he were still alive. Katherine was in my mind's eye, too.

There was no time to entertain my ghosts, no matter how precious they were. I lifted my hand and rapped good and hard.

The door swung open. Standing there was a woman I recognized, an acquaintance from before. I stepped back, surprised.

She squinted at me as though trying to place me in the large network of people she knew.

"Jeanie Arthur." I extended my hand toward her. "It's been a while."

Cora Hillis broke into a broad smile, her kind eyes lighting as she finally recognized me. "I knew it was you on sight, Jeanie. I was simply stunned to see you, is all." She took my muddy paw in a firm grip and pumped it with both of hers. I felt relief in her kind reception, as though I'd been waiting for someone to treat me like a person, like I still mattered.

"Come on in, Jeanie. I'm just picking up some donations from Mrs. Mellet. She's agreed to help me gather clothing and household items for the poorhouse and for Reverend Shaw. They have nothing over there, and the children are running the streets, and…well…I can't be idle in allowing good children to lead poor lives. There's just no excuse for society to allow…" Cora raised and lowered her shoulders before she stepped to the side and glanced at her hand. "Well. I'm running at the mouth when I should be asking about you. How are you, Jeanie?"

I could see the dirt I'd transferred from my hand to Cora's, and I waited for a scolding word or expression. But Cora didn't even wipe her hand on her skirt, didn't even pretend to need to wipe it on the apron that tightly wrapped her shape.

"Fine, Cora." I felt my throat go dry. I couldn't remember the last time someone asked me that and really wanted an answer. Her eyes dug deep into my gaze, her face soft with interest, and I couldn't speak. I didn't know what to say that was informative yet still appropriate. Launching into years of all I'd done to ruin our family, all that Frank did to help me ruin it, was not polite, yet it was all I could think about. It was as though I'd never made small talk with her or anyone at the club, anywhere.

She took my hand in hers again, making me suck back my breath.

"I'm sorry for your loss. All of them. Especially your amazing James."

I nodded without forming words. I wondered if she'd heard of the divorce. She appeared much too at ease with me to know that my marriage had ended in that way.

I searched my memory for interactions I'd had with Cora. Looking back, they weren't flattering to me. I'd been rude to Cora time and time again, or at least aloof to her, if nothing else. Now, thinking back, recalling all she'd undertaken on behalf of others, things I'd discounted as a waste of time, she seemed godly to me. She was wealthy, the wife of a lawyer who came from decent money but who had always been interested in lifting up those who had less than she did.

She had taken in her ill sister and spent her time tending to those who needed it. I noted Cora's fine silk dress. She was indeed generous and smart, but that didn't stop her from enjoying a fine dress, I suddenly recalled. This woman should have been someone I had adored all those years, not ignored for the likes of Elizabeth Calder.

I may have lost nearly everything that mattered to me over the years, but I'd learned that personhood was far more than what someone wore or the china they served their food upon. Elizabeth had been as shallow as a mud puddle, and Cora was deep and still and precious like a fine, still lake.

Cora patted my hand and let it go. "Is that Tommy?" Cora rose to her tiptoes and looked over my head, waving at the children. "I thought that was him. I could swear I saw him the other day—at the river."

At the river.

"Oh, maybe it wasn't him. Boys at that age have a way of all looking alike, don't they?"

I nodded.

"But," Cora shook her fist, "we have to do something about this river and the children swimming in it! In this day and age, there should be a pool. It's ridiculous that children are swimming in this dangerous river. You could help me, Jeanie. You're powerful with your words. I could really use someone like you to help me assist the downtrodden. It is not a one-woman show."

I felt bowled over by her compliments, the emphatic, casual way she passed them off to me. It was as though I were going from being buried, hidden under someone's boot, to suddenly being seen, pulled up off the muddy street as Tommy had done just that day.

"I mean it," Cora said. "Let's do something about it. Sitting around discussing art at the Women's Club is a fine thing if you have safe places for children to swim, but we could really make a difference in society if we built a pool, if we helped mothers who needed it."

I drew back from Cora's fervor, but then was energized by it. Would it be possible that she might really invite me to work with her? Could it be that this woman I'd never really thought of at all had opportunities for me? Could I even do it if I wanted to? Would the women at the club allow it— women with far more in common with Elizabeth Calder than with Cora?

"Cora—"

Yale let out a bellow, drawing Cora's and my attention behind me.

I whipped around and held up my hand to stop the children from coming closer. I needed to handle this matter without any interruptions.

Tommy swung Yale onto his shoulders. I gasped, afraid such an act would frighten my delicate girl.

"*Was* that Tommy at the river?" Cora asked again, standing on her tiptoes, lifting her hand to wave at him, but he was headed in the opposite direction.

"Tommy's been boarding with a Mr. Babcock, who owned a farm just a few miles away, while waiting to meet up with us. We've just… Well, I don't want to bore you. You have important work to do."

Cora narrowed her eyes and shook her head as she began to speak. She stopped herself before getting anything coherent out, appearing confused. "Well, of course, Tommy was boarding at the farm, waiting for you. That explains it."

I was about to ask her what she meant, what exactly was explained, when Mrs. Mellet stepped into the hall behind Cora.

"Why," Mrs. Mellet said, "you've arrived." The woman clamped her hand around the top of a cane that shook under her weight. She released her knotted fingers for a moment to reveal a carving of a rose inside her grip. I stepped forward to support her. The woman jabbed her cane at the floor. "No. I need to do for myself. That's what they tell me, anyway."

I nodded. This woman, this once-hardy, mountainous being, now shrunken and stooped, her face softened, folds of skin like scalloped drapes, had aged decades in just the last few years. Even her eyes were softer, as though someone had chipped away all the hardness, sculpting a completely different person. I immediately lost all doubt that the woman who wrote to me was this woman, the person who could and would restore our lives.

Cora smiled at the old woman. "I have all that I need for now, Mrs. Mellet. Thanks so much for helping those who are suffering. It will make a significant difference, I believe. This came at just the right time. Reverend Shaw is mighty grateful."

Mrs. Mellet pointed her cane at Cora. "You just get that Women's Club to do more than hang artwork all over town. We need someone worried about the poor and weak. Well, I don't have to tell you."

Cora nodded and ran to Mrs. Mellet, swallowing her in her arms, holding her so tightly, the old woman choked. I had never seen anyone treat Mrs. Mellet with such warmth. I became more convinced that something had certainly changed in Mrs. Mellet's life. "I'll send a wagon tomorrow for the other items. I'll let the reverend know you're in full tilt with the plan. He'll be thrilled."

Cora sighed and walked to me, taking me by the shoulders. "I'm so happy to see you, Jeanie. I'm sure I'll see your byline in no time flat now that you're back."

I began to protest but then stopped myself. Was it possible? I hadn't gone so far as to imagine myself writing for pay again. Perhaps with Mrs. Mellet speaking up for me, I could write again. Quintessential Housewife would no longer work as the title of my column, but certainly, I had more to say now than I ever had.

I reached out to shake Cora's hand. She yanked me into an embrace. I was self-conscious of my uncleanliness, but she did not seem put off. "Thank you, Cora." Those were the only words I could get out.

"So you *will* write?" Cora asked.

I nearly said no because I feared what might come from it, putting myself out there to be seen and heard. "I think I might. Well, if we're here, I suppose I will." For the first time in years, I thought it was quite possible.

Cora pulled away. "Well, good. Good. I will see you around." She bounded past me, down the porch steps, full of the vigor of a teenager. I adjusted my hat to shade my eyes as I watched her stop at the children, smiling, smoothing Yale's hair.

Tommy pulled his hat over his eyes and spent more attention on his feet than in greeting Mrs. Hillis. His big body had suddenly taken on a toddler-like shape, head bent, his big paw pressed to the top of his hat to keep it on, his posture more boy than man.

Maybe Tommy hadn't had a good experience with Cora back when we lived in Des Moines. More of my past opinions of Cora rushed back to mind—I'd thought she was serious and dry, worried about people who shouldn't be worried about. What a difference a few years made in one's perspective. I had been a shallow, awful person. I watched through the front door as Cora hopped into her carriage and signaled her horses to proceed.

"Well, come on." Mrs. Mellet swung her cane through the doorway that led into her library. "I'm glad you made it before my footbath and nap. Lots to discuss."

I was shutting the front door when I saw Tommy move away from Mrs. Hillis as she left. He romped around, Yale on his shoulders, whinnying like a horse. My breath caught when I heard Yale laugh, the sound rising on a gust of wind, shocking me. I couldn't remember ever hearing Yale squeal like that. I wanted to join them in their frolicking, to enjoy my family. Soon I would.

Mrs. Mellet had limped over behind me. "Those are my prized roses you just jumped into, Mr. Arthur!"

I drew deep breaths, measuring what I would say next. As a younger boy, Tommy had often been thoughtless in his conduct, apparently something he hadn't grown out of while boarding with other families.

Tommy removed his hat and held it to his belly. "Yes, ma'am."

Mrs. Mellet chuckled. "Reminds me of my son, Maxwell. Boys are all the same, I expect. Like God knew they would be too much trouble to make them all different. They're all trainable in the exact same way."

Disagreeing with that statement but not wanting to say so, I exhaled and saw that Tommy and Yale had disappeared behind the house.

I knew manners required that Mrs. Mellet take the lead in discussing finances, but since my son had been killed and my marriage destroyed, abiding niceties seemed like a luxury I no longer enjoyed. I knew it was hypocritical of me, but too bad, I thought.

I watched the shuffling woman. "I'm sorry about the bushes. He was just trying to entertain Yale so we can settle our accounts, and then we can get out of your hair."

Mrs. Mellet jerked her head to the side, indicating that I should follow her into the next room. As we crossed the threshold into the library, I scanned the soaring room, smiling at the feeling that I'd stepped back in time, stepped back into my own home. Three full walls of books, fifteen feet high, covered every bit of space but the two doorways. Images of my early life shot to mind. I'd passed countless hours each day reading and writing in a library much like this.

Mrs. Mellet nodded. "Yes, money and your family name. Much to discuss."

I grimaced at her flat tone and searched her face for lack of sincerity. Had it been a trick?

"I've contacted Mr. Halsey about loosening up the ties on my money, to give you what's yours."

"Yes, thank you. I'd appreciate that. The sooner we are steady on our feet, the better."

Mrs. Mellet hobbled to a bookshelf and brushed the spine of one tome with her crooked finger, giving me the impression she was holding back.

"Mrs. Mellet?"

She pulled another book from its slot and moved it two books down. "It's still going to take some time to raise the funds from selling property, and, well, I won't bore you with the details. More time than I thought when I wrote you."

My stomach contracted, releasing a flood of acid I'd come to feel as reliably as the day turned to night. I pressed my belly. "I trust we can settle all matters before long. Tomorrow, at the latest. You were very generous with the train fare, but I'm down to my last bit of money."

Mrs. Mellet shuffled to her Windsor chair and turned. A basin of water sat in front of her. Her eyes were rheumy but warm, obscuring her once sharp, stabbing glare. Her current amiable gaze seemed genuine as she grasped the chair arms and lowered herself into the seat. "I have what you need, so just settle in and stay here with me, and in due time I'll fix your problem as promised. It won't be long."

I balled my hands at my sides, but kept my voice cordial. "It's been long enough. I'm done with this phase of my life."

Tommy flew into the library, Yale whimpering in his arms. "She wants you, Mama."

He knelt down with Yale, and she plopped to her bottom and then struggled to her feet, toppling over several times until she was upright, clasping on to my leg. I bit my lip at the sight.

"Ahh, a little one." Mrs. Mellet perched a forearm on her knee and stared at Yale. "I do love little feet pattering around the house." Mrs. Mellet pointed her cane.

I picked up Yale and kissed her cheek. This little one didn't do much pattering around, but she was as sweet a child who ever lived. Tommy lifted his canteen toward me. Water dripped down its side, wetting the canvas that wrapped the metal.

I held Yale's hand, letting her wrap her little fingers around my thumb. "No, thank you, Tommy. Why don't you and Yale go see the gardens while I finish up with Mrs. Mellet? She has the most stunning gardens in the back, if I recall."

"Best in six counties." Mrs. Mellet stabbed her cane into the floor.

"Yes, ma'am." Tommy clutched his hat tight to his chest. "I'd love to accompany my sister on a promenade around the grounds."

Tommy's wording brought me a giggle, but I smothered it with my hand. I relaxed, relieved that Tommy was being so attentive to my wishes. He had changed so much.

Mrs. Mellet pointed her cane at one bookcase after another. "Bring back memories, young man? Jeanie? A library like this?"

We both nodded in agreement. The floor-to-ceiling warmth of leather-backed tomes full of the world's best ideas was something I missed—much more than silken, embroidered dresses and fine jewelry. "It does," I said. "You can't imagine what we've lost. But none of it compares to my son, James. His loss is…"

Tommy's face dropped. The pain he felt in his heart was showing in his eyes.

"We all feel James' absence." I squeezed Tommy's shoulder, wishing I could take his pain away as much as my own.

Tommy nodded. I handed Yale back to him, guiding them both from the room. "Just give me a few minutes with her," I said as I patted him on the shoulder. He nodded and left.

"I know of many of your losses," Mrs. Mellet said. "That's why I contacted you. Once I heard, once I fully understood, I couldn't allow myself to let things go with my hand in what resulted in your ruined name and dead son."

I moved back to where she was sitting.

Mrs. Mellet shifted in her seat. "I'm the only one in town who would take you in, you know. I'm sorry. Soon I'll have nothing to lose. Once I tell everyone my part in the failed investment, no one will have me in her home, either. I understand that. I'm ready. I know the years you've been away have been God-awful." The old woman's energy seemed to rise now that she was sitting, her voice as pointed as her stiffened posture.

My lips tightened as I fought to recall what I had rehearsed, but I couldn't remember; the rising gratitude mixed with ever-present sadness distracted me. I'd never felt such a rush of unexpected gratitude toward a person.

"Thank you. For realizing that." I was hopeful that the nightmare that had started in Des Moines four years back was about to end. It wouldn't bring James back, but restoring my accounts, my name—that felt like an enormous gift.

"Your divorce," Mrs. Mellet said, "makes reentry into society thorny even with my revelations." She shook her head. "But nothing is impossible. I've prayed that in giving you money that was yours, in speaking publicly about your innocence in your husband's stupidity and your father's crimes, I will make your life easier than it's been. I hope your children haven't turned delinquent, that—"

I stepped closer to Mrs. Mellet. "Katherine and Tommy are fine children."

"Where is Katherine—Tommy's twin, correct?"

I nodded. I wish I knew. "She had to conclude her business with the family she was helping. But she is exceptionally smart, hardworking. No matter what they've been through, they haven't soured; they're far from delinquent."

Mrs. Mellet reached for the footbath and batted at the water with one hand, clenching the armrest of the chair with the other, bending toward her foot and nearly tumbling from the chair. "Good as she may be, where *is* Katherine?" She steadied herself and glared at me.

Embarrassment burned my cheeks. How can a mother not know the answer to this question?

"You don't know." Mrs. Mellet drew figure-eights through the water, creating a wake.

"It's been a long few years but she's due here in just a day or so. But no. Right now, I'm not sure exactly where she is. She's on her way. That, I believe."

Mrs. Mellet shifted back in her seat and shook droplets from her fingertips. "Well, that's good news for all of you, isn't it?"

I smiled at her and squatted in front of the water, wanting to cut off this line of conversation. "Let me move it closer."

Mrs. Mellet straightened and looked away. I felt the old woman's discomfort at needing this type of assistance.

"God put our feet too far from our hands, didn't he?" Mrs. Mellet said.

I smiled. "I suppose He did."

Mrs. Mellet nodded and swallowed hard.

"Let me do this," I said.

The woman mouthed the word *yes*. I knew that sensation, the helplessness that was expressed in this woman's posture. I would act as though her inability to clean herself were nothing. It was all I had to give in return for our name. I lifted my weathered calico skirt and slipped to my knees. I grabbed the toe and heel of her shoe and wrenched the expensive form from Mrs. Mellet's foot. As I did so, her toes pushed through openings at the end of her stockings, her feet seeming to expand several sizes, showing me I was not the only woman who'd suffered bouts of shoe pride.

As Mrs. Mellet's gnarled feet were exposed, a sour smell rose upward. I put the back of my hand to my nose before I could stop myself.

"You're laughing at my feet?" Mrs. Mellet said.

I shook my head. "I was just recalling the day we first arrived on the prairie years back." I sat back on my knees and closed my eyes. "Oh my—I remember my dainty, silken shoes. They bloodied my feet inside of three hours on that hard land, they did."

I opened my eyes, but my mind was still back there, taken by the memory of the first time I laid eyes on Howard Templeton, his gentle hands on my bloodied feet, how mortified I was when he removed his shirt to rip it into bandages. He had been such a nice man at a time when Frank had been so awful. I still heard from him from time to time, but I knew my chance at love with him or anyone else was long gone.

Mrs. Mellet patted my head. I leaned into the comforting caress for a moment then I rolled up the woman's skirts to her knees, being careful to be discreet.

Mrs. Mellet moved her bottom to the edge of the chair. "I doctored my stockings. For easier work on my feet. Doc Allison said it might help if I do these daily footbaths and cut off the feet of my stockings for the time being."

I nodded. "Clever." I pushed the stockings up over the woman's knees and worked my cotton blouse sleeves up to my elbows. I lifted Mrs. Mellet's right foot into the bath and then her left. I shook the fragrance and the salts into the water and gently stirred the water with my hands.

Mrs. Mellet relaxed, settling back in the seat. "Isn't it something when a person finds herself in her own life yet completely unfamiliar with its terrain?"

I stopped mixing the salts and met Mrs. Mellet's gaze. I probably shouldn't say anything at all. I should just take Mrs. Mellet's comment as rhetorical, leave my nod as affirmation I understood.

"I'm familiar with being unfamiliar with my own existence. Yes. I know that condition," I said.

Mrs. Mellet's lips turned up, and her cheeks swallowed her close-set eyes with the smile. Her one eye went lazy, not tracking with her stronger one. Old Crooked Eye was what frightened or annoyed children called her.

"Why, yes, you would be familiar. That's why you've ended up where you are, Jeanie Arthur."

I reached for the cloth beside the bowl and pushed it into the water. I lifted one foot and began to work the cloth over Mrs. Mellet's skin, between her toes, never having imagined that I'd be intimate with the landscape of another woman's foot any more than I'd had to become friendly with my own life going off in all the wrong directions. For three years, I'd been a train without its track.

But honestly, I had to admit that even though Des Moines held so many bad memories for me, the fact that James hadn't died here meant I could pretend he would pop around a corner any second. For some reason, that illusion was comforting to me in a way I had not expected.

Mrs. Mellet slid back farther in her chair, relaxing her grip on its arms. "I'm making apologies all around, to you, to Cora Hillis—that's why she was here today. I plan to place an article in the *Register* about you, about the state of the poor and the orphans. Just as soon as I've finished the article, it will be published. If I could do my life over, I'd be more like Cora Hillis." Mrs. Mellet straightened, grasping at the arms on the chair, startling me from the footbath.

"I'd be more like you, Jeanie. Yes, a combination of you two, I think, would be lovely." She fell back into the seat again. "I just hope it's not too late to set things right. Forgive me, Jeanie Arthur. Please."

"Yes. I do."

Mrs. Mellet sighed and closed her eyes.

I rubbed and washed and cared for this woman who wanted nothing more than an opportunity for redemption. Her sincerity was weighty. I could feel it; I trusted it. And I could understand her needing to do this. I'd learned that from an old friend named Ruthie. Just one lesson she'd taught me. So if I could play a part in Mrs. Mellet's spiritual restoration, I would.

I thought again of Ruthie. Yes, I had learned the hard way what happened when one's heart was battened tight, unwilling to offer forgiveness. I wouldn't do that to another person as long as I lived. I was sure that it wasn't the person who needed the forgiving who suffered but the one who disallowed redemption who would be cursed to live her life mired in filthy regret. That, I would never do again. But there were limitations to what I would suffer at this point. I couldn't move on to another town without Katherine. But I would be sure to keep my reckoning in the forefront of Mrs. Mellet's mind. She brought me here for a reason, and I would need my accounts restored much sooner than later.

Chapter 25

Tommy

1891—Des Moines

Tommy was worried about his sister Katherine. He would not admit that to his mother, but he hoped she was all right. He hadn't thought anything of not receiving letters from her lately, not until his mother mentioned it. Seeing her face, the way it creased with worry, or fear shot through her eyes as though she was seeing something he could not, made him aware of how odd it was not to hear from Katherine.

Tommy was not thrilled about staying in Mrs. Mellet's attic, as they were supposed to do while they waited for the money, but having his family one step closer to being together was satisfying. And he liked seeing his mother smile when she saw him. He liked how he felt being back with her.

He'd borrowed Mrs. Mellet's buggy and gone to his camp to gather any of the items with value: his gun, the stove, and the supplies. He left the tent made of branches standing but took the canvas sheet. He went to the area of the creek where it met the river and saw that the meat was gone. He guessed Pearl had come back for it, or someone had stolen it.

It didn't matter now. His mother was to come into money from Mrs. Mellet, and soon he would be working at the Savery. As he stared at the rope with nothing on its end anymore, he apologized to the deer again, as if its soul was present, as if it had a soul at all.

Back from breaking down his camp, he stood in Mrs. Mellet's kitchen and drank down a glass of water in one gulp.

He wanted to please his mother. He wanted to tell her about his letters from his father, that the two of them were trying to gather enough money to pay Frank's debts and get him back to start again. He wanted them all together, and perhaps this was a good first step.

But for now, all he wanted was a few moments of peace down by the pond near Mrs. Mellet's woods, where he could fish and bring everyone dinner. He set the glass on the counter and turned, nearly barreling right over Mrs. Mellet. Old Crooked Eye was how he referred to her in his mind. She forced her lazy gaze on Tommy, poking at his chest with her bony finger, ordering him to milk the cows, weed the garden, feed the chickens, and do anything else she bade him to do. She seemed more harmless now that her age had taken her sting away. But that didn't mean he wasn't suspicious. Was it possible for a person to change so fully after living her entire life one particular, angry, mean way?

He hadn't meant to flinch away from the orders she'd given him. He was not afraid of working hard for money. But something about this arrangement bothered him. He didn't trust anyone with a promise that wasn't scratched out on paper. Old Crooked Eye caught him with her cane, pinning him against the kitchen cabinet.

"You're being good to your mother, aren't you?"

Her holding him against the wall called up the feelings of panic that came when he felt any sort of trap at all.

Mrs. Mellet backed away and rapped Tommy's leg gently with the cane. "Wake up, sonny. I have other help. But they're indisposed this week. So I got you until we wrap up this bank matter. And I think you're a nice boy, Tommy. I can see these things about people. Tough as you think you are, you're still a boy who needs his mother. Don't disappoint her. Show her you're a good son, not a lily-livered boy who's always in trouble."

She started to hobble from the kitchen, and Tommy went after her.

"What do you mean 'always in trouble'?"

She nearly fell as she left the kitchen, her cane flying down the hall. She gripped the table she was passing, nearly going down herself. He sighed, wanting nothing more than to run out the door and take to exploring the woods, but she had dropped her cane, and that was it. He picked up the cane and offered his arm, wanting to be sure she was steady.

They shuffled to the parlor.

"You're not a complete brute."

Tommy shrugged. Of course he wasn't.

"What did you mean by saying 'always in trouble?'"

"All boys are always in trouble. Don't be so quick to appear guilty."

He looked away. Could she know he'd spent time in jail, of all things? Of course not, but it felt as though she knew.

"Unless you *are* guilty of something."

"'Course not."

She smiled at him. He wasn't sure which eye he should turn his gaze to, but he settled on the one that appeared the strongest.

She smiled a lopsided smile. "You could have just handed me the cane, you know. I'm not a weakling."

"I know," he said. She was a mean old bird, but all Tommy needed was to catch the smallest glimpse of weakness in a person, a sliver of vulnerability, and he would find himself helping that person out. He hated himself for being such a sucker, but he couldn't change it. It was his burden. And he tucked away the thought that Mrs. Mellet was all there in the head and decided whatever babbling she had offered in regard to his mother's plans for the family was full of holes like a moth-eaten sweater might be.

"Your mother told you about the chores you'll do while you're here, right? The animals, the stalls, the stoves."

Tommy shook his head and started out the door, wondering whether performing these chores would ever result in her handing over what she'd promised his mother, envisioning his peaceful camp by the river.

**

Tommy was not looking forward to sleeping in the attic. He wanted to be excited about the prospect of living with his mother and sister, but he wasn't sure the attic quarters would be spacious enough to allow restful sleep for him. Until he'd known there was even a chance of seeing his mother and sisters so soon, he hadn't realized how much he'd missed them. Like the sore ribs that kept his attackers' fists from damaging his fleshy organs, he suspected he'd been granted a shell for his heart, his soul, his hope. With them beside him, the shell had softened, and he wanted Katherine with them more than ever.

He hoped Mrs. Mellet's attic was roomier and airier than he suspected and he wouldn't have to explain the unbidden, blind fear that struck him in confined spaces. He'd tried to stay with Yale and his mother in the boardinghouse room the night before, but even that was too confining. He hated that he couldn't control the blinding fear that took him when he felt trapped, even when he was not actually ensnared. Mr. Babcock had understood his plight. He'd allowed Tommy to stay in the barn. He made him a warm, comfortable area, telling him he'd shared Tommy's fear of small places, even bedrooms and closets in banks that were being held up.

Babcock had explained his similar experience during the War Between the States. Tommy had looked at him in awe, wondering how this man could know all he did about Tommy's inside fears and worries without Tommy breathing a word of them. Mr. Babcock said he'd known it the minute he saw Tommy blow out of that closet in the bank and save them all. He said only a man with a fear bigger than the fear of being shot during a robbery would do what Tommy had done. He didn't make him feel bad or small for such a thing. Instead, he allowed him space to start to feel something better: peace.

Tommy wasn't so sure his mother would see his irrational panic in the same way. He worried about embarrassing himself in front of her, of appearing like a small boy who needed protection rather than a man who could not offer his family what it needed.

Tommy set out to do Mrs. Mellet's chores. Barn duties were first on the list. It was a nice size, with a decent loft— something he'd become accustomed to assessing anytime he entered a barn. He fought off the kernel of worry pitting his belly like a grain of sand inside a shoe. He thought of his woods, the openness, the opportunities he found there. Scouting on the riverbanks or in a cave or a clearing surrounded by protective walnut trees, he'd find what others left behind. He always found a way to sell a lost hat, cast-aside saw, or a forgotten watch for profit in town.

But it was the creatures of the woods that he found comforting—the squirrels, the mice, the rabbits and fox and deer. He loved them all—they were his pets, his family when he had none. At times, he understood the idiocy of thinking that he meant something to wild animals, that somehow they understood him... well, he thought that when he was being childish.

There in the stinky barn, shoveling horse manure, he tried to make a game of it. He would see how large a load he could take, how far he could throw it and still get it on the pile, dashing back and forth to see how fast he could take five shovelfuls, hands in the air, finding himself champion of…well, victor of something.

He dreamed of the job waiting for him. It was about time for him to check back in on the start date to be a bellboy at the Savery. He'd get eight dollars and tips.

The position as bellboy would allow him to see the glamorous visitors to the city and would pay him wages enough to take care of his family and fund his father's trip back to them. He could not wait to surprise his mother with the news that they—all the Arthurs—would soon be together like they were before. He could not wait to see his mother's face when he surprised her with the news of his plan, when he offered her a big sack of money and the letters his father had written declaring his desire to reunite.

He stopped for a minute and put his hand in his front pocket, feeling his Indian Head. He tapped his back pocket— the place he kept the letters from his father. There had been only seven letters in the last year, but each was clearer: Frank wanted to come back and reclaim them as his. But his mother had arrived before he'd set things up. He was off-kilter a bit with her arrival, but mostly he knew it was good to be together. It would give him a chance to soften her toward his father.

His father had grieved James' death in a way his mother misunderstood. But three years had passed and Tommy was sure his mother could clear a corner of her heart and invite his father back in.

He sympathized with his mother's state of mind. But his father was drowning in the same grief, and she would see that if she just opened her eyes and really looked. He'd seen his father's head drooped, his shoulders slumped in sadness over their loss. He couldn't work; he couldn't move for the pain it caused. He remembered when his father had returned to the prairie to get them all and his mother had turned him away. Tommy could still see his father's broken posture, his gaunt face. And he could envision his mother's angry expression, hear her unforgiving words. She had held her grief tight against her, not allowing anyone to share it, to show their pain their way, and she had allowed it to change their circumstances, to change them all. But as Tommy had forgiven her over time, he knew she could forgive his father.

He thought of his father's words. It wasn't long before he'd met with bad luck in Texas—that's just the way things went for his old dad. After cotton had been such a stellar investment, after it had grown like weeds—beautiful, white, fluffy, moneymaking weeds—the weather turned and his cotton crop was a bust. In an instant, gone. He had written that he'd left Texas with some debt still attached to him and had gone east to find work to pay off his debt in Texas. Bad luck seemed to be his father's staunch companion the last few years, and Tommy thought he, now a man, was just the person to turn his father's luck around.

Tommy picked up a shovel and pushed the metal tool forward, grunting as he lifted it and carried it toward the growing pile of waste. He poked the barn door open with the shovel. He stood at the threshold, leaning his chin on the handle, thinking of all the things he'd rather do than shovel waste for free. He wanted to be good for his mother, to work hard for her. He knew he could not blame her for everything that had gone wrong in their lives. But there, shoveling horse-manure, breaking his back in the heat of the day, when it was only the first thing on a list of a dozen to do that day, he felt a quiet rage gurgle in his blood.

Anger always fed on his recollections of how everything had fallen apart. He hated that part of himself, the part that might turn toward unforgiving if he let it. So he chose to redirect his thoughts and repeat his list of things to do, his real list, not this one Old Crooked Eye had made up at the sight of him.

One: He'd make all the money he needed. Two: He'd bring his father back. Three: He'd make them all see that he was just as special as his brother had been. He was diamond and ruby and black pearl special, he was. He knew it deep in his soul, and soon everyone else would, too. James was hard to measure up to. He'd seemed to be there for their mother when she'd needed him to be.

Opposite of his brother, Tommy was often wayward. He'd find himself enjoying the prairie air, returning with water his mother requested and then becoming distracted by a quick game of tag with the Zurchenkos, forgetting his family's needs. And the times when he was there to help, like the day they'd left Des Moines, his mother downplayed, forgot, or never noticed his reliability in the first place.

That day, it had been Tommy who'd guided their mother out of their house. It had been Tommy who'd spirited the trunks away before the looters found them. But with the chaos, it was as though it never happened.

James had found joy in books and ideas that he could share with their mother, doing every blessed thing she needed when she needed it. Tommy had hated the way he became tongue-tied when trying to express his thoughts about something he read.

Now that James was dead and his absence had been carved in Tommy's heart, he felt ashamed for his competitiveness, his desire to be loved as much as him. That didn't stop Tommy from being thrust into an invisible competition still to that day. He held no ill will toward his brother for being seen as better. He just wanted his own chance to be seen as great, or to be good enough, at least that.

He couldn't wait to make his mother's eyes light up when he handed over a bunch of money to her. This would be the last attic for all of them.

Tommy wiped his brow with his hat and repositioned it on his sweaty scalp. He knew his mother would not approve of his plan—she would want him in school, not gallivanting around town scraping together money for her, for Frank. But he had a say in his future at this point. He saw himself as a man.

Tommy considered one moment in particular when he recognized he'd entered manhood. He didn't think of it often due to the way the memory wormed into his heart, making him clasp at his chest every time, as the pain it caused was exactly what he imagined a heart attack to feel like.

Once, at one of the first homes he'd boarded in, Tommy had been asked to run an errand for Edgar Nutt. At that time, Tommy, Katherine, and their mother were all still in Yankton, though each was living with a different family. His errand took him just past where his mother had been boarding. He'd snuck in the kitchen door and up the back staircase, hoping to surprise her by leaving some fresh-cut flowers for when she returned to sleep that night.

He'd crept upward, silent as a mouse, completely unnoticed. He had assumed his mother would be out doing her shopping chores for the family. He imagined her face when she finally went to bed and found his flowers and loving note.

As he reached the attic, he heard muffled crying. He stole closer, drawn to the sound, something about it familiar and sickening, though he knew it was impossible. They were not crying people.

He couldn't breathe as he worked his way down the hallway. He knew there were other maids and a laundress in the home. He should have turned and left whichever of them to her private cry. His mind went blank, unable to convince himself that he should be running the other way. Finding the source of the crying, he peeked into the doorway that led to a small bedroom. A candle lit the room, silhouetting a figure in the bed. A woman lay there curled into a ball as her baby nursed.

At first he'd thought he was wrong, that the frail woman could not have been his mother. He had started to back down the hallway when the woman said through her tears, "My sweet James. I've left you behind." He froze. It was her.

He wanted to comfort her. To tell her that even though James was gone, he was there, and he would do whatever he could to be the son that James had always been, her favorite.

We're not crying people. He looked around the corner again. Her body was so small; just a thin nightgown clung to the bones of the woman who used to be robust and sturdy as iron, this figure, this person with matted hair knotted around her scalp as though it hadn't been brushed in years. That crying. The recollection of it caused him to squeeze his eyes shut and cover his ears. "We're not crying people." His mother had said that a thousand times that year on the prairie.

And there she was crying—no, wailing like an animal dying in the forest. It was a sound that met his ears and swam through his body, weakening every inch of him. He knew his mother's will, her pride and strength, and seeing her this way filled him with fear he'd never felt before. Even with his father leaving, there was something about their mother's determination that had kept him strong, too. Now, seeing this, he knew she was bad off; she would not want to be seen like this by strangers. He silently begged her to stop, to find her mettle like she always did.

He found himself on his knees, his forehead against the wall, nauseous and frightened in a way that turned his skin winter-cold, raising goose bumps and slamming his lungs shut. He didn't know how he finally found the strength to move, but he knew he had to comfort her. Maybe that would help. He stood and eased around the corner of the room to find that she had fallen asleep. Yale had given over to satisfied sleep as well. Tommy shook his mother's shoulder, but she didn't wake.

He noticed a quilt had been balled at the end of the bed. He shook it out and then held it against himself, trying to warm it before he laid it over both of them. "Mama." He shook her shoulder again.

She did not stir. A lump formed in the back of his throat and he was overwhelmed at the sight of his mother so incredibly…not herself. He shook his head. He petted her hair and kissed her cheek, tucking the quilt tightly around her and Yale. He put the flowers on the small wooden box across from the bed. He reached into his coat pocket for the note he'd written, but it was gone. He looked around for something to write on but saw nothing.

This unsettled him further, struck with a deep fear, the kind that dizzies a person, blurring his vision. He'd learned to expect the unexpected in recent years, but he'd never have thought it was possible to find his mother so utterly broken.

He drew a deep breath. He understood then that it was he who must find a way to piece their family together. He needed to find his path in life and drag the rest of them with him. Something had shifted in the world, and the last remnant of the way things were before the family lost everything had just disintegrated, lifting into the air like brown fall leaves scattering in the wind.

He shuddered, wanting to climb under the covers with his mother and sister but knowing he could not. It was time for him to prove his worth to the world, to his mother. It was time to grow up. And in doing so, in seeing that his mother actually needed something, someone, he thought he would do his best to care for himself so she could get well, so she would not have to worry about him. He lay his head on his mother and squeezed her tight. *I will save us, Mama. I will find a way.*

Voices coming up the stairs had alerted him that he needed to leave. His mother did not stir as he rose and hid in a shadow, and when the laundress and a maid passed, he ran down the stairs, right into the cook. She batted his arm with her wooden spoon, and he ran out of the house and all the way to the general store, where he bought the nails and ordered the lumber for his boss' project.

It wasn't until late that night, when he was under the bedframe where the Nutt boys slept above him, shoved as close to the wall as possible, where the brothers couldn't squash him fully as they jumped on the mattress, that he let his mind process what he'd seen, more fully understand what it meant about his mother, his life.

With the brothers on the mattress, jumping and harassing him, he decided his mother would not rescue him. It fully settled onto him that she was not capable; she was worse off than he was. Right that moment, he had to begin to shape his life and find a way to take care of the family he loved.

He wracked his mind for ideas. He'd heard there was high-paying work in Des Moines—even coal mines were paying men's rates for boys who could pass as adults.

And he knew right then that was exactly what he was supposed to do. It was taking him much longer to achieve his goals, to be the man who could provide, but the goal was there; the will to succeed was wide and deep in the man he was becoming.

It took him a while to figure out his plan. He knew his weaknesses—that he wasn't book smart like James—but that didn't mean he was something to kick off the bottom of his mother's boot. Tommy knew his mother needed him. It was clear as the crystal that had once graced his Des Moines dinner table. And he would make her proud.

Tommy chortled at his current position. If only he could go back four years to when the Arthurs lived at 2050 Grand Avenue and they had a stable boy who chucked the animal excrement into giant piles. If only there had been another choice besides lighting out for the prairie to live like animals in a home cut out of the side of a hill. If only that, they might be doing just fine—the family still intact. No matter, he scolded himself. He was going to be her savior and his father's, too.

**

The sound of scratching on wood made Tommy turn. He scanned the space and saw nothing. He went back to shoveling but heard it again. He froze, listening. He heard it a third time, and the hair on Tommy's neck stood up sharply. He turned slowly, noiselessly, to see a skunk just two feet behind him, sitting on its haunches.

"Oh no," Tommy said, and began to slowly back up, smooth steps, soft as possible. He reached a hand out as though the skunk would understand he wasn't an enemy of any sort—heck, he couldn't even skin a deer he accidentally shot.

The skunk stretched, standing on its hind legs, and Tommy felt his breath return. It didn't appear rabid, but he certainly wasn't going to wait to find out. Tommy took another step back, and without any warning growls or stamping or any sign at all, the skunk spun around and lifted its tail. Tommy tried to run but tripped over his feet and fell backward, taking a good dose of spray over the front of him.

The stench filled his lungs, choking off his air. The pain in his eyes felt like sand grinding into the delicate tissue. He could not believe the discomfort. He crawled out of the barn, coughing, blind, trying to scream for help. Nothing came out. He was disoriented, forgetting exactly which direction to head in toward the house. He moved on all fours, heading for where he heard the horses congregating. The water trough. Tommy thought he would suffocate before he got there. It was as though someone had reached inside his body and gripped his lungs, preventing them from working at all.

Wheezing and having to force air in and out of his body, he looked through squinted eyes for the trough. He tossed some dirt as he moved forward, hoping to scare off the horses, worried one might accidently step on him as he scuttled up to the trough. He moved faster, gripping the trough with shaking fingers, pulling himself up, telling himself to ignore the pain, to splash the water over his face and remove the oily spray.

"Tommy!" He heard his mother's voice rising behind him. He could tell she was running. Old Crooked Eye's voice joined his mother's, telling her not to go near him, that the stink would transfer to her and be carried into the home. Tommy heard his mother's feet stop behind him. Was she going to listen to the old bat? He could hear her gasping for air. Tommy stopped throwing water on his face and waited, heaving, wondering if his mother would really abandon him just so Mrs. Mellet would not have to smell the very skunk that lived in her own barn.

"Mama?" Tommy was surprised at how childish his voice sounded to his ears.

Nothing.

"Mama?" Tommy spat into the trough, the spray working into the crevices of his tongue and throat, making him feel as though he were suffocating. He turned and tried to look at his mother through his blurred vision. Would she listen to that old crone? He could see his mother's shape but couldn't make out what she was doing. Before he could cry out for his mother again, she was beside him, bending him over the trough, splashing them both with water. Tommy bawled like a baby.

"Oh, my Tommy, my sweet boy." She rubbed a cloth over him, trying to remove the oily stench before it fully sank in. He felt at once the worst he ever had and at the same time never more loved. His mother had chosen him even at his filthy worst. She cradled and loved him as he never thought she would.

She shushed him and splashed water onto his face, patting him with another cloth, reminding him of when he was still a little boy. Once she'd washed him down as much as she could with plain water, she stopped and stood straight, taking him into her arms. Tommy collapsed into his mother's chest, though he knew he was polluting her clothing even more.

"I'm sorry, Mama," Tommy choked through his words. "I didn't tease it. I swear. It just sprayed without warning me at all. Normally, I have a way with animals." He sputtered and clung to his mother like a baby.

"Hush now, Tommy, my sweet. You're going to be fine. Just fine. Not a boy in the world who hasn't been sprayed by a skunk."

"But Mrs. Mellet?"

"No need to fret about her. You just do as I say, and you'll be fine. I promise."

Tommy nodded into his mother's shoulder, realizing he had to bend down in order for his mother to cradle him. His body had grown into manhood, but the rest of him, his insides… well, all that bawling taunted him with the idea that he was still part boy. And he was a boy who was glad his mother was there to take on his troubles for the first time that he could remember.

Chapter 26

Katherine

1891—Storm Lake

The Christoffs and Katherine had emerged from the cellar to find the home remarkably intact. They looked skyward, the Christoffs praising God they were alive. Katherine closed her eyes and inhaled the sweet, cleansed air. The land bore the scars that the air did not. There were ruts dug into the soil where the tornado had seemed to bounce along, setting down here and there on its way east. It uprooted trees and destroyed homes in a strange diagonal line, missing one home and ruining the next one.

The storm wore itself out somewhere well into Ohio, they eventually heard. Since the storm, Katherine had found the atmosphere at the Christoff home changed, as though the tornado had done its work inside as well.

Mrs. Christoff had put distance between the family and Katherine—something that was not unwelcome to her. Yet it put her on edge and made her want stability and to find her mother even more. A few nights after the storm, she walked into the keeping room that butted up against the kitchen and shared its fireplace to finish her work for the day.

She eyed the socks and stockings that hung by the fire but sauntered past them as though they weren't waiting for her to darn them. Before settling in to work, Katherine needed to revisit her sketches—if even for a moment. She wished to dive back into her drawing. Something about the fluid movement of her hand released the knotted worries in her mind and lightened the burden in her heavy heart. She dug behind the laundry tubs and pulled the mismatched patchwork satchel she'd sewn from discarded wools, knits, cottons, and even a canvas wagon cover from its resting place.

She pulled some of her papers from the satchel and honed in on one, turning it toward the firelight to examine the scene of a boy and a fallen deer. She'd made the drawing after the tornado. Her hand had flown over the paper, the elements of the scene rushing at her like the winds that had barreled past the house.

Before she even realized it, she'd sketched out a scene full of sadness. Just looking at it caused tears to well up, and she swallowed cries she could not explain. Mesmerized by the fact that she had created such a moving tableau, feeling that it was born of pure imagination yet profoundly familiar, she reminded herself that the confusion she felt could not stand in the way of her assignments. Not if she ever wanted to get back to her art.

Her fingers moved quickly, riffling through her collection of drawings. She gently stowed the sketch of the boy with the deer between two sheets of butcher paper, managing to discard the heavy mood it brought. She hoped to one day purchase paints that would allow her to fully capture the scene, trusting that somehow she could animate the boy, to more wholly tell his story, whatever that tale was.

Mrs. Christoff's feet tapped across the floor of the room above Katherine, reminding her that she wanted no reason for her keepers to become interested in the only thing that kept her sane and hopeful—her art. Since the storm, the elder Christoffs had kept their distance from Katherine, even keeping Hannah so busy, she was with them only at meals and when she fell exhausted into welcome sleep.

Katherine hugged her satchel to her stomach, not wanting to part with it just yet. She promised herself that someday she would work unfettered. One day, she would have a studio belted floor-to-ceiling with windows that opened like doors into a courtyard, with woods and a stream just a short walk back. She could envision herself in a linen apron splashed with every hue.

She would create her work in peace, the only interruptions gentle breezes calling her gaze outward. Knee-deep in the richest paints, with scores of the finest brushes in every size, Katherine would happily break to eat; her cook would bring her tea and apples and pears for snacks, joining her for light conversation. Then she'd take her luncheon in the dining room, her cook sitting with her long enough to enjoy a meal of chicken stew, fat, buttered biscuits, and the brightest forest-green beans.

Katherine heard Mrs. Christoff's footfalls escalate from tapping to stomping, and her voice cut into Katherine's daydream. As usual when Mrs. Christoff was angered, she screamed. Currently, she voiced her disappointment in the Murrays canceling on their plans to have dinner with the Christoffs.

Apparently, the fact that half of the Murrays' home had been torn away by the tornado did not provide enough of a reason to send word they would not keep their date. Mrs. Christoff suspected it was that the Murrays heard of their tax problems, not that they were patching their house back together. It hadn't occurred to Mrs. Christoff to pack up the dinner, take it to the Murrays, and stay to help *them*.

Katherine sighed. *Someday my life will be my own.* She placed the satchel back near the laundry soap, stacking boxes and bins and washtubs in a way that wouldn't draw attention to her cherished possessions.

As Mrs. Christoff stomped around in the room above, the sound of something crashing caused Katherine to startle. She stuck her head into the hallway and listened for descending footsteps. But the angry footfalls stayed upstairs. Down the hall near the front door, the plum-shaped ball that hung from the finial jumped and whirled at the bottom of the old chandelier, almost as though it, too, wanted to escape the tension created by the Christoffs. The crystal festoons shivered and the almond pendants jangled, just as Katherine's insides did every time Mrs. Christoff's anger rose up.

Katherine told herself to get back to her chores. She grabbed the darning egg, reminding herself to mend the yawning holes in a way that did not cause friction in the shoe. Standing in front of the fire, she fought the urge to pull out her charcoals and paper to capture the way the flames bobbed and weaved behind the laundry, making her mundane chore appear somehow beautiful.

She shook her head and snatched each sock and stocking from the roping, the warm woolens heating her arm as she laid each onto her skin. She set the kettle onto the grate and could already taste her evening tea, sweetened with the honey she and Hannah had harvested earlier that year. For most, laundry day was a prison sentence. For Katherine, it was her only opportunity of the week to find some peace, some solitude to go with the loneliness she carried even when in the company of the whole Christoff family.

The stone floor of the keeping room warmed her toes right through the pitted soles of her slippers. She marveled at the way the slate floors held the heat from the fire, which had remained lit all day for the laundry.

The laundry ritual made her think of her mother. Katherine hoped her mother's heart still held her love for her in the same way the fire stayed with the slate. She wondered if somewhere right at that exact moment, her mother was mending socks, with the water on for tea, anticipating her own store of honey that would be drizzled into hot amber liquid.

The week before, Katherine had been able to hang the laundry outside, where warm spring weather had settled. But in the days since the tornado had materialized like a ravenous, mythical monster, consuming everything in its path, the air had carried a nip that blunted the arrival of spring and the happy fever that often arrived with it.

With the stockings warm in her lap, Katherine selected one of Mr. Christoff's wool socks and shoved the darning egg into it. She drew the threaded needle from the pincushion and stitched the sock, the needle smoothly sliding in and out of the fabric.

A gust of wind banged a shutter against the siding, taking Katherine's mind back to the day of the storm. She winced, recalling the power of the tornado. She shivered as she remembered James appearing, demanding she run for shelter when there had been no sign to warrant seeking it.

She stopped sewing and gazed toward the window across from her. The night blackened the view, and the orange flames reflected in the glass. In the quiet of the keeping room, Katherine pictured the expressions of fear and confusion on Mrs. and Mr. Christoff's faces when the tornado passed.

Katherine had felt the very same things and was sure her face must have communicated it. Only Hannah was overtly relieved and thankful to be alive, a guttural laugh having gripped her once she realized she was not harmed in the least. Only Hannah had not seen what had developed before the storm and had sent them all running across the soil for the safety of the house, and she bore none of the confusion the rest did.

"Mr. Christoff needs those socks for work tomorrow." Mrs. Christoff's voice came from behind Katherine.

Katherine sat up straight and turned her body to see her keeper loitering in the doorway. The usual venom in her words was missing, but Katherine understood the order. "Yes, ma'am," Katherine said, fixing her gaze back on the sock, beginning her stitches again.

A shadow fell over Katherine, and she looked up at Mrs. Christoff, who had extended a book to Katherine. She took it from her and turned it over to see *Holy Bible* embossed in the black leather. They'd given Katherine a Bible when she arrived. Why another?

Mrs. Christoff patted it. "This one's been blessed by the reverend."

Katherine nodded, confused by the gesture. She took it from Mrs. Christoff and noticed newspaper clippings had been inserted in different sections. Mrs. Christoff dug her finger into the book where one particular clipping extended. She laid the open book on top of the stockings in Katherine's lap.

"Start with that one. The article and the verse."

Katherine narrowed her eyes on Mrs. Christoff. Was she inviting Katherine into a more familial role? Katherine was about to tell Mrs. Christoff she was still planning to find her mother and return to her family, not become part of theirs, when she realized that was not what Mrs. Christoff would have been offering.

The woman nodded and backed out of the room, keeping her eyes on Katherine. Once in the doorway, she gripped the moldings on either side of her. "We'll be having the minister and the Murrays to our home night after next. Now that the minister will come, so will the Murrays."

Katherine nodded, more confused by the moment.

"So read. Study."

Katherine looked at the Bible and set the sock she had been stitching on the table beside the rocking chair. She noticed that Mrs. Christoff had used a pencil to draw an arrow to Revelation 21:8. "But as for the cowardly, the faithless, the detestable, as for murderers, the sexually immoral, sorcerers, idolaters, and all liars, their portion will be in the lake that burns with fire and sulfur, which is the second death."

Katherine looked over her shoulder, back to where Mrs. Christoff had been standing in the doorway. She was gone. Her footfalls quick, her feet pounded up the front stairs. Katherine could hear the chandelier rattle again, as if announcing her departure. Katherine felt cold and moved her rocker closer to the fireplace.

She reread the Bible verse, then stared into the fire. The Christoffs had been stern with their Bible readings, using them as harshly as their own words and the punishing hands they used to keep order in their lives. But this was different. All of these topics had been lectured on over the course of the time she'd spent with the Christoffs. She couldn't put her finger on what was happening that was eerily different from before.

She remembered her instructions to read the newspaper article that had been used as a bookmark as well. She lifted it up and read the headline.

Fortune-Teller Heads for the Hills

Katherine squinted at the article. She wondered if she'd misunderstood Mrs. Christoff. Perhaps she'd simply used the scraps of paper as bookmarks. She knew Mrs. Christoff would quiz her on her assigned readings, so she put her finger on the first line of text and began to read.

Myra Tannenbaum bilked her last customer, escaping to the west after committing a fraud. She invited Mr. and Mrs. Jack Bumstead to her home and accepted their money, telling them their futures using cards, a smooth crystal orb that rested on a black stand, and even their own palms. While Judge McCaffery pronounced her customers nearly as much to blame as she was, he sentenced her to a two-week stint in jail. But Ms. Tannenbaum used her significant confidence skills to convince her jailers to allow her to gather tea leaves to tell their futures. Excited at the prospect of winning lottery numbers, the two deputies didn't notice she was more interested in leaving than in tea leaves. Mr. Bumstead was irate when he heard of her escape. "That woman told me we had three days left before rain would come. I put aside my planting because she said she knew there was no weather on the way. That very day, the tornado laid its lashing tail over my house, my fields, and I knew she was a shyster of the very worst kind." The crowd gathered around Mr. Bumstead, shaking fists, yelling all manner of discontent at services they had paid for without receiving anything of

> value in return. The mayor
> declined to comment on his
> deputies consenting to have
> their fortunes told, to having
> lost their prisoner. While many
> citizens feel as though they
> have been taken for fools, the
> leading and righteous citizens
> feel no sense of swindle, as
> Mrs. Jackson declared: "Those of
> us find our life instructions in
> the Holy Book, not in the parlor
> games of wanton women. We,
> therefore, are safe in the word
> of our Lord, Jesus Christ."

Katherine's hands quivered as her eyes fixed on specific words in the article—*fraud, fists, wanton woman, fortune.* She rubbed her eyes and reread the Bible verse, this time the word *sorcerer* riveting her eyes. She looked back to the empty doorway. It was impossible. She paged through the Bible, flipping to the other verses that had been marked. Deuteronomy 18:10–13, "Anyone who practices divination or tells fortunes or interprets omens, or a sorcerer or a charmer or a medium or a necromancer or one who inquires of the dead, for whoever does these things is an abomination to the Lord." *Sorcerer. Tells fortunes.* She looked back at the newspaper article and scanned it. She didn't have to go farther than the headline to have it all click in her mind, heavy as a wet wool bedcover. Was it possible they thought she was a con—or worse, some sort of witch?

Katherine went back over the events that led up to the tornado. It was true something had made her leave—*no! Stop it*, she told herself. James had told her. She held her breath. Was it true? Was her dead brother really sending her messages? She thought of the mother and baby who had appeared to her in the kitchen the night she was sneaking food. She looked back at Deuteronomy. "One who inquires of the dead, necromancer…" She was not sure what that even was, but the word sat ugly on her tongue, turning her mouth sour. "For whoever does these things is an abomination to the Lord."

She did not inquire of the dead. They inquired of her. She flipped back to the first article. Were the Christoffs warning her? Were they going to turn her in to the authorities? Katherine's eyes burned. *Mama, please bring me home,* she prayed but then stopped herself. *Abomination.* Was it possible she, her very life, was an affront to God? She closed her eyes and drew a deep breath, waiting for the calm. But then she realized what it was she was doing: inquiring of the dead.

She shot up to standing, causing the stockings and the Bible in her lap to crash to the floor. Before she could bend to gather them up, the kettle began to scream. She dashed to the fire and pulled it from the grate without grabbing a potholder. The copper handle burned her palm. She dropped the kettle and screamed. She fell to her knees and cradled her burned hand.

It was reddened, but no sign of blisters appeared. She blew on her skin, studying the way the outline of the handle was inlaid into her skin, the paisley design embedded there.

"You read palms, too."

Katherine jumped and fell on her bottom. Mr. Christoff walked into the keeping room and squatted down in front of Katherine.

She smoothed her dress over her legs, pulling her knees in to her chest. "I burned my hand. I wasn't reading it."

Katherine's gaze went to the Bible, which had splayed open when it fell to the floor near the rocker.

"My wife wants you to read the full complement of the noted passages."

Katherine shimmied her bottom backward.

"You follow her orders or she'll have you sent to jail."

Katherine got to her knees, still cradling her arm against her belly. After reading the verses and just one article, she knew what he meant. She finally understood why they'd all kept such a wide berth of her since the tornado. "I didn't do anything."

He scrutinized her, his brow furrowed. Katherine tried to slow her breath, to stop her shoulders from heaving. He cocked his head as though he were discerning whether she was a human or a fish.

"You knew that storm was coming. No warning for anyone. Sky ripped open and that funnel dropped down like a ton of lead."

Katherine thought back to the odd sensations she'd felt in the field, to James—seeing him there, feeling him right at her shoulder. Still, she knew enough not to believe it was anything more than a child's way of comforting herself. She should not be blamed for something she did not do, for something she did not understand herself.

She wrapped her arms around her legs, wanting him to leave the room. Her loneliness, her desperation at being abandoned gripped her throat. She did not understand what she did or did not do. Something told her she was not safe. James, probably. But she understood that sounded insane. She knew what they did to lunatic women. She smoothed the wool skirt over her knees and straightened her back. "I saw the black clouds. Right before you."

He grimaced. "I didn't see a thing. Not until we'd already run three hundred yards toward the house."

"You simply weren't looking in the—"

He grabbed her arm. "No. You knew that storm was coming as though God himself whispered in your ear."

Katherine almost corrected him and said her brother was an angel, not God.

"Devil's got your tongue all tied up. You're mute and holding secrets."

"You're hurting me."

He smiled and released his grip as though her arm were as hot as the kettle handle that had scorched her skin earlier.

"Look at that finger. That's the mark of the devil, isn't it?"

Katherine rubbed her smarting arm and looked at her finger. "It came from frostbite. That's all. I wasn't born with it like this."

He stood and loomed over her. "Mark of Satan, either way." His body was threatening, but Katherine lifted her gaze and snuck a look at his face. And there she saw fear. "You read that Bible." He swatted his hand through the air. Katherine knew he followed the teachings of the Bible only when convenient or in the company of his wife. And she knew that no matter what the truth was about how she'd come to understand they had been in danger that day in the field, the truth even she herself did not fully trust, it was clear something had happened.

"Mrs. Christoff has required my presence upstairs. But be assured. I have ways of ridding my home of evil." He looked her up and down again. Katherine had wished his fear might keep him from touching her ever again. He was certainly reticent to approach her in the way he used to, but she imagined that would only last so long. It wasn't as though she was evil, as though she were performing witchcraft. He would come for her again, she was sure.

He rubbed the inside of his thigh and a slow smile worked over his face. "You are evil. I'm not sure if I agree with my wife about what that means, but for now, I will abide her tight rein. Neither of us wants her to react out of fear. Not in regard to either one of us."

Katherine did not know exactly what he meant by that, but it was obvious that the Christoffs had discussed the matter fully.

As he turned and went into the hall, Katherine stood, unable to move, shocked that Mr. Christoff could be frightened off as he'd been, that he could be discouraged to approach her by his belief that Katherine may be evil or fear of his wife. Her mind turned to where it did when she was scared, to James, to that place where she found peace. But something stopped her again. What if the devil were attached to her somehow, creating in her the very same abomination that was written into the Bible?

What if it wasn't James protecting her, but the devil luring her in the way the articles said Miss Tannenbaum lured her marks? And that one thought erased all the comfort that her calming used to bring.

That one thought made her ignore the sensation of James' presence, to turn away from his form when he appeared by the fire. She loved God, but she could not accept that James was sent from the devil, that he was anything other than her loving, protective brother. Still, her own fear had settled in and she was no longer sure how to find her way.

Chapter 27

Jeanie

1891—Des Moines

I drew a deep breath. The distinct scent of mold in Mrs. Mellet's attic was oppressive. I hadn't noticed it earlier, but now that we'd settled into it, it seemed to rise up, entering the room like a person carried the bouquet of the outdoors when coming in on a crisp fall day. Worried about Katherine, I needed to keep busy. I pulled the bed away from the wall and took my vinegar-laden rag to the wood.

Ever since the year in the dugout in Dakota, well, the smell of earth inside a home had been too much for me to take. On those days when I did nothing but sleep and nurse Yale, I would manage to scrub away any sign of filth I could locate. But that was it—that was all I managed, feeling crazed, knowing that was how I appeared.

That day in the attic, worried about Katherine but trusting in the God who'd saved my life on the train trestle, I told myself Katherine would be with us soon. I could not bear any other possibility. Tommy reassured me that he would check for letters and telegrams at the post office every day.

I thought of the delay in getting the money Mrs. Mellet had promised. I felt she was sincere, but I'd misjudged people before. Still, what choice did I have but to believe she would deliver as she had vowed? I pushed the white muslin curtain aside on one dormer and looked at the barn.

After Tommy had been punished by the skunk, Mrs. Mellet demanded he sleep in the barn. It broke me to think that the second night we had the chance to be under the same roof, Tommy would have to be put aside, that he would have to sleep like an animal in the barn. But I did not want to alienate Mrs. Mellet and take the chance she would pull back on her promise.

Before I could even break the news to Tommy, he suggested the barn as the place he would sleep. It was as though he was relieved to not have to stay in the attic with us. That hurt, sending a wave of disappointment through me, but then I reminded myself it would take time for us to come together as though we'd never been parted.

On all fours, I worked my way around the attic room, searching for moisture at the baseboards and around the window frames, scouring, pulling up green pollen that had probably been there for weeks. The steady motion soothed as I decided I would give Tommy a haircut the next day and would also shave his thin beard. Mrs. Mellet said he could bathe, and she would give him clothes that her son, Maxwell, had outgrown. All of that should help cut the choking fetor of the oily skunk discharge.

I hauled a bucket of vinegar water across the room to scrub the windows and woodwork. Yale lay on the bed, her knees up, hands busy with a wooden spoon that she seemed to be using as a dolly.

She did not speak a word aloud, but her lips moved as though she was conversing for the doll and herself, moving the spoon in a way that mimicked walking. I rubbed the baseboard, turning the blackish mold gray, then yellow, and then gone.

I thought of the friends we'd made on the prairie. Howard Templeton and Greta Zurchenko were two whom I'd kept tight in my heart over the past three years. Howard was a kind man who had befriended James, treated him like a son. When the image of his kind face passed through my mind, it would cause my stomach to seize. But not in the pained way it did when I was troubled.

On the prairie, he had been every single blessed thing Frank was not. Howard was optimistic, like I had been. He had hauled a piano from back east and had insisted on building a plank home in a land where if the fire and snow didn't take your life, crop, and sanity, the grasshoppers did. That was the beginning and end of his impracticality. He was steady and wise and always there, offering a hand to whichever neighbor needed it. Oh—the conversations we had, the friendship that bridged our souls.

Beyond that friendship was the way that every time Frank disappeared or was swallowed into the scorched earth of the inner sadness of his black soul, Howard would pop up to fill in for my wayward husband.

Frank broke promises as easily as we snapped summer tinder. The crack of his fragmented vows echoed in my memories of that year as he turned away from duty to anyone who needed him. Sometimes Frank would even "get lost" on the way to the Zurchenkos to help tend their fields. Howard was always there when expected.

Or Frank would take sick with a fever I could find no evidence of beyond his being rolled into a ball on the bedstead, arms up over his head, sweating—but only because he forced the heat with blankets and maybe fear someone might drag him from his nest and require him to behave as an adult. Somehow, even with his own claim to tend, generous Howard Templeton could be called on to swing by and do what Frank had not managed on a given day.

There were times Frank found his vigor and would disappear for far too long at the Moore sisters' home, helping them do something they should have done themselves—if helping meant making love to Ruthie Moore, the woman I'd made my trusted friend. Frank found comfort in a warm bed with another woman. He left his children and me to cultivate our home as though I had no husband at all. It was at those times too, Howard would arrive to fix a broken wagon wheel or fetch extra water with the children.

And there had been the bathtub that Howard had hauled all the way from Yankton. My, my... The one and only bath I'd taken that year in a tub... I had luxuriated for those few moments. It was heaven right inside my grotesque, awful, earthy hut. I knew no one was perfect, not even Howard Templeton, but he had certainly been dependable in a way my own husband had not. That mattered. That stuck with me like sweet, restorative honey.

I shivered and stopped scrubbing, sitting back on my knees, peeking over the windowsill, watching one dark cloud hang over the setting sun, causing orange to burst through one small spot, warming my face. I closed my eyes. Templeton had been a match for James as well, teaching him how to read the indications of the weather, how to predict what types of clouds should send us running for cover before one drop of rain hit the dirt, sending pillows of dust into the air.

James had learned that the winds pressing down from the west were different from those swirling up from the south, and well, except for the blizzard that exploded with no hint it was coming and killed so many, James had learned just about everything a person needed to know about predictions, and much more than a person wanted to know. Perhaps if his father had been more interested in his children rather than in Ruthie Moore, our son would still be alive.

I grasped the windowsill and dropped my chin to my chest, pained, numbed, and weakened by the memory of my son's death. I shook my head like a dog shaking off water, trying to force away the thoughts of James. Now was not the time to let them sweep in and swallow me whole. I had three living children.

Would I ever have a day when I didn't expect to see James appear around a corner? Hear his laughter in a crowd? Probably not. But it was time to notice my own living children who appeared around corners, who still laughed aloud, who still had beating hearts.

I dropped back to my hands and knees and crept farther down the wall, scrubbing the baseboard with the rag, checking it for more mold. I did not have to bury myself with James. I could allow myself the chance to mother the others, to help them grow into productive adults. I could free myself from the clasp of pain I'd locked myself with while mourning.

Dust coated my tongue and I cleared my collapsing throat and told myself to continue to breathe, to continue to live, for Howard had proven what a fine man he was, and in doing so, he'd lifted the clamp that held my heart closed, and the feeling when I let myself experience it, well, that love was like nothing I'd ever had with Frank.

I scrubbed and looked at the cloth, moved farther along and scrubbed again, my knees aching on the unforgiving floor. *Katherine.* I needed her with me. I needed to know she was well and on her way.

Yale stretched and yawned. I stood, my knees aching as I did, hobbled to Yale, and rubbed her belly in a circle with the palm of my hand. "What do you say we move the bed over there by the window? Then we can see the barn."

Yale looked back at me, her gaze seeming to affirm my thought. And so I moved one end of the bed and then the other, making progress to where we could lie and take in the

view of the sky and the barn where Tommy would be
spending the night alone.

**

Out in the barn, Tommy tried to get comfortable on the
prickly hay. Mr. Babcock's loft had been made comfortable
for Tommy. He'd laid a featherbed down for him. It was
Tommy's job to air it out nearly each day to keep vermin from
joining in his slumber. But everything Mr. Babcock did let
Tommy know the man understood what he'd been through—
that although he'd had difficulty, he was a good young man.
Not some guttersnipe, someone who should be shoved under
a bed and tortured by the boys who slept in relative comfort
above him.

Though being sprayed by a skunk had been what
nightmares were made of, he was glad to sleep where he had
access to open air. He did feel a bit ostracized, even if it was a
good thing to sleep alone. This was the first time that his
sleeping outside meant he was not where he *should* be, with his
family so close.

He rolled the old coat Old Crooked Eye had sent out for
him to use under his head. He balled it up and punched it.

He flopped onto one side, head on his bent arm, hoping
the skunk incident wasn't a sign of his luck turning bad. He
knew bad luck led to misunderstandings, doubling up the
badness in a way that changed entire lives if the fortune was
awful enough. Like it had with their father. None of the family
ever really understood him. Except for Tommy.

He knew his father never went looking for trouble—it
simply found him. He read all of the letters from his father
and then lay back. When he couldn't sleep, he pulled his lucky
penny from his pocket and traced its subtle peaks and valleys,
hoping the act would open a portal to his father, that in

touching it, Frank would know Tommy was thinking of him, cheering him on.

Tommy knew deep in the back corner of his soul how his father felt bearing the burden of such bad luck. It didn't matter that he hadn't seen his father in years. He knew him as though they'd been together every second since they left their life in the dugout. He shared the kind of knowing with his father that Katherine and James had with their mother.

Tommy flipped to his back, causing the skunk secretions to waft into his nose. It turned his stomach inside out. Tears came to his eyes and he told himself not to cry, that he was not a baby—hell, he wasn't even a boy anymore. Yet there he was, fourteen, a man, crying as though he was three years old. He turned on his side, trying to move away from his own stink. When that didn't work, he curled up, arms tight around his legs.

His stench was getting to him. So he went to the hay door in the loft and pushed it open with his feet, scooting to where he could dangle his legs over the edge of the opening, wanting to say prayers, hoping they could bring him peace like they had so many times when he was younger, like the prayers he'd sold with Hank and Bayard seemed to do for the folks who bought them.

As he looked up into the sky, short gusts of wind stung his cheeks. He rubbed his arms and watched the stars flicker, wink, and blare, as though they were begging him to notice, to make him remember the Lord created this great universe, and it was God who would show him his path in life.

"God, help me…" He looked away from the stars, shrugged, and took a deep breath.

"Dear God, *please* help me…" Tommy had once prayed so easily; now, he couldn't conjure prayers for himself in the least.

The glow of a lamp in the attic across the way drew Tommy's attention. He saw his mother near the window, pulling covers back on the bed.

The sight made him feel isolated, lonely in a way he hadn't in ages. He'd actually been fine on his own, he had to admit. Yet right that moment, in that barn, watching his mother with Yale on her lap as she smoothed her hair back the way she used to smooth his, jealousy stabbed at him. He rubbed his chest, feeling as though he'd aggravated his tender ribs when he tried to escape the skunk.

"Mama!" He lifted his voice, cutting through the evening silence.

His voice didn't carry far enough. They didn't even flinch in his direction. All he saw was the mutual admiration of a mother and daughter, the way she looked sitting there on the bed, as if being with Yale was the most important thing his mother could have ever imagined.

He looked back at the stars. He searched his heart for goodness, hope. Thoughts of Pearl popped into his mind. He smiled. *Pearl.* Tommy realized right there on that cold, skunk-sprayed night, that he was no longer the person he had been when they'd separated years back. He'd known he'd grown up, but the separation, with his mother so close, now felt so real.

He was too old, had been through too much, to believe his mother could do anything for him but hug him and kiss him and tell him things would change. After that day he'd snuck into the attic and seen her cry so hard she fell into a deep sleep, he had decided he would leave her any thread of dignity she had left. She had been so accomplished, powerful, proud. Though he'd wanted to wake her and tell her to get up and work and do all the things she'd once done better than anyone, he could not risk shaming her. Something told him that if she knew he'd seen her at that low point, she would never be able to come back from it. And like his father, who needed his space to mourn, he saw right then that she must have needed hers, too.

He'd known leaving to find boarding on his own would mean one less thing for her to worry about. And he'd been right. Since he'd left to find work and lodgings on his own, his mother had found her way back to living. And though her clothes were tattered and her hands rough, her posture was regal again, her words full of power. And he knew he'd done the right thing. It was his first step into manhood, and though he had cried like a baby just hours before, when the skunk had fouled him, he knew that was simply a lapse in manhood, his soul exhaling and recognizing its full transformation.

The mesh of confused feelings stirring inside him had momentarily thrown him off the steady path he'd created for himself. But now he saw the confusion as a mark of the growth he'd known was happening all along.

Sitting there in that loft, smelling like the ass of a skunk, he knew he was in control of his life, and he had no doubt that he'd show his mother she could be proud of him, and she would love him, like James, finally.

"Tommy!"

Tommy looked up, squinting at the back door of the house. No one was there.

"Psst! Can you see us?"

His gaze shifted upward to the attic window. There, framed in the window, was his mother, waving, blowing kisses to him as though it were the most normal thing in the world. She lifted Yale's hand and waved it at him.

"Hey, Mama. Hi, sweet Yale," he said, waving back. And he knew they loved him. As long as they had been apart, as distant as they still felt right then, he was sure that his family was strong, that this was just the beginning of something better.

Chapter 28

Katherine

1891—Storm Lake

Katherine gripped the dresser in the bedroom of the Christoffs' home. The missus yanked on Katherine's corset ties, causing her to jerk one way, then the other. Katherine pushed her stomach out as far as she could, hoping that once the garment was secure, she would have a little room to breathe. She was confused and unsure about the dinner plans for the evening but knew better than to ask for clarification. She would be given more information when the family deemed it necessary.

Mrs. Christoff finished the lacing and spun Katherine toward her. Hands on her hips, she analyzed Katherine from top to bottom. The older woman bent down, a groan escaping as she folded over her thick belly and plucked a loose thread from the bottom of Katherine's new flannel petticoat, which had been layered over the cotton one she usually wore.

"You've memorized the verses I marked in the Bible?"

Katherine's breath caught in her closing throat as she recalled her orders to memorize portions of the Bible. She hadn't been able to memorize everything with her workload, but she nodded anyway.

"Don't mess up this dinner, young lady."

Katherine gripped her petticoat in both hands, trying not to give away her confusion and fear. As usual since the tornado, the Christoffs had kept many of their discussions behind urgent whispering and cupped hands, as though she might not notice. Something was different about this dinner, and though she did not know why it was different, her orders to dress for it set it apart from any other meal she'd been preparing, serving, or eating. "Everything is either finished or nearly cooked. The oven was fussy earlier. It wouldn't get hot enough for the—"

"I don't care for excuses." Mrs. Christoff grabbed her skirt and whisked it to the side as she sauntered to the closet, where the dress Katherine was to wear hung on the door. "And I don't mean the food, Katherine. I mean your behavior, your appearance, your… Well, just don't say anything except when directed, and then be sure your pious, pliable nature shines like the summer sun. If you have any interest in continuing to work here."

Katherine put her fingers to her mouth and nodded. Her plans to leave were immature, but her churning nerves told her that she might have to run before she was fully prepared. All she needed was money, warm clothes, and her letters and sketches. Nothing else mattered. She stared at the woman as she unbuttoned the blue silk dress and slid it from its hanger, carrying it with her hands in the air so the hem would not drag.

Since coming to the Christoffs', she had never been given the opportunity to wear anything other than bland, ill-fitting calico dresses. Then, suddenly, this gown appeared in the home, the sapphire blue shocking against the room, which was darkening as the sun set.

Katherine had tried to ask Hannah what was going on, but the Christoffs had sent her to the McMillan home to help while their daughters were away with relatives. When she arrived back home earlier that day, she was ordered to stay near Mrs. Christoff, her every word and action monitored. Two positive circumstances had arisen out of their shunning of Katherine. One was that Mr. Christoff kept nearly a room's width away from her since the night he'd approached her while she was sewing and reading the Bible.

Ostracizing her as they had had also given her stolen moments to sketch. She'd become adept at falling into a peaceful condition that produced scenes and figures and landscapes of places she'd never seen but had somehow created with charcoals. She thought this experience must be akin to what the authors of fairy tales and novels had when writing.

And James, he appeared in her art as much as any of the nameless figures that sprouted from her imagination. Though she could not get the scathing Bible verses or articles about women who attempted to use the occult to tell fortunes and steal money out of her head, she had decided she would not accept that the God she believed in would see James appearing to her as evil or as having been born of the devil. And while she had never courted any sort of otherworldly power, she would receive the presence of her brother with an open and, she thought, pure heart.

Mrs. Christoff snapped her fingers in Katherine's face. "Wake up. We need to make a good impression." Katherine felt a sense of foreboding, confused about Mrs. Christoff's orders. When had she not created a good impression on anyone but her?

Mrs. Christoff handed Katherine the corset cover, which had a high neckline with ruffles that circled the base of her throat. "Let's make sure you are modestly displayed. That dress is of fine quality, but it's not fit to your figure." Katherine pulled on the frilled, dingy corset cover and began to button it.

"I would feel better serving in my plain dress." Katherine lifted her arms and Mrs. Christoff slipped the dress over her head. As the gown brushed past her nose, Katherine caught the scent of something rancid. Sweat-stained armholes told her the dress had been worn many times.

Its round skirt, which would not have taken a bustle, as well as its crinolines and hoops, told her the dress had been stowed away for some time. The stiff stench of perspiration filled her nose. Her stomach turned, and a sense of dread gathered heavily in the room. Katherine could see the cotton lining of the dress had been patched with several different types of cheap fabrics, its guts revealing rough wear.

Mrs. Christoff whirled Katherine back toward the dresser and began to work the buttons upward from the small of Katherine's back. "Reverend Banks and the Murrays want to get to know you better. They are deacons now. Very important people.

"The Reverend would like Mr. Christoff and me to coordinate next week's revival. So if he wants you to dine with us, you will serve and share. I would like for him to see you in the role of a grateful boarder, willing to help the family but capable of dining with all the manners required."

"Oh, galoshes," Katherine said, feeling nauseated. She covered her mouth.

Mrs. Christoff expelled air as she worked her way up Katherine's body. "I hate when you say that. A curse is a curse is a curse, even if you've disguised it in something as ordinary as a rubber covering that keeps a shoe dry in the rain. You mean it as a curse word. So find your manners, and let's make our guests atwitter with having dined at our home, with having selected *us* as examples for Christian life."

"I can do the buttons, Mother," Hannah said.

Katherine and Mrs. Christoff turned to see Hannah in an ice-blue brocade dress trimmed in royal blue cording that was similar in shade and intensity to Katherine's cheap gown.

Katherine smiled at the thought of talking to Hannah after not seeing her for so long. But she knew better than to let it show, for Mrs. Christoff would surely deny her any pleasurable company.

"You wait in the parlor for our guests."

Katherine looked at her hands and pushed a cuticle back on her thumb. She would not have her chance.

"Oh, Mother." Hannah swept farther into the room. She took Mrs. Christoff's hands and swung them back and forth. "The Lord would like us all to breathe now and again. You're flushed." Hannah put the back of her hand to her mother's forehead. "You know the Murrays will flee like rats from a sinking steamer if they suspect you are tubercular or suffering scarlet fever."

Mrs. Christoff looked back at Katherine and placed her hand at the base of her neck. "You're not ill, are you?"

Katherine shook her head. "Flushing is not evidence alone of illness. But you've been working so hard. Slaving, really. Perhaps a rest for just a moment," Katherine offered as she picked up on Hannah's ploy.

Mrs. Christoff swept her arm forward, moving Katherine aside. She bent into the round, pedestaled mirror that sat atop the dresser, turning her head back and forth, blotting at the small bit of exposed chest that showed above her very modest neckline.

"You're right, Hannah. It's as though I've been blotted with red ink."

Hannah rubbed her mother's shoulder and turned her toward the door. "You just need a moment's rest. Close your eyes for a few. I'll bring a wet cloth for after your nap."

Mrs. Christoff looked to her daughter and nodded reluctantly. Hannah ushered her toward the doorway. When they reached it, Mrs. Christoff turned back, appearing worried. She started back into the room, and Hannah gripped her hand. "Oh, Mother, so red."

Mrs. Christoff looked down again. "Yes. Well, finish up dressing and help Katherine with the verses we discussed. May all our souls be cradled in the light of God's love."

And she left the room, the rustling of her dress growing fainter as she descended the stairs.

Hannah ran to Katherine's arms. They held each other. "Your hair smells like an orchard of the sweetest apples," Katherine said.

Hannah pulled away and studied Katherine's face. "Mother had me freshen up every part of my body for this dinner."

"What is happening? Why am I wearing this rancid gown?" Katherine held her hands out. "I can barely stop from retching. Do you smell that?"

"It's stunning on you, Kat. Really. No matter that the cut is wrong and you wear no bustle." Hannah shrugged.

Katherine covered her mouth and swallowed rising bile.

"What's wrong?"

Katherine shook her head. "I don't know. I just feel sick. The dress smells like…well, like a dead rat. I want it off my body."

Hannah sighed. "You can't do that. Turn around. Let me finish buttoning."

"Why is your mother dressing me up after all these months of ignoring my dress?" Katherine asked as Hannah started gently working where her mother had left off.

Hannah gripped Katherine's waist and rotated her. "I think they want to save you."

Katherine whipped around. "What?"

"I don't know that for sure. But Mother is petrified. She thinks you've mingled yourself with the devil and somehow brewed up some sort of sorcery. Right under her own roof. The way you knew about her sister and then predicted the dangerous tornado coming when no one else for miles even saw a cloud in the sky."

"But—"

Hannah took Katherine's hand and held it softly. "I know. They're wrong. It's impossible. You just felt the shift in weather. I believe you. But you need to convince *them*."

"Why on earth would your mother put me in this dress and ask me to sit for dinner if she is so frightened of me?"

Hannah sighed. "I don't know. She won't tell me anything."

Katherine nodded.

"Just be cheerful and sociable. The minister will never believe that such a stunning girl as you—pliant, pious—could ever have entertained a single thought of the devil, let alone have courted him."

Katherine shook her head, her stomach acid curdling. "I don't think I'm going to be able to serve dinner feeling like this." She put her hand to her forehead and felt sweat pouring down from her hairline.

"You look like death. That alone will make Reverend Banks think he should steal you away to save you. It's one of his favorite types of healings—stealing a child away to put the love of Christ back in him or her."

Katherine shivered at the thought. "Hannah? They sent you away before?"

"Not me. But others, yes. Surely you heard them talk in Sunday school."

Katherine had heard rumblings and warnings, but not stories.

"Don't let him see that you are ill in the least."

Katherine wanted to ask Hannah to help her leave, to get Katherine some money to take a train back to… Well, anywhere might be better than this. She would start looking for her mother back in Yankton, where she last knew she lived.

But something made her keep her own council. Hannah was a little girl, after all.

Hannah went to her mother's dresser and opened the top drawer. She fished around inside and turned back with a canister of powder in one hand and a feathered puff in the other. "Let's just use this powder. It will take up some of the moisture at your brow."

Hannah stepped closer, dipping the puff into the powder.

Katherine gripped her wrists and stopped her. "Your parents need my hands around the house. They won't send me off with Reverend Banks." Hannah couldn't possibly be right about this. Katherine was the Christoffs' best tool, cost-efficient and hardworking.

"I won't go." Katherine wanted to explain to Hannah why she must join her family but was worried that confiding in her might not be smart.

Hannah stared at Katherine, her folded brows finally softening as her mouth began to quiver. Hannah's face paled, her lips formed into a tiny o, and horror transformed her expression. "You can't leave me."

Had she given a clue she was thinking of running? No. Katherine would not say she was leaving soon, that she had begun to plan her departure. She needed more time to hide away money, to find a safe way to travel without a chaperone. Yet she didn't want to lie straight out.

"Someday I'll leave," Katherine said. "It's the way of the world."

Hannah swallowed hard. "You can't leave *me*."

Katherine exhaled, sorry at the thought of having to leave the girl behind. Katherine certainly understood how it felt to want to hold on to someone with an iron grip. She hadn't realized the degree to which Hannah had begun to depend on her, to like her. She thought of her mother having to separate from her children. A twinge of understanding stirred. "Well, I can't stay forever, Hannah."

"But for now?"

"For now," Katherine said. But not much longer than that. She would die if she stayed beyond the time she needed to obtain money and a way out of town.

Hannah's face grew bright with satisfaction at Katherine's reassurance. "Let me do your fringe," Hannah said. "Curled fringe is still in vogue."

Katherine touched her hair. "My hair doesn't take a curl. It never has. That's why I don't cut fringe into my hair."

Hannah grasped Katherine's hand and led her to the fireplace, settling her on a small wooden chair. Hannah wrapped a flannel swatch of fabric around the handle of the round iron, pulled it from the fire, and waved it at Katherine. "Everyone's hair curls when the iron is hot enough."

Katherine put her hand up and drew back.

Hannah came at Katherine with the iron. "Let me try."

Katherine sat on the stool in front of the flames as Hannah pulled a section of Katherine's hair from the chignon that held it back from her face. She twisted the strand around the heated cylinder, then pressed the iron against Katherine's forehead.

Katherine gasped and drew back, causing Hannah to drop the iron. It hit the floor with a thud. Katherine pressed her fingers against the smarting skin. The section of hair that had been wrapped around the hot iron was warm but still straight as the fire poker.

Hannah's mouth hung open. "Well, I'll be… Your hair didn't take a smidge of curl. Not one bit."

"I told you."

Hannah cocked her head.

Katherine shrugged. "Now, don't you start thinking I've been practicing some sort of black magic."

"I don't think a thing."

Katherine went to the mirror on the dresser and worked her rail-straight hair back into the chignon at the nape of her neck. She turned her face back and forth, touching her cheeks. She was gray with nausea. She wasn't sure she could make it through a meal. She didn't know which would be worse—staying with the Christoffs or being pawned off on some other farmer. If only Katherine knew where her mother was.

"I just wish my mother hadn't stopped writing to me. If I knew where she was, it would solve the problem for all of us. I could certainly earn my keep with her as much as with your family."

Hannah came up behind Katherine and began to fuss with the fabric at the small of her back. "Wouldn't solve *my* problem if you left. Your mother is clearly preoccupied and not ready to accept her children back into her home. Besides, you're *my* sister now. You said how much you missed your sister. Well, here I am."

Katherine heard the shattered catch in the girl's voice. Katherine certainly understood why Hannah would want Katherine to stay. She also understood that Hannah was too young perhaps to see her father's lustful gaze follow Katherine. And though Hannah could see her mother's sharp distaste for Katherine and knew the punishments they gave her were extreme and unwarranted, she might not fully grasp the sense of desperation it caused Katherine.

Another wave of nausea rolled through Katherine. She couldn't imagine deceiving Hannah. It wasn't fair. "Well, of course I will do my best, Hannah. But it sounds as though your parents have made up their minds. I don't know what to do."

Hannah looked in the mirror and twirled her spiraled fringe around her forefinger. "Nonsense. You'll stay here. That's what you'll do. Just be compliant and holy at dinner, look pink and healthy so he sees no reason to take you for soul-cleansing. I will take care of you, and you will take care of me." Hannah patted Katherine's shoulder as though she were the older girl.

Katherine exhaled. She forced a smile at Hannah. Soul-cleansing. She'd witnessed the minister nearly cleanse a girl's soul to death at the last revival. The thought of being subjected to such a thing made her squeeze her eyes closed and pray to the God she knew was good, asking him to make her well, to pink her cheeks and keep anyone who was there for dinner from thinking she was anything other than an angel descended right from heaven itself.

Chapter 29

Katherine

1905—Des Moines

Katherine had sketched through the night following the funeral, falling asleep only as the sun was rising. Now its rays beat down on her hard, her head pounding as she tried to open her dry eyes. She stretched her legs and turned so she was flat on the iron daybed in the art studio. She had not even tried to make her way back down the hall to her bedroom and Aleksey that night.

She reached over her head with her arms and yawned as the door to the studio burst open and her children rolled in, bouncing on her, demanding she get up so they could eat. Katherine laughed, filled with familiar contentment as Beatrice snuggled into her side and Andrew lay on top of her, vying for the most real estate, the most affection. Asher stood in the doorway, arms crossed, small smile on his face. "Dad's waiting, Mama. Says we're to go to brunch."

It was then Katherine's mind rewound to the funeral, to the emotions it had stirred.

"Uncle Tommy?" Katherine wrapped her arms around both children and squeezed.

She lifted her head to see Asher shrug. Katherine was struck by a sense of dread and heaviness. Though Tommy was no stranger to sleeping out, she had been hoping that he'd come back to sleep sometime during the night. He wasn't a teenager anymore, and she worried that he was unsafe.

She struggled to sit while Andrew and Beatrice fought to stay latched on to her. "Go on, children. Get dressed properly, and I'll do the same. Check again to see if Uncle Tommy returned in the night, and waken Auntie Yale. We'll have a magnificent breakfast." She tossed them onto the ground one at a time, and each rolled dramatically away as though they'd been harmed. Then she raised her arms and flapped her fingers, calling them back toward her.

"You, too, Asher," she said. He sauntered over, hiding a smile.

"Nuzzle one." Asher tipped his head toward her and she smothered his cheek in kisses before he could pull away and pretend to wipe them off. "Nuzzle two." And so she went down the line until each had been covered in kisses. Aleksey appeared in the doorway, his arm up high on the doorjamb. His blond hair was tousled, and his stubbly chin and bright smile made Katherine feel warm inside.

"I told you not to paint. You're going to get sick if you don't sleep."

Katherine sat up and opened her arms, winking at Aleksey. "No paint. But I had to sketch."

He sat beside her on the daybed and pulled the knapsack onto his lap. "You dug this out?"

"I had to. You know. All those memories taking me back to... I just needed to see the drawings again, to dig through them, to remember, is all. I feel like my mind is a series of tunnels with an above-ground entry, and once I head down one, I have to follow its underground twists and turns until I remember what I'm supposed to or I do away with whatever bad feeling I have."

"And did you manage all that?"

She shrugged. "I don't know," she said, chuckling. "I'm still too tired to really know what I'm feeling. But I had to be here. I feel like my mother's here with me. And I really needed to draw whatever came to me instead of what I've been commissioned to do."

"Mama. Someone's knocking," Beatrice said.

"You get dressed," Aleksey said. "We're all starving and looking forward to some good eggs and bacon at the Lighthouse. I'll see who it is."

Katherine went to their bedroom and began to clean up in the adjoining bathroom. The fresh fragrance of lemon water woke her up more and refreshed her. She looked in the mirror and traced the outline of her face. She closed her eyes and thought of her mother. "No matter what I missed in your life, I love you and I'm sorry," she said to herself, feeling warm as she revisited forgiveness. "And, God, please let Tommy find his."

Aleksey poked his head into the bathroom. "You better hurry. There's someone here to see you."

Katherine blotted her face with a hand towel. "Who?"

"A man and a woman—a married couple. They want to offer condolences."

"More?"

"They just arrived on the train, so they couldn't be here yesterday. That's all they would say."

Katherine nodded. She felt a surge of excitement at the thought there were still more people who held a piece of the puzzle of Jeanie Arthur. She smiled, her curiosity piqued in a way that made her grateful to be alive.

**

Katherine lifted her skirts and rushed down the stairs. When she entered the parlor, the couple was at the window, pointing and gazing at something out of Katherine's view.

"Hello? I'm Katherine Zurchenko. Jeanie Arthur's daughter."

They turned toward her, and each grinned.

Katherine studied the pair. They looked at each other and back at her, clutching each other's hands. Katherine felt off-kilter, as though she'd seen them before, but she could not place either of them. She'd met so many people in the last day that all faces were beginning to look similar.

"You knew my mother?" Katherine asked.

They glanced at each other again and then back at Katherine.

The woman stepped forward. "It's you, Katherine. You're the one who we knew."

Katherine cocked her head. "Me?"

She looked closer at the woman and then at the man. In her residual fatigue, she had trouble believing what she was seeing. There was something in the way the woman moved her shoulders and flashed her smile. Seeing them took Katherine back in time and finally saw their faces not as they were right then in the year 1905, but how they'd appeared in 1891.

The woman reached out, her hand shaking. "Kat, it's me."

She hadn't been called that in ages. She stepped forward gingerly to be sure her eyes were not lying. "Hannah?" Her hands trembled as she stared.

The woman flew forward, crashing into Katherine's arms. They rocked each other back and forth, giggling like little girls. "It's me. It is me!" Hannah said.

Katherine felt a rush of joy at the sight of this woman who used to be a girl, the girl who'd helped Katherine escape from her very own dreadful family.

Katherine gripped Hannah's shoulders, staring at her as though she were not sure she was flesh and blood. "Hannah Christoff."

Katherine could hardly believe that Hannah was standing there, but she really couldn't fathom what on earth she was doing with *him*. Could it be true? Katherine slapped her hands over her mouth and then threw her arms wide open. "Will! What on earth?"

He tossed his head back and let out warm, rumbling laugh. "Oh, it's quite the yarn, Katherine. A great, tale, I must say."

And Katherine pulled them both to the davenport, sat between them where she could embrace every word of the story they had to tell.

Chapter 30

Jeanie

1891—Des Moines

I could smell the mix of vinegar and partly removed mold in Mrs. Mellet's attic before I saw it. I stirred before the sun rose, opening my eyes as the deep blue night turned bright sapphire, tucking the bright stars away for later. On the other side of the bed, my Yale slept, her arms flung open, one tiny fist laid on my stomach. *Please let Katherine be safe*, I prayed. I hoped this new day would bring news of her whereabouts. I needed to know she was on the road back home to us.

I kissed Yale's hand and settled it under the quilt. I sat up, my bare feet on the planked floor, toes cold against the wood. Afraid of black depression crippling me, I made a deal that morning. I gripped the featherbed and waited for it—the sorrow. It rose up, choking me.

I shuddered as the tears welled, stung, then dropped down my face. I tried to swallow the sob, but it escaped. I would allow myself to feel every inch of James' loss for just a bit each morning. Then I vowed to tuck it away and finally function for the sake of the others.

Surprised that the deep sadness lessened with the deal I'd made that morning, I exhaled. I kissed Yale awake and squeezed her legs, making her giggle. "Time to clean up for morning," I said. I removed the soaker that covered her diaper, silently thanking Mrs. Stevens for seeing Yale had proper underthings while still toilet training. She had done well during the day, but night was still difficult for her.

I carefully set the safety pins aside and sat her on the chamber pot. When she finished, I dipped a cloth into the water bucket and wrung it out. I swabbed Yale's bottom and legs and pulled on her drawers, underskirt, and a clean dress.

Once Mrs. Mellet and I realized my comforting Tommy had ruined my dishwater-gray mourning dress, she'd sent me into her daughter's old room on the second floor of the house. She and I had selected four costumes for me to take. One was a dress made of challis. It was ruffled around the neckline and cut across my shoulders and would require a blouse underneath for daily use.

The background was an impractical cream, and it was printed with brown, orange, and mauve flowers, stems, and strawberries. Its cut was large skirted, awaiting the push of an 1880s bustle. My height made up for my only having drawers, a chemise, underskirt, and bodice instead of the mounds of fabric that had been intended to go under it. It did not matter; I felt like a queen when I slipped it on.

The second dress was printed cotton with ribbons of windblown posies, leaves, and paisleys against a brown background. The third dress was of lavender silk jacquard with pinstriping in a deep purple thread. It came in two parts—a skirt and a bodice—cut better for a woman of the seventies than the nineties, but it did not matter a wit to me. I was awed by the gift. Finally, to wear for daily chores, I was given a blouse with a rounded collar and a plain navy blue skirt that did not cover my curled black boots. I would have to wait to replace my shoes, for nothing in her closet fit me.

Dressed and washed up with fresh water, I lifted Yale into my arms and headed to the kitchen to find my list of things to do for the morning.

Yale yawned as I set her in one seat at the table and gave her a day-old biscuit with marmalade. While she nibbled on the treat, I emptied the chamber pot, washed up again, and then set about readying breakfast for Mrs. Mellet. There was a note on the marble baking table stating that I should serve the day-olds along with clotted cream instead of making fresh and that I should head to the garden to dig some red potatoes and fetch the eggs, as well.

I wrapped one hand around Yale's and another around a pail as we moved through the paths that defined outdoor rooms in the Mellet gardens. Clearly, she'd had her gardeners in at some point that spring, for the boxwood was shaped perfectly and the roses were precisely pruned and blooming, tossing their perfume into the morning air like blushing debutantes on the day of their entrée into society.

But then I saw the dead plants. I bent down in front of a bed of dead tulips—browned and flattened to the ground after their spring bloom. I lifted the limp stems.

"My, my, Yale, these must have been magnificent when they were blooming." *Everything is beautiful in full bloom*, I thought. I squatted and tore a dried stem from its root and made a browned daffodil move as though it were a doll of some sort, giving it a voice. "You should have seen me, dear Yale. My petals were as big as your head when I was first alive!" I tapped Yale's forehead with the flower, and the dark-haired beauty curled away, laughing.

"My, yes, this garden was exquisite once." I stood and surveyed the grounds, the paths that cut it into sections. I headed to the irises—russet, dry and slumping—crocus carcasses, still-pink peonies trampled by cows that had found a hole in the fence, and I wondered what had caused Mrs.

Mellet to let parts of her garden go. We ambled through the grounds, turning and bending and reaching for interesting plants, patting the dying ones as though they were pets or people on the last go-around of life.

"Morning, ladies."

I jumped at the sound. I turned to see Mrs. Mellet limping toward me, hand around the fat brass knob that topped the cane she had chosen that morning. Mrs. Mellet's knee gave a little, and she caught herself with her cane and the back of the bench to her left.

"Here." I took Mrs. Mellet by the arm. "How about the seat under the oak? We'll dig the potatoes while you enjoy the early sunshine."

Mrs. Mellet shook off my helping hand and grumbled as she shuffled to the bench. I watched with my breath held, waiting for her foot to catch on one of the scraggly roots that rose out of the dirt.

"I listened to your monologue over there. A gardener, now, are you? From what I heard tell, you Arthurs and the rest of that cohort in Darlington Township couldn't grow prairie grass to save your lives."

I chortled. "That's what you heard tell, did you?" I thought of the fires, the grasshoppers, the drought—all the reasons, in addition to our lack of skill, that might have contributed to black thumbs on the prairie. Coaxing any crop to fruition had been nearly impossible, and when success had been achieved, I thought the occurrence might be given over to having more luck than skill. Except for the Zurchenkos. They knew what they were doing. I shrugged. "You heard right."

Mrs. Mellet grunted. Yale grabbed at a rosebud on the bush nearby and caught a fistful of thorns. Her face crumpled in pain, and she let out a little yelp, but not much else.

I tugged each thorn from her palm, naming them as I did. "This one is Henry. He says, 'Help me out of here!' This one is Samuel, and he says, 'Let me be—this girl is sweet and warm!'" Once they were all removed, Yale giggled and pushed her face into my thigh, her arms tight around one leg. I swung her up, her feet flying in the air, then covered her face in kisses before I settled her on the bench near Mrs. Mellet. "You sit still, Yale. The roses aren't ready for cutting, anyway. Make Mrs. Mellet's life easy, if you please. Mama will be done in a short time."

I jammed the pitchfork into the ground and pushed back on the handle, popping four potatoes up with the dirt. I glanced over my shoulder to be sure Yale was not causing trouble. I was waiting for the perfect moment to ask Mrs. Mellet if she had a sense of when the money would be available, and if so, whether she'd made her family aware of her plans, for there was nothing worse than sons and daughters scorned.

Mrs. Mellet cleared her throat. "Get them all up. Might as well."

I narrowed my eyes on her. "You don't want to harden them off?"

"The future for me is now, Jeanie Arthur."

"Why not a few? Surely you'll have some to store."

She patted her forehead with her hanky, then stuffed it back in her pocket.

"Are you all right?" I asked.

"Oh yes," Mrs. Mellet said, her voice thin and unconvincing to me.

She flicked her hand at me. "Keep on with the potatoes."

I turned back and released the unearthed red potatoes from the plant.

"I know," Mrs. Mellet said, "you were busier writing and whatnot than gardening when you lived here. Just how do you know anything about chemicals and rot and how to rid roses of fungi and all of that I heard you say?"

I sat back on my heels. "Well, you heard right about my ability to grow food on the plains. But in one of the homes where I boarded in Sioux Falls lived a woman with the greenest thumb in the universe I've come to see. She was a kind soul. But she didn't have much except her gardens. She was losing money hand over fist in bad deals and selling off furniture and silver place settings until we ate dinner with mismatched utensils. Down till the last night I was there, I ate my beef with a fish fork, of all things, and she ate with a giant ornate serving fork. But her gardens. She sank every last penny into antique roses sent direct from London and lilies from the Orient."

I set the potatoes into a bucket at my feet and dug the pitchfork a little ways down the row of potato plants. "She created these miraculous gardens. Seeds—people sent her seeds from the world over, and she'd make them grow right there in the middle of nowhere, in that horrid little town." I shook my shoulders, trying to throw off the bitterness that had pushed out of me right then. I didn't want my thoughts and words to be distasteful or unappreciative. That was not the image I wanted to put out to the world. Right then, I realized there would be times when the still-dark, leached soil of my soul would give rise to poison thoughts that sprouted on suffocating vines. It was my job to prune them away and reveal what was still good inside me.

"I learned a lot in the last years. That's what I mean." I turned to see Yale had inched closer to Mrs. Mellet, nearly on her lap. I bent to retrieve the potatoes. "And that little lady, Miss Yale, has the second greenest thumb in the universe, I've come to see."

"Well," Mrs. Mellet said.

I worked with both hands, not looking back, taking Mrs. Mellet's relaxed tone to mean Yale was not bothering her.

"This young lady's thumb may be green, but I suspect her mind's addled. Good to have a strength, I suppose."

The woman's tone wasn't sharp or harsh. I turned back, ready to pounce if Mrs. Mellet was doing something cruel to Yale. They were simply sitting, faces turned to the rising sun as if they were at the wellness resort a few towns away.

Pluck, pluck, pluck, the potatoes came apart from their roots. "I think Yale is just fine. She's just a slow mover. Some people are like that. They, well, they're like the iris. They need ten months in order to grow, to be ready to bloom. That's my Yale. She's just iris-like, that's all."

"*Hmph.* I suppose that could be the case—a slow learner. Just as long as she's no trouble to you."

I stopped working. I felt anger close my throat. I wiped my forehead with the back of my hand as I was reminded how Yale would sometimes wander off. The way her disappearance even for a moment stopped the beating of my heart as though God himself had lifted his hand off of it. I realized I was balling my skirt in my fists and nausea was filling my stomach. Yale had been through a lot. I was lucky she was alive. She did not need to be a genius, too.

"You don't talk much," Mrs. Mellet said. "You were chatty before you left town. If you weren't littering the town with your written words, you were speaking at the Women's Club, about how to do this and not to do that."

I stood and looked at my feet, brushing my palms together to remove the dirt. The toes of my worn shoes peeked out from under my hem. I turned my gaze back to Mrs. Mellet, startled at the sight before me.

There on the bench sat Mrs. Mellet, but Yale had climbed onto the woman's lap, facing her. Yale's hands cupped the woman's cheeks like she did to me so often. I was about to scream to leave Mrs. Mellet alone at once, but then I saw Mrs. Mellet smiling. A warm expression softened her face, her weathered skin appearing pillowy, joyous.

Mrs. Mellet met my gaze as Yale's tiny hands created a web over the woman's cheeks. "I like you better this way." Mrs. Mellet playfully nipped at one of Yale's fingers. She giggled in response. "To be honest, the old, rich, know-it-all Jeanie? I didn't like that girl much. This version of you, the woman who arrived in rags with pretense thrust aside, *now* you're interesting. Now I like you. You're hard evidence that secrets and lies are poison." She nodded as though needing to agree with her own words.

I felt a burst of affection for Mrs. Mellet, an odd emotion to feel for someone who had been party to my family's demise. Maybe it was simply a case of optimism, the kind I hadn't felt in years. The old woman was right—secrets could be crippling.

"Yes, I'm happy to do this for you, Jeanie, for your family. I'm even more contented to relieve my weight in secrets. They are cancerous, eating away like hungry parasites…"

I nodded. "Thank you. It changes everything for us that you are willing to make amends." My voice cracked, so I cleared my throat and gathered my gumption. "Along that line, could you tell me whether your children are aware of your plans for a significant amount of your fortune? Just so they don't find themselves flushed with haughty anger when you tell them after the fact. They know, right? About your plan to right this wrong?"

Mrs. Mellet nodded with her eyes closed, now hugging Yale as though she were her granddaughter.

"You told them?"

She waved her hand at me and smiled. "People believe what they want to believe and interpret things in any manner of ways. The same story is told and ten people hear a different message, don't they? You know that."

I stepped closer. "You told them about your plans to repay me, right?" I felt the tingle of a lie settle into my bones. Was it possible that Mrs. Mellet had called me back for nothing more than a private apology?

"Oh, now you're back to Old Jeanie, pushing and prodding for the exact right match for what you want to hear. You just finish with those potatoes. Yale and I will get us the eggs. I'll be ready for luncheon at the rate you're working, staring at me like I'm priceless artwork or something. I said I was setting matters right, didn't I?"

I turned back to the potatoes, plucking and plunking them into the pail hand over fist. I rolled Mrs. Mellet's words over in my mind, a smile creeping over my face. Mrs. Mellet was ready to set the record straight, to redeem herself, to prepare her soul for the day she might find her opportunity to plead her earthly case at the pearly gates.

And part of that must have meant turning the Arthur honor back to the rightful owner. I wasn't sure if the woman was truly being nice, but her kindness toward Yale was enough for me to carry on, to be sure we would leave her house as promised, with what I'd returned to get. I nodded. This was the beginning of something good for all of us.

"Mrs. Mellet," I said.

"Yes, Jeanie?"

I turned to face her. "Thank you for the dresses and for housing us here for the moment. But I have to be clear. I insist that you and I go to your lawyer's office today and formalize the papers. I've—*we've*—been through too much to have this fall through. I need to be clear."

Mrs. Mellet smiled down at Yale and then met my gaze. "You are clear as this blue sky. We will meet with him today."

I exhaled. "I'll send word with Tommy this morning, and we will go this afternoon."

Mrs. Mellet nodded, and I felt as though just those words to Mrs. Mellet were an accomplishment. I turned back to finish my work. There was no time to waste, and as much as I did not mind doing some work for Mrs. Mellet if absolutely necessary, it was not going to be my destiny.

**

Tommy woke with the sun, the soft morning rays poking through the planks in the loft door, calling him to consciousness. He rolled onto his back and stretched, remembering when he had been a little boy and his mama's sweet voice, the rise and fall of it, had sounded as she nudged him to rise and shine.

Oh, how Tommy had loved that life they'd once had in Des Moines, when he had been just a boy of ten. Once they'd moved to the prairie, he had done his best not to think of it much, as it pained him several times over when he did.

First it was the missing of their breakfast table, laden with ham and bacon and chicken as well as golden eggs, sweet rolls thick with cinnamon and sugar, fresh milk, and apple juice when the apples were ripe and they'd had so many, they couldn't eat them all or give them all away. Most mornings, there was even eggy toast or slapjacks drenched in syrup sent direct from Vermont. A meal like that even made the school day that followed bearable.

Then there was the pain he felt in recalling his mother's reaction when he even hinted at the notion he was recollecting such a morning feast on that dry, hellish prairie they'd lived on for a year. She acted as though he weren't human for calling up memories of such a lavish life, as though suddenly she was ashamed they had lived it.

It was just another way his actions forced her face to harden, her eyes to widen, her skin to flush with anger or crinkle in incomprehension that this son, Tommy, just didn't seem to fit the mold she'd created for him. He had not seen any of that since they'd met back up two days before.

He rolled to his side and yawned. A sharp breeze ran over his skin, assuring him that spring had not yet given over to summer. He told himself to get up and do his chores. He knew that he would not be excused from his duties simply because he stank of skunk. The burning in his eyes had mostly dissipated, and that alone made him more willing to work. Not to mention he *wanted* the work. He hoped he could impress Mrs. Mellet and get her to pay him some cash in addition to room and board.

His stomach growled and tumbled, aching for something to fill it. He inhaled. What was that? Yes, he knew. The taste of eggs, toast, and bacon came on a burst of wind, up through the hay door. Tommy rolled onto his side, his head resting on his arm as his mouth watered with anticipation. He squeezed his eyes shut and told himself to buck up about the chores.

He imagined his father, who'd said he'd spent many breakfast-free days to save his pennies to buy more cottonseed, to pay more fellows to help him pick it. Boy, his father had suffered a great deal, and it was this thought—the idea that it would be he who saved them all—that made the thought of chores palatable at all.

He reached deep in his pocket, his fingers searching around for his lucky penny, the Indian Head his father had tucked into his palm, folded his fingers around, and told him was a promise of the wealth that would follow once Frank made his mark in cotton.

It was gone. Tommy shot to his feet. Where was it? He jumped up and down, dug back into one pocket and then the others, tossing the silver salt well, a tiny hairpin with a jewel at its end, tangles of twine, a pocketknife, everything that wasn't attached to the fabric, out. No penny.

Back down on his knees, he pushed hay to the side, this way and then that, searching the area where he'd been lying. Nothing. Maybe he'd put it in his coat with the letters? No. He'd removed the coat before he worked. He spun around, pushing and pulling hay aside, his hands picking up dirt, his nose filling with it. He sneezed. It shook his body, and in the process, the sneeze jarred loose his final thread of composure, and he began to cry.

He bent over his knees, head tucked onto his legs, and he shuddered, sobbing for the second time in less than twenty-four hours. He tried to suck it all back inside, his fear, anger, worry, sadness. All of it. But in the loss of this penny and one quaking sneeze, it had all been released into the world, and he couldn't stop it if the force of a train was bearing down on it.

"Tommy?"

He hadn't heard his mother come into the barn.

"My Tommy," Jeanie said. He could hear her race up the ladder to the hayloft. She knelt beside him, trying to wrench him upright. He stayed tight in a ball. He didn't need to add humiliation to his list of overwrought emotions.

He felt her pull away at his reluctance to let her comfort him. It would figure that she would give up after one try. It wasn't like he was James or something. It wasn't like he was dead. Or her favorite. Heck, if pressed, he couldn't say for sure his mother loved him at all compared to the others.

Tommy tried to stop crying. He held his breath and felt the congestion settling into his head. And in the silence, he heard his mother sigh. "Oh, Tommy. It's going to be fine. Let me give you a haircut and a shave, and you can take the buggy to town with a letter to Mr. Halsey. We are going to seal this deal today, Tommy."

The cows mooed below, reminding Tommy he was due to milk them before they were turned out. His mother rubbed circles into his back, moving closer to him, wrapping her arm around him. He could feel her chin dig into his shoulder blade, then her cheek, nuzzling him as much as he would allow her, and he felt satisfaction in her comfort but wished he had not been such a baby. She needed him to be grown, not another baby to care for at such a hard time in their lives. And yet he wanted that Indian Head penny as though it were a security blanket. He wished his mother could understand. Could he explain to her what it meant? Or would her face go sour at the mention of his father?

**

I had been on my way to the barn with Tommy's eggs, toast, and bacon when I heard shuffling and crying in the hayloft. My first thought was that he was tangling with another skunk or being bitten by a snake. But as I climbed up the ladder and found him crumpled into a ball with no antagonist in sight, sobbing, I couldn't imagine what was happening to him.

He had been on his own for so long and clearly wanted to be a man, to be independent, and I hadn't considered that he might still need to be held and rocked by his mother. I couldn't recall him ever crying as a child, not really, not like most children. He'd responded to the loss of James, the divorce, the separate living quarters for the last three years as though he were a thick-skinned politician winning and losing seats, as though the loss of his family was just some game he understood and played. He'd spouted off Bible verses, said prayers aloud, exuding some sort of ordained faith that the rest of them might have liked to possess, but perhaps it had all been an act. A way of not accepting the loss. But there he was, bent over, weeping.

"It's all right, Tommy." I rubbed his back while he tried to hide his red, tear-stained face from me. "Katherine will be with us soon. We'll have money. We can—"

"I can't find my penny!"

"It's got to be here," I said.

"The Indian Head Father gave me when he left us…when you…when we split up." Tommy's shoulders began to heave again, his eyes growing wild. I shook my head, mystified at what he was referring to. He got on his knees and began pushing hay this way and that. "I have to find it. It's like a portal between him and me. If it's gone forever, I just know it'll mean bad luck for us both. More for him. He won't make it if he has any more bad luck, Mama!"

I watched this desperation cloak Tommy as though it were a hooded garment that allowed only for his frantic eyes to be seen, and right then, a chill climbed up my arms and around the back of my neck like spider feet. I shivered and rubbed my arms. I felt the recognition of Frank right there in my son. I couldn't breathe. His irrational belief that this penny meant something to his useless father, that it somehow would keep them both safe and provide a connection was pure insanity.

And it was as though I was staring at a young Frank Arthur, the man I'd mistaken for passionate and full of the gusto other men lacked. But this was the other side of such determination—it fizzled and died and dropped under a thick, black existence that allowed Frank to function only if stimulated and tantalized by something enticing and grand, like another woman or an enormous project that would surely, in his mind, bring fortune and save them all. Air castles on one end of his moodiness and cavernous depression and fear and anxiety on the other. And here it was in my son.

I wanted to scream at Tommy as he crawled around the floor, burrowing, rummaging for the penny. But the tension in his back, the desperation in his breathing, the dismay in his eyes tore at me, made me sorry for him having Frank's blood coursing through his body. But I could not blame him for his father's sins, so I dropped to my knees and joined him in weeding through the hay, looking for the penny.

My fingernails scraped at the wood planks, and dirt collected under them. One tore off. I shook my hand and bit the spot where it throbbed. Anxiety rose inside me, matching Tommy's, taking me by surprise. Tommy's vulnerability stripped away any facade I'd built to cover my own pain. It felt as though it were all new again, the loss, the grief of the past four years.

I went to the loft door and opened it wider. The sun moved from behind a cloud and its rays caught something in the hay, causing it to glint. "I think that's it." I grabbed Tommy's arm. "By the ladder." He kept searching, ignoring me.

"There! Tommy, between the boards."

I ran to it, and finally Tommy joined me. We both knelt above, our heads butting into each other as we tried to wedge it out with a too-thick stick, then a piece of stiff straw. We each held a piece of straw, and together we lifted the penny from between the boards as though performing battlefield surgery.

When we finally got it all the way out, Tommy snatched it, slamming his fingers shut. He pressed his hand to his chest, and his face bore all the relief I would have expected to see if he had saved the life of a human being.

My hands shook as I pulled him into my arms. I wanted to convey how loved he was. His unsettled breathing evened out, and he seemed to be comforted. I kissed the top of his head and pulled his shoulders so I could look directly into his eyes.

"Now, now." I cupped his face and dried his tears with my thumbs.

He cleared his throat. "I'm not a baby."

I exhaled deeply. "Oh, I know you are not a baby. You've lived on your own, and you've grown big and strong despite having been… I know you are going be great, Tommy. I can see it."

Tommy squeezed his eyes shut.

"You may have had a scrape or two since we left the prairie. But you are a good boy. Nothing changes that, not even a misstep or two." This felt like the perfect time to talk of moving on if Des Moines was too suffocating. "We can move east, west, we can go north. But we are going to make our way in the world, Tommy."

He turned his back to me and put one hand against the loft window. His back tensed, and I could see from the tightness in the back of his neck that he was grinding his teeth. "East, north? Not until I get Father here." Tommy's shoulders rose and fell with deep breaths. He cleared his throat and shook off a final sob. "We need to be here when he comes back."

I wrapped my arms around him again, holding tight. "I know it's hard. I do. If you do your chores, dump your clothing at the well, and wash up, you should be fine coming back in the house. I set some tomato juice near the well for your hair. We will cut it and shave you. Don't tell Mrs. Mellet. She's tight with the canned goods, and I don't blame her, but I won't have my son sleeping in the barn like a dog."

Tommy looked over his shoulder and sniffled. "I like it outside. Why don't you ever mention my father?"

"Tommy." I don't know why this question surprised me. In all the moments I felt the loss of my family the past three years, few of them involved sadness at having split with Frank for love's sake. I rarely considered how much the children would feel his loss because he had done so little for them. But I should have known they would have more questions about his situation than I did—that his absence would mean something different to them.

Tommy turned and smiled at me. "Let's stay here until he gets back."

"There are so many places we could go."

Tommy's head whipped around and he glared at me.

"We aren't leaving."

"We don't have plans laid to leave, but we could start over completely somewhere else."

"Father's coming back. Here."

My stomach twisted. I had struggled with how to handle the downfall of Frank Arthur. Because my father had been a large part of the investment swindle that caused the fancy class of Des Moines to lose massive amounts of money, homes, and jewelry, and then his suicide… well, I knew what it meant to find out your father was not who you thought he was. I hadn't wanted them to ever feel that crippling pain.

Because when that happened, why, you might as well rip away everything that person thought about herself or her world, her accomplishments and abilities and destiny. I had done my best to protect my children from knowing their father had impregnated another woman, promised her he would leave with her and their baby, and was the cause of their brother's death. How would any child recover from knowing such things about their father? In lying to them, I saw now, plain as that penny glinting in the sun, that I had complicated the circumstances even more.

I wasn't sure that spilling the whole truth would salve the damage I'd done in letting Tommy believe his father was *not* a scoundrel, so I hedged what I said. I didn't think I would ever be able to inflict that demoralization on my children. I would hold Frank's secret for as long as I breathed, for as long as it was needed to allow my children to be whole. Still, there were practicalities to consider.

"He's not coming back," I said. "He promised to write me when he settled, and he didn't. He's just gone."

Tommy reached into his back pocket and wrenched a set of letters from his pocket. "He's coming and he wrote and I'll be there waiting for him. As a matter of fact, I'm going to get him, if need be. We will be a family again. Including you."

I stared at the letters in his fist. Panic welled inside me. What did they say? I couldn't grasp that Frank had kept in touch with Tommy or that he could possibly say anything to convince me he was willing to reunite.

"He wrote you?"

"'Course. I'm his son."

I tried to steady my voice to hide the way this news jarred me.

"He wants us back. I told him I'd come get *him* if necessary. Once I save up. And I know that once you see him again… I would have come to get you both once I had enough cash."

I smiled. "Oh, Tommy. You are big-hearted, aren't you?"

But it worried me that he was invested in the idea of his father living with him again. If Tommy was corresponding with Frank, I wanted it to be comforting for him, not fuel and escalate Tommy's desire to see his father and me back together.

He pushed the letters into my hand. I read all seven of them in a few minutes. The letters were full of typical Frank Arthur air castles and promises that would never be kept. It was plain to see. It roiled my blood that the man would leave a trail of hints that he needed help from his son.

The nerve of him to manipulate Tommy into thinking all that stood between this family's prosperity and its splintered state was Tommy raising money to help him come back. It was then that I fully saw how Tommy had one foot in adulthood and one in childhood. The problem was, when it came to family and fathers, that one foot in childhood might end up anchored there forever.

"You'll have school in the fall. Your father can take care of himself. Once you have an education and a job, you can help him any way you like, but until you have means, I will not allow you to focus on something so utterly—"

"I have plans for us, for all of us. And none of them involve going east or north willy-nilly. I can make you proud and put us back together. Father wants you, Mama. He is so sad. He lost some money on the cotton, and he didn't come back here because he didn't want to face you. He lit out for Florida, of all places. The Everglades. Catching alligators for shoes and bags and such. It nearly tore me up to hear he was afraid to come back, that he felt the need to go farther away. I know as soon as you see him that you will forgive him. You're a good woman, I told him."

I covered my mouth. Perhaps I should enlighten Tommy regarding just who it was that was good and bad. I hadn't meant for him to form a negative view of me in the absence of Frank.

"Tommy, I think you're reading into his words a little. Yes, he loves you. I wouldn't doubt that ever. But I'm not sure what you're seeing in these letters is what he is saying—"

Tommy swung around, face red, a vein pressing up through the skin at his temple. The anger flinted in his eyes, and he looked as though he was going to pounce on me. "You drove him away!"

"I didn't drive him away, Tommy."

"He came back, you two talked, and then he left again," Tommy said.

I thought of the letter I had found in Ruthie's pocket when she died. He had come back for her. I wanted to scream that out. But I couldn't. I could weather his blame for now. It would pass.

I put my hand out to him. "Things are complicated, Tommy. It's not a matter of me driving him away. He's a grown man. He had decisions to make, and he felt it was best to leave. He didn't fight to stay. Perhaps when he's ready, he will tell you his side of the story."

Tommy looked at my hand but did not take it. "The letters say he loves us. He loves me. Maybe not clear out the way we say it to each other. But maybe he just needs to keep some dignity and he will return when it's fully intact. Sometimes people need that."

"It could be all that, yes." I was not prepared to unearth the truth of what happened between Tommy's father and me. Not right then, not when I was overjoyed to have him with me, when I was still so worried that Katherine was not yet here.

Finally, he took my outstretched hand. He lifted his eyes to look at me. "I'm sorry, Mama. I didn't mean to sound so hateful."

"I know. It hurts, and people say things that sting when they feel pain."

Tommy nodded. "Thank you."

Tommy's comprehension of a person's need to keep their pride felt mature, and I was proud of him. If only he hadn't placed such faith in a man who never once worried about his dignity, as far as I knew.

Tommy straightened his posture. His face grew serene, as though these words meant something far beyond what I knew, as though he'd been wanting to say them to me for a long time.

I couldn't force a swallow down my constricted throat. It had been so long since I'd had to try to absorb Frank's failures so that his children could see his luster that I'd forgotten how hard it was to do—like a barrage of punches to the stomach.

Tommy took my other hand and held it, too. "When he left us back at the dugout, you said he just needed time to grieve over James. You said he just needed time. That he could do wonderful things when he followed through. And I believed you then. And I believe that now."

"I did say that." I should not have said that.

"And then you divorced him. You let him let you divorce him."

I shook my head. "It wasn't for no reason, Tommy. Do you really believe that I divorced him simply out of boredom?"

Tommy's eyes were puffy from the difficulties of the last day. Clearly, he hadn't slept well in the barn, but I had seen his posture lengthen, the transformation in his demeanor as he calmed. "Until my father returns, I am the only man in our family." He poked at his chest but avoided answering my question.

Mrs. Mellet's voice lifted through the hayloft door.

"Go on." Tommy waved his hand through the air. He pulled me by the shoulders and kissed my cheek. "She probably needs her toenails bitten off."

He chuckled.

"That's repulsive, Tommy," I said and I laughed along, the tension shattered. I patted his chest. "I have a plate for you for breakfast. We'll clean you up, and tonight you'll sleep inside with us. Your family."

He sniffed under his arms and grinned. "I can handle the barn. Nice breeze, fresh gusts of lavender and hyacinths perfuming the near-constant stream of air that shoots through this here hay door."

I squinted at him. "Nonsense. You'll come inside tonight."

"I'm all right, Mama. I swear."

Mrs. Mellet's voice came again, more urgent. I hesitated to descend, not sure he was okay.

"Go on. I'm fine, Mama. I'm fine." He opened his arms and laid open one of those grins that had come so easy until he'd been doused by the skunk.

I squeezed the ladder as I moved down a rung. I was losing something as Tommy was finding it. I tapped the ladder with my forefinger. Tommy growing up was a good thing, not a loss like that of my James.

That was a loss, and no other disappointment I could encounter in the future could compare. Having seen the letters, I was sure that Tommy would never leave to find Frank because there was no address, no solid information other than allusions to a certain town or scheme.

I felt the heavy disappointment Tommy would experience when he found out his father was not waiting for him in any particular locale. That innocence in him just knocked me back. He had physically transformed into a man. I saw hints of responsibility in him; I saw that he had grown up in many ways. But these tears, they were evidence of a still-growing boy.

"I know you're a man now in many ways."

"I took care of myself, if that's what you mean."

I remember what it was like to feel so right, so righteous. I knew I needed to let Tommy know somehow, let him down easy so he wasn't smacked in the face with it later, but first I just needed to get him to trust me again, the way he seemed to trust Frank. I knew the deep regret at having bought into Frank's dreams and hopes. But for now, I would let Tommy have his delusions. For now, that was the kindest thing I could do.

As I stepped down the next rung, another glinting object caught my eye. I stepped back up a rung and reached across the floor, grabbing a small silver piece. I looked at it closely. A silver salt well engraved with the letters ACO.

"Tommy? Did you see this? Where did it come from?"

He turned and his eyes widened; then he swallowed hard as though he recognized it. Just as quickly, his face went blank again, and he shrugged. "I guess Old Crooked Eye was entertaining in the hayloft?"

"I doubt this is hers. Wrong initials. You never saw it before?" I don't know why I asked the question again, but it didn't quite make sense to me that it was up there.

He turned to the hayloft door. "No."

"I'll take it to the house. Maybe a relative passed it down. Or a crow brought it from someone Mrs. Mellet knows. They steal shiny things, you know. Crows do."

"I know," Tommy said.

I headed down the ladder, leaving Tommy to do his chores and scrub off the stink.

"Mama?"

I looked up to see hay dropping where Tommy's feet kicked it clear of the loft.

"Thank you. For seeing me as a man. For believing in me."

I nodded and smiled before blowing him a kiss through the tears that filled my eyes. He had tangled the idea of me believing in him with the idea that I should also believe in his father. I would need to work hard to teach him that the two things were not tied together at all.

Once Katherine arrived, I told myself, I would not split us up again, and I would not allow Frank's careless trail of crumbs to nowhere interfere with yet another son's future.

Oh, how I wanted to tell Tommy that his father's straying eye, busy hands, and careless behavior had caused James' death, that men like Howard Templeton were the exact opposite of Frank in morals and conviction. I'd never been so close to telling Tommy just what kind of man he was holding up as an idol, but I couldn't. It simply wasn't the right time. And as I left the barn, I wondered just when the right time would be.

Chapter 31

Katherine

1891—Storm Lake

The meal the Christoffs hosted for the reverend and the Murrays had provided the best-tasting dinner scraps that Katherine had eaten in a long time. Not that she had been permitted to sit at the table with the guests, but she had been able to skim off the serving platters once she'd doled out the meal to those at the dining table.

Due to the Christoffs having to struggle to get the farm up and running, to restore this home, they had been forced to sell their good silver. Earlier that day, Katherine had been required to scrub and polish the inexpensive tin as much as she could.

When they all sat down to eat, Mrs. Christoff announced that she had been particularly charitable and had given away their silver to an organization that arranged to use the proceeds of its sale so that a family in South Dakota could purchase the tools and seed they needed to start a farm. The reverend was particularly impressed at hearing this, and the Murrays inquired as to how they might be able to give away the extra set of silver they had but never used.

Katherine knew that information would never be disclosed, but she chuckled to herself, envisioning all the ladies of the church unloading their precious dinnerware for a cause that did not exist.

Once that lie had been discussed for an appropriate amount of time and praised as a selfless act of generosity, the Murrays took the lead in discussing the surge in criminal activity in town, that it was often children carrying out the illicit behavior. They blamed the parents, but it seemed to depend upon how loyal the parents were to the church as to how the child was viewed—as the devil's spawn or simply a child in need of the belt.

Katherine was collecting the dinner plates, doing her best to stay out of reach of Mr. Christoff. His fear of her seemed to abate in the presence of others. And, whereas Katherine would have thought dining with guests might protect her from his exploring eyes and roaming hands, she found that he became brave and enjoyed the chance to try to touch her right under the noses of the people who claimed to best understand evil and the shape it took in society.

She was focused on how to best collect his dinner plate and tinware when she heard the word "revival" mentioned in conjunction with her name. She froze momentarily, reaching to collect the knife. Had she heard it? She walked slowly toward the hall, then stood just outside the doorway, where they could not see her, and listened.

There was a pause in conversation, as though they were waiting to be sure she was gone. Then they started again.

"Why, yes, a revival with your Katherine at its center might be just the thing to drive our funds to the most holy of sizes. Provided she's willing to be moved by the spirit," Mr. Murray said.

A chair slid across the floor in the dining room, and Katherine flew down the hall with the dirty dishes. She scraped them and then stood at the pie safe, doubled over with stomach pain. Had she heard them right? That she would be the focal point of the revival the Christoffs had been put in charge of? Mrs. Christoff's knife-sharp laugh rang out from down the hall; the rhythmic rise and fall of Reverend Banks' voice filled in around it.

Katherine began to quake. She clasped her hands together to stop them from shaking as she remembered the Spring Up! Revival they had attended. The girl who had been hauled to the pulpit, her feet circling in air as she twisted and fought off the adults who were bringing her forth to have her soul scoured of the devil.

If only she had found a way to still herself, to stop wrestling free. Katherine had wished for her to find a calm center inside, to let the chaos around her swirl without feeding it. If only she had, Katherine thought they would have put her aside, become uninterested in her. But even as Katherine had prayed for the girl and tried to will a sense of peace to settle over her, she had thrust and wrenched and choked on her fear, creating a froth at the mouth and glee in those who had pinned her to the ground, in those who'd claimed to want to help her.

Katherine swallowed hard, closing her eyes, opening up to the calming. But then the words of Scripture rang in her mind. Was she summoning something otherworldly? Was she courting the devil himself? She put her hands over her ears. *Stop it. Stop it. Stop it.*

A grip on her arm startled Katherine, and she whirled around. "Hannah." She exhaled, free of the confusion that had clamped her down. "Did you hear them?"

"Hear what?"

"Your mother and Reverend Banks. They declared *me* the object lesson for the next revival."

Hannah scrunched up her face. "No, no. They didn't say that. I was sitting there. They said you could greet the congregation. They were talking about music and—"

"I heard them!"

Hannah's eyes widened and welled with tears. Her lips quivered, and Katherine realized how young Hannah actually was. She could be so mature and engaging in many ways, but even she, who saw her parents' foibles, ignored them. Katherine reminded herself of the struggling girl. *Stay calm. Let it pass. Don't let them have a reason to hold you close. Just do your work.*

Katherine turned and opened the center screened door on the safe and started to pull out the cake tray when Hannah's voice rang out.

"I'll do that. You sit, Kat. Just sit for a moment. You can't go back out there all riled up for no reason. You'll be giving Reverend Banks cause to haul you right out of the house."

Katherine nodded. She was fearing the same thing. She sat at the worktable while Hannah pulled out the cake, set the tray on the table, and then returned to the pie safe. She opened the screened door on the left and shuffled a pie and the plate of jelly-filled roly-polies around.

"I'll help," Katherine said.

Hannah froze, then looked over her shoulder at Katherine. "Just cleaning up some crumbs—you sit."

Katherine ignored the feeling of her body being dragged into the ground by five sets of hands and began to cut the cake in front of her, placing the yellow confection with its creamy frosting onto china dessert plates.

When she finished, she rose and began to arrange the plates on a tray. Hannah finally tore her attention from the pie safe, latched each screen door, and took up the two plates that didn't fit on the tray.

"Keep your smile bright. I see Reverend Banks and the Murrays looking at you, but their faces bear no sense that they believe you are possessed by any demon at all, let alone the devil himself. So far, I don't think they've even noticed you're ill. I've seen Mrs. Murray in a lather about people she feared or disliked, and she shows none of that tonight. They don't think anything bad about you at all."

Katherine patted her forehead with a linen cloth, hoping she did not look as horrid as she felt.

"Just smile. They'll not look past the smile," Hannah said.

Katherine exhaled, but she did not trust Hannah's assessment. Staying even another few nights at the Christoffs' would ensure she could at least leave with a semblance of a thought of where to go. She could not afford to be hustled off to Reverend Banks' for a soul-cleansing.

Katherine thought Hannah's young age was showing. She'd clearly overlooked the searing gaze of the minister, who watched Katherine's every move, even when all attention was on Hannah's recitation of historical events of the Dakota Territory from 1860–1871.

Hannah also overlooked her father watching the minister become mesmerized by Katherine, and Mrs. Christoff staring at her husband as he repeatedly requested Katherine bring him fresh water, a new napkin, or a clean spoon. Katherine told herself to stay calm, that no matter what anyone had decided about her purity or sinfulness, she was leaving. That thought alone gave her a sense of hope that none of them could tamp down.

She and Hannah entered the hallway, and a thick breeze pushed the front door open, making the chandelier rattle, the ball swinging wildly at the bottom. Katherine set the tray on the entry table and pushed the door closed, moving the latch to hold it steady against any more wind.

She turned to see Hannah studying her, making Katherine feel uncomfortable, as though she'd been discovered in the hallway in her bare feet, wearing nothing but her chemise.

Katherine turned her face to the jangling chandelier. "That thing is hanging by half a wire, it seems." She forced a laugh, and Hannah's gaze went to the still-swinging light. She narrowed her eyes on it. "Katherine, is that—"

"Let's go. We still have to get the coffee for the cake."

Katherine picked up her tray and made her way into the dining room with Hannah trailing behind. They stopped at Reverend Banks first. Hannah settled the plates she was carrying in front of him and Mrs. Murray. Then she assisted Katherine by removing plates from the tray, placing one each in front of Mrs. Christoff and Mr. Murray.

But when it was time to place the cake for Mr. Christoff, Hannah took hers and headed for her seat, leaving Katherine to hold the tray in one hand and bend down for Mr. Christoff to select the piece he wanted. Katherine pushed the tray toward him and he studied the two pieces left as the others chatted at the table.

He glanced around the room, then pointed at the piece closest to Katherine. She began to lift it up with her free hand, but he waved her off. "No, no. The other one." She nodded and set the plate down before beginning to lift the other, wishing he was still shaken by what happened on the day of the tornado. Perhaps he felt that in the presence of the reverend, he was safe from the evil they attributed to her.

She felt her skirt shift and Mr. Christoff's palm underneath it, against her knee, his calloused skin catching on the stocking as he rubbed circles. Her hands shook, causing the plate to clink on the silver tray. She looked around the table. Didn't they notice?

"That's precious china, Katherine," Mrs. Christoff said.

Katherine nodded and backed away, forcing Mr. Christoff to drop his hand. She looked around the room.

Were they fine with him handling her this way? No. They did not see. Mrs. Christoff was mesmerized by Reverend Banks' dissertation on just how God showed himself in everyday life, in everyone who was open to him.

Sweat poured down the sides of her face, and her mind grew light and unfocused. She worried that she would pass out if she didn't leave the room right then. "Coffee," she said, placing a plate in front of Mr. Christoff before dashing off to the kitchen.

She opened the back door to allow a breeze to enter the kitchen, then put the kettle on the fire. She drew the coffee grinder from its place in the cupboard above the dry sink and put the beans into the glass chamber, the aroma clearing her mind just a bit. She went to the pie safe and opened the screened door that normally revealed the sugar cone and the pinchers used to break it up.

She pulled out the paper-covered cone but couldn't find the pinchers. She reached deep into the safe, her fingers tapping this way and that, waiting to feel the metal tool. Finally, she felt them and pulled the tool out. That was odd. Hannah must have changed the order of things when she was shuffling items this way and that earlier.

Katherine sighed and turned the handle on the coffee grinder. The sound of crunching and the release of thick, wonderful coffee filled her nose. It was then she heard it. The chandelier down the hall was rattling. Katherine poked her head out of the kitchen to have a look. There didn't appear to be anything happening that would cause the chandelier to quake, and yet it was.

She shrugged and went to the sugar cone, peeled away some of the paper that encased it, and began to clip at it, using the nippers to break off tiny shards of sugar, placing them in the china bowl.

There it was again—the clanging chandelier. She was drawn to the sound, wondering how the Christoffs and their guests weren't made curious by the noise. This time when Katherine stuck her head into the hallway to have a look, she saw the ball at the bottom with the diamond-shaped facets cut into it winking sapphire blue like her dress, blazing emerald green, throwing amber splotches against the wall, dancing with shades of white and ruby, drawing Katherine farther down the hall, toward the warm lights.

Her measured, soft steps carried her forward. She passed the staircase, and the mahogany door blew open again, a gust of wind pushing her dress back against her legs. Katherine passed the dining room and glanced inside. No one seemed to notice the wind pushing through the house, the jangling chandelier, or her walking by. She quietly closed the door, and the air stilled. She turned to see the kaleidoscope of colors still shimmering against the cream damask-papered walls. She clasped her hands together at her waist and moved back, stopping when the chandelier was directly above her.

She squinted at the light show bursting off the ball, feeling as though the unusual colors being cast about the space had the ability to warm her from the inside out. She heard the door blow open behind her, a crisp gust pushing at her back, cooling her sweating skin. The crystal swags vibrated as though churning in boiling water. Katherine couldn't take her eyes away from the sight. Now the entire chandelier was shuddering. The medallion around the base at the ceiling began to chip; the white plaster snowed down.

The wind coming from behind made her shiver. She turned her hands palms-up, looking at the plaster as it hit her hands. Then, as she looked upward again, transfixed, the chandelier made an even more emphatic shake, and the pendant dropped from its chain, falling right into Katherine's upturned hands.

Katherine stared at the ball. Three golden links were attached through the hole at its crown. She looked back at the chandelier rocking in the breeze. The orb was cool to the touch.

"What is all that racket?" Mrs. Christoff's voice rang out as she stuck her head into the hallway from the dining room.

Katherine closed one hand around the ball and put it to her side. She nodded toward the front of the hallway. "The latch on the door must be broken. Wind blew it right open."

Mrs. Christoff rolled her shoulders back and frowned, looking past Katherine at the door. "Well, close it and get back to that coffee. We're nearly finished with our cake."

Katherine walked to the door, waiting for a hand to close on her shoulder, to demand the crystal ball. She pushed the door shut softly and turned back. Mrs. Christoff's gaze was attached to the still-swinging chandelier. She did not seem to notice some of the plaster had hailed down and did not mention that the pendant was missing. Katherine closed her hand around it tighter, each fingertip fitting neatly over a smooth facet.

"Just get on with it," Mrs. Christoff said. "Our guests are wondering what you're up to."

Mrs. Christoff swept back into the dining room, leaving Katherine alone. She walked back toward the kitchen, already pulling her skirt up so she could tuck the faceted ball into the secret petticoat pocket, as though somehow keeping the ball would feed her, as though somehow she would not suffer Mrs. Christoff's wrath once she finally noticed it was gone.

**

Katherine finished drying the last dinner plate, setting it gently in the sideboard in the dining room. The minister and the Murrays were long gone, but Katherine could still feel their presence in the dining room. Part of that was the lingering of Mrs. Murray's rose perfume. Another portion of what Katherine was experiencing was fear—the sort that embedded itself in her bones and shook her from the inside out. She could not stop the images of the little girl who'd been dragged to the pulpit at the revival. Her screams and the wild audience added to Katherine's distress.

From what she'd overheard that evening, Katherine had about two weeks to leave before she would become the center of attention at the next revival. Mrs. Christoff had wanted it sooner, but Reverend Banks cautioned against having two revivals too close in time, in not honoring the hard work the folks were doing during planting season.

Those extra days would give Katherine enough time to gather up some money or hide away items she could easily sell for railroad fare. She did not intend to stay any longer than she had to. If only she knew exactly where she was headed. She rubbed her belly and entered the kitchen.

Above her in the bedroom, she heard the family moving around. Katherine had been ordered to finish cleaning and to organize the fabric for the next clothing orders before going to bed. She was about to put out the lantern in the kitchen when she saw the basket of rolls was still sitting out.

She nibbled on one and eyed the pie safe, not believing her luck. In the Christoffs' rush to bed, they hadn't checked for the padlock.

She began to put the basket in its place and her mouth began to water. The lemon frosting on the cake that was stowed there smelled like a little piece of heaven. She licked her lips and pushed back the dishtowel that covered the confection. She bent forward and inhaled divine citrus.

She ran her finger across the frosting, digging into the yellow goodness. She pulled out a section of the cake and tried to eat it slowly, to savor the taste, but once the sweet frosting hit the back of her tongue, the tangy lemon caused her mouth to flood with saliva.

She couldn't stop herself from taking more. She removed the cake from the pie safe and shoveled the white-and-yellow heaven into her mouth with her hands, nearly choking. She could not risk eating the entire thing—even this had been too much.

She stepped back from the table, breathing heavily, her fingers caked with frosting, crumbs adhering to her skin. She stared at the cake, its crumbling sides no longer neat cuts.

She patted the cake back into shape, smoothed the icing with her finger, and covered it with the towel again. She pushed it back and shut the screened door on the pie safe. The tray extended so far that the door wouldn't close.

She pressed it shut again, unable to latch it.

"Oh, galoshes," she said. She wiggled the tray and pushed it in again. "For goodness' sake." She sighed and took the tray out again and tried once more. No luck. She pulled it out again and set the tray back on the table. She reached into the safe and walked her fingers around the dark space, searching for what might be keeping the tray from properly fitting.

Her fingers swept over some paper. She grasped and pulled. She stared at the clump in her hand—envelopes. Katherine went to the window where the moonlight cast the sharpest beams. It was then she could read the return address. *Sioux Falls, South Dakota. Jeanie S. Arthur.*

Katherine's full belly turned. Her hands shook as she reread the envelope. Nausea cramped her insides. She looked at the postmark. The top letter was dated just a week back. The others were from several weeks and months back. Her hands shook as the realization settled in. How was this possible?

Why would they have hidden these letters? She rubbed her eyes.

Katherine's hands dropped to her sides. She knew why, whether she wanted to believe it or not. They would not want her talking with her mother because they wanted her with them, earning all the extra money she did with her sewing for half the church.

The bed creaked above, and Katherine held her breath, waiting to hear feet. Nothing more sounded out, but unable to track them in their complete silence, she hoped one of them was not sneaking down.

If someone did come down, she could simply pretend she was seeing to the stove. She rushed to it and opened its belly. She poked at the dwindling fire and blew gently on it to reignite the flames. It was barely warm. She snuck to the back door and attempted to quietly slide the bolt. It wouldn't move. She held her breath and lifted up on the handle while she jiggled the bolt. This time, it squeaked and moved.

She froze, praying no one would think the sound to be out of the ordinary and decide to investigate. She glanced at the cake carcass on the table and the secreted envelopes now strewn beside the tray.

Please don't come down.

She went to the doorway and poked her head into the hall. The chandelier was still, the front door closed tight. She patted her hidden pocket, where she'd stowed the crystal ball that had fallen earlier that night. She exhaled. She needed more wood just in case.

She opened the back door and stepped into the crisp air. The sharp wind sliced through the dress as though she were naked; her toes felt wooden as the cold seeped into her skin, burying itself in her bones. She grabbed a log from the pile and scurried back to reenter the kitchen.

She pushed the wood into the dying fire and opened the flue just enough to stoke the flame. She bit her nail as she took up the letters, the newest one first. She snaked her fingers inside and slid the letter from its pouch. Katherine stood by the window, reading the latest letter first.

My dearest Katherine,

Where are you? Where are you? I haven't received word from you for months. I am sick in eleven different ways at not knowing where you are. I'm desperate and frightened and oh, please write me and tell me you're okay. Please forgive me my poor performance at... Well, I am sorry. There are no words to better our past predicament. But I hope the words that follow—I know the words that follow will alter everything that has been wrong ...

Katherine's breath quivered and tears sprouted from her eyes, dropping onto the letter, splashing the ink. She'd never felt such relief, such affection from someone who was not even in the same room as her. She lifted her head, savoring the sensation of love that seeped from the words her mother had written. She looked at the ceiling, sniffled, and swallowed a sob. Her mother hadn't forgotten her. Katherine was not alone in the world. Jeanie Arthur hadn't been unconcerned. She had been looking for her daughter all along.

Circumstances have changed, and I can now assure you and Tommy that I will have the funds to keep us all. Finally. Please give me a chance to explain. Meet me in Des Moines as fast as your feet can take you there. When we reunite, I'll explain everything, but I will say now that Mrs. Mellet has written to say she will set our name right, that she will pay back some of what she took from us, that she desires to relieve some of our suffering!

Home! We are going home, and that means we will live together, putting all that has been awful to its grave, buried far away from our minds and our souls. Here is enough money to get you from Yankton to Des Moines. I have not heard from you in some time, but I assume you are still there. I know it has been hard, but please keep your heart open to mine and meet me in Des Moines!

I love and adore and miss you to the very depths of my being. Please send word when you have your ticket. Thank the Turners for their care. Send them my gratitude for having kept you warm and safe while I could not. I will be at the depot in Des Moines on May ____, arriving just after noon. Please send word to the post office there, and I will retrieve it. I'm sending letters to each of the places I know you were staying…One of them should reach you.

Katherine, Katherine, Katherine! I Love you forever—as wide and deep as the earth's crust,

Love from Mama

Katherine stared at the letter, checked the dates over and over. She could not make out the date her mother had promised to meet her—her tears had blurred the ink. But it did not matter. She now knew her mother had received none of her correspondence, and she knew where her mother would be. Katherine reached into the envelope a second time, searching for the train fare. Nothing. The address it had been sent to was the Turners' home in Yankton.

How had it found its way to Storm Lake? It must have been sent along with the others or picked up when Mr. Christoff took his trip to Yankton. Katherine looked at the other letters, a chill rising in the kitchen although the new log grew hotter. Her teeth chattered as she opened the remaining letters, turning them this way and that to capture the moonlight.

Her mother had not forgotten her. Her mother had been desperate to reach her. Katherine had felt used by the Christoffs, biding her time until she could buy her way back to her mother, but she had not fully understood the depths of what they were willing to do to keep her in their home. Their cruelty dug in further, past the pinched arms, sharp words, and cold tone, reaching deep inside her, chilling in a way that soundly convinced her that very evening that leaving was the best thing she could do.

Katherine heard the groaning of the Christoffs' bed as one of them must have turned. She looked to the ceiling, waiting for a sign that they were sleeping or getting up out of bed.

Nothing. She exhaled. But the relief passed as she heard feet on the floorboards above her. Katherine sprang up and shoved the letters inside the bodice of her dress, then thrust the cake tray to the back of the pie safe with shaking hands.

The stairs creaked. Katherine held her breath and took up the basket of rolls. She could pretend she was still putting them away. She turned from the safe, nearly in tears, preparing to defend herself, when Hannah stepped into the kitchen. Her muslin nightgown gently wafted as a draft came down the hall, pushing against her shins in an almost ghostly way. Her hair formed a flyaway halo—evidence of a fitful sleep.

"Kat?"

Katherine's breath returned. "I was just having some water."

Hannah narrowed her eyes on Katherine, glanced around the kitchen, then shrugged.

Katherine stared at Hannah. Had she seen her hiding the cake?

Hannah gestured to the pump. "I get thirsty at night, too."

Katherine sighed.

"So I won't tell."

"Thank you," Katherine said.

Hannah's gaze went to the table, to the scavenged lemony crumbs that Katherine hadn't cleaned up.

"I won't tell of that, either." Hannah pointed to the table. She moved toward the table and plopped a lemony crumb into her mouth. "Let's get those swept away before my parents waken. That divine smell will surely rise up the stairs and alert them that we had a treat."

Katherine couldn't speak. Hannah had always been friendly, but now Katherine was beginning to feel as though they were actually friends despite their age difference. Perhaps *ally* was a better term. Perhaps Katherine shouldn't have been so quick to believe in such things, but she needed to trust someone.

Katherine rubbed her arms to create heat. "I'm sorry, Hannah."

"For what?"

"That your mother is cruel and mean."

Hannah sighed and looked at her bare feet, wiggling her toes.

"Your mother isn't sweet as lemon cake, either, Katherine Arthur."

Hannah's use of her full name gave Katherine pause, as though Hannah was telling her that she had power in the house over Katherine. She might have readily agreed on this matter of her mother possibly being not so sweet until just an hour before. But how one hour had changed everything about the way she felt toward her mother. Jeanie Arthur hadn't forgotten her daughter. Jeanie Arthur had means and a plan to reunite their family. Jeanie Arthur was nothing like Hannah's mother.

Nothing. Still, Katherine resisted the urge to put her trust in Hannah, sweet as she had been. Katherine took Hannah's hand. "Your fingers are ice. Let's get you back to bed."

They started toward the hallway, but Hannah stopped, gripping Katherine's hand, making her halt as well. Katherine turned.

"Please don't go, Kat. Please."

Katherine exhaled, relieved that Hannah used her pet name again, feeling any distance from earlier close again. Katherine thought of all the time she'd spent feeling sorrow that her mother had stopped trying to reach her. She was awed that the loneliness that weighed on her, that gripped her hardening heart, was suddenly lifted. She could not agree to stay. But she worried Hannah might tell Mrs. Christoff if she confided that she had plans to leave. Katherine could not afford to have them keep closer watch, to let them have even more control over her. But she wondered if Hannah had seen the letters. She wanted to ask her. She had been rooting around in the pie safe earlier. Had she seen them? She thought the girl would admit it if she had.

"Go? What would make you say that?"

"I feel like you're going to leave me. I don't know where the feeling comes from. But I just don't want you to ever go."

Katherine felt tiny cracks of pain, like the crevices that form in china as it ages, carve into her heart. She didn't want to hurt Hannah. But she couldn't risk being forced to stay. She wasn't going to tell her about the letters or ask if she'd read them.

"I'll stay, little friend. For you."

"They won't let you go, anyway."

Katherine searched the girl's face for a smile, a sign that her words were the joking kind. But there was none of that in Hannah's face. Katherine would not leave out the front door of this home. But she would leave for sure.

Hannah's face lit up, her eyes warming Katherine's heart and shaming her also. But Katherine had been alone long enough. Life was hard, it hurt often, but it was time for Katherine to do what was right for her. It was time for little Hannah to learn the world did not break open with gold and diamonds just because that's how she wanted it. Terrible as it was to learn, it was true.

"They don't need me."

"They need you for the revival."

Katherine shook her head. "Go back to bed, Hannah. They will scold you for roaming the house. I'll finish the kitchen and be right up."

Katherine bit her lip. A lie. There was no sin inside a lie one told to stay alive. No God could find fault with that type of logic.

Chapter 32

Jeanie

1891—Des Moines

Mrs. Mellet's kitchen was bright and airy. I couldn't help wishing to buy a home just like it as soon as was possible. After I fed Tommy his cold eggs, with Yale on his lap, I clipped as much of his hair as I could so that it looked presentable but also got rid of a good deal of the skunk excretion. He had entertained Yale with the wooden spoon, playing along with it like a dolly, making it run across her legs, over her shoulders, and fly through the air like a fairy.

If only Katherine had been there, if only I knew she was safe, I could have more fully enjoyed the moments of laughter, the unusual guffaw from Yale, as though she was just now learning that people, in fact, find humor and laughter in the world. It pinched at my heart while heartening me simultaneously. I felt more alive than I had even in the days since realizing I'd been part of a miracle.

I put Yale onto the floor so I could safely shave Tommy. "Now, don't forget to check the post office after you drop the letter to Mr. Halsey. My stomach aches at the thought of one more day not knowing where Katherine is."

I stopped shaving to spread more cream on his face. He shifted in his seat. "I know, Mama. We'll get word soon. I know we will."

I thought of the morning, the angry words, the sadness I'd seen in Tommy's face. And I was so grateful that those moments had passed and we were relaxed together, as though the tension had never even been there.

"Thank you for being so helpful, Tommy. I can't say how reassuring it is that you're here." My voice cracked. Tommy looked away. *We're not crying people.* Those words seemed to hang in the kitchen air. I knew Tommy probably needed to see me as ever strong and capable, that he was reassured when I was just that. So instead of allowing the threatening tears to flow, I pushed them back and continued with his shave.

After he was cleaned up, Mrs. Mellet allowed Tommy to select a few shirts, pants, socks, underthings, and shoes from her husband's and son's closets. I drew him a warm bath, and while he scrubbed his skin, Yale and I went to milk the cows out back near the pond. By the time I put them out to pasture and returned to the kitchen, Tommy was dressed and appearing as handsome as a man drawn into a storybook tale.

When he saw us enter the kitchen, he spun around and finished with a two-step. "How do I look?"

"All grown up and handsome as anything I've ever seen," I said. He held me tight. "We'll get word from Katherine today. I just know it," he said.

I nodded and pulled away, a jumble of nerves dancing in my stomach, telling me I was not so sure I agreed.

Chapter 33

Katherine

1891—Storm Lake

Katherine's body quivered, but she tried to mask it from Hannah. She did not want to elicit any suspicion on the girl's part. She walked Hannah back to the bottom of the staircase and promised she would be up in just moments. She kissed her forehead and smoothed back her hair. "Sleep tight, little angel sent from above."

Hannah wrapped her arms around Katherine and hugged with all her might. Katherine patted the girl's back and rested her chin on the top of her head.

Did she know? Would she stop Katherine if she suspected?

"Go on," Katherine said. She patted Hannah's backside and the younger girl ascended. Katherine heard the bedroom door close and then she ran for the keeping room. Her heart thrashed inside her chest. She tossed aside the piles of material and boxes. *There it was.* She reached for the bag that held her sketches and pencils and clutched the bag to her. She needed something to sell. She scanned the keeping room. Nothing there besides andirons, washtubs, washboards, and clothes pegs.

If the Christoffs hadn't sold their silver just to survive, Katherine knew the dining room would have held the items that would garner the most money and ensure her passage home. But with the silver gone, what could she sell? What would be easy to carry? A teacup? No. She paced the room.

Where did Mr. Christoff keep his money? She thought of the last time he returned from town, from the bank. He had immediately taken to the cellar. Katherine went to the door on the left side of the keeping room and pulled it open. The darkened cellar emitted a moldy, suffocating foulness. She lit the lantern and reminded herself she'd been in the basement plenty of times to collect the roots, to shovel coal into the stove. There was no reason to be frightened of all the things that had brought fear to her since boarding with the Christoffs.

She raised the light and saw a mouse run down the wobbly stairs. She shuddered and lifted her skirt, her hand brushing past the crystal orb, taking odd comfort in just knowing it was there. She set each foot carefully as she descended and then stepped left into the room that led to the coal cellar.

There were more washtubs down there, and a commode and sink near the back. Katherine shined the light, turning this way and that, searching for something in the cellar that would have served as a place to hide money.

She dug through a cupboard that had been built into the wall, the place where apples and squash had been stored before they were eaten. There were several drawers. She opened them, but there was nothing inside. It was no use. She would have to hope to pocket something from the dining room that she could trade for money. She told herself not to be glum, that the most important thing that could happen, had—she knew for certain that her mother was waiting for her. And that was all she needed to know.

Her mood steady, she decided to head back upstairs, to arrange the materials as had been ordered and sleep. She was certain with some rest she could plan her escape long before they desired to have her as the central saved figure of the revival.

Katherine turned and walked smack into Mr. Christoff. Her body felt as though it were alight with fire as surprise stunned her into silence.

"What are you doing down here?"

She opened her mouth but had nothing to say.

He stepped forward and put his hand against her face, his thumb rubbing her cheek. Katherine drew back, her muscles tense; fear tasted like iron on her tongue.

"Let her stay down here." Mrs. Christoff's voice came from the stairway behind Mr. Christoff.

He froze, his thumb hard against her cheek. He hesitated, and Katherine could not imagine what he was considering. But then he smiled and brushed his thumb over her lips. She pulled away, stomach churning with disgust at his touch.

He nodded. "Yes, Ida. That sounds like a fine idea."

Katherine wanted to protest but couldn't speak, for fear had numbed her tongue.

He took the lantern from Katherine, backed away, and turned as he headed toward the stairs.

As they climbed upward, Katherine heard them mumbling but could make out only one clear sentence. "We'll all sleep better if she's stashed away here," Mrs. Christoff said just before the door clicked shut.

**

Katherine had stood for some time in the same spot she'd been in when Mr. Christoff went upstairs. She listened for the sound of rodents, for the growl of monsters, for all the things that every human feared at not having comfort and safety in life. She shivered and rubbed her arms to make some heat. The coal cellar would be warmer with the stove running inside it.

She turned in the direction of that space and squinted. Moving gingerly, she entered the space and stretched over a dwindling mound of coal, reaching for the door that led outside. Perhaps she could squeeze through it. She held her hands from one end of the opening to the other. Even with her slender shoulders and even if she could get up high enough to try to push through, she would have trouble fitting. She slid the latch and pushed it open.

A view of the stars greeted her, the crescent moon framed perfectly. She tried to memorize the shades of navy blue, sparkling, shimmery silver stars, the way the moonlight appeared smudged around its edges the farther it went out from the crescent.

She moved nearer the stove and sank down to her bottom, accidentally sitting on the crystal ball. She removed it from the pocket and held it in her palms, feeling the facets. Perhaps she could sell it? She looked down at the glass and turned it, catching the moonlight, causing colors to jump. *Mama, Mama, Mama.*

Katherine pulled her legs in and balanced the ball on her knees. A gauzy veil of clouds cleared the moon, and it lit the basement brighter, the light catching on the orb. With one finger, she moved it back and forth, making it look as though it were lit from within.

She closed her eyes and buried her face in her knees, clutching the ball against her head. *Please, God. Help me.* She repeated the prayer and finally felt the calming. She lifted her head and saw James squat down across from her. A smile spread across her face. The glowing warmth overtook any colors that had been dancing, and it grew warm in her palms. James' hands were around hers, the light emanating through their fingers. And in that moment, she knew she would find a way out. Somehow, her brother was watching over her, and somehow she would make her way back to their mother.

**

Katherine found a gourd that had made it through the winter and used it as a pillow. She woke with her neck crooked, her muscles tight, and her bones heavy, as if someone had injected them with lead while she slept. She moved slowly, her aching muscles making it difficult just getting to standing. She shoveled the coal into the belly of the stove and went to the top of the steps, listening for a sign of life in the house. She tried the door, but it was locked.

She banged on the door, but no one responded. Finally, she used the chamber pot that was set in the farthest, darkest corner of the cellar. Back at the top of the stairs, she bashed her fists against the door, calling for someone to unlock it. Finally, after hours more sitting at the top of the stairs, intermittently listening for someone in the house, she heard the key turn in the lock.

The door opened, and the light streaming in the keeping-room windows forced her eyes closed. But not before she saw it was Hannah who was letting her out. Katherine got to her hands and knees and crawled into the keeping room as her vision adjusted. The warmth of the fire told her she was near the middle of the room.

Hannah squatted down and hugged Katherine, their arms tight around each other. Katherine had gone long past feeling like crying. Determination at leaving was all that fueled her heart.

"Oh, Kat, I'm so sorry they locked you in. They're just frightened. You have to give them a chance to realize you are not, well…you know."

Katherine couldn't respond.

"Please don't," Hannah said.

"Don't what?"

"Leave."

Katherine looked down at her dress, filthy from the night in the cellar. Had she not been so cold, she would have taken it off.

"I see it on your face. I know what you're thinking."

"I'm thinking I need to clean up. Did your parents grant you permission to release me?"

"No. Father's in the field. Mother went to the feed store and the grocery and to see Reverend Banks."

Katherine's heart sped up at the thought. This was her chance.

She hopped to her feet and ran upstairs, Hannah following close by. "Kat, please. Stop!"

Katherine reached behind her and tried to work the buttons on the dress.

"You don't have any money," Hannah said. "You don't even know where to go."

"Oh, I do know where I'm going now. Your parents hid some letters, but I found them. And I know exactly where my mother is."

"But there's no money in the envelope—"

Katherine froze. No money in the envelope. How would Hannah know that? She turned, anger flaring at the possibility, the betrayal. Was it true? Could the girl who called her Kat so affectionately, the girl who wanted Katherine to stay with her forever and be her sister no matter what, have betrayed her?

Hannah looked at her feet.

"What did you say?"

Hannah bowed her head into her chest as though hoping to disappear right into her own body.

"You read the letters."

Hannah lifted her head, tears welling.

Katherine gripped her skirts. "How could you do this when you know how much I want to be with my mother? You're just like them."

Hannah shook her head wildly. "I'm nothing like them. But you're all I have. They don't care about me, but you do. You treat me like…"

Katherine sighed. "Like a sister."

Hannah nodded.

Katherine thought of all that the Christoffs had done to her. Hannah had been exempt from most of the poor treatment. But what if that changed when Katherine left? The thought chilled Katherine from the inside out. "Come with me," Katherine said.

"I can't."

"You can."

"They're my parents. I couldn't do that to them."

Katherine felt sad and worried for Hannah, but she would not risk her own life to stay with those religious lunatics. "They aren't my parents."

"It will get better if you stay. I promise it will. I'll make them treat you better."

"You don't get it, Hannah. Do they think my mother won't write again? Clearly, from the letters, she's desperate. She's not going to just lie down and die and forget me."

Hannah shrugged.

Something in Hannah's demeanor struck Katherine as wrong. "What is it?"

Hannah began to sob.

"Hannah. Tell me. It's no use hiding things from me now."

She swallowed hard, her throat straining from veins popping out. "I hid the letters before they even read them. My parents don't even know they exist."

Katherine began to remember the way Hannah always insisted on getting the mail with her mother, on being the one who went into the post office, as though she were saving her mother an errand. Hannah's shame was etched deep into her face, her eyebrows knitted tight.

Katherine needed to run, but she did not feel anger toward Hannah. Though Hannah had not been treated like Katherine, she suspected she had never felt loved by them. Katherine could understand the desperation that loneliness brought. She took Hannah into her arms, smoothing the back of her hair.

"Don't tell them about the letters, Hannah. If you really think of me as a sister, you need to let me leave and don't ever mention seeing the letters."

"I'll be all alone."

"I'll send for you. I'll write. I'll make sure you're not alone. Please. For me, do this. Let me leave and don't breathe a word. Maybe they were planning to hide me in the basement until the revival. They won't even know I'm gone."

Hannah nodded. Katherine kissed her forehead. "Now, help me change out of this dress and into something that is fit for travel."

"Kat." Hannah pulled a burlap knapsack from inside a drawer in the dresser. She stuffed an embroidered sampler she'd been making inside. "To remember me by." Katherine nodded.

"Hannah!" Mr. Christoff bellowed. They froze and stared at each other.

Katherine's mouth went dry. If he knew she had been let out of the basement, it would mean great punishment for Katherine, but probably also for Hannah. The younger girl surely could not withstand what Katherine had. About to surrender to Mr. Christoff to save Hannah from punishment, Katherine turned.

"Lunch, Hannah. Don't make me wait."

"Coming!" she yelled and dashed across the room, yanking a walking suit from the closet. She stuffed the tweed jacket and skirt into a suitcase and added a shirtwaist, chemise, drawers, and stockings. "He doesn't know you're out of the cellar."

Hannah buckled the straps that held the case closed and shoved it at Katherine. Katherine felt a swell of affection for her little friend. The love was spiked with sorrow, though, as she could not believe she would leave the girl behind.

She took the suitcase handle and pulled Hannah into an embrace. "Come with me. My mother will care for both of us."

"Hannah!"

Hannah pulled away. She took her straw hat from the top shelf and plunked it onto Katherine's head, tying the ribbons around her chin.

"I'm sorry for hiding the letters."

Katherine nodded.

They started toward the staircase. "I'll go down the back staircase. You take the front."

"I have to go to the keeping room before I leave."

"Take the watch in the box on the mantel—it's buried under the buttons. You can sell it for train fare," Hannah said. "I'll keep my father busy eating until you're gone."

Katherine nodded. "They will punish you."

Hannah shrugged. "I'll tell them you stole it all—that you tricked me and crept away. They'll believe me."

"They'll think it was the work of the devil."

"That's the only way they'll believe I wasn't involved."

"Then tell them that."

Katherine felt a darkness settle in around them. "Run away with me."

Hannah shook her head. "I just can't. They won't hurt me."

"I don't believe it," Katherine said.

Hannah pushed her shoulders up to her ears and then let them drop. "Write me. Tell me all about the blizzard, the cow, and how Aleksey held one hand while they cut your finger off the other, how his crystal-blue eyes held yours like love and promises."

Katherine held up her hand. "Half a finger, Hannah. Just half. And I never said a word about love."

Hannah's face creased in tears. "Oh, it must have been love."

Katherine would not argue this with her at such a time. They gave each other one last squeeze. Hannah whispered, "Walk along the creek at the edge of the woods. They won't see you, and you'll have enough time to make it to the train before they even know you're gone." Katherine nodded, and they held hands as they crept into the hallway. As they turned toward the separate sets of stairs each would take, they dropped hands, fingertips the last to let go, and each disappeared from the sight of the other.

This was it. Katherine descended, noticing the weathered chandelier. *Please don't let him hear me.* Each step downward made the suitcase sandwich the crystal ball against her leg, reassuring her that it was still with her. She snuck down the hall, nearing the doorway to the kitchen.

She stopped there and heard Mr. Christoff coughing. She stole a glance and saw he was seated at the table, back to the doorway. Hannah stood to his side, pouring him coffee. Katherine lifted her hand and wiggled her fingers. Hannah smiled at Katherine, eyes watery. Finally, she mouthed the words "Good-bye, Kat."

And Katherine broke the spell and stole across the doorway, passing the opening without drawing a bit of interest from Mr. Christoff.

Katherine entered the keeping room and drew her stash of sketches from their hiding spot. She tucked them into the knapsack and went to the mantel where the box with the watch sat. Katherine pulled it down and opened the lid. She flicked aside the buttons, finally uncovering a tarnished watch. Katherine wasn't sure she could sell it easily, but it was the only item worth anything.

She replaced the box and went to the door that led into the back of the house. She passed the cellar entrance and shuddered, as though her body were shaking off the dark desperation that came from being locked in it.

She thought again of the money she knew was hidden down there somewhere. She looked at the watch in her hand. No. Searching the cellar again was not worth the risk. She would have to make do with the watch.

She grasped the door that led outside.

"Where do you think you're going?"

Mr. Christoff's voice came from behind.

She spun around.

He was glaring. "I was just heading downstairs to check on you. And what do I see? You've escaped through a locked door." His eyes widened. "You *are* keeping company with the devil, aren't you?"

"Let me leave and the devil will be gone from your home for good."

"I wish I could do that."

She turned the handle behind her. She could run much faster than him. But to where? Surely he would get his horse and chase her that way.

"I'll show you what the devil has planned for us."

He rubbed his crotch.

"No."

He chuckled.

She grasped the watch in her hand tightly.

He stepped toward her.

Katherine lurched forward and threw the watch as hard as she could. It landed between his eyes with a *thunk*. He put his hand to his forehead, a confused expression spread over his face, and then he collapsed like an empty coat, right on top of the watch.

Hannah stepped into the room and went to the floor next to him. Katherine joined her. They tried to shift him and get the watch, but he was too heavy to move.

Katherine saw blood well up and stream across his brow.

Hannah untied her sash. "Grab that twine to tie him. Then tie me with this. Quickly, or you'll lose your chance."

Katherine's hands flew, securing Mr. Christoff and then doing Hannah's wrists. She fell over to her side. "I'll pretend to be knocked cold on top of being tied up."

Katherine stared, wary of leaving her in such a predicament.

"Take the gig and go," Hannah said. "The only danger now is in staying. I'll be fine." She winked at Katherine before she closed her eyes and played injured as she suggested she should.

Hannah was right. This was Katherine's last chance to leave. She bent down and kissed Hannah on the cheek. "Thank you," she whispered in the girl's ear.

Katherine swallowed her reluctance, leapt up, and burst through the back door, loping toward the barn, hoping to hitch the horse and be gone before the man found a way out of the ties and gave chase.

Chapter 34

Tommy

1891—Des Moines

The law office was paneled in thick, gleaming wood. It smelled of polish and ink and books. Tommy tried to imagine what it might be like to work in such a place. All of the intelligence in one spot must have made for all sorts of high conversation. He could handle sophisticated conversation but the books? Reading sophisticated ideas was not as fun as discussing them. These shelves were not like a family library. No, he did not have to crack even one of them open to know he would not enjoy poring through those in pursuit of a weekly paycheck.

Tommy delivered the letter his mother had written to Mr. Halsey and was told he would have to wait an hour for the man's reply. Tommy used the time to finish most of the household errands. Returning to Mr. Halsey's office exactly one hour later, the receptionist handed Tommy the envelope.

With that envelope safely stowed in his pocket, he knew he should hurry to the post office to check for mail and telegrams and head back to Mrs. Mellet's so she and his mother could ready for the assigned meeting time.

With the short distance between the law office and the post office, Tommy left the buggy where he'd parked it and kicked stones down the road, hands stuffed into his front pockets.

"Hey, Tommy!"

Tommy recognized Hank's gravelly voice without even turning around.

"Say, fella, how are you?" Hank elbowed Tommy. "We've been looking for you to write some of them poetic-like prayers. Turns out there's quite the market for prayers that say more than Bible verses."

Tommy grimaced, remembering the silver salt well his mother had found in the hayloft.

"You guys left some of your stolen stuff in my pocket and it fell out, unbeknownst to me. Let's just say I was questioned on the matter, and I do not appreciate that."

Hank shrugged. "Aww. That mean you're not gonna pen no more of those magic words like you done the other day?"

"I can pen some prayers when I get the time. I don't mind that. But I don't want any part of stealing. I just—"

Hank patted Tommy's shoulder. "I know, Arthur. The first time in jail is the worst. I smell what you're cooking on that."

Tommy stopped and looked at Hank. "Look. I have half a dozen errands and chores to do before the sun sets, and then perhaps I'll be in better humor. It's not that I don't want to help. Especially if I've inadvertently, without much effort at all, raised the quality of your prayer product. It does flow naturally." Tommy grinned.

Hank readjusted his hat. "Right from some spring of spiritual goodness from the depths of your soul."

Tommy squinted at him.

"Reverend Shaw said that," Hank said. "We had to tell him what you done when Mrs. O'Malley called on him, requesting more of that good stuff from the handsome, educated, polite boy."

Tommy raised his eyebrows.

"I knew O'Malley wasn't talking about me and big ole Bayard," Hank said.

Tommy whistled. "You're really greasing the wheel, aren't you?"

Hank shrugged. "Think about it. I've got another cold body waiting on me and Bay." He stuck his hand out. "Friends."

Tommy looked at his hand, the blackened knuckles and calloused fingers. Despite the dealings that were not legal or moral, he thought Hank was a good fellow down deep. And sometimes the only friend in sight is one that you weren't expecting would be there when you needed him. Tommy shook his hand and headed toward the post office while Hank went who knows where to retrieve and deliver who knows who to their final resting place.

**

Tommy pushed through the post office door expecting to see Pearl seated behind the counter or busy behind it, inserting mail into the slot that would ensure it arrived in the hands of the addressee.

He knocked on the counter. "Pearl?"

A plump man rounded the corner, coming from the back room. "Hey there, Sonny. What can I do for you?"

Tommy was suddenly nervous that Pearl was not there. He hadn't realized he'd been looking forward to seeing her, yet he felt a pull of attraction. His stomach stirred, and he became worried that he would not see her. "Is Pearl working today?"

"She's workin', all right. But not here right now. I got her on an errand to meet the mail train."

"Oh," Tommy said. A flash of Pearl, her verdant eyes and her big smile, came to mind. He pushed away his disappointment that he would not be seeing her in person. "I'm looking for mail and telegrams. Addressed to Tommy or Jeanie Arthur. From Katherine Arthur. My sister."

The man slid down one side of the cubbies and then the other, moving his finger along as he looked. He turned and said, "Nothing."

Nothing. He was not looking forward to delivering that bit of news to his mother. He knew how unnerved she'd been about not hearing from Katherine. She believed her to be safe and sound with a nice family, but Tommy could hear the catch in her voice when she mentioned her, when she suggested they send off another telegram or letter.

And so he patted the envelope in his pocket that contained the response from Mr. Halsey. At least his mother would feel good about taking care of the matter with Mrs. Mellet. Then perhaps they could better plan how to find Katherine. If she wasn't going to show up, at least the money would give them more resources with which to look for Katherine. At least there was that.

**

Tommy unhitched the horses, watered them, and was heading toward the house when he saw his mother coming from the back door, her face full of hope that he had heard from Katherine. He smiled at her and saw how pretty she looked with the wind grabbing bits of her hair from the bun at the nape of her neck. She appeared younger than she had just a few days back, when they had first reunited. And she certainly looked healthier than the morning he'd found her crying in her bed in Yankton. She was still lithe and light, but today, she looked pretty again, the way he remembered her when they'd lived in Des Moines.

When they reached each other, she clasped her hands at her waist and smiled. "So? Tell me."

Tommy pulled the envelope from his pocket. "This is Mr. Halsey's response to your letter."

She took it and began to slide her finger into the corner of the flap. "And news from Katherine?"

Tommy didn't want to tell the truth. But there was no choice. "Nothing."

His mother stopped opening the envelope and lifted her eyes to Tommy. He saw that she had to force a swallow down, that the news was paralyzing.

She looked to the sky as though doing a complicated math problem.

"Tomorrow, Mama. I know it." He wanted so much to ease the sadness he saw folded into her face. "And I got us some bread while I was waiting for Halsey's reply. Now you won't have to bake."

She pushed a smile at him. "You did a fine job, Tommy. But I worry since I sent so many letters to Katherine. I should send more, though. And then as soon as we get money, we will make full speed after her. We'll retrace every step she took since I last knew exactly where she was."

Tommy nodded. "Open the letter. You'll feel better once you meet with Mr. Halsey."

She jumped as though she'd forgotten she had the letter in her hand. She tore it open and pulled the paper out, unfolding it. It didn't take long for her to close the letter back up, so quickly that he thought perhaps she hadn't even read it. Her hand shook as she stuffed it back into the envelope.

"What is it, Mama?"

She shook her head, held up her skirt, and ran toward the house. Tommy followed her. When they burst into the kitchen, his mother stopped. He could see how hard she was breathing, shoulders rising and falling.

He stepped to her side. "Mama. Let me see."

"Halsey's going on vacation and will get back to us when he returns. In three weeks."

Tommy took the letter and read the three short sentences. He looked back at his mother, her pale complexion, the worry cutting into her brow, and all the light and happiness he had seen in her earlier had been sapped away. This angered him.

He took her shoulders and turned her toward him. "Now, you listen, Mama. He may be going on vacation, but it does not sound like he's gone yet. Let's get Mrs. Mellet into the buggy and head over there. This is not a matter that will wait."

She put her hands over his, a wan smile appearing.

"We won't wait," he said.

She nodded. "You're right. I'll go up and waken her from her nap and get her downstairs inside of twenty minutes. Like it or not, it is time for her to follow through."

Tommy kissed her forehead. "I'll take care of the horses and gather umbrellas. Looks like rain."

She grasped him like he was a child, holding him so tight, he coughed. "Thank you, Tommy. Thank you so much for all of this." Right now, this boy who strived for a strength he didn't always feel realized he was, in fact, the very pillar his mother needed to lean upon. This fueled his sense of importance, made him sure that his path was smoothing out, straightening, taking him to where he would be whole again.

And Tommy ran from the kitchen, determined to help his mother get what she deserved.

Chapter 35

Jeanie

1891—Des Moines

Tommy's news that Mr. Halsey was leaving for vacation smothered the air right out of me. The thought of how slowly Mrs. Mellet moved amplified the worry in me that we might not reach the law offices in time. But if I coaxed her properly, perhaps I could get her into the wagon inside of fifteen minutes. I took the back staircase from the kitchen two steps at a time. When I hit the landing that led to the hallway feeding into Mrs. Mellet's rooms, I stopped.

I forced myself to count to ten and collect my words. While Mrs. Mellet owed me a debt—she indicated that she believed the same—there was something that told me to watch my tone, to massage the discourse in a way that reflected the manner she had demanded to be treated nearly her entire life.

I knocked on Mrs. Mellet's bedroom door. No response. I rapped again and pressed my ear against the wood. Nothing. I moved down the hall to the dressing room door and did the same, to no avail. She had to be inside, and I was not going to let her sleep the day away while Mr. Halsey took off for a relaxing break somewhere that was already warm and sunny.

I dashed back to the bedroom and slid the door open, peeking inside. She was sitting in her chaise lounge reading softly aloud with Yale lying against her, listening to the words of Yeats. Irritated, I cleared my throat and entered.

"Mrs. Mellet."

She closed her book and stared. Her eyes flashed with irritation. Yale smiled at me around her thumb.

"Can't you see we're busy?"

I smoothed my skirt at the waist and calmed my breath. Now was not the time to come across as crazed. I lifted Yale onto my hip. "News from Mr. Halsey. I know you want this matter dispensed with as soon as possible. I'm quite sure you want your life back without children under your feet and you want to settle our account, as you outlined so beautifully in your letter to me. I'm sure you want to nap in peace once again, without the distractions of a young mother."

Mrs. Mellet swung her legs around, putting her feet on the floor. She rubbed her backside. "I've been sitting there so long, my buttocks are asleep."

I reached out with my free hand. I was not going to rub her bottom no matter how numb it was. "Let me help you stand."

She batted my hand away. "I'm fine here." She scooted forward, grimacing as she rubbed harder.

My sense of hearing dulled as rage grew inside me. She kept speaking, but I could not even make out the words. I'd been through years of loss, followed by hope that had been decimated only to rise again, pulling in more resentment and doubt with every incarnation.

And this time, this optimism I had held for us—this time I would not simply let it go because of a man's vacation plans. I pulled the dressing room chair over so I could be eye level with her, Yale on my lap. I smoothed Yale's hair and tried to calm my voice so as not to scare either one of them. "Mr. Halsey indicates in his note that he is leaving town soon for three weeks."

Mrs. Mellet cocked her head, and her lips parted. "Why, yes, I do recall him mentioning that."

My lungs grew heavy with breath that I could not release. I squeezed Mrs. Mellet's wrist.

"Ouch," she said.

I released it. She rubbed it and eyed me, her lips pursed.

"Well, then, let me get you dressed. We need to catch him before he goes. We need to formalize the papers you mentioned. You've indicated that you understand the urgency to me."

She spread her hands. "Look at me! I'm still in my dressing gown."

I set Yale back on the chair and traipsed to Mrs. Mellet's closet, flinging open the door, my hands shaking, my whole body quivering with years of anger. "This is *my* life, Mrs. Mellet. I will not allow you to casually delay my future as though it were nothing more than the next appointment at the engraver's." I tried to keep my voice even and unemotional even as my insides were quivering. I yanked a tweed walking costume out. "Let's get you dressed, and we'll catch Mr. Halsey before he goes."

"He's gone."

I dropped my arms, the costume puddling at my feet. "*Gone?* Tommy just brought the note." Again I kept my voice as calm as possible. "Five minutes ago."

"What time *is* it?" Mrs. Mellet looked over one shoulder and then the other, as though she'd forgotten where the clock in her own room was located.

I looked to the bedside table. "Twelve thirty." I rolled my eyes.

She waved her hand through the air and lay back on her chaise. "Halsey's long gone—leaves for vacation every first Thursday of every third month of the year at eleven forty-five on the dot. He's as reliable as Eastern Standard Time. Tommy probably hadn't even gotten halfway back here before old Halsey had a nip and nap in his carriage."

I grabbed the back of the chair to steady myself. The world spun and shrank simultaneously, a funnel cloud spreading over me from the head down. I had the sudden thought that she had indeed brought me back to Des Moines simply to say she was sorry and nothing more. I would have had to have lost half my sane mind not to see this now.

I tossed the costume at her feet, less concerned about keeping my subservient place any longer. I did not believe Halsey had left yet at all. I pointed at her. "You get moving. I will not let Halsey leave without us having settled this. You promised. I trusted."

She shot up and pointed back at me. "You're not in a position to tell me what to do."

I turned to the window and wiped the sweat from my brow.

"I'm upset, Mrs. Mellet. This is no longer about my place in society. It's about my family's survival. I will not lose another child simply because you don't want to take a buggy ride to town. There must be someone at his office who can show us the filed document."

She pulled her ear and scratched her neck, glaring at me. She settled back in her chair. "Of course. Katherine. Yes, you want to make plans to bring her back, too. Of course. Halsey's secretary must have filed the letter. Tomorrow. You can read that copy for yourself."

I waved my hands up and down through the air. "I can't wait anymore. I have paid my debt with my entire life. Why are you doing this?"

"It's not me. I said I was sorry. I said I would make things right. But you're bullying me." She struggled to stand and hobbled toward me, her nostrils flaring.

"You have no right to be rushing-bull angry at me, Mrs. Mellet. *You* invited *me* here. You said you would make things right. I'm simply claiming what we agreed upon."

She began to shake, her jowls flapping as her gray eyes held mine, our anger lashing us together.

"I need that money, Mrs. Mellet. You said you understood. I need to find Katherine, and I need to put our lives back together. This is not me asking for you to restore my accounts so I can go shopping for a summer wardrobe. This is life and death for my family. And I've allowed the world to have its way with me long enough. I demand you follow through with what you promised." I felt my body strengthen with each word.

Mrs. Mellet reached out to Yale and rubbed her thumb over the back of Yale's hand. She knew I was unsure about Katherine's plans to meet us, but perhaps she did not understand my desperation. Now was not the time to take my place low on the social hierarchy. "I need money to find Katherine. I've waited for word from her, and I'm at the point where I need to fund a search for her. And that money is mine. I'm not asking for something you didn't offer, for something that isn't owed me."

Mrs. Mellet sighed. Her shoulders slumped, and she petted my head. I did my best not to flinch away. "I am not dead *yet*, Jeanie Arthur." Her voice was cold steel even as her hand was gentle.

"I still control this situation, and I know for sure that even if we met with Halsey today, he wouldn't have all the information regarding my accounts. Yes, he has the signed and witnessed copy of the letter, but he's busy selling stocks and gathering up bonds. That's part of what he's doing on the way to his lake home." Her voice began to rise into a yell.

She pulled her quaking hand away from me and tried to straighten her frail back and shoulders. "I believe he's even liquidating my holdings in a coal mine, of all things. My husband did fine by me. I know there is plenty left to share with you, Jeanie Arthur. But we simply need to keep decorum and be patient." She raised her fist to me. "Be patient, *damn it*. And take your strangling hands off my neck."

I wanted to kill the woman right then. I wished I had my hands tight around her throat. Her mercurial mood and perplexing promises and delays caused me to have to fight back the urge to just sit on her chest and pretend not to notice her air was slowly squeezing out of her body.

I breathed deeply. "Well, you said there's a copy of the letter. Can I see the one you have? I'm assuming you have one here? I would feel so much better if I just saw the letter."

Mrs. Mellet collapsed onto the chaise as though she'd just run to town and back several times. Her chest jumped with labored breath. She closed her eyes and flung her hand over her forehead. "Of course, Jeanie. Of course." Her voice was thin like tissue paper in a spring wind. "Just let me nap. Let me rest, and I'll show you the letter. It's in my letter box with everything else."

She was asleep in seconds. I bent my fingers into the shape of claws and shook them at her as though pretending to strangle her. She turned her head and moved her shoulders, getting more comfortable in her lounge.

"Mrs. Mellet?" I shook her shoulder. Some things in life should not have to wait. Her mouth fell open, and a stabbing snore gave me her answer. I looked at her grayed skin, and if she hadn't looked so frail at that moment, I would have deemed her faking sleep. I shook her again. Nothing came but another snore. I stood and rehung the walking costume. As soon as Mrs. Mellet was awake, I would have her tell me where the letter was, and we would most definitely go to the law office tomorrow just to check on matters.

Yale had pulled her wooden spoon from under the chaise and was marching it across the floor. I scooped her up and she nuzzled into my collarbone, yawning. I stared down at Mrs. Mellet. She looked vulnerable and small when asleep, clothed in a nightdress. Her curled bare feet were exposed. I reached for the knitted blanket on the end of the chaise to cover her feet but stopped. If she grew chilled, she would wake up faster, and then we'd sooner be paging through the paperwork. I'd had enough of this. I walked out of the room and closed the door behind me.

In the hall, I could hear the old woman snoring like a saw eating away at a tree trunk. But even with my upset still roiling, I thought of her exposed feet.

I stalked back into the room and covered her legs with the blanket. Then heading up the stairs to take Yale to the attic for a nap, I plotted out the rest of the day. Before I did anything else, I would tell Tommy about the delay and make the lunch I knew Mrs. Mellet would request upon waking. Angry and impatient, I would flavor the meal with my ire, convinced that it was the fury that kept debilitating sadness at bay. It was the wrath inside me that kept me from collapsing right there, curling into myself again, afraid to face the world.

Chapter 36

Katherine

1891—Storm Lake

Katherine could barely breathe. Her vision jumped as her mind reeled through everything she needed to remember in order to be safe from discovery, in order to find her way back home. She hitched the mare with trembling fingers and tossed her belongings into the gig, tearing across the land as fast as the winding route near the stream would allow.

Mr. Christoff would not be unconscious long, and Katherine knew that his humiliation and ire would be too great for even a raging headache and having been tied up to slow him. He would most certainly take off searching for her once he was free. Katherine did not know Mrs. Christoff's plan for returning home, but it could be anytime.

Hannah had advised heading for the railroad. She would do that, but not the Storm Lake depot. Surely he would track her there easily. So she rode the horse as hard as she could, cheering him on as she cut east across Iowa, where she could catch a bend in the Raccoon River and follow it to the first town where a train would stop. Once she had some distance between herself and the Christoff farm, she stopped the gig and jumped off. She would change her clothes there in the woods so that when she arrived in town, she could hide until she secured some sort of money for train fare. Perhaps she would even ride the gig the whole way to Des Moines, as she saw no way to raise the funds to purchase anything at all.

She looked down at her dress and remembered when Mrs. Christoff had dressed her in it a few days back, the nauseous wave that had coursed through her. She could not wait to remove it, to get rid of the heaviness that seemed to go with it. The dress had partly been unopened by Hannah, so she reached behind her and tore at it, the buttons flicking off and releasing her from its tight embrace. She dropped it to the ground and stared at it, the hole-laden cotton lining yellowed and grayed. She stepped away from it and noticed a piece of paper jutting out of a pocket in the lining. She lifted it out and read it. "Loretta Hughes—1827–1844—Burial Frock. The dress she always wanted but did not get until she perished." Katherine's eyes trailed down the list: Sarah Louise, d. 1851; Mary Paige, d. 1852; Jane Marie, d. 1865; seven more names followed, with a death date beside each.

Katherine's eyes blurred. She gagged, realizing that the parade of corpses that had worn the dress explained its out-of-date cut, the poor condition of the lining, the feelings of dread and illness she'd experienced while wearing it. An urge to stomp and beat the dress against the ground came over her. She put her hands on her hips and stared at the dress. She picked it up and heaved it overhead, wanting to beat it against the river rocks. But with one end of the dress in her hands above her head and the other trailing down her back, she was suddenly filled with deep sorrow and compassion.

She lowered her arms and held the dress against her chest. Drawing deep breaths, she felt as though she'd been freed of an iron yoke. She shook her shoulders, then folded the gown and set it on the rocks with the discarded underclothes neatly on top.

The mare whinnied and bowed its head for a drink at the river's edge. Katherine popped open the suitcase and cast off her chemise and drawers. She would wait to change her stockings until the pair she was wearing was fully played out, and she would keep on the petticoat with the pocket that held her round crystal. Katherine put on the shirtwaist, pulled on the tweed skirt, and buttoned the jacket. The skirt was a little short since it was Hannah's, but Katherine's starved living meant she could fit into the waist and the rest of it fine.

Katherine got back into the gig and drove as fast as she could to the train depot in Maple Springs. She was just outside of town when the wheel on the gig lost a gasket and began to wobble, making it impossible to go on. She unhitched the horse and walked it the rest of the way into town. She would hitch the horse to a post and leave the gig to be found later. Though she had gone past the Storm Lake depot to the next town, she still felt nervous.

She glanced around, searching for a sign that one of the Christoffs had figured she would not go to Storm Lake and guessed her path, beating her there somehow. But she saw no sign of anyone familiar. She petted the mare, putting her head against its nose. "Thank you for keeping me safe." She touched her hair, looked at her body for something, anything that she could trade for money. She could ask passersby for a loan. Though thin and unkempt, the walking suit lent her an air of civility and honesty that might be just enough to get someone to lend her money.

She saw a family with three children milling around the ticket window. The father was clean-shaven, and the children wore fresh, perfectly fitted clothing. Katherine knew that if the children's clothing was fine and tailored, money was not an issue for this group.

She sidled up to them. "Excuse me," she said.

The mother turned, her face folded into confused creases, as though she was stunned someone was speaking to her.

"It looks as though you're headed to Des Moines. I need to go that way, but I've had my purse stolen." The woman's gaze flicked over Katherine's body. Katherine straightened her posture, pushing her shoulders down, lifting her chin in just that way she'd seen her mother do a million times.

Once the woman processed that Katherine's clothing was decent, if not luxurious, that her carriage was cultured, a small smile spread her lips.

The woman began to speak, but as she did, her husband announced they had no spare change.

"I can watch your children on the train."

"We have a girl," he said and pointed to a woman who had at some point stepped up to the children and was wiping one mouth and then the next with a handkerchief. The mother shrugged and turned away.

Katherine went to the ticket window. "Sir, is there some work I can do in exchange for fare?"

He stopped counting money in his drawer and cocked his head at her. "You mean like scrub the outhouse? Shovel in the hay?"

She would have done anything.

He smirked and looked back at his money drawer.

"Yes, yes. I can do that. Please. I just need fare to Des Moines."

He waved a dollar at her. "Listen. I was pulling your leg. I don't have authority to give you work for a ride. Move along."

"But—"

"Paying customer behind you."

Katherine slid out of line and wandered back to the mare. The sun was setting, and with only the empty suitcase and the knapsack packed with her sketches, she thought she was doomed to either be returned to the Christoffs or subjected to finding work in the hotel across the street. She set the suitcase down and sank onto the wooden sidewalk near the hitching post.

She picked up her drawings and paged through them. She began to sketch, her hand flying over the paper as the world receded, and with the flick of her wrist, feathering shadows and shapes began to reveal figures. She held up the drawing as the night began to close in on her. She turned it this way and that. A mother tossing a boy into the air, his hands out to the sides, feet bent up behind him, both with giant smiles on their faces. It reminded Katherine of her mother with them, the joy she'd seen on her face when laughing and enjoying her children before everything changed.

She rolled up her skirt and pulled the crystal ball from her pocket. She balanced it on her knees as she had the night before, watching the night tighten around her like velvet in a jewel box. She could feed the horse and then head back to the river and follow it the whole way to Des Moines.

The horse would have water. She would leave the hobbled gig and just go as fast as possible, making it home before the week was over. Days—she was days away. She looked up at the horse and felt sorry she was so hungry. Katherine stood, the ball and sketches tight against her side as she rubbed the horse's neck. "Can you do that? Can you take me home?" The mare nodded her head, making Katherine giggle.

She would need to secure a saddle if she didn't want to take the gig—she could travel faster on horseback alone. She looked down the line of horses and wondered if she had the backbone to steal someone's saddle—even if it was her only choice?

She would go to the pump for water and make her decision from there. She had no choice. She turned to cross the street and ran smack into someone's chest.

The jarring collision made her drop the suitcase, sketches, and crystal ball. She chased after the rolling sphere and found it stopped inside a muddy wagon rut. With head bowed, she turned to gather up the sketches and suitcase. But the man had already picked up her things. He was setting the suitcase down on the sidewalk and paging through the sketches.

"I'm sorry," Katherine said, rubbing her thumbnail over the muddy facets.

"So, my lady. We meet again."

Katherine's head shot up so she could meet his gaze. The person she'd originally thought was a man was indeed the size of a man, but his face was younger than that. She knew him. She studied him, cocking her head as she fought to recall the situation in which she'd met him before. His red hair, the color of hot fire, was familiar. He crossed his arms and widened his stance, looking over the horizon, and it became clear where she'd seen him before. At the revival—the only person besides her who hadn't been enthralled and entranced.

"They sent me to get you. Hannah's distraught. They're incensed. All this talk of your missing finger and the storm you predicted. The US government can't even predict a rainstorm with black clouds in the sky. And you called one before there was even a wisp of wind."

The thought of Hannah having to suffer for Katherine's sins was not going to work. She began to feel panic swell. "Hannah? She's all right?"

"She is."

"Well, I didn't do anything wrong. It was they who were—"

"You stole the gig."

She shook her head. "Borrowed."

Her eyes began to burn. Her arms and legs grew heavy as frustration set in.

She shook her head, fear drumming at her skull as blood rushed through her body. "Please let me go. I'm not doing anything wrong."

"Stealing is wrong. In everyone's book. That's wrong."

"I didn't steal a thing."

"I beg to differ."

"He was going to rape me." Katherine squeezed the crystal and shook her head. "Please. I just want to go back to my family, where no one touches me and no one starves me while they eat like pigs. I will send them money for the hobbled gig. I have no intention of taking anything that isn't mine. I just want out of there. That is all."

He pointed to the crystal in her hand. She put it behind her back.

She rubbed her neck where the tension pulled tight. "Hannah gave it to me."

Katherine drew deep breaths. She couldn't go back. She closed her eyes, wanting the calming to come, wanting James' spirit to somehow arrive and take her away. She'd done nothing wrong. She'd done only what came naturally for her. She would not be blamed for the Christoffs' fraud.

She shook the knapsack from her shoulder and offered it to him. "Take a look. There's nothing there. No money."

He dug around, pulling the rolls of drawings out, setting them at their feet.

"That's it." She pushed her chin toward the sack. "You can take the suitcase back. This just has my drawings and pencils."

He stared at her and then looked at the pictures again.

"You drew that?"

She nodded. "Please. Let me go. I didn't want to do any of that. I didn't know how to leave. Or where to go."

"But now you do?"

"My mother—they hid her letters. She's been writing. I would have run to her sooner, but they didn't let me know she was writing."

"Your mother contacted you?"

Katherine saw a figure emerge from the end of the alley. The plump, stooped shape was that of his mother. She was sure at first sight. The woman shook her finger at the redhead.

Katherine smiled.

"You're hardly in the position for a chuckle."

"Your mother."

He grimaced.

"She's here, isn't she?"

He looked from side to side. "She's six feet under, back in Halifax."

Katherine covered her mouth and held the orb against her stomach. It was warm. She looked down to see it glow between her fingers as it had the night in the cellar. Katherine was flooded with the glow she saw coming from the orb.

She looked back at him. "No. She's here."

He looked around again. "I believe in the Holy Book, but I think you saw that night at the revival that I am hardly moved by religion as it plays out in the Bible."

Katherine crinkled her nose. "She's got her arm around you and is patting your belly."

"They said you were one with the devil. I think you're simply crazy."

His words stabbed at her, but she looked back at her hand, the light emanating from it. She felt as though the crystal ball had become something tangible for her. Something that comforted, that helped bring the calming that let her connect to James. And now this...this woman. He looked fearful. She knew if she said more, she could cause him to drown her in the river for fear that she was dangerous. But the warmth in her hand ran up her arm, flowing over her shoulders and down her back as if she were wearing a cloak warmed by the fire.

"Tell him," the woman said.

"She said stop your drinking or your ulcer will burn a hole right through your belly lining."

His eyes widened as he looked away, his jaw tensing. Katherine held her breath. "You are much too young to have an ulcer, in my estimation, but she insists you have one. Do you?"

He looked at Katherine with an expression of shock, then quickly tried to cover it up by turning away and wiping his hand across his mouth.

"Look me in the eye," Katherine said. She needed to know, to be sure for her own sake that she wasn't hearing voices that were not there.

He snapped his gaze to her.

She drew back, lifting her hands. "Those are her words, not mine. The woman. Your mother, I believe, said that. Not me. I'm just, well…" For the first time, Katherine felt she understood what was happening. "I'm simply mediating her message. To you. But I need to know if…" *I need to know if I am sane.*

He looked at the orb in Katherine's hand and took it from her. Its glowing white color disappeared, and he bounced it in his hand; it rotated in the air, catching the moonlight.

"You're delivering messages? Like a postman?"

She shrugged.

The next time he tossed the orb, Katherine snatched it out of the air before he did. He looked back at the drawing.

Katherine watched as the woman moved closer to her son. "She has her arm around you. She's patting your head, kissing your forehead. Three times—no, four."

He put his fingers to his temple.

"One for good measure," he and Katherine said at the exact same time.

Katherine nodded. "Yes."

He cleared his throat. "She's not angry?"

Katherine closed her eyes and let the feelings tumble over her. "Not a bit." Katherine looked at the orb again, its warm glow taking on a golden sheen. It was then Katherine felt the connection deepen between what she saw with these folks who turned out to be the spirits of loved ones, her calming, and now the crystal orb. Though she had nothing to her name, no way home, and was possibly faced with being hauled back to the raging-mad Christoffs, she felt shrouded in safety. As though she could face anything that came her way.

He looked at the drawings again, paging through them.

Katherine closed her eyes again. "Nothing but love. That's all she feels in regard to you." Katherine opened her eyes to see the redhead swiping at his eyes as though he'd been weeping. She took his hand, put the crystal ball in his palm, and placed hers over the top.

"Feel that?"

He looked down.

Katherine waited. *Please, God, let him feel what I do—the warmth, the love.*

And after a few seconds, he nodded, the waves of warmth coursing between their hands growing stronger. A crack of thunder cut through the soothing connection.

They leaped apart, the ball back in Katherine's grasp.

He removed his hat and ran his hand through his hair.

He looked into the raging sky. "The way I see it," he wiped his brow with his forearm, "is punishment is due."

Katherine's eyes began to burn with rising tears. *Please, no.* She hadn't meant to hurt anyone.

He snatched the knapsack from the ground. "The others won't be far behind. They borrowed the Leyheys' carriage and took off behind me. They stopped in Storm Lake and sent me on to see if you were here."

Katherine gasped.

"Take my horse and follow my directions." He dug in his pocket and pulled out money. "You're going to leave my horse at my sister Lynne's place on the old mill road. I'll send word to her. You can trust her."

Katherine nodded.

"I'll return the Christoffs' mare and let them know the gig is stuck in the woods. I have business near Lynne this week. I can get Bernie then. Take good care of him. He's like family to me. Staying with my sister overnight will give you a delay and the Christoffs will quit looking. They won't want the hassle. I'll make sure of it."

Katherine's throat tightened. Could she trust this stranger? Was she being naïve? She recalled him at the revival, the way he had not been caught up in the fervor with the rest of them. She closed her eyes for a moment and got a sense of how she felt about him. She breathed deep. *Yes.* She heard his mother's voice clearly. And then she knew.

She threw her arms around his neck and kissed his cheek. "Thank you. Thank you."

She pulled away.

He took her hand. "No. Thank you."

She could see him force a swallow down.

He squeezed her hand. "I wasn't as good to my mother as I should have been. I regret that. Thank you for this… well, whatever it is you just did."

Katherine nodded; the full measure of what her ability could do ran through her. She'd never really understood what was possible in it, but there, in that moment, feeling this man's grace and appreciation, she knew.

He surveyed the area then refocused on Katherine. "You need to listen closely."

She nodded.

He took her by the shoulders. "You need to be brave."

Katherine straightened under his grip. "I will."

"I'm going to report that I saw you purchase a ticket for Dallas."

Katherine shook her head. "They'll check. That clerk will remember."

"He won't remember a thing. I'll make sure of it."

Katherine swallowed hard.

"You take my horse, Bernie, over there. Go east and ride him to the Raccoon River, heading south to Middle Raccoon River. Then ride to Swan Lake. It's a small town. But my sister is there. Don't breathe a word of what you've told me about our mother. My sister is a good person. But don't risk it. You'll go to the Parise farm and you'll ask for my sister, Lynne. You'll sleep one night. She'll tell you what to do next."

"But it's about to storm."

He looked over his shoulder. Near the depot, Katherine saw the Christoffs had arrived, craning their necks and stretching to see into the windows of the train that was loading passengers.

"There's plenty of storm right here, Katherine. You need to be on your way. You can do this."

She looked at the crystal in her hand. Then she finally nodded.

"Bernie can ride one hundred miles tonight. But you need to go only about half that far. Stay near the water. He can go without food, but not water."

He reached into his pocket and pulled out a fold of cash. He shoved a clump into her hand.

She stared at it. He closed her fingers around it.

"I'll pay you back," she said.

He nodded.

"My drawings." She started to bend down, but he grabbed her arm.

"Just go," he said.

"I need them," she said.

"You need to move fast."

"But they're part of me... They're..."

"You have to go. Now. Hannah covered for you, but I saw the lie in her eyes. I knew."

"Hannah." Katherine's voice cracked. She couldn't imagine having to live with her awful parents for one more moment.

"She'll be all right. I promise," he said.

Katherine pulled away from him and dropped to her knees to gather the drawings.

"All right." He squatted down. She held the knapsack open and he shoved a bunch into it.

"These aren't fitting. I'll take them." He said. "This one with the boy in the air... My mother commissioned a painting exactly like this when I was a boy."

Katherine looked at what he held. She knew he wanted to ask how she could possibly have drawn that, but they both understood the answer without speaking it.

He shoved her. "Go on. Now. Run."

"Send word to Des Moines. Please? To Jeanie Arthur."

"I will. My sister will as well."

Katherine nodded, pushed the shoulder straps of the knapsack over her arms, lifted her skirt, tucked the crystal into the pocket, and tore away. It had been some time since she'd mounted a horse, but she did it easily, the air lifting her as though one hundred angels had made her weightless, protecting her.

She clicked her tongue at Bernie, and he began to trot. She turned him east and looked over her shoulder to see the man who had saved her arguing with the Christoffs, Hannah slouched between her parents.

Katherine pulled on the reins, stopping Bernie. She wanted to turn back and get Hannah, to just be honest and explain her actions.

But as she considered going back for Hannah, the hair on the back of her neck stood up. She felt the presence of her brother James. She heard his voice, sweet as ever, telling her to go, to just ride on and never look back. She nudged Bernie with her heels again, and with tears in her eyes for Hannah but glee in her heart for escaping, she rode.

Bernie hit his stride quickly, pulling over the rolling land as though equipped with wheels instead of legs. Katherine patted his neck. "Thank you, Bernie. Thank you."

The encouragement seemed to make him run even faster, smoother, as though he and Katherine were one. The rain stung her cheeks and the wind tossed her hair behind her, the thick, drenched ribbons beating her back with each step Bernie took. She finally let her emotions fully embrace her. She had not realized just how trapped she had been since she had last had the chance to feel the sensation of breakneck speed, to feel the freedom under the huge sky above and rolling hills beyond.

Chapter 37

Jeanie

1891—Des Moines

With Yale settled in for her nap, I went down to the kitchen and heard the sound of Tommy pulling the buggy around back. I pushed through the kitchen door to tell him that we would not be going to Halsey's that day. "Leave the rig here while you have some lunch," I said. When he entered the house he offered me a loaf of bread and a hesitant smile. The sight of him cut the rage I'd been feeling quite a bit.

I was flooded with gratitude that he was there, that his walking in the door with bread seemed like the greatest gesture I could have imagined. I rushed to him and grabbed him up. "Oh, Tommy." The smell of skunk had lessened with the scrubbing, haircut, shave, and new set of clothes. But the oils must have settled into his exposed skin to some degree. "Oh, that skunk."

Tommy squeezed me tight and patted my back like I'd done to him so many times. "It'll be gone soon, Mama."

I nodded, comforted by his hug, hoping I was comforting him as well. Finally, I pulled back. "Where did you get the bread, anyway?"

"Bakery on Muldoon. I made three deliveries inside of an hour in exchange for this day-old."

I was pleased at his industriousness. "Very good job, Tommy."

He squinted at me. "It's not a bar of gold, you know. Just flour and yeast and a bit of cinnamon, it looks like." He set it on the table.

I was overwhelmed with emotion, a mix of love for him and hate for Mrs. Mellet. I covered my mouth.

"What is it, Mama? I can help. Tell me what we need to do."

I shook my head. I could not comprehend how Tommy had grown into this man. The idea of having him right in front of me was finally settling in. Just hours before, he'd been crying over a lost Indian Head, and now here he was, seeming like a grown man again.

I knew this pendulum of behavior was the way of adolescence. I had impulsively run away and married Frank at Tommy's age. I understood the ebb and flow of ripe, new emotion, but I was grateful for this more mature side of Tommy.

He picked the bread up again and tilted it back and forth. "More bread? You want more bread—that's it, isn't it? I've left you speechless upon arrival with bread. And here I thought it would take diamonds and rubies to render you speechless."

"Oh, Tommy." I took his face and kissed his nose.

He smiled and pulled a newspaper from his back pocket. "Thank you. I'll read later on."

"Did Mrs. Mellet have more bad news?" Tommy asked.

I sighed and sat at the table, my head on my fist. "I'm not so sure she's going to do what she promised."

Tommy sank into the chair across from me. He removed his hat. "I knew it. Old Crooked Eye couldn't have changed that much. I know better than to trust people to—"

I shook my head. The burning in my eyes made me wish I was hot with anger again. "She wrote a letter that outlines what she wants us to have and also the details of her failings and what that means for us. She has a copy here, she said. We'll look at it after her nap. The other copy is at the lawyer's office. She said we'll go tomorrow, that we can see it even if Halsey isn't there. And we can check on the liquidation process."

"So that's good, right?"

I nodded. Something had dug into my gut and kept me from feeling certainty that any of this was good at all.

"You told her we are not going to wait around, playing slave for her, right?"

"I was direct. Yes."

"Well, good. The old Jeanie Arthur would have been very direct."

I cocked my head at him. The old Jeanie Arthur. I had never heard him characterize me that way, never knew that he really saw the difference in me in terms of before and after.

"Yes. Well, you're right about that," I said and squeezed his hand, feeling more connected to him than I ever had in my life.

**

I cleared the remains of the toast and jam Tommy and I had eaten for lunch. Day-old bread had never tasted so good. I suspected Yale would waken soon, and I hoped that Mrs. Mellet would, too. I put my hand at my belly. That was the spot where I could always feel my emotions stir—excitement, anger, worry, sadness—that then crept up my esophagus. The small seed of anger that had earlier exploded and traveled into my bloodstream had called its tentacles back, tucking the explosiveness inside. The seed was still there, like a tiny heart, beating with mad blood, reminding me it was there even if not scorching hot at the moment.

I replayed the argument with Mrs. Mellet. Even with the level of anger I had been feeling at the time, the upset I'd displayed at her, I hadn't said anything that couldn't be taken back. A flicker of fear came to me, familiar. *Don't let it take over. All is not lost.* Katherine. She was lost. I pulled a piece of paper and a pencil from a drawer in the pie safe and sat at the table. A list. I would delineate my next steps—three sets of actions. One set for if the money comes in the next few days, one set if there is an extended delay, and one set if the money never comes at all. At the top of each column was Katherine's name. *Katherine, Katherine, Katherine.* If only writing her name or saying it aloud could conjure her right into the kitchen.

From there, I drew brackets where I would fill in the measures to take to locate her given each circumstance. Perhaps if the money were delayed until Mr. Halsey returned and signed off on all the liquidated investments, it wouldn't be the worst thing to stay at Mrs. Mellet's.

We were warm, we could eat, and at least Tommy was with us. The pungent residue of skunk would dissipate, and Tommy would join us inside the house. Considering where I had been a week back, thinking of how I felt that night on the train trestle, this much progress was a miracle—yes, the evolution of the miracle I first recognized that next day but had already forgotten. I squeezed my eyes closed, calling up that feeling when I realized I was still alive. Appreciate and move forward.

I looked at the clock over the doorway and began to head up the stairs when Tommy called to me. "I'll round up the cows."

I nodded.

He had opened the back door and had begun to walk through it.

"Wait."

He turned back. I went to him and took him in my arms, inhaling him, coughing as the spray burned my throat, but still picking up a modicum of the scent that was undeniably him. "I love you, Tommy. Love you so very much."

He looked at me as though confused. "I love you, too."

"Well, go on. I'll wake Yale and hopefully Mrs. Mellet will rise very soon."

Tommy had turned and headed back through the door again when a crash coming from upstairs made him stop. We both looked upward.

"Yale?" I yelled and ran up the stairs, Tommy on my heels.

We got to the attic and jogged to the end, where the bed was set up. I poked my head inside that space and nearly fell over at the sight. Yale was sprawled on the bed, limbs stretched in every direction, sleeping as hard as could be.

Tommy and I looked at each other, stunned.

"Mrs. Mellet," Tommy said and turned, running for the staircase.

I followed, taking the stairs as fast as my skirt would allow. When I emerged into the second-floor hall, I saw Tommy knocking on her bedroom door. "Mrs. Mellet?"

I reached him and pushed past, opening the door. My gaze flew to where she had been sleeping. The chaise was empty. The bed was empty. I headed through the space and into the connected dressing room. Collapsed in the middle of the floor was Mrs. Mellet, facedown.

I flew to her. "Mrs. Mellet! Are you all right?"

Tommy and I turned her to her back. I tapped her cheeks with my hands. "Mrs. Mellet?"

No response.

I slapped her hand. One and then the other. "Mrs. Mellet?"

Tommy hunched closer and put his ear near her mouth. "I can't hear her breathing."

"Wait. Watch her chest," I said.

Her body lay still as a board, her eyes open and fixed on the ceiling, her lips slightly parted.

"Here," I said, putting my arm under her shoulders. "Help me sit her up."

Tommy did, and we each took turns saying her name, pressing or prodding some part of her body, trying to nudge her back to life. Finally, we set her back down.

"Go get Doc Hamilton."

Tommy shook his head. "He's dead, Mama. He died before we left for the prairie."

I could not remember that simple fact for the life of me. "Then head to the first house or business you see and ask them who is doctoring these days, and get that man out here immediately."

Tommy sprang to his feet. He nodded and looked over his shoulder as he was sprinting out of the room.

I saw it in his eyes and in Mrs. Mellet's body—prone, grayer than she'd been before. There was no need for a doctor. She was dead, and there was nothing we could do to change that a bit.

I wasn't sure what to do as I waited. Feelings of fear and worry ran rampant, but also sorrow for the dead woman. Had our argument caused this? I went to the chaise lounge. The knitted blanket was still draped across the bottom of it. I picked it up and held it to my belly as I went back to the body. Just minutes dead and Mrs. Mellet had already crossed over to the point of being *the body*.

I shook out the blanket and let it waft down, covering those twisted blue toes. I pulled it up to her shoulders, tucking it around her as though she were merely napping.

**

Tommy had arrived back at Mrs. Mellet's just seconds before a man named Dr. Allison came roaring in on his horse. He moved quickly, saying hello as he bolted through the door and followed Tommy upstairs. We watched as Dr. Allison pronounced her dead by way of old age. He'd been caring for her for the past two years and was not surprised to find her dead. He'd warned her that her weakened heart would not allow for much more life on earth.

"At least she was a God-fearing woman," Dr. Allison said.

Tommy and I made eye contact.

Dr. Allison scribbled some notes into a black leather book, then set it aside and pressed his fingers into her wrist and neck all over again. Kneeling beside her, he closed his eyes and moved his lips in what I supposed was a prayer. He sprang up and walked us from the room, asking us what our roles in her life were. Upon our satisfactory responses, he went on to explain the timeline of what was to follow.

I assured him that we would send telegrams and letters to family and keep the house until her son arrived for the viewing of the body and burial. Dr. Allison would send the undertaker to prepare the body for the funeral, as well.

"Well," the doctor said, "though you and I have not met before this, I think it's quite fortunate to have you here to tend to the details, to allow the grieving family to remain distant from such distasteful responsibilities."

I agreed with him but did not look forward to the duties ahead.

Around the time the doctor was leaving, Yale stirred and cried for me. I found her sitting on the chamber pot when I got upstairs and nearly collapsed from shock. She had even managed to spare every bit of fabric from any fluids. I tore a few pages from the newspaper, wiped her, and then washed our hands. "Oh, my Yale. You are such a big girl." It was as though she had sprung forth years in terms of development in just a few days. I did not have the time to fully weigh what that said about my parenting up to that point.

I took Yale and started downstairs. Though I was about to pass the second floor and head into the kitchen to prepare the telegrams that needed to be sent, I couldn't stop myself from heading into Mrs. Mellet's bedroom. I closed the door to the dressing room so we would not have to see her lifeless body. Then I quickly began to work my way around her room, searching for addresses, names, and, of course, the box that Mrs. Mellet said held the letter she had written about me and the money she had promised. Mrs. Mellet would no longer have to fret over things like finances and housing, but I had no such luxury.

I easily found the addresses but saw no sign of the letters. I ignored the disappointment, knowing it was best to make use of the addresses in order to not lose time. Downstairs, I wrote the letters and telegrams that I wanted Tommy to send. I found some change in a tin in the kitchen and gave that to him to use at the post office.

Once Tommy was on his way, I was free to search more fully for the letter that would mean my financial freedom, if not simply a reprieve from grinding poverty. I burrowed into every cranny of Mrs. Mellet's bedroom and finally made my way to the closet. There were several boxes on the top shelf, and one of them held the letter on crisp, linen parchment. My hands shook so hard, I could barely read.

To Whom It May Concern,

I hereby ask you to allow Jeanie Arthur entrée into society once again. As an upstanding member of such society, I have *realized that redemption is required—both giving and receiving it—to live a full, rich life. I am sure that she will make good use of the funds I've set aside for her in the amount of fifty thousand ($50,000) dollars. This money is being liquidated as per Mr. Halsey, Esquire's direction. In his care are the details of the matter.*

Forgive, forget. I have done so. You should, too.

I was taken by a torrent of conflicting feelings. The letter held no confession of Mrs. Mellet's role in the bank and investment failure. There was no mention of my not having a single wisp of responsibility in the matter. Her request to admit me to society was limp, at best. That was maddening. But my eyes flicked back to the amount of money repeatedly. It was enormous. Enormous. It would not even matter if I had entrée into Des Moines society. That amount of money would mean my children and I were free to reestablish our lives wherever we chose. Fifty thousand dollars. I couldn't stop repeating it.

I clasped the note against my chest. Then I looked at it again. Her signature was missing, but her handwriting? I paged through other items in the box, half-written letters, what looked like journal entries, household notes. The writing was an exact match. And there was the copy that the lawyer had formally drawn up that was stored at the office.

I nodded and sighed. Yes. This was it. No one could deny what was due me. Finally.

**

Tommy had hung around the post office long enough
that he was there when a return telegram came from Mrs.
Mellet's son, Maxwell. He thanked me for contacting him and
asked that I meet with the undertaker until he and his wife
and sister could make it to Des Moines.

Tommy replied to the telegram, saying of course we
would do what was needed. I wished Maxwell had rehired the
staff that Mrs. Mellet had recently let go. They would have
been better to handle the arrangements, as I felt significant
discomfort in this role. I had no idea what Mrs. Mellet had
told anyone in regard to me and her invitation to me to come
to Des Moines. But I assumed she hadn't told many. Mrs.
Hillis knew I was there. Dr. Allison knew. And the
vacationing Mr. Halsey.

I would not feel settled until the will was read and all
matters were resolved. Still, I realized a woman had died. A
woman's family was about to gather to say good-bye, and that
family would probably not be excited to know they were
going to share some of what they must have thought of as
theirs alone.

**

On the day of the funeral, the extended Mellet family
members would be arriving just as the body was readied for
viewing. Reverend North from the First Presbyterian Church
was to oversee the ceremony. I had not been looking forward
to seeing the friends who would come to the funeral. I'd
written the invitations myself and could not even eat breakfast
that morning at thinking I would have to face so many
families who, when I last saw them, had been digging through

the drawers of my dressers and pulling paintings from my walls.

As family began to arrive, I collected hats and wraps and arranged them neatly on a series of coatracks I'd found stashed in the basement. My hands lingered on fine silks and luxurious velvets, at the men's hats stitched with expert hands. I resisted the urge to put my nose against a brand-new bowler. I'd forgotten I'd ever cared how fresh felting smelled. I looked over my shoulder at Mrs. Mellet's body, watching her children and grandchildren huddle around the casket, whispering. Maxwell Mellet, the old woman's eldest, stood with his arms around his wife and sister while his children huddled off to the side of them.

I bowed my head, touched by their quiet loss. The tone was markedly different from that of the burials we'd had on the prairie. So many children then. *James*, I thought. *I hope you are warm. I hope your soul is safe.*

A squeal of laughter from one of the Mellet grandchildren who didn't understand what was happening startled me and reminded me to get to the kitchen to tend to the food.

In the kitchen, I found Yale halfway in the bottom of the pie safe, pulling utensils and linens out onto the floor as she created a nest for herself inside. My heart stopped at the sight. I rushed there and put my head inside, looking for any sign of rat poison or any powdered substance, as Yale had a habit of quietly getting lost and finding just the right thing to nearly drop me dead on sight. With the small steps toward independence she'd made since we arrived at Mrs. Mellet's, I was more concerned than ever that she might very quietly disappear like little Anzhela Zurchenko did on the prairie.

I brushed back Yale's hair. "Where's your brother?" Yale's slow gaze met mine, and her lips lifted into a lazy smile. She pointed upward.

"Is he getting dressed?" I folded Yale's hand into mine, knowing there would be no answer.

I heard voices coming from the hallway.

"Shh, shh," I said to Yale. I pulled out a stack of linens and patted another set, signaling that Yale should tuck herself into the space and lay her head on the soft fabric. I showed her a wooden spoon and moved it as though it were a doll. "Here's your dolly, Lily. When we leave here, I will add hair and eyes and a pretty dress like yours. We'll make a sweet doll just for you." I clutched it against my chest. "But until then, you just hold her like this. Nestle her against you while you both take a sweet nap." I put my finger to my mouth, letting her know it was time to be quiet. I closed one of the doors to the bottom of the pie safe, leaving the second one open slightly so that Yale would feel secure.

I stood and turned, my arms loaded with linens and small copper gelatin molds, which I'd removed to make room for Yale. Maxwell Mellet entered the kitchen.

"Where is that lemonade? My aunt arrived with no one to take her wrap and no one to offer her something for her parched throat."

I scooted to the icebox. I hacked at the ice block in quick succession, causing chips to fly in every direction, pricking my face with cool pellets. I filled a glass with the biggest fragments, then splashed lemonade into it, garnishing it with mint cut from the herb garden. There was no point in explaining to Mr. Mellet that Tommy should have been at the door but wasn't.

I shoved the glass into Maxwell's hand. "My apologies." I made eye contact for a moment, then looked away, my face filling with heat, wishing I could erase my history in Des Moines. "Should I ready a tray? Or another lemonade for you?" My breath steadied with a glance at the pie safe, seeing that Yale had fallen asleep for her nap.

"Well, no. There's plenty for the family for now. It seems as though her friends are otherwise engaged. Except for Mrs. Hillis. She's out there. But I suspect she's angling for donations or whatnot. This house is nearly empty. What was my mother doing this past year?"

My throat dried at his accusing words. It may have been improper, but he had broached these topics, and I felt as though I should discuss my stake in his family's money. Still, I would wait for the lawyers.

"Your glass is empty. Let me make you a fresh drink." I stepped back, gesturing toward the icebox. I knew what Maxwell thought of my family since the scandal. He'd made that very clear the day we were pushed out of town. But I doubted his mother had confessed her role in the swindle. I wasn't even sure how she figured in other than her announcing to me that she had.

"My mother said she'd hired you, called you back from the Dakotas. Said your pitiful life had turned even worse than any of us could have predicted. Shows crime does not pay, for sure."

I dropped my hand and lifted my chin, trying to keep my anger from creeping into my face. Crime? I thought of my dead son, my missing daughter.

"Yes. She said you'd been hounding her for three years to allow you to work and board with her."

Did he just say that? "I hounded her?" My hand shook as I put my palm to my forehead.

"Said she had a change of heart and wanted to help you since you weren't exactly the one who lost our money. She'd heard you were tossing around Sioux Falls, moving the children hither and yon. Trouble, trouble everywhere."

I thought of the letter she had written to me, the note in the box upstairs. My missing daughter. Rage shook me and would not allow me manners. Not this time. I shifted to face

Maxwell head-on, fingers laced at my waist. "That's not true. That's not the story." I squeezed the words out, disgusted with myself for having said them with his mother's dead body just three rooms away, but I could not stop myself.

"I'm quite sure you don't know just how awful the rest of the story is." *Let him have this time with his dead mother. You don't have to tell him this now.*

"Oh, I can imagine how a divorced woman has to get along in the world. I have heard."

I gouged the ice so hard that I split off a chunk the size of a newborn baby and it crashed to the floor before I could catch it, splintering over the wood. *He doesn't know his mother was involved.*

I looked over my shoulder to see Maxwell staring at me as though I were three-headed.

"Don't get crazy, Jeanie. I don't want to ask you to leave."

I abandoned the ice and strode across the kitchen, my emotions taking hold as they had when I'd argued with his mother. "There's a lot more, Maxwell. And I'm afraid you're not going to appreciate the news I have to share."

He put his hands up and backed a step away. I realized I was holding the ice pick in a menacing way. I dropped my hand to my side.

"Well, I'm sure with the time that has passed since your family did so many friends and family in, I will manage to hear your story with less angst than you clearly suppose."

I chortled. I tossed the ice pick aside, afraid I might plunge it into his chest. "Don't be arrogant. I'm not any less a person simply because my purse is so much less than it was. Your mother called *me* here to confess *her* part in that swindle you are referencing. She promised me money and she promised a public apology. I have a missing daughter and a dead son, and I will not help your family as I just have for the last week and allow you to condescend to me. Your mother was complicit in our loss."

Maxwell's face went bloodless. He opened his mouth and then closed it, unable to speak.

I stepped toward him. "Can't swallow, can you? That lump in the back of your throat? I know the same lump, and you can just get used to it, Maxwell. The world turns on an axis that does not always align with what you want."

He looked as though he was going to pass out. I took his arm and led him to the hall. "I'm sorry to have told you that right now. But you pushed me, Maxwell. And way too much has happened to me to allow you to condescend. Simple, mutual respect. Get to know it. You're going to need it."

I gave him a little push in the direction of the parlor, where his family was mourning, then went back to preparing the little cucumber sandwiches his wife had decided were needed to send Mrs. Mellet into the afterlife.

I stood over the sink, wiping my hands, feeling incredible strength take hold. When had I last felt this? I turned my memory back. When? I could not find the memory, the event, the place, but for once, an overwhelming crash of emotion was positive. I felt strong. I could do this. I was worthy of all that Mrs. Mellet called me back here to reclaim. Finally, that realization settled, and I was sure it would not be shaken again.

Chapter 38

Katherine

1891—Somewhere along the Middle Raccoon River

Katherine finally reached the farm and home of Will's sister, Lynne Parise. Katherine was famished, wet, and shaking when she knocked on the door. Lynne had cracked the door a sliver, held a lamp up, and studied Katherine for a moment. Her hair was matted against her cheeks and back and her lips felt swollen with the chilled, sodden spring air. After a short hesitation, complete with Lynne's confused expression, Katherine spoke.

"Will. He sent me."

With that, Lynne threw open the door and yanked Katherine into the home, rubbing her arms before ordering her out of her clothing and under a blanket in front of the fire.

Lynne's husband returned from the barn after Katherine was settled in the rocking chair, watching the flames lap at the thick logs. He was quiet with busy, whittling hands and watchful eyes. Once Katherine was warm and in a dry sleeping gown, they made a nest of fresh, warm quilts and a soft featherbed near the fireplace.

Katherine had thought she would fall into immediate deep sleep, but running from the Christoffs and the ride on

Bernie had lit her mind like a lamp illuminates a dark closet, her obstinate thoughts ignoring her body's yearning for sleep.

She stirred and flopped back and forth and finally just sat cross-legged by the fire. She pulled her knapsack onto her lap and removed her paper and a charcoal. She sketched lovely families with smiling children gathered at their parents' feet. One drawing, which Katherine had intended for Lynne's family, contained a dog sitting near the fireplace.

Wanting the sketch to evoke the Parise family in particular, Katherine had erased the dog and drawn him again twice. The family had no dog, but when sleep finally pulled her away from her art, she was too tired to erase him again, and so she left the yellow dog with the wide head and almost human-like face sitting protectively at the children's feet. She'd drawn his head resting on the little boy's lap, the hound's eyes full of the kind of canine woe that forced even the most animal-averse person to scratch it behind the ears.

Katherine's bones were heavy and she curled into a ball, the fire now offering only a small glow between the logs. With her drawings and pencils back inside the knapsack near her feet, she pressed her crystal ball against her chest, her finger tracing the faceted planes. She felt safer than she had in years.

Her warm, soft bed, away from the snores and gropings of the Christoffs, made Katherine think of Hannah. Poor girl. *Please keep her safe, God.* Katherine told herself that Hannah would be unharmed. Her parents had never given a hint of malice toward their daughter, not in the same way they had Katherine. She sighed. There was no way to change the way things had unfolded, and Katherine would have to believe that Hannah would grow up happy and ready to move into marriage just as soon as a match was made.

It was true that Katherine wanted to see her family again more than anything. But she could never have guessed the sensation that would come from merely being free of the

Christoffs, of the life she'd lived even before that. Freedom was the only way she could characterize what she was experiencing. She silently said a prayer of thanks for Will, Lynne's brother, and a prayer of hope that her mother would still be waiting for her when she arrived in Des Moines.

In the morning, Lynne filled Katherine with golden, buttery eggs, biscuits, and jam. As Will had said, other than Katherine telling them that he had sent her there, his sister nor her family pried for answers as to why she had arrived in the night, soaked and alone. They arranged for a Quaker neighbor who was headed to West Branch to drop her at the Des Moines train station, where she would meet her family.

They were tucking her into the neighbor's coach when Katherine stepped back out. She could not leave without saying more, thanking them better. She opened her arms and hugged the Parise children so hard, each sputtered and choked. Then she wrapped her arms around Mr. Parise, who blushed and sputtered that it was his pleasure to offer respite. And finally, there was Lynne. Katherine wrapped her up and swayed back and forth, the woman grasping Katherine just as tightly. When they let each other go, both were tearing up. As Katherine had felt the Christoffs' disdain in thick, bone-chilling ways, she felt an unexplainable love from Lynne. It was as though they'd known each other forever, as though each had needed some part of the giving and taking that had happened over the span of just hours.

"I haven't slept so well in years," Katherine said. "Thank Will again, and feed Bernie an extra apple for me. Apples can make up for a lot, you know. That horse is magnificent."

Lynne smiled and tucked Katherine's hair under the hat she'd given her. "I'll let my brother know of your immense gratitude. Now, enjoy that hat. Don't give it another thought."

Katherine nodded. She grasped Lynne's hand. It did not make sense that Will would have tied himself up with the

Christoffs or that church in Storm Lake when he could be near this wonderful family. It just didn't fit. "Thank you so much."

"Of course."

"Do you think your brother will have gotten that telegram off to Des Moines?"

"If he said he would, it's as good as done. Will does not suffer fools, cruelty, or wasted time. If he promised, he did. And I will send one to the name and address you left for me."

Katherine put her hand over her heart. Lynne's confidence in Will had filled Katherine with the same trust. "Give him that letter and that drawing. The other one is for you. I left it on the table in your keeping room." Katherine shrugged. "I don't have any other way to say thank you. I will someday. I think… I know, actually, that there will come a day when I can thank him properly."

Lynne took Katherine's elbow and helped her into the coach. "I believe that. And thank you for the drawing you did of our family. It's really quite stunning."

Katherine squeezed Lynne's hand and the woman closed the door and stepped away from the coach as it began to roll toward Des Moines.

Katherine watched the Parises until they were small as peppercorns. When the coach moved so far that the family disappeared into thin air, Katherine settled into her seat and laid her head against the window, trying to find sleep again. As she did, she thought of Tommy, her mother, and Yale. Each face came to mind and calmed her worry, let her rest her bruised and tired heart on the thought that the worst was nearly over. As she headed east, she sighed and fell asleep, headed back to the family she loved so much.

Chapter 39

Katherine

1905—Des Moines

The parlor was still filled with the hardy scent of funeral flowers. The hot sun cut through the gap in the sheers and splashed over Hannah, Will, and Katherine. She had been shocked over and over again at the funeral as strangers—other mourners—stood by the dozens, proclaiming their gratitude for her mother. But now, the next day, in the low tide of what had been drowning grief, she had awakened to find the two people who had helped save her so many years ago had come to visit.

Sitting on the davenport, Katherine and Hanna clutched at each other as her mind unraveled memories, finally unleashing and releasing the worry she'd held for Hannah over the years. But then she only became more confused, as she could not understand how Hannah could be here with William. "Hannah Christoff. How are you? What are you and Will doing together?"

Hannah put her hands on Katherine's shoulders, smiling wildly. "Well, it's Mrs. Will McIntyre now."

Katherine looked to the man next to her with the bright red hair.

It was really him. "Will."

He squeezed Katherine's hand. "I'm so glad you're safe and alive."

Katherine went to the cart that held a pitcher and poured the two a glass of water. "I just don't understand," Katherine said. "Aleksey said you were here to offer condolences for my mother." She handed them glasses and pulled a chair over so she could sit and see them both at the same time.

"Well, that part of the story is just lucky, we think. We still had a small worry that Katherine Zurchenko was not the same as Katherine Arthur. We thought if it turned out you were *not* you, we could just say we knew your mother when, and then take our leave without much harm."

Katherine shook her head. "I am just stunned. There's so much going through my mind that I don't even know what to ask. I mean, you two made it possible for me to go back to my mother."

Will and Hannah looked at each other and grabbed each other's hands again. "And you made it possible for us to be together."

Katherine drew back and tried to remember how that could be true. Hannah was at least four years younger than Will. Katherine remembered thinking how nice his sister and her family had been to her, but when she wrote to them over the years, she never heard back. She remembered thinking how odd it was that Will might be wrapped up with the Christoffs when he came from such a wonderful family—a family who'd made Katherine feel as though she were one of them. "I don't understand. How did I get you two together?"

Will slid to the end of the settee, his forearms resting on his thighs. He began to talk, then stopped, appearing as though he were reeling back his memory like a fish on a line, searching for exactly what he wanted to say. "When you ran from the Christoffs that day, and then when I sent you on

Bernie to my sister's place, I had to go back and explain to the Christoffs that you were not at the station."

Katherine straightened as though she'd been poked in the behind. "I remember. I saw them there, looking. I saw you, Hannah."

Will nodded. "That's right. I thought for sure they saw you because you stopped and turned back. I knew then you were truly worried about Hannah. But I managed to convince them that someone fitting your description had boarded a train for Dallas."

"I remember you saying you would tell them that," Katherine smiled.

"And," Will said, "that was when I saw how the Christoffs treated Hannah. I saw how angry they were at you, Katherine, and that they didn't believe Hannah was innocent in helping you."

Katherine covered her mouth, knowing Hannah had helped her.

Hannah smiled.

A chill worked up Katherine's spine. She reached out for Hannah. "Did they put you in the basement, or did your father…"

"No. No."

"To me, the trouble wasn't whether they believed Hannah helped you that day. It was that they believed you worked magic or sorcery."

Katherine remembered the newspaper articles and the Bible verses they'd made her read. She rubbed her arms, chilled even though the day was growing hot and sticky.

"I was supposed to leave town and get work on the railroad, but something told me not to. I kept checking back on Hannah. They didn't feed her for days, claiming that they thought your amputated finger and your escape into thin air was more evidence of your being evil. The devil was your kin, and they were worried that Hannah had somehow retained your evil and that it would sprout up like daffodils right out of her skin for all the world to see."

Katherine thought back to her last days in that house. She knew what they had wanted to do to cast out the devil. "The revival?"

Hannah nodded.

Katherine slid onto the settee, moving Hannah closer to Will. Katherine wrapped her arms around Hannah. "Oh no. I knew you should have come with me."

"Well, I knew you weren't evil," Will said. "What you did when my mother… well, you remember, right?"

"Of course." Katherine thought of the crystal ball they had grasped between them that night at the train station. She remembered the way his mother had come and warned him away from drink, to care better for his acid stomach.

"Well, I made a promise to Hannah. I told her that I was a gentleman. I confided about you and what happened with my mother in that alley. I showed her that drawing you did. Do you remember?"

"The one of the boy being tossed into the air?"

He nodded. "I vowed to her right then that I would not harm her, but I knew whatever they did to you to make you run would eventually be worse for Hannah. So I offered my services as a gentlemanly escort, and we left for Oregon. And over the years, we fell in love. My sister and I talked of you often, and every once in a while when Hannah and I returned to Iowa, we would put an ad in the paper seeking you."

"This time," Hannah said, "we happened to see your mother's obituary. We remembered your name as being Arthur and thought it was worth a shot, though we didn't believe it would be the connection we wanted. But Will's sister had the receipt from the telegram she sent way back in 1891. And there was your mother's name, Jeanie Arthur."

"I tried to write her for years from Darlington County. But I never heard back."

"They moved. Fire took the farm one summer and nothing was left."

Katherine nodded.

Will pulled some paper from his wife's satchel. "And here are those drawings you did so long ago." Katherine traced the images, the boy being tossed into the air by his mother. The family with the dog.

"I remember them."

"But what you don't know is that if not for these drawings, I don't think I would have gone back to help Hannah. You drew something about my mother and me that you could not have known. And you did the same with my sister's family. That dog died a year before you were there. And Lynne was quite sure there was no cause to mention a dog. She showed it to me when I went for Bernie. I knew then I had to get Hannah away from her parents. I don't know what her life would have been like if I hadn't, but I know mine would not have been filled with the love she's given me."

Katherine's shoulders collapsed. She covered her face with her hands. "Oh, my goodness." She drew a deep breath and made eye contact with her guests again. "I thought of you all often. I knew there was a reason my mind kept going back to those years, to the knapsack. The old drawings."

"You have a gift, Katherine. I'm sure you know that. But we wanted you to know that your ability to… Well, whatever it is you do, it is good and it changed our lives."

Katherine could barely swallow she was so moved. She always marveled at how much easier it was for her to sort through other people's lives than it was to use her ability to fix her own.

Will flipped open his pocket watch and shot up to standing. "We're due back to the station. Our children—"

"Children!"

They both threw their heads back and laughed. Hannah took his hand and stood. "Why, of course, children, silly girl," Hannah said. "They are six and four years old. And they are wearing their aunt and uncle into the carpets."

Katherine pushed up off the settee and hugged them both tight, breathing in the lavender from Hannah's freshly washed hair, wanting to be able to remember it later. "I can't say thank you enough for coming here and telling me all of this."

They handed Katherine a piece of paper. "Our address. Please, please keep in touch. I can't believe I finally met your Aleksey. But I need to hear more! The whole story! I thought you were never getting married."

Katherine chuckled, remembering the way Hannah would make her retell the story of the blizzard, Aleksey, and the cow. How much life had changed since that story was told to Hannah. Katherine had been years removed from even seeing Aleksey, let alone having the chance to marry him—let alone wanting to ever marry anyone at all.

"I will keep in touch, and I promise. The story will be told, Hannah."

And then Hannah and Will left, leaving in their wake a sense of the world righting itself just a little bit more. Jeanie Arthur's death cleared the way for another reunion, a new way of revealing just how people's lives went on, one without the others, but affected by them all the same. If only there was a way to share some of that with her brother. His life seemed to be in shambles. His anger, tangible at times. And when Katherine went to call everyone down to finally leave for brunch, the only one missing was Tommy.

Chapter 40

Tommy

1891—Des Moines

Tommy's belly was a jumble of nerves. Hands in his pockets, he approached the post office. He attributed the butterflies to the thought that his mother was at the reading of Mrs. Mellet's will. As he hadn't all along, he did not trust that woman to have done what she promised.

Now that he was older, he felt like he was seeing varied sides of his mother. When he was small, however he'd seen her at any given moment was the depth and breadth that he attributed to her. For a while, she was a demanding mother, then a distant one, a harsh mother, a loving, laughing one; then she became a distracted mother, a strong mother, an intelligent mother, a beautiful mother, then an angry, yearning mother.

Now he realized she was all those things all at once. Like a faceted jewel, she appeared different depending on the light and the angle it hit the stone, but she carried all those attributes inside her, always. With this revelation and seeing her handle Maxwell Mellet as she had the day of the funeral when they did not know he was there, Tommy had come to believe his mother was magnificent.

No matter that a side of her may be unpolished or revealed at a given time; Tommy would cherish what he'd witnessed when she bellied up to that pompous jackass, Mellet.

Tommy had seen her iron core, the love of her family, the intensity he'd forgotten was so powerful when experienced in person. And it was in that moment that he knew bringing his father back to join the family was what his mother deserved—a man who loved every side of her, a man who could release the loneliness Tommy knew had been buried under the strength, under all the other things that made her who she was.

He'd been expecting another letter from his father that would update Tommy on his status and ability to travel back to Des Moines. A letter or telegram from Katherine would go a long way to relieving his mother, and him as well. He had a feeling the good news was at the post office, waiting for him. He felt it in his gut that Katherine was on her way. Even though he and his sister were twins, she often seemed more attuned to James than to him. But Tommy knew they were tied together in a way that would last forever, even if it went overlooked from time to time.

Tommy entered the post office. The bell on the door announced his arrival, and at the sound, Pearl looked up from the counter. Her face broke into a glowing smile. Tommy didn't know how to stop his own grin from making him feel as though he were a circus clown. He covered his mouth, rubbing the new stubble that had grown since his mother shaved him.

Pearl let out a whistle. "Look at you. Shined up like yer headed for a bank loan to buy yourself a pot o' gold."

He lifted his hands and looked at his new set of clothes as he approached the counter.

When he reached it, he sidled up, trying to lean casually against it.

She wrinkled her nose. "You tangle with a skunk since I seen you last?"

He moved his head in a motion that was half nodding, half shaking.

"That's why the shave and cut?" she asked.

"Part of the reason."

She brushed the top of his head with the palm of her hand. "Well, ya look nice. More like yer mother's son now."

"I have to agree with that," he said. His stomach took a little tumble as he caught her playful gaze. "Hey. Did you take the deer meat? I broke camp and saw it was gone."

"I traded it for... Well, I *reckoned* you weren't going to eat it, seeing as, well, you know the whole thing that happened that day that I—"

Tommy lifted his hand to stop her. "All right. All right. I know what you're saying." Tommy knew she was implying that since he'd been upset when she saw him, he wouldn't have eaten the meat. "Traded it for what?"

"None of your business, nosy."

"It was my meat, too. And I'm not the nosy one."

She tilted her head and raised her eyebrows. "You weren't gonna have none."

He exhaled and rolled his eyes. He didn't want their conversation to end. "Oh, all right. I don't like meat much— you're right."

Tommy spun the paper she had been writing on so he could read it. She snatched it away. "You are the nosiest human being I've ever met."

"I beg to differ. You hold that title. We both know that. What are you writing on that paper?"

She held the paper against her chest and hesitated before slamming it back onto the counter. "Just a list of places I'm gonna visit as soon as I have the funding for it."

Tommy ran his fingers down the two stacks of envelopes that sat beside her paper. "What's all this?"

"Just looking at postmarks. All these places where people are writing from. Letters from Ireland, England, Vermont, the Florida Keys. What is that, even?"

"Islands off the south of Florida."

She sighed and tossed her hand at him. "I bet there ain't a single question I could ask you that you ain't got the answer to."

"Well, I was forced to study a heck of a lot at one point in time. I do know answers to—"

"Well, not everything." Pearl smiled a wicked smile. "I won't be asking you how to gut a buck anytime soon."

He scratched his neck, marveling at how he wasn't flooded with shame at what she knew about him. "I guess you got me there. But lock that in the steel trap." He put his lips near her ear and whispered, "And don't say that out loud again."

She held her pinkie out and shook it.

"I'm not doing that again."

She stepped back and stuck her hand into her apron, shrugging. "It holds. Pinkie promise doesn't need to be redone."

Tommy pointed to the other list. "What's that there?"

She shrugged and stuffed it into her apron pocket.

"Come on. Show me."

She shook her head. "You looking for mail? Maybe a telegram?"

"You're changing the subject. But yes, I am."

"Well, here." She handed him a thin envelope.

He pulled it out of the sheath and read. The message filled him with joy, and he pumped his fist in the air. "Yes!"

"Yes, what?"

"Nosy, are you?"

"Now, come on. Tell me."

"What's that list you hid away in your pocket?"

She pulled it out and shoved it toward him. "Words."

"Words."

"Lovely, majestic, flamboyant, huge words I want to know and use and write. Someday I will speak the way these rich folks write."

Tommy was enamored by this. She could spout off flowery, descriptive words like those in a list, but her typical language was more apt to contain the word *ain't* than the word *majestic.* "Now, Pearl, I admire your ambition." Oh, he was beginning to revere so much more about her than that. Her green eyes sparkled at him like when the sun rose on the river. Her smile lit him up as if it were his own. But he didn't want her to get in trouble. "You can't keep ripping into people's letters just to gather up their words like water in a bucket. They're not yours."

"Mind yer own business. And tell me what's got you so excited."

"My sister's coming! Should arrive later today."

"Your sister?"

Pearl took on a wistful look as she sighed, retreating into her own thoughts. She held a letter out to him. "Katherine, right?"

Tommy took the letter and drew back. "You read the telegram?"

She shook her head. Then, with her lips pulled tight, she slid another telegram out from behind the counter. "Here's another. From a Lynne Parise."

"You read that one and also a letter. You read my letter. I can tell. You said you never did."

"I said nothing either way. You must have mentioned her name. Or yer mother did that day you both came in. I told you I don't read mail that is not for my eyes."

Tommy rubbed his brow.

"So who's Will McIntyre?" Pearl asked.

Tommy realized she was referring to the person who'd sent one of the telegrams on Katherine's behalf. The thought that she might have read letters from his father or seen some of the sad letters his mother had sent before made him self-conscious. He didn't like the feeling. He knew he shouldn't worry about Pearl knowing things about him. In most ways, she was more vulnerable than he. But still. He was a private type of man.

"I don't know who he is," Tommy said. "I'll ask her when she gets here. But…" He pulled himself partly over the counter and whispered as loudly as he could, worried that her boss might be in the back room, "You're gonna get yourself in trouble. Big stuff trouble. So cut it out. Or I'll tell on you, Pearl, I will."

Pearl looked as though Tommy had punched her in the belly. Of course he wouldn't, but he wanted to scare her.

She spun around on her stool and jumped down, ignoring him. She went to a bin and began to place the letters into slots.

Tommy waited for her to say good-bye or acknowledge him again. It took him only a few seconds more to realize she was ignoring him. He didn't need her digging into his mail, but there was something about the way she became irritated by him that made him want her attention, that made him want her to smile instead of scowl. Was she sad? Angry? "Aww, Pearl. I didn't mean to make you mad."

She plunked the letters into the cubbies so hard they bounced halfway back out.

"Please? Just say you're not mad."

"I ain't mad." Her voice was flat.

Someone tapped Tommy's shoulder. "You going to talk all day, or can I get some service from the nice girl?"

Tommy looked at the man and back at Pearl, who had turned to face them but was focused on the gentleman, not Tommy.

"Oh, hey, Mr. Saur."

"Nice to see you, Pearl. How about my mail?"

She handed it over.

He paged through the envelopes and leaned onto the counter, setting most of them in a pile. "Woo-wee, Pearl! Take a gander at this one. *Salinas, California.* Now, that sounds like a place to put on the list."

Pearl made a face at Tommy as though to say, *See? Not everyone thinks I'm awful.*

Tommy felt a stab of jealousy. Who was this old-timer acting all sweet to Pearl as though they were friends, as though she would care about an old man who pretended to care that Pearl had a list of places she wanted to visit?

He didn't have time for more chatting. But this stab of jealousy had turned flood-like and coursed through his body like it was two thousand degrees of molten lava. He wiped his sweaty brow. The man and Pearl were enthralled with his letters, and she did not even notice that Tommy had swiped a piece of paper and a pen. He ran through all the places his father had been recently. *Salinas, California. Please.* He dipped the nib into ink and wiped the excess off, waiting for Pearl to show that she knew he was still there.

When she was drawn deeper into conversation with the man with all the most interesting postmarks in America, he grew more frustrated. He scribbled on the paper, trying to keep his naturally sloppy cursive as neat and attractive as he could. *Tahiti.* He drew a lavish curlicue under the word, remembering that his father had said he might want to sail there someday.

When Pearl and the man showed no sign of pulling out of their conversation, he debated whether he should ball up the paper and stuff it into his pocket, leaving Pearl to live without ever hearing of a place so exotic even Tommy knew very little of it other than that it was an island in the Pacific.

But as he watched Pearl sweep her red hair out of her eyes and level one of her wide-open smiles on this fella, he decided to leave it. He had things to do that day.

He sauntered to the door, wanting to push through it without looking back, without risking her seeing him do it and knowing that he cared. But when he got to the door, he couldn't resist. He turned back and saw the man was busy shuffling through his envelopes. And Pearl had the paper Tommy had written on in hand, her finger tracing the word, a small smile lifting her lips, a special smile he'd never seen on her before. The sight of it made him dizzy. And as he pushed through the door, he thought the Indian Head was finally doing its work.

And so he headed back to Mrs. Mellet's with the best news he could have imagined—Katherine was returning. With the reading of the will, the Arthurs would find themselves with one special day to cap off what had been a difficult separation, making all that went wrong seem suddenly unimportant. All of this sitting right on top of Pearl's smile when she saw the word *Tahiti.*

Chapter 41

Jeanie

1891—Des Moines

I sat in the front parlor of the Mellet home while one of Mr. Halsey's young partners, a Mr. Harris, shuffled papers and cleared his throat. Even after the contentious conversation I'd had with Maxwell the other day, he had allowed Yale and me to stay in the attic and Tommy to stay in the loft one last night. Tommy had gone into town again to check on mail and telegrams from Katherine. I hadn't eaten that day, sick at the thought we might go another day without hearing from her.

I sat on the edge of the settee, hands in my lap, fingers folded over the letter Mrs. Mellet had written outlining her plans for repaying us. The single lie I was willing to tell in this situation was that Mrs. Mellet had given me this letter rather than my having dug it out from the box she'd told me it was in. I exhaled deeply and glanced at Maxwell, his wife, and Maxwell's sister, Isabelle. Part of me wanted to be invisible, to recede from the room, to keep from intruding on their private pain.

Mrs. Mellet's body had been removed from the room, but miasmic death still permeated the space, a thick sourness that collected in my mouth, so overwhelming that I wondered if it originated inside me rather than from the now-absent body.

I shuddered and noticed Maxwell Mellet staring at me.

I tried to convey my condolences to Maxwell with my expression, my eyes, a nod. I reached up my sleeve and took my hanky from it and dabbed my eyes. A bead of sweat formed at the nape of my neck and dripped between my shoulder blades.

Mr. Harris cleared his throat, looking every bit as nervous as I felt. "Well, now. I am very sorry for your loss, for what you're going through. But it's good to see you're all in good health and spirit." He stretched his neck and rubbed it as though his muscles were cramping. He cleared his throat again and shuffled his papers.

Maxwell leaned forward while his sister clung to his arm as though she needed him to stay upright. "Ah, yes, well...here we go. I do hereby leave the house and the listed accounts, the bulk of what I own, to my son, Maxwell. I bequeath my jewelry, silver, and clothing to my daughter, Isabelle." The siblings nodded at each other as though it made perfect sense.

My throat closed, but it was time. I slid forward in my chair and lifted the letter toward the attorney. He looked over his glasses at me. "You have something there?"

I nodded and stood, walking to him.

I could feel the Mellets' collective gaze hot on my spine. My hand shook as the letter passed into the attorney's grasp. I could not bear to turn around and take my seat again. My nerves bundled, pulling into a knot in my stomach. I straightened against the fear that cuffed my whole body.

Mr. Harris cleared his throat. "Oh, yes, Mr. Halsey mentioned this to me. It reads 'To Jeanie Arthur, my apology and a sum of fifty thousand dollars.'" The attorney looked up from the letter and made eye contact with me and then the

Mellet siblings. I knew this was a strange thing to have happened to them, that it would feel wrong to them.

I deserve this.

"This can't be right!" Maxwell said so quietly I almost didn't hear. I turned to him. I could understand he might feel odd that his mother was giving anything to a non-family member. Still, he should understand why it made sense that she did. Isabelle swayed in her seat.

The attorney was fixed on his papers, paging through them, searching for something. "Now, just hold on a moment. Let me find… Yes. This goes with the miniature chest."

"I will take this whole mess to court. Where is Halsey?"

"Vacation," the lawyer and I said simultaneously.

Maxwell jerked his shoulders as though he'd been seared with a hot poker.

"Sit down, Mr. Mellet," Mr. Harris said. "You need to hear this out."

The lawyer hoisted a miniature dome-topped cedar chest from under his coat, which had been draped over it. It was a shocking blue, but the paint and its Dutch-like flower decorations were wearing through to the dark wood underneath. The lawyer held it up. "This was Mrs. Mellet's. She stowed it under the seventh and eighth floorboards in her bedroom, and I have retrieved it as per the instructions."

The Mellets joined me as we gathered around the box, our heads bent in, touching so we could get a clear look.

The hinges squeaked as the lawyer lifted the lid. Inside were pins that a woman would wear: a Christmas tree, a wreath, a spring bunny, even a ladybug. He flicked those around and picked one up, holding it into the light. "Costume jewelry. Just as it notes."

"As *what* notes? What *is* this?" Maxwell spat.

The lawyer lifted the Christmas tree pin up and dropped it again. "This is my first reading of a will, Mr. Mellet, so please give me a moment."

Maxwell crossed his arms and looked away.

There were buttons and seam rippers and a few blank pieces of paper. He lifted those out and exposed crumpled-up dollar bills. He smoothed each one on the table. "Looks like nine dollars."

Nine dollars sounded good to me. Fifty thousand and nine dollars! I could already imagine the tiny house we would buy with the lush gardens in the back. We would have hens and cows and fresh vegetables most of the year.

The lawyer held his hands up. "All right. The last time Mrs. Mellet came into the office, Mr. Halsey let me know, just in case something happened, that this was complicated and that I needed to—if it were me who was here to handle this— that you have to be patient."

"I have a job in Chicago. I can't sit here waiting for Mr. Halsey to return. Not like some of us can." Max glared at me.

"Well, I remember the letter being mentioned and imagine there is a copy in the vault."

"The vault you can't access?" Maxwell said.

"That one, yes," he said.

"Anyway, the letter is quite legitimate, I believe," Mr. Harris said. "I personally was not aware that she was planning to leave you so much, Mrs. Arthur—"

Maxwell shot to his feet. "How could Mother do this? Giving our money away as though it were pages from the *Farmer's Almanac*."

I stepped toward Maxwell and gripped his arm. "Mr. Mellet, I understand that you feel upset about this. But I have the letters your mother wrote *me*." I pulled them from my apron pocket. "I didn't ask her for anything. She knew she did wrong and she wanted to help make my life better. That's not a bad thing."

"Let me see that letter you gave Mr. Harris."

The lawyer handed it over. Mr. Mellet scanned it and slammed it back onto the desk in front of Mr. Harris. "It's not signed."

"Is it valid?" Isabelle asked. "That amount of money simply can't go to a stranger, a woman with questionable motives."

"My motives are just." I was angry and at the end of my generosity for showing understanding. No one knew what it was like to lose something that was mine more than me, but they were still getting a substantial amount. My take would not leave them penniless in the least.

"And there's more for Mrs. Arthur."

"This is crazy!" Maxwell threw his hands in the air, his face contorted.

Mr. Harris ignored the outburst, speaking over the grumblings and Isabelle's quiet sighs.

"This was the box I was ordered to retrieve, and this was what was under the floorboards. But Mrs. Mellet had Halsey write in that you were free to remove any of her plants that you desired from the garden, Mrs. Arthur."

"Plants?" I stared at the crumpled money in the box.

"Yes, the contents of this box and plants. She thought you'd learned so much about yourself in the past few years— that you'd truly bloomed into a new person and that you adored gardening—"

"And an apology? She said she wrote something for the paper?"

"It's not like you were her child, you know," Isabelle said. I turned to see her blot her eyes with her handkerchief.

My face fired with blood rushing like a train. "She told me she was going to repay what I lost when she and my father—"

"She and your father?" Isabelle said.

I felt like I was being held underwater. All I could get straight in my head was the sound of Mrs. Mellet's voice telling me I would have all that I was due.

"I don't want anything other than what I am owed."

Max shook his head, his shoulders shaking as well.

I went to Isabelle, thinking she might be easier to talk to. "Your mother promised if I came that she would restore my accounts and my name. She told me she wanted to make amends." I pointed toward the back of the room, in the direction of the gardens. "We sat on that garden bench by the greenhouse, and she told me she wanted redemption and wanted to—you two must understand my circumstances. You must."

I blotted my eyes with a hanky. "I don't want to add to your pain."

Maxwell ran his hand through his hair. "You think we're not going to protest this will? We can't verify anything you're saying. Yes, my mother took a recent fondness to you. She was kind that way, toward animals, toward—"

I held my hands out, fingers spread. I told my mouth to stop moving, but it was too late. The words had already been released. "She was *not* kind. She knew she was dying, and she was trying to keep her feet from eternal fire."

Silence swept through the room. My chest heaved. It had to be said. I'd stomached enough shame and embarrassment of my own over the years. I would not suffer under it any longer, and I surely would not accept someone else's on their behalf.

Isabelle stood and moved toward me. I could smell the woman's breath, that she'd taken some drink to get her through the day, but I would not back down.

Mr. Harris stepped in between us. "Now, that's enough. There's no way to address your concerns today. Clearly Mrs. Mellet loved her children and assigned a significant amount of money to you, Maxwell—two hundred thousand dollars. Her jewelry was worth a fortune as well, Isabelle. And yes, Mrs. Mellet obviously felt sorry for you, Mrs. Arthur, but there's nothing that can be officially handed over until Halsey returns and opens the vault. I agreed to do this as a favor to you people, just to reassure you that there were inheritances coming. But I've had enough of the condescending attitudes and arguments."

Maxwell shoved his nose in the air and fussed with his lapels as though putting himself back into order. "That handkerchief Mrs. Arthur has stuffed up her sleeve is my mother's. I don't recall a mention of that in what you read."

I looked down at the clothing I wore. Apparently, neither Maxwell nor Isabelle recognized my clothing as having come from the Mellet closets.

"Wait just a moment, Mr. Mellet. Mrs. Arthur worked for your mother. She even cared for her feet for the last few days. The hanky is hers and also the small domed box and its contents. But past that, none of this matters. Not until Halsey returns."

"How long will that be?" Isabelle asked.

"About three weeks," Mr. Harris said as he cringed away.

Maxwell and Isabelle shot another glance my way before collapsing their attention like a circus tent over Mr. Harris. They shouted and cried and wondered how it was possible for their mother to have given so much money to a virtual stranger, how it was possible that Mr. Halsey could have taken leave for so long with no measures in place to make things right.

Their words passed over me like the Des Moines River current on a hot summer day. The ranting did not stop long enough in my mind to be processed or responded to; it was simply the background noise of the moment.

I took deep breaths and gripped the velvet arms of the chair. I willed myself to stand. Everything was fine. I collected the blue box and headed to the stairs. I ascended the stairs, the shouts punctuating my steps upward. Three weeks? To me that was a blink. I'd gone years with nothing. The nine dollars was more than I needed until the rest was released.

Once in the attic, I looked at Yale on the bed, playing with her wooden spoon. I thought of Tommy, a young man who was capable of contributing to our family. And Katherine. I revisited my list of things to do in order to find her. I would have no time to wallow. I had the steps I needed to take to make my life right. That sum—fifty thousand dollars—looped through my brain. We could move on. Head back east to Chicago or Boston or Pittsburgh. Fifty thousand dollars made anything possible, and three weeks would be nothing in light of all we'd been through already.

Chapter 42

Tommy

1891—Des Moines

Tommy rode Mrs. Mellet's horse as hard as possible. When he arrived back at the house, he dismounted, set him out to pasture, and added water to the trough. He dashed into the house through the kitchen and could hear arguing in the front room.

He snuck down the hall and peeked around the doorway to see into the room. Maxwell and Isabelle Mellet had cornered a frightened-looking man, who, Tommy guessed, had something to do with the will. The anger in the room was thick, and Tommy felt a surge of excitement. Their hostility could mean only one thing: The will had clearly outlined the money that would go to the Arthurs. This, on top of the news he'd received from Katherine, gave him pause.

He bowed his head. *Thank you, God, for delivering me this news.* He shrugged. Was there a God? He thought of all the times he'd recited Scripture, almost using it as a weapon against people rather than a source of comfort or contemplation. But that had been long ago.

He'd thought at one time he believed the Bible to be true, convinced that every word had been laid down by God and the Holy Spirit. But it didn't take long once he was off on his own to realize his use of the Bible had been to irritate his family more than anything. And it didn't take long for him to realize that he could believe in a God and not think those words were magical, were the truth. "Thank you, God. Thank you for this, for bringing my family back. For the money that is ours." He drew a deep breath and straightened. Then he bowed his head again. "And please let my father write soon and tell me where he is. Please."

Tommy's long legs propelled him up the main stairs like a lion up a mountainside. He tore down the second-floor hallway to the back stairs until he was standing in the room where Yale and his mother were lying on the bed. He had expected to see her packing, to find her nearly as excited as he was. But, of course, she had only half the good news, so perhaps she was simply placid, not yet fully joyful due to not knowing where her daughter was. It was just the third time he'd been up there, and immediately he felt the walls close in. He went to the dormer and threw open the window beside the bed.

When he turned back, he saw his mother's eyes were sleepy slits. He went to her side of the bed and knelt beside her. "Mama? Are you all right?"

She stretched. "Just tired, Tommy. That's all."

Tommy took her hand. "I saw the Mellets downstairs. And I know there must have been money left to us, for the anger in Maxwell Mellet's face could fuel a train from here to Chicago and back."

His mother got up on her elbows and opened her mouth to speak.

"Mama, wait till you hear."

She swung her feet onto the floor. Tommy got up from his knees and sat beside her, taking her hand in his. He kissed her fingers.

"What is it?" he asked.

"It's the money."

Tommy saw the whole story in an instant in her eyes. Three little words—*it's the money*—and he knew it was not going to be their money.

He put his arm around her and pulled her in to him. "Oh, Mama. What happened?"

She sat up and turned toward him. "Mrs. Mellet's intentions were clear verbally and also in the unsigned letter. It's fifty thousand dollars."

"Fifty thousand dollars!" Tommy's mouth dropped open. He wagged his head as though trying to rid himself of a fly that had landed in his ear. He couldn't believe the idea. "Fifty? Thousand? For us?"

She nodded.

"We could live modestly forever. We could get Father. We could—"

His mother squeezed his hand and shook it. "Listen to me." She exhaled, her eyes darting away from his gaze.

Tommy's belly tightened. Something wasn't right. "What is it?"

"Apparently," she said, "with Mr. Halsey out of town, we cannot have access to the money for weeks. And the Mellets aren't happy. I fear they might fight our share of the will."

Tommy agreed. "Maxwell Mellet's hot under his collar—you're right—but I'm sure it's not as hot as where his mother's feet are resting right now."

His mother shook her head and leaned in to him, her head on his shoulder. "Oh, Tommy. I do think Mrs. Mellet was sorry. But someone like her just can't untangle the awful that she wrought. Even when she wants to. It doesn't appear as though she wrote the letter to be posted in the paper. There won't be a public declaration of our innocence in the swindle. But none of that matters. We have each other. We'll have enough money to start over anywhere we want."

"You have kinder thoughts toward Mrs. Mellet than I," Tommy said.

"Oh, I'm angry, Tommy, but I've learned I need to let go of that when I can. I've been going over my list of things we need to do and how we will get Katherine—"

Tommy felt a measure of satisfaction at hearing his mother's positive outlook. He grabbed her up and held so tight, she lifted off her feet and let out a little cough. This money would make their lives easy in many ways. Not the way it had been when they first lived in Des Moines, but simple and abundant compared to the last four years. He set her down and grinned at her smiling face.

Tommy smacked his forehead. "Mama!" He had forgotten to tell her his news. "It's Katherine. She's on her way."

His mother's eyes went wide. Her lips quivered, her dark eyes filling. Her hands went out to her sides a little as though grabbing the air for stability.

He took her hands. "Oh, Mama. She's coming back today. We're to meet her at the train station."

His mother's awestruck face filled him with even more joy. He saw the worry leave her as he never had before.

"Which train?" She whispered as though she hadn't the energy for full volume.

He shook his head. "No train. She's coming on a coach. There was a telegram from a man named Will and his sister, Lynne. Apparently, he sent Katherine to her farm—the Parises, and they then arranged to have Katherine ride with a gentleman headed to West Branch. I don't really know more."

His mother covered her mouth. Her body softened and she fell into Tommy, her hand gripping his forearm tight.

He wrapped his arm around her shoulder. He felt like a man, more than he ever had.

"Oh my God," she said softly. "She's coming. She's coming."

Tommy's mother felt small in his arms, as though she were now the child.

"Mama, I'm so sorry about earlier. What I said about you and Father."

She straightened and took his face in her hands. "Oh, no, no, no, Tommy. I am sorry about all of it. All that matters is that you are here, that Katherine is coming, that Yale is here."

"I love you, Mama." Tommy thought back to the day he'd seen his mother crying, the day he'd realized it was time for him to take control of his destiny. It had been a hard road, but he'd managed to tread it well. And now, with his mother in his arms, he felt he'd achieved some of what he'd set out to do—to help make his family whole again. His father had yet to be returned to him, but he could not have anticipated how good it would feel to see his mother's pride in him, to experience the kind of love he'd always thought she held only for James.

"I love you, too, Tommy." She pulled him in and kissed his forehead. "Look at me, Tommy. I want you to hear this and understand it right down to the very core of who you are."

Tommy nodded. "All right."

"I am proud of you. I could not imagine this moment without you. I could not imagine you being more of a gentleman than you are. And I want you to embed that in your mind somewhere deep, where you can always find it. I love you and I am proud of you."

Tommy's spine lengthened and he felt a shift inside. His mother's recognition of him as a source of pride, her words full of love and emotion, changed everything for him. He would be her protector. He would show her every day that he was the man she'd just said he was.

She embraced him and kissed his cheek. "I don't know what I would have done without you."

Tommy let his mother hold him as thick pride spilled through him, plumping the very cells that formed his body. He was so happy that he almost spoke aloud the thought that soon he would find a way to get Father to join them, but even as he began to speak it, he managed to drag it back in, unheard.

His mother had been through so much and still harbored ill feelings toward his father. He would not ruin this moment of happiness for her, for them. That was the least he could do. And he saw himself right then as a man, as someone like his brother, James, had been. Someone who put the feelings and desires of others before his own.

Chapter 43

Jeanie

1891—Des Moines

Fifty thousand dollars. The sum banged around my skull like dancers at a ball, twirling, rising, and falling with intensity. But now, when I thought of the delay in retrieving the fortune, I simply reminded myself that Katherine was on her way. Between Tommy and myself, we had eleven dollars. That would be enough for us to rent a room and eat dinner and breakfast and find a place to board tomorrow.

We were back at the train station where I'd met Tommy a little over a week before. And now it was Katherine who would join us. I paced the depot with Yale on my hip. I glanced at the enormous clock that hung near the ticket booth.

"What time did the telegram say Katherine would arrive again?"

"Five thirty, Mama. But they might be late if they stopped to water the horses and eat."

I nodded. That made sense, but I couldn't help thinking something had gone wrong again. *No, don't think that way.*

I stole a look at Tommy. He gave me a reassuring nod. His easy confidence made me smile, took away some of my fear that the world had become too powerful for we Arthurs to manage. *No need to fret.*

Like the day at the poorhouse when I recalled how Elizabeth and the mob of former friends and neighbors had taken all our worldly goods, I remembered Tommy guiding me from my bedroom, helping me understand it was time to let go. He had been there for me that day. *He is here now.* How proud I was. It was now time for me to make it up to him and Katherine. My grief had been so deep and suffocating, I could not see far enough in front of me to even wonder how hard James' death would be for them. It was as though I had been infected with a virus that overtook every bodily system, blinding me to everything except my own existence.

The clock at the watchtower ticked forward. Six o'clock. Two coaches pulled up behind a wagon full of people who began unloading their luggage onto the depot.

Katherine.

Did one of those coaches hold her? A man with a top hat and shoes so shiny they gleamed from fifty feet away lent his hand to a woman with blush-pink shoes and a damask gown.

Katherine?

The man helped the woman from the coach, her black hair and unfamiliar dress emerged from the coach. Of course I wouldn't recognize her clothing. Perhaps her hair had darkened with age?

Katherine?

She faced us. Her close-set eyes and thin, straight lips told me that was not my daughter.

The driver for the second coach hopped down and opened its door. A brown boot punched through the doorway. A woman wearing a tweed walking costume stood, her chestnut-brown hair sweeping down her back as she offered her hand to her driver. She tilted her head a certain way and pushed her hair over her shoulder.

My breath caught, and I knew.

Katherine.

She reached back into the coach and pulled a knapsack out, slinging it over her shoulder. She had grown taller, but not much more shapely at all. I wanted to run to her, but I could not move. Tommy was looking in the other direction, his hand shielding his eyes from the setting sun.

I strained to see the woman's hands better. Could I see her missing finger? They were covered in gloves, and I could not tell if the woman's little finger was halved.

She turned, and her eyes searched the station, stopping on this face or that before moving on to the next. I couldn't breathe. It was her. But she was so thin that it looked as if she would fly away on a dandelion seed if it came up under her. She was taller, lithe. Her carriage was graceful and her skirts swayed back and forth as she walked, waltzing in between people, her gaze searching the faces of those who passed her by.

Her face was pale rather than creamy, but as the sun was setting, the glaze hit her face and her eyes lit up like jewels, all the colors of the prairie lands held there. Her face was still round but shaped by exquisite cheekbones. As she moved down the depot, I watched people stop and stare, moving out of her way as she searched. I had never seen someone so beautiful. I'd never felt someone's presence so fully.

Tommy turned and took my elbow. "Mama, what are you waiting for?"

I couldn't speak. He took Yale from me and pressed the small of my back. "Go on. You've waited long enough."

Suddenly, I had my breath back, my voice. I raised my hand and motioned to her. "Katherine."

She stopped. Her gaze settled on mine, but I could see that her eyes kept searching, seeing me but not sure it *was* me. I was suddenly self-conscious. Had I changed that much? Aged so much? I touched my cheek. Could the weight of the last four years be seen on my very face? Was I recognizable?

"Mama." I could see her lips form the word.

I nodded and started toward her. Someone stepped in front of me, nearly falling over my feet.

I steadied the man and continued toward her. "Katherine," I said.

And I could wait no longer to have her in my arms. I broke into a jog, and she did as well. When we met, we slammed into each other, arms clasping. "Oh, Katherine, Katherine. You're back."

"Mama," she said. We rubbed each other's backs and began to laugh. We pulled apart and I took her hands and stepped back to have a look at her. She was taller than me, but her frame was nearly emaciated. I could see the joy on her beautiful face, the tears that were clearly happy, not sad, but I couldn't help wondering if she'd eaten in days. "Oh, my Katherine. I have missed you so."

She started to say something, but it came out garbled. "Oh, galoshes, Mama." Her lips quivered as she tried to hold back tears.

I drew her in again. "You don't know how long I've waited to hear someone say that silly thing."

She nodded against me, choking, her body's tension releasing as she softened into me.

"It's all right, Katherine. You can let it out. I am here."

And she collapsed further into me, her body shaking with tears and the same relief I felt. She was home, and we would find a way to make our lives work. This time, we would do it. This time, I knew we would.

Chapter 44

Katherine

1891—Des Moines

Katherine, Tommy, Yale, and their mother had rented a room for the night she arrived. Not far from the train station, the hotel was run-down but clean, offering linens, a bathhouse, and even breakfast with the four dollars it would cost to stay. That was worth it for them, as they needed a good night's sleep before embarking on what would be an important day—finding a place to live where they could all be together.

Katherine's mother and Yale were each heavy into sleep, each in one of the beds in the room. Katherine and Tommy were seated by the fire, not ready to sleep yet.

"Tomorrow I should hear if I have the job at the Savery Hotel. It will mean room and board and pay. It should really help us out. I am declining the room, so that should allow me to make even more."

Katherine smiled and brushed some lint from his shoulder. "You've really become a handsome man, haven't you?"

He narrowed his eyes on her and lifted one side of his mouth in a wicked grin that Katherine guessed made girls he wasn't related to swoon.

"I can't get more handsome, Katherine. We both know that."

She chuckled, taking in the feeling of being with Tommy. She'd grown tall herself, but he stretched beyond six feet. She couldn't believe how much he'd filled out. But it was his manner, his smooth countenance and humor that struck her, that reminded her so starkly that this young man, her Tommy, was not someone she could say she knew well anymore. In some ways, she saw flashes of James in him, flashes she'd never seen before.

She grabbed his hand in both of hers.

"You're still cold," he said.

Katherine shushed him, clasping tighter.

Tommy shifted his feet. "What?"

Katherine felt sadness course through her body, shooting right through their joined hands. She pulled away and blew out her breath, understanding that he had probably experienced the exact same loneliness that she had.

"You're looking at me funny," he said.

"It's just that I missed you so much. And Mama. And Yale and still James, of course." She thought of James' spirit, which would come to visit her, infusing her with a sense of presence that she did not get from the other living family members who just weren't there but were still alive. "I wasn't sure this would ever happen—us seeing each other again."

He tapped the end of her nose, making her smile, and she swatted his hand away. "I always knew we would."

"I always enjoyed getting your letters. When you managed to send them," she said. "But they conveyed none of this humor and charm you wield so easily, like a weapon of manners and destruction all at once."

"I sure loved getting yours." He shoved his hands in his front pockets. "Sounds like you had a rough time lately. When they stopped coming and I moved, I just thought that was the path we were taking—full estrangement. Tell me about the last few months."

Katherine looked into the fire. She would elaborate someday on the awful things that had happened while she was with the Christoffs and the Turners before them, but not yet. She was so exhausted from leaving the Christoffs and the travel that followed that she couldn't imagine revealing the insanity of the past months, the past few days. She knew her brother loved her.

She could feel their connection in a way that she'd lost over the past two years. It was back in just these hours since they'd reunited. But that didn't mean she was ready to reveal what she'd experienced. She remembered the way he turned to Scripture in times of worry or sadness. That was too close to what she recalled about the Christoffs. She could not make herself vulnerable after all she'd been through.

She would keep her secrets to herself. How could she say the words, "James has never left me even though we buried him. I had a conversation with my brutal keeper's dead sister." How does a sane person reveal such a thing, even to someone who was least likely to hold it against her?

Much as she wanted a confidant, someone who understood her worries, who saw her strengths, who loved her for exactly who she was, who *believed* her, it would be too risky to confide. She cleared her throat. *No.* She'd learned to depend on herself, to protect herself, and that was all she needed to know for now.

Surely though, she could enjoy having her brother back, as this grown, amiable version was lovely to behold. She looked back at him. "You're even a more fluent charmer than I originally gathered, aren't you? Dangerous with all that charisma at your disposal. Probably not fair to all the other young men in your vicinity, is it?"

Tommy shifted to face Katherine and flashed a grin. "I can't deny I'm refined and debonair."

Katherine relaxed, her shoulder leaning against his, growing more comfortable by the second. Their shared history sprouted up around them like spring tulips, filling the space with silent beauty. Their rich connection accounted for way more than the time they hadn't communicated. It was meaningful and strong even if she had begun to doubt it at one point. She looked over her shoulder at her mother and Yale.

"Mother is so tired," Katherine whispered. From this distance, with space between them, but not so much that she couldn't see her, Katherine felt warmth and love for her mother perk inside her.

"I have a plan to make her world, all of our lives, just right. Like rain, right as rain in hot August," Tommy whispered. He added another log to the fire.

She tipped her head toward his. "You mean that job at the Savery?"

"That's just part of the plan. I'll save every penny so we can get our father back for Mama. And we'll all live together once again. Just like you've been wishing for years. He is so excited to come back. He can't wait."

Katherine pulled her knees against herself, wrapping her arms around her legs. She hadn't been expecting this—that Tommy had been corresponding with their father. "Father wrote you?"

He squeezed her shoulder. "He wrote you, too. Didn't he?"

Katherine couldn't look at Tommy. There was something shameful about her father not writing to her, as though it were her wrongdoing, not his.

"Well, don't be angry. I assumed he was writing to both of us. Maybe he thought I was sharing them with you."

Katherine grimaced. That was ridiculous. She thought of the Christoffs and imagined for a moment that her father had swooped in on a horse, rescuing her from her evil captors. But she had been forced to save herself.

Tommy's voice grew quieter, like he realized this information might hurt Katherine. "He's so busy. I'm sure he wrote. Perhaps the letters got lost? He's had much success, some travels—"

"Success?" Anger curdled in Katherine's stomach. She silently begged James to come and sit with her, to help her find that spot where nothing penetrated her heart but feelings of love and comfort. Nothing came to her. She winced as a sour taste sprang up on her tongue. Where had her letters from her father been?

She closed her eyes and tried to find that space inside her where peace prevailed no matter what was happening around her, that space that opened between the living and the dead, where she found comfort and knowledge that escaped others. She'd been so good at using that space for the benefit of others. Perhaps her father had been trying to get in touch with her all these years and the mail had been lost?

Really, she had been so busy surviving that she had not put her thoughts on her father much at all. She realized right then how little of a part she must have thought he could play in making her life better. It was her mother whom she had yearned for, in the same way Tommy clearly yearned for their father.

She moved closer to the fire, feeling the growing flames against her cheeks. She loved her father, but there was something about the manner in which their family had fallen apart that made it easier to disconnect from him.

Still, she felt a sting at not hearing from someone who should have wanted to hear from her. "So Father... He sent word to you? Father's successful?"

"Success, what else? He's a man with a vision as big as the blue sky and as long as a summer day. He said to send his love to you in every letter."

Sweat beaded at Katherine's hairline. She dug out a handkerchief and dabbed the moisture from her temples, shifting away from Tommy. He pulled his arm from around her shoulder. She patted the back of her neck with the hanky. She didn't want to speak poorly of her father. She loved him. But if he was successful, shouldn't he have brought the family back together long ago? If he had, she wouldn't have had to stay with the Christoffs at all. She knew it was more complicated than that, but still, she knew her father would not keep quiet about any success he could claim as his.

Yes, there was something she labeled as affection for her father deep inside her, but if she thought real hard about the time they'd spent on the prairie, *success* was not the word that came to mind when she thought of him. As much as her mother tried to make him out to be, well, the same man of vision that Tommy imagined him to be, Katherine had seen the cracks in that invented facade as sure as she was drawing breath. Still, though, she'd always wanted his attention, to know he loved her.

She'd written her father, but she'd never known if he got the letters, and she'd certainly never received any response. Could it be true that he wanted to come back? She'd never considered it. She understood this news should bring happiness, contentment, something good to her, but it didn't. She looked over her shoulder at her mother. What would she think of this?

Tommy pulled letters from his pocket and fanned them like playing cards, then shoved one under her nose. "This one just got here when I got your telegram. Father is sad we're not together. He wants us back. All of us."

Katherine took the letters and ran her finger over the peaks and valleys of the crinkled envelopes that must have been clenched in his hand or shoved deep inside a pocket. She peeked at her mother again. Her sleeping posture was languid, peaceful. Her sleeping breath was deep and even, her face soft and untroubled.

Tommy elbowed her. "Mama's not real happy to hear of my plan to bring Father back." He held up his hand to Katherine to forestall her response. "I love Mama. I understand more now, but, boy, when I get our father back here, I know she will just see him and fall in love all over again. I just know it. With that money from Mrs. Mellet, it will be even easier to get Father here."

I bet it will be, she thought. No, her mother would not like this news for many reasons, Katherine suspected.

"You understand love, do you?" Katherine said, poking him in the side.

Tommy rolled away, a big dramatic display of pain that was not there from her playful jab. He sat back up, a big smile coming over his face. She could see that he was trying to stop it but couldn't.

"You don't have to be in love to understand it, to see it right in front of you." Tommy squeezed his eyes shut as though he was picturing something happy. Katherine was moved and surprised by his desire to bring the family back together, that he'd taken the initiative to make it happen. She suspected he felt his own love for someone to be so idealistic about it, to not have seen any of the nuances of their parents' relationship, to believe so fully in what his father told him.

"Anyway," he said, "we'll be happy again, all of us. The way we were. That kind of love, I have time for. I feel it now. You should have seen how happy Mama was when she heard you were coming. I can still feel it—her joy. And she was actually proud of me."

"Of course she's proud of you. Why wouldn't she be?"

Tommy shrugged. "I think we can really make a go of this, we can go back in some ways. I know it."

Katherine nodded, not wanting to argue or question at this moment, so soon after they'd all come back together after so long. For now, this was enough. Tommy folded the letters into a neat square, matching each corner precisely before tucking them into his pocket as though they were gilded treasure, his tongue coming out of the corner of his mouth as it always had since he was a little boy when he concentrated. His determination was evident to her.

The way we were.

The sentiment lifted her skin into goose bumps. Without James, nothing could ever be the same. And she didn't trust any such sentiments sent through letters. Especially when she considered the dates she saw on his collection of correspondence from their father, dates spaced out over what looked like years, if she'd seen the postmarks correctly. She'd gotten plenty of letters that burst with promises from her mother. Words on paper were nice to pass the time, but they didn't amount to promises kept, families reunited.

"You must have had dozens of suitors," Tommy said. "Look at you. There can't be a prettier girl in the entire country. You must have fielded several proposals by now."

"Oh no. No suitors. Not that I worry about it. I won't ever get married. Never," Katherine said so quietly she wasn't even sure she'd spoken aloud.

"Never marry?" Tommy said.

Katherine shook her head. She studied her nails. "Well. I can't imagine a man whom I would love, who would let me be exactly how I want to be. So I'd rather just not think of it, not want it at all."

She laid her head against the foot of the bed. Was Tommy being cruel to their mother by trying to bring back their father? No. He was a forgiving believer. He would find no use for cruelty to anyone, she was sure, let alone their mother. She drew a deep breath and tried to open to the calming that should come when she needed it.

She thought of Hannah, the church members, the revival, and the storm. She recalled the woman in the kitchen with the baby, James' warning, Will's dead mother appearing at the train station. It was as though they'd all come to her at just the right time to guide her where she needed to be. *Angels.* She felt as though her world had suddenly been peopled with angels. Poor Hannah. She wanted so much to help her, but knew that she could not, not right then. Perhaps that's what her mother had felt when she didn't come for Katherine. Perhaps she told herself Katherine would be fine, that she could protect herself or that angels would watch over her. Maybe it was that. Katherine sighed. She told herself that Hannah would have her own angels. She had to believe that, for she had no other choice.

She closed her eyes and tried to get a feel for Hannah, for what she might be experiencing right at that very moment. She patted the pocket in her skirt where the crystal ball was hard against her leg, wishing she could take it out and read it, draw comfort from it as she'd done in the last days.

She considered taking it out and showing Tommy, seeing if he could understand what had happened to her, how she was sure she had angels who stepped in and out of her life in just the right moment. Will. Even he would be counted among those who were divine in Katherine's eyes. *Thank you, God, for all of them.*

But in the end, she knew it was lunacy to try to explain. And she could not put him in the position of his religion coming between them. What if he thought she was evil like the Christoffs and the minister had?

She had time. She didn't need to reveal her entire life in a few seconds. No. She could allow herself the time just to enjoy them all being together. She folded her hands in her lap, one hand covering the other, hiding the pinkie finger that had to be amputated after the blizzard, and she just allowed her surrender.

"Katherine, Tommy," their mother said from the bed behind them. "Are you two all right?"

Katherine turned to see her mother up on her elbow, waving them toward her. "Come on to bed. We have to find a home tomorrow."

Katherine turned and got on her knees, rubbing her mother's foot, which was covered by the quilt, warmed by the fire. "Come sit with us here at the fire, Mama."

Her mother hesitated and then drew back the blanket, joining Katherine and Tommy on the floor, sitting between them. They pulled the quilt from the bed and covered all three of them. Underneath the quilt, her mother held her hand and squeezed it three times.

Katherine kissed her mother's cheek. "I love you, too, Mama. I am so happy."

And they talked through the night. They danced around painful truths of the years that kept them apart. The fire blazed, reminding Katherine of the warmth she felt when James or the other guides came. The bobbing hues of blue and red flames reminded her of the crystal ball before it fell from the chandelier, the golden glowing flames like the night she held the crystal ball with Will and his mother came to talk.

Nothing in her life was perfect. But there before the fire, with as much of her family there as possible, she realized that she had what she needed even if it was not in the exact way any of them wanted it to be.

Love had found its way into their worlds, drawing them back in a way that Katherine could not deny. For right that moment, she felt happy. And all that happened before could be subjugated. All that happened before no longer mattered. The Arthurs were together, and that would change everything.

Katherine's mother had fallen asleep on Tommy's shoulder. He carried her back to bed and put her next to Yale. Katherine hadn't realized how slight her mother had become in the years of separation. Not until she saw how easily Tommy lifted her and settled her into bed. She watched as Yale scooted her backside into her mother's body, and they were molded into one, intertwined like tree roots pinning a great oak tight into solid ground, like any child and mother should be.

Katherine kissed her mother and Yale and tucked the fire-warmed quilt tight against them. Her mother still had a regality about her. Katherine supposed that kind of bearing didn't chip away even with the rigors of poverty battering at a person. But still, she saw her mother's smallness for the first time ever. Katherine pressed her hand to her heart. If only her mother had an angel. If only Katherine could bring her one.

"I'm going out," Tommy said in a whisper.

"What? No."

"I told two fellas I'd help them deliver coal in the morning. There's a list of forty homes due for delivery."

"Not yet," Katherine said, latching on to Tommy's wrist.

He squatted down. "You get some sleep. I'll be back for breakfast." He kissed her forehead.

She shook her head. "You need sleep."

He smiled. "It's morning, silly Katherine. We've been talking all night." Katherine sighed and watched him leave. He turned to smile before he closed the door. Katherine exhaled. She picked up her knapsack and moved to the empty bed. She sat cross-legged and withdrew her drawing materials. Though her limbs were heavy, as they'd been the night at the Parise farm, her eyes were not. The air she shared with people who loved her seemed to fuel her with vigor that could be drained only through the drawing she loved to do so much.

And as the sun began to rise, outlining around and under the dark green blinds at the window, Katherine began to draw her sleeping mother and sister, feeling as though doing so would mean she could hold them safe inside her heart forever.

She studied them, their perfect, peaceful posture.

"Katherine," her mother said from the other bed.

Katherine smiled at her and rubbed her eyes. She'd been so absorbed in her drawing that she hadn't even realized her mother had wakened and pulled back her covers. Katherine watched as her mother re-tucked Yale's covers and then she scooted over in the second bed to make room for her mother.

They both laid down, her mother's arm under Katherine's head and they both looked at the drawing Katherine had started. Her mother traced the charcoal lines. "Wow... I just can't believe you can do this. Your art has always been so beautiful, but this..." her mother shook her head. "It's like magic. I feel like we could get up and walk off the paper."

Katherine laid the sketchbook down and turned on her side to look at her mother's profile. Her dark hair was loose at her temples and Katherine pushed it back. "I think my drawings kept me alive in a way. I could just go to them and my mind would spin something out through my hand and for those moments I was drawing, I was at peace."

Her mother turned to her. She traced Katherine's jawline, her gaze tight on Katherine's. "I don't even know how to say how sorry I am. I can't even begin to tell you how—"

Katherine heard her mother's voice crack. She could see her vulnerability—something she had never witnessed before. Not like this. She didn't know where to start, either, how to make her mother understand none of it mattered right then.

They were getting a second chance to start again. They could reshape everything they knew about each other. There was much she wanted to tell her mother, but she couldn't mend together words that would make sense.

"We're together, Mama. We can rest now." Katherine took her mother's hand and they clasped them together, held between their two bodies, near their healing hearts.

"I want to tell you everything, Katherine. I want to know everything," her mother said.

Katherine's eyes were heavy, fatigue hitting her hard now that she was tucked in warm with her mother. "We will, Mama. There's time for all of that." Katherine opened her eyes quickly before they closed again. She had seen her mother's tears welling, she saw the smile, and she felt her mother smooth back her hair as she promised to keep her safe.

Katherine found the energy to nod in response. She'd never felt so comfortable falling asleep. Her mind registered every inch of their connection, their feet entwined, their hands melded, their foreheads touching.

Katherine let sleep take her as she decided yes, Jeanie Arthur must have had her own angels. After all, it seemed like a miracle that they had found their way back to each other just when they couldn't shoulder the separation even a bit longer.

And Katherine could not forget that on that final leg home, in the carriage driven by the man headed to West Branch, she had come to believe that the Arthurs' winding path may have dipped into the fringe of hell, but the path must have been lifted by something as pure as an angel, as powerful as the love of a mother and daughter trying to find each other again. *That* she could believe.

Chapter 45

Katherine

1905—Des Moines

Katherine and her family ate a hearty brunch at the Lighthouse. But Katherine's mind left often, thinking of where Tommy might have gone. He was no stranger to sleeping out of doors. For all she knew, he'd slumbered in the back field with the cows for pillows. Just the way he liked it as a boy.

But when they returned from brunch, Tommy was not in the kitchen, backyard, or his room. They even checked the attic, but he was not there, either. Finally, Katherine decided to steal a few minutes in her studio before she started to make the bread for dinner.

She entered the studio and stopped abruptly. "Oh my, Tommy. You scared the life out of me."

He turned but kept holding the button that Katherine had strung onto twine and hung from the window latch. He looked exhausted, his eyes swollen and red.

"Can I have this?" he asked, lifting the twine off the latch.

She nodded. "Of course you can have it." She felt a surge of relief that he would want such a thing.

She rushed to him and held him tight. "Where have you been?" He shuddered in her arms.

He shrugged. "Barn." Then he chuckled. "I don't know how to handle all of this, so where did I end up last night? Right back where I used to go when I was a boy. How can I have aged nearly twenty years and when at my worst, my only way to cope is to run to some barn?" he asked.

Katherine squeezed his arm. "Well, I can't really criticize." She swung her arm toward her knapsack. "I was up all night, knee-deep in my charcoals."

Tommy smiled. "I feel better, then."

She nodded, feeling as though more and more of the layers of distance were peeling away, like dirt scrubbed off prairie skin. She felt a glimmer of happiness at the thought that maybe Tommy would stay longer, that perhaps he'd call for Emma and they both would move back here.

Katherine patted his arm. "We'll send a telegram to Emma. Or send Aleksey for her."

"No!"

Katherine snatched her hand back. "What's wrong?"

He looked away, then down at the button, running his finger over it.

"Tommy?"

"I already sent one." His voice was soft. "She's not coming. She's sick, but I think she's really just sick of me. And I can't blame her. Look at me. I've cried like a baby all night. We're not crying people. Remember that? And all those people, those strangers in your house, describing all this loving, wonderful stuff our mother did for them. And I sat there feeling as though I were not even her son. I couldn't share any of that. I had nothing. And now my wife won't even let me go get her."

"What on earth did you do, Tommy?" She'd seen his rough edges when he arrived just days before their mother died.

He fussed with a stack of canvases, setting them up against the wall one by one.

"Tommy, just tell me."

"I found out she was pregnant again and I left. I took a temporary position at a church in Webster when their reverend passed."

"Why would she be so upset at that? Why didn't she go with you?"

"Doc said if she was going to make this one take, she needed to sit and not do anything. Not even take a buggy ride into the next state."

Katherine closed her eyes and tried to imagine how that might feel if it had been her. She wouldn't have handled it well, but Emma was different. Emma wasn't the type of woman to be emotional or feel put-upon. But perhaps that was the same mistake Tommy had made.

"Did you ask her if she was supportive of you leaving?"

He nodded.

"And she said to go?"

"No."

Katherine's shoulders sank. "Why on earth did you go? I can't imagine that Emma has ever asked anything excessive from you."

Tommy pushed his hand through his hair. "You're right. And that's exactly why I'm in this spot with her."

"You know they could have found another minister to take the church in the interim."

He looked at the ceiling.

"Well, why did you do it?"

Tommy turned his gaze to Katherine.

She raised her hands. "All right. All right. It's not my business."

"I just can't talk about it until I settle it with her. It will take some doing…"

"Well, you better do right, Tommy."

He rubbed his chin, his whiskers rough under his fingertips. She could see his jaw quiver as he tried to restrain his tears.

Katherine pulled him to the daybed and cradled him in her arms. "Oh, Tommy. I'm so sorry. But you can make things right."

He shook his head and sniffled. "When I got that call to go and she announced the pregnancy, I got scared. I could feel that it wouldn't work out. Her face was lit up like candles on Christmas Eve, and all I could do was picture what her face would look like when she lost this one, too. And then I thought of Mama and Father, and in my mind I saw Mama's disappointment on Emma's face and I panicked. I thought she'd be leaving me soon. A woman wearing that disappointment on her face doesn't stay with a man who makes her feel that way."

Katherine held him tight. "Emma isn't Mama. And we don't have to beat ourselves up over the past. But we do owe our families of today. We need to move forward without repeating the same mistakes."

He sat up. His swollen eyes looked as though he would not be able to hold them open much longer.

"Did you sleep at all last night?"

"Not a wink."

Katherine didn't know what to say. She didn't want to scare him off, but she wanted to know more about what was wrong, wanted to know that he would attempt to rescue the part of his life that was wrong but still carried a beating heart. She wanted him to see that his feelings for his life before should be used to better the present. She knew that sounded self-righteous. She knew she had discovered that too late herself.

She drew a deep breath and exhaled, and for the first time since the agitation of the funeral, Katherine felt the presence of James, felt again, for sure, that their mother was at peace.

She grabbed Tommy's hands. "She has forgiven us, forgiven everyone she needed to, Tommy. It's our turn."

He nodded, clearly choking back a sob. He looked at their hands, joined between them.

Katherine squeezed his hands. "Well. You can stay here with us. You can have the barn loft. You can go back to Emma. But I won't allow you to just run anymore. That woman loves you, and it's time for you to put her first, ahead of the church, ahead of yourself."

He drew a deep staccato breath and met Katherine's gaze.

"Can you feel her?" he asked. "James, too?"

She smiled. "I can."

Tommy looked away.

Katherine could feel his resistance softening, knew her words were having impact.

"I'll send word to your church that you're needed here. I will make this work so you can finally sort through all that's wrong. Or you're going to lose your wife, your life. And that's not going to make anything from our past any better at all."

He nodded, and they sat near the window. She wove her fingers into his, her head on his shoulder, thinking of their "twinness," the magical closeness that many feel but that had eluded them for many years. In those moments, she felt their connection deeply. They watched the birds through the window as they flew back and forth, feathering their nests.

"You always did love birds," Katherine said.

"I did, yes."

"Can I tell you a story?"

"That'd be nice," he said.

She relayed to him how Hannah and Will had arrived and how they brought the drawings she'd done, how it was Jeanie's death that brought them to Katherine. "I really believe that means something. I don't know what. I still have knotted, confused thoughts and feelings about Mama. There's so much I want to know and feel angry about. But something shifted for me when I allowed it to. And I think if you just let yourself open not to what you can see, but to what you can feel, you just might find the same peace that I have."

Tommy sat up straighter, and Katherine wondered if he would leave again.

"Will you consider it? For me?" Katherine asked.

His eyes darted around the room as though mirroring the confusion he must have been feeling inside.

"Let Aleksey and me help. Just for a little bit."

And he began to nod. "Okay. For you, Katherine. I'll give it a try."

Katherine pulled him into yet another embrace, feeling as though his concession to simply try to listen to his heart might provide enough space to open up to a miracle.

For she believed in her heart that miracles were the stepping-stones that had led her through life. Even the small ones, the ones others barely noticed, were there, were guiding her along, helping her all the way. Her guides, her angels, her James. All of them reached out for her and pulled her along. And she would not believe she was the only one they were looking to protect.

She was sure her mother was with James; she could feel them both in the studio as Tommy rubbed his temples. She reached into her knapsack and grasped the crystal ball. Tommy went to the daybed and lay down, his head propped against the bumper that softened the iron arm. By the time Katherine had lifted the crystal ball to show it to him, he was deeply asleep. She held the faceted sphere into the light that bathed the room.

The triangle faces flashed with a rainbow of colors, splashing them over the floor. She pulled her knees in to her chest, clutching the crystal ball as she had that first night they'd all met back in Des Moines in 1891. She went to Tommy and pulled a light blanket over him, smoothing back his hair as she would her child.

Tommy, Tommy, Tommy. I will take care of you until you can take care of yourself. You just have to let me. Just open up to the idea life can be better, and I know it will be. I know it can be.

Katherine sighed. There were so many unanswered questions for her, for her brother, for Yale. She thought of Cora Hillis, the fact that she wanted to meet with Katherine and give her some things Jeanie had left, more pieces of the past that Katherine had ignored or not even known existed.

She had seen her sister as a burden for so long that it startled her to realize yet again that Yale was a gift. Katherine thought of all the people who'd come to bid her mother good-bye. She thought of Yale's eulogy, the eloquence in the innocence and simplicity of the love she had shared with Jeanie Arthur. Katherine knew she could not recapture the past or replicate what Yale had shared with their mother.

But a lifetime of mediating between the living and the dead had taught Katherine that one's death did not have to mean the end of knowing a person, of setting things right. She understood that her mother had passed over, but also understood she would always be near.

She did not know if she would share such things with Yale. Her sister was educated for a person with limited mental acuity, but that didn't mean she would process what it meant for a body to die but a soul to continue to live.

Going forward, Yale would be as much a part of the Zurchenko family as any of them. But it was what Yale seemed to hold in her heart, in the very skin that enveloped her bones, that Katherine was most excited to share—the love of a mother, which no one could completely take away. And it was Katherine's connection to her mother in death that she might be able to share with Yale as well. Jeanie Arthur would live on in both Yale's memories and Katherine's mediation. And that was something Katherine could not have imagined would be true just weeks before. The love that had been there all along would not die, and that was all Katherine needed to know at that moment.

The End

Readers,

If you have not read *The Last Letter* and are interested in how the series began, the first novel in The Letter Series is available in print at any retailer as well in eform—Kindle, Nook, Kobo, ibooks, Smashwords, and more.

For more in the saga of the Arthur family, please look for an early 2016 release of *The Garden Promise*, Book 3 in The Letter Series. Here is a rough and short excerpt for your reading pleasure...

... Up on my knees, I couldn't see her in the children's garden.

"Yale!" I sprung up and spun around. There was no sight of her brown dress or black hair, no sound from her. My mind flew to Greta, who'd lost her two-year-old in the high grasses of the prairie. I struggled to breathe and dashed around the space, doubling back to the area I'd ordained as Yale's garden.

"Yale!" The sound of a cow mooing made me snap around. Standing there near the porch was a female cow. Yale was under it, pulling her teats, squirting milk into her mouth. I was elated and horrified. She could have easily been trampled by a cow that hadn't noticed her or that wouldn't appreciate small hands yanking.

I ran to Yale and scooped her up. She wrapped her legs around my waist and roped her arms around my neck, fitting every inch possible against my body. "Yale, are you all right?" I examined the little girl's face, her arms, every inch I could get to without setting her down. Her wet bottom moistened my forearm.

When I settled into a normal breathing pattern, I opened my eyes and saw a man pushing through the gate that stood off to the side of the porch. I stared, feeling as though I'd seen him before.

Was he looking to rent the house, looking for someone who lived there before? "We rented this home the other day. It's no longer for the taking," I said.

He removed his hat and smiled. "I'm Reed Hayes."

"Reed Hayes," I said. The name rang nicely in my mind. I couldn't remember hearing it before even though I knew I'd seen him somewhere.

He turned his hat by the brim, then his eyes flashed. "I didn't realize *you* were Jeanie Arthur."

"You know me?" Had he been an acquaintance of Frank's? A friend of the family she had forgotten?

"Well, not really. But—"

I was certain I appeared confused as I drew back from him, not sure what he wanted, not really having the time to find out.

"I know *of* you," he said. "Let me start over. Two separate things happened. One—I saw you the at the train station that day with the boys who were hassling the child with the violin." His face appeared as though he were awe-struck and happy at the same time.

With the mention of the boy with the violin, I placed Mr. Hayes immediately. That day at the train station, he hadn't noticed that anything was wrong with the boys until I went after the awful bullies. "Why, yes," I said. "I remember now. I was meeting my son, Tommy, there that day."

Mr. Hayes placed his hat back on his head and nodded. "Then today, I saw Cora Hillis in town and she introduced me to your Katherine. She said she was trading her fresh bread for a tiller. But of course I didn't know that her mother, Jeanie Arthur, was you, the woman from the train station."

He looked down at his feet shyly for a moment. "Until now." His voice was soft as he met my gaze again. "Now I know."

The woman at the train station? The idea that he'd kept the image of me in his mind as someone he'd met was fascinating. My mind went back to the train station. I had been so preoccupied that aside from trying to help that little boy, my mind didn't register any sort of attention from a man at all.

The cow mooed behind us and I felt a rush of embarrassment flush my cheeks. Had he seen Yale under the cow, witnessed my panic when I didn't know where she was? Had Tommy not closed the gate and allowed the cow to get into the yard?

Reed walked over to the boxwood that lined the outer edge of the yard. He reached through and nodded. "It's the fencing on the other side. It's broken in several places, and the cow could easily wander in."

"Oh." I said, wanting to take Yale inside to change her wet clothes. "My son will fix that right away. Thank you."

"I'm sure you're not new to the experience of the wandering cows, what with having lived in Des Moines before?"

"Of course not."

Reed stepped toward me. He held my gaze. "I appreciate the trade—the bread for tilling. I look forward to having something with jam for breakfast."

I felt as though I couldn't form words. His closeness excited me in a way I hadn't felt in ages, but his mention of my having been from Des Moines made it clear he knew of my past. Both conditions made it nearly impossible to pull appropriate wording from my snarled thoughts.

"Thank you," I finally said. "We appreciate the trade as well." I pointed over my shoulder. "I did some work near the rose bushes. But as you can see, well, I had some trouble here in the kitchen garden."

He nodded and adjusted his hat as he craned to see where I had first pointed.

"Looks like a lot of work for one day."

"Yes."

We stared at each other for an awkward moment. "Well," I said, "you can take the tiller back there. I'll get started with it in a few minutes."

"Oh no," he said.

Perhaps he wasn't planning to bring the tiller that day. "Oh, I'm sorry. I didn't mean—"

"I'm here to do it. I *have* the tiller, and I *am* the tiller."

Katherine was an exceptional baker, but we didn't have enough on hand to hire someone to do the tilling itself. "We don't have enough in trade for a tiller, the man. We can trade for the tiller, itself. The tool."

He waved her off. "Nonsense. I'm teaching at Drake and nearly done with my dissertation. It's been too long since I've hand my hands in the dirt and this is the perfect way for me to welcome an old friend of Cora's back to town."

His use of the words "hands in the dirt," gave me an excited chill as I felt a connection to him, felt as though he understood something about me by his using the phrase. I rubbed my arms. I couldn't stop a smile from coming to my face so I looked away, not wanting to seem giddy in front of an unfamiliar man.

He pointed at the journal on the ground. It was open to the page where I'd sketched some paths and plantings. "It looks as though you have some ideas there."

"Yes," I said.

"May I?"

I nodded. He squatted down and picked it up. "This is good." He paged through it. "I can see exactly what you want to create here. And in the back of the property."

Suddenly, unease settled inside me. If he knew Cora, then he must know of my background. In the reflection of my past life, I saw every detail of my current tattered one with sharp focus, my failings obvious to all who cared to notice.

He smiled down at what he read.

Don't let your pride interfere. He didn't come here to court you. No need to be nervous. We needed the help and if Cora Hillis recommended him, well, then I would say all right.

"I need to change Yale and then I'll be back outside to discuss the plan. What I've written so far is not complete."

Mr. Hayes didn't seem to hear me as he flipped through the rest of the journal, biting on his thumb in between page turns. I decided to tend to Yale and headed up the stairs to the kitchen door.

"Mrs. Arthur."

I turned back.

He strolled toward me. The connection I felt between us was as real as the boxwood that lined the garden. It didn't make sense that I felt such a thing. I wouldn't be childish enough to assume he felt it as well, but I basked in the warmth for a moment; I allowed myself to appreciate it.

He put one foot on the bottom stair. "I look forward to this tilling project. I've been cooped up studying and writing. This fresh air, this opportunity has… well, it's like a burst of goodness. And I look forward to knowing *you.* Any woman who takes matters in her own hands like you did at the train station with that little boy who was playing the violin is worth knowing." His eyes darted away, then he clamped back onto my gaze like shackles on wrists. "I mean," he said,

"I didn't even notice what was happening until you were halfway to solving the problem."

I shaded my eyes with my hand and squinted at him. *He wanted to know me? Worth knowing?* My breath caught; a thrill pulsed through me. I exhaled and chuckled. He was a friendly man, the sort who would help out a stranger for someone like Cora Hillis. But to know me? That would take more than weeding through the overgrown gardens. I didn't expect anything of his niceties, but I knew I should at least return them.

"Your dissertation? You're a professor without his PhD?"

He shifted his feet and cleared his throat. "I'm almost there." He held up his forefinger and thumb to show a tiny sliver of light through them. "I'll defend my work by the end of the year. But I'm more than just a professor without a defended dissertation. I have interests in many other things. Like your writing. Mrs. Hillis shared it with me. I would like to discuss your articles with you, the way you wove fact into anecdote and turned the monotony of household duty into something enviable. That's quite a feat. If you don't mind?"

My writing? I was so stunned at his statement that I lost my manners. I patted Yale's back. "Why on earth?"

He shrugged as though my hearing his words confirmed that he really had no good reason for wanting to discuss home-keeping columns that were years old. "Good writing is good writing. Academic or otherwise."

My wariness dissolved at his complimentary words. That, accompanied by a flash of uncertainty that crossed his face, endeared him to me without my even knowing him. "Perhaps that's right," I said.

"We can talk while we work." He raised his eyebrows.

"Writing talk while tilling?" I asked. "There's a topic for an article."

He broke into a smile that crunched up his eyes and lit up his face in such a way that I knew he was honest, just in seeing the openness in his expression. *And Cora sent him.* There was that.

"We can do both. I assure you," he said.

I could not hide my grin this time, feeling a lightness enter me like a spirit moving right through my skin. I shivered, speechless, unable to access anything other than awkward mumblings. I entered the house to change Yale. Was *he* still smiling?

I peeked back at him over my shoulder and saw that he was. I could barely breathe as I disappeared into the kitchen and out of the sight of Reed Hayes, his presence still with me, as though he'd joined me in the house, as though he'd offered something much more than to till my garden. He'd seen beyond what I'd lacked. Somehow, he'd called forth the person I wanted to be again.

Acknowledgments

The list of people I need to thank for helping see this book and all the others through is extensive. I will leave people out, I know, and then I will circle back and fill in the gaps, but please know if you helped me, I know it and I will thank you here and/or in person.

To take this book from a seed of an idea to the point it is in your hands was an enormous job. Mostly because I did not know there would be a sequel to *The Last Letter* when I wrote it. But so many readers wanted to "see" more of what happened in the seventeen years that separated the two timelines in *The Last Letter* that I could not refuse at least exploring it. So first, it's the readers I need to thank.

All of your enthusiasm, support, and virtual affection is priceless and tucked away in my world like precious jewels.

Thanks also to Susan McClafferty, Jenny Toney Quinlan, Penina Lopez, Susan Helene Gottfried, Julie Burns, and Marlene Engel for your professional input. Each of you has a hand in this book's release, and I would gladly recommend you to any author looking for a set of eagle eyes and open minds for their work. I can't say how many times I thought "this book is done," and then one of you found all the ways it was not even close. Thank you so much for all you do. The rich layers, emotional character journeys, and clean proofing are firmly rooted in the work you all helped me do better than it would have been with me alone.

Thanks to Lisa Gavran. Endless plot talks and readings you have done spark the entire process. You see what I can't and I thank you for all your hard critiques and kind adjustments over the years. More than anything, you are just the best friend a person can have.

Thanks to Melissa Foster for your friendship and all the back and forth on each of these books!!!!! Never-ending and deep appreciation to you. I can't wait for the Sweetheart Series to launch in 2015!

Thanks to Natasha Brown for the endless cover revisions. Your work is beautiful and heartfelt, and I can't say thank you enough for squeezing me in and making this work the way it needed to.

Thanks to Rachelle Ayala. Your formatting is superb and fast and I am always indebted to you for making sure there is time to rework each book. Thank you a million times.

Thanks to Kelli Uhrich and everyone at Booksparks. The launch is always better when not alone!!! Your hard work is much appreciated and will ensure that readers can find the book in the first place!! Thank you!

To all the Mindful Writers who understand that none of the marketing and promotion matters if you don't write the book. Thank you for all the laughter while working. It's the best combination I can imagine for writing.

Thanks especially to Lori Jones, Madhu Wangu, and Larry Schardt for making the Mindful Writing opportunities happen.

Thanks to all my friends who tirelessly buy and sell my books to other readers. It means the world that you care enough to do it.

About the Author

Bestselling author Kathleen Shoop holds a PhD in reading education and has more than twenty years of experience in the classroom. She writes historical fiction, women's fiction, and romance. Shoop's novels have garnered various awards in the Independent Publisher Book Awards, Eric Hoffer Book Awards, Indie Excellence Awards, Next Generation Indie Book Awards and the San Francisco Book Festival. Kathleen has been featured in *USA Today* and the *Writer's Guide to 2013*. Her work has appeared in The Tribune-Review, four *Chicken Soup for the Soul* books and *Pittsburgh Parent* magazine. She lives in Oakmont, Pennsylvania with her husband and two children. For more information, go to kshoop.com or visit her on Facebook or at @kathieshoop.